D1826085

Fade to Black

Steven Bannister

Copyright ©2012, 2014 Steven Bannister

ISBN: 9781478387190

This is a work of fiction. Names, characters, places
brands, media, and incidents are either the product of
the author's imagination or are used fictitiously. Any
similarity to persons living or dead is purely
coincidental.

All rights reserved. Without limiting the rights under
copyright reserved above, no part of this publication
may be reproduced, stored in or introduced into a
retrieval system, or transmitted, in any form, or by any
means (electronic, mechanical, photocopying,
recording, or otherwise) without the prior written
permission of both the copyright owner and the above
publisher of this book.

*Be sober, be vigilant; because your adversary the devil,
as a roaring lion, walketh about, seeking whom he may
devour: 1Peter 5:8-9*

Chapter One

Glastonbury, southern England

Eighty-seven-year-old Albert Mortlock shuffled once more from the bench in his tiny farmhouse kitchen to his living room. The hip reconstruction he'd had four years ago hadn't yet healed. An overfull teapot in hand, he sank with a low groan into his favourite chair, a 1931 chesterfield original.

It had commanded the corner of the room by the wood-framed window since the day it had been delivered. Like its owner, it was cracked and grey with thin leathery skin bulging in the wrong places. It had been his father's chair and Albert had been forbidden to sit in it until his father had passed away. Fifty one years he'd waited, but that was his father – rules were rules. He frequently found himself thinking about his father and how hard he'd made not only his own life but that of Albert's. He fretted over how it wouldn't be long before he joined his father in that other world. He had no desire to see the bastard again.

The fiddly, time-stained glass panels of the window ushered in the yellow summer moon, by whose light he could see his roses in full white and red bloom. Even pruning his babies had become more challenge than pleasure these days.

The cottage Albert had inherited stood on a tiny parcel of land which had once been part of a much larger farm that, according to family legend, had been owned by the Mortlocks under one name or another since the Middle Ages. The landholding had once spanned the marshes to the foot of Wearyall Hill. But that was history. Albert was happy enough with the acre he'd been left. The cottage, perched on slightly higher ground here in Ashwell Lane near Stone Down, met all of his modest needs.

Albert looked past the roses to the slight hump in the neglected lawn, accentuated in the evening light and which he alone knew marked his wife's grave. Forty six years after her burial, the grass was still a little greener under the willow tree. He approved of the view but thought for perhaps the hundredth time that his father really should have dug a little deeper.

German-born Marion had insulted them publicly one too many times; and his father, a World War I veteran, had finally snapped. He shivered at the memory and adjusted the faded wool rug around his knees – even in summer he needed an extra layer. Whenever he thought of Marion, and it was quite often these days, he also remembered his son. They boy had been put up for adoption at just six months old after his mother had 'mysteriously run out' on them. Albert had been known to speculate along with the townsfolk about where she could have run off to and with whom. Had even one of them bothered to visit him at Ashwell Lane, they'd have discovered the truth.

The years had passed and the townspeople he had known had all died; now there was nobody around who remembered Albert had ever been married. He'd never heard from his son, and that was fine with him. The child had probably been spared the same fate as his mother. He reached to pour himself a fresh brew, spilling some of the hot, weak liquid on his rug. He puffed a little more than usual at the effort – his emphysema from a lifetime of pipe smoking was poised to claim his lungs.

Lifting the hot tea and blowing it gently as he always did, he turned to look up through the larger window at a view of which he never tired. Glastonbury Tor rose almost from his backyard and, from this vantage point, it seemed to touch the now fully-risen gibbous moon. He saw it then. An intense, crimson light hovered directly above the tower at the summit of the Tor. It remained for a few more seconds, as he knew it would, and descended the side of the Tor nearest his cottage. A ripple of anticipation teased him as it crept steadily towards him. Albert had not expected to ever see the light again, but he knew now that his years of mumbled prayers had been answered. Albert's father, his grandfather, and his ancestors stretching back a thousand years, had seen the light and played their role. Albert wasn't about to break that tradition.

That light, Albert knew, lived forever. He waited calmly for it to come to him. It arrived at his window, pulsating as per the ritual. As was expected, he rose to his feet, clutching at the arm of the chesterfield for support. He faced the light and bowed to it. After a moment, the light stopped pulsating and grew impossibly, *painfully,* bright before moving steadily away across his back garden to the west. Albert stood for a few more moments, then manoeuvred himself easily back into his chair – his hip perfectly functional, the emphysema in his lungs banished for his remaining years. He had, like his male ancestors, given permission to the crimson light – to *it* – to live among mortals once again in exchange for physical redemption.

Albert knew that as a consequence of his actions ordinary, decent men, women and children would forfeit their lives in unimaginable, *terrible* ways until permission was withdrawn from the light. The townsfolk had come to know him as the kindly old gentleman who'd served so earnestly in the Glastonbury post office for nearly seventy years and to whom they'd once given a civic service award; but he knew the truth – he was a killer; just like his father.

TV news: BBC Four, Roseanne Palmer:

'Once again, Glastonbury Tor has excited paranormal fever in Britain. It seems that on Saturday and again last night, strange lights were seen orbiting the Tor and fourteenth-century St Michael's Tower which sits at its peak. A flood of calls on both nights to Glastonbury's

Centre for Paranormal Studies has experts again scratching their heads. According to the reports, reddish lights were seen hovering above the Tor on Monday night at 10:14 p.m. and, exactly twenty four hours later, an intense white-blue light appeared. According to many the lights seemed to actually enter the tower. Earlier today, rector of Glastonbury Abbey, Reverend Nevin Creeley, dismissed the sightings as "overactive imaginitis" and reminded everyone that re-runs of the X-files and Alien movies had been screened on free-to-air television this week.'

Palmer to camera left: 'In the studio tonight we have arguably Britain's foremost authority on Celtic myths and legends, Professor David St. Clair.

'Professor, is Reverend Creeley right? Are we looking at a bad case of "imaginitis"?'

St. Clair (laughing): 'Well it's a great word, Roseanne, but I'm not sure it does the good folks of Glastonbury justice.'

RP: 'So you think the strange lights are real then?'

St. Clair: 'Well, I understand fifty or so calls have been received – it's doubtful in my view, at least, that so many people would have been so stimulated by sci-fi movies that they somehow joined in a mass hallucination.'

RP: 'Interesting – so what could the lights be?'

St. Clair: 'What they could be has been a matter of speculation since the fifth century – that's how long people have been ascribing mystical powers to the Tor. Of course, that coincides with the new spiritualism and awareness of "other-worldly" possibilities that seemed to take hold at that time – particularly in southern Britain.'

RP: 'Could the mysterious lights around the Tor have triggered the beliefs?'

St. Clair: 'The Tor has been at the centre of many legends and beliefs – not all of them concern mysterious lights.'

RP: 'Such as?'

St. Clair (smiling): 'Faeries for one – and not the cute winged variety found at the bottom of the garden. It's said they have caverns and magical springs associated with the home of Gwyn ap Nudd, the Faerie King, and of course there are those who believe in ley lines, celestial pathways from the summit, not to mention the big one – the connection to King Arthur.'

RP: (chuckling) 'There's a lot to explore on this one then, Professor St. Clair, but we'll have to leave it for another time – maybe in a galaxy far, far away! Thanks for coming in.'

St. Clair: 'My pleasure, Roseanne.'

Chapter Two

New Scotland Yard, London.
Tuesday, 2:00 p.m.

Allie St. Clair had been an acting detective chief inspector for exactly thirty seconds and it already felt right. She'd earned this. Seven years of making a drunken sod look good had finally paid off. Two weeks ago, DCI William 'Billy' McBride's liver had made his decision to retire an easy one. Her immediate elevation to the head of a murder investigation team under the aegis of Homicide Serious Crime Command was gratifying and she quietly hoped her promotion enjoyed the unanimous support of the hierarchy at New Scotland Yard.

Her former boss had been a legend with the metropolitan police – at least in his own lunchtimes. At fifty two, Billy had barely served enough time to qualify for a pension. But barely was good enough, and now he had passed out of Allie's working life. The farewell booze-up for him at his beloved Old Star just off Broadway, conveniently located not one hundred yards from Billy's office, had been put on hold as he'd been admitted to hospital five days ago to undergo a series of tests.

She'd heard his photo now hung above the bar at the Old Star. *He's earned that, all right,* she thought. It was ironic that the very thing he loved to do most, which had elevated him to some kind of hero status, had brought his career to a sodden halt.

She ran her fingers over the new warrant card which Detective Chief Superintendent Ellen Carr had just presented to her – the cheap plastic feel not dimming her prickle of anticipation. Around the central meeting room the rest of her team stood in their respective positions of support, admiration, mistrust and jealousy. This was life. She had worked hard, played it straight down the line, and tried to do the right thing by those colleagues whom she respected and liked. But there were those who felt she wasn't ready for this responsibility. She was, after all, just thirty years old and, horror of horrors, she hailed from a background of conspicuous wealth and privilege. Her team, many of whom she'd worked alongside for some years, had no way of knowing she eschewed her father's wealth and struggled like everyone else with a hefty mortgage. She even rode an old motorbike as buying a decent car on her salary to date had been too much of a stretch.

Carr was winding up her congratulatory remarks and Allie prepared herself to respond. She thought again about McBride. She'd never actually hated him, and in some ways had felt sympathy for him and his condition, but he'd belittled her too many times and taken credit for her work as a matter of course. But, she reflected, she could even have lived with that for a while longer. What she couldn't abide, however, was his refusal to care about anything but himself. To Billy, victims of rape had 'asked for it'; battered women were just weak; and murder victims, the majority of whom were homeless or hopelessly drug dependent, were a nuisance at best, interrupting his drinking time. He was a sad man – and that was a fact.

Carr's awkward speech came to an end. '. . . one of the youngest officers ever to achieve the rank of detective chief inspector! Allie, congratulations!'

The twenty-strong team applauded as they should and, as tradition dictated, she was invited to 'say a few words'. Allie St. Clair now faced them as their new superior officer.

She was conscious of the fact that even her first words today would have an effect on how she was perceived by her new team. She paused for a moment to survey the room and simply enjoy the moment. She noted young DC Jacinta Wilkinson's beaming smile and thumbs-up gesture directed at her. She smiled her thanks. No such acclamation from Detective Sergeant Rachel Strauss. She was clearly agitated; shuffling and looking anywhere but at Allie. There could be no mistaking the ice in that corner of the room. It was unlikely their friendship would ever be rekindled. Their initial friendly rivalry as trainee detective constables seven years ago had disintegrated over time into outright enmity. Allie had been given recognition for having largely cracked a murder investigation that Rachel had worked on for months, but to no obvious avail. Allie had genuinely sympathized with Rachel and had approached her superiors more than once to have Rachel's role in the investigation acknowledged.

Even Billy, with whom Rachel had a close working relationship, had done nothing to correct the injustice. Rachel was never to know that Allie had tried hard to act in her interests. The problems between the two women had been compounded a couple of years previously when Allie had been approached by the Met's advertising agency to feature in a series of recruitment ads to run in the nation's press. It had been no secret that the agency's hierarchy had felt that Allie's thick, lustrous black hair, slim physique, and clear-skinned good looks were exactly the 'look' they were after to attract higher-calibre male applicants. Allie still regretted her decision to pose for a test photo shoot. Mere days later, a huge, full-colour poster had been hung in full view of the public and her colleagues.

A friend in the force had confided to her that Rachel Strauss made loud, croaking, vomiting noises every time she passed the poster. Rachel made no secret that Allie's near-perfect white teeth and searing green eyes were hard enough for her to cope with in real life, but photoshopped and ten feet tall, she was nothing less than an assault. Allie had already withdrawn from the campaign by then; she'd been uncomfortable with the whole concept from the outset and had only initially agreed under pressure from her superiors at Homicide Serious Crime Command. Her withdrawal neither won her points from HSCC nor assuaged Rachel Strauss's bitter reaction.

It was only some months later that Allie had learned Rachel had thought her own shaggy blonde hair and impressively packed uniform might have 'fitted the bill', as she was fond of saying, and she actively sought to be the face of the Met. Had Allie known at the time, she would have gladly stepped aside.

She looked now to the corner of the brightly lit room where a bevy of male detectives gathered. She knew some would also have a problem with her new status. The Met was a male domain, despite well-publicized efforts to correct the impression. As genuine as those efforts were, it would take time.

She thanked those who had helped her along the way and expressed hope that they would all work together as an effective unit. She even thanked Billy for everything he had done for her, wished him well, and said that she planned to visit him at the hospital soon. In fact she'd been very surprised to receive a note from him the day before asking her to come and see him. She'd been wondering whether he would welcome a visit from her and the note had eased that concern. What *was* interesting was the unmistakable sense of urgency in the tone of the message.

At the end of her speech, she didn't invite everyone to join her for the customary celebratory drink. She knew this was bad form and didn't miss the raised eyebrows in the room. She felt it wasn't appropriate given Billy's condition. At the last moment she added that perhaps drinks could be postponed, 'Just until Billy's well enough to join us.' This drew a few nods and a general murmuring of approval. 'Perhaps in a week or so,' she suggested. She drew her speech to a close with a simple, 'Thank you once again and see you all tomorrow!'

There remained, of course, the details of changing offices, phone numbers and so on, but all that would happen the next day. Most of the team stopped by her office individually as the day drew to a close, to again offer their congratulations; Strauss an expected exclusion. Allie found that Strauss's attitude disappointed her more than she'd expected. Prior to their falling-out, their friendship had been one Allie had valued.

Everyone had drifted out by 6:00 p.m. and she decided to head for home, but not before promising to have lunch the next day with two of her closest friends from British Transport Police which was headquartered just across the road, also in St James' Park. On a whim, she suggested they gather at the nearby Feathers Inn on Broadway at 1:00 p.m. Leaving her fourth-floor office and ducking down a brick lane behind the St. James' tube station, she rounded the corner and unchained her motorbike from the iron security post. Her phone pinged. Groaning, she dug it out from underneath her heavy leather riding jacket. She read the message,

Congratulations Allie

-Michael

Michael? No *Michaels* sprang to mind. Stuffing the phone in her zip pocket, she sorted the bike chain, fired up the six-year-old Yamaha cruiser and decided that rather than cook tonight, she'd treat herself to a meal in one of the restaurants in Putney High Street near her home by the Thames. Maybe try the new Spanish restaurant, The Matador, or was it the Toreador?

Traffic was lighter than normal, so she decided to head out through Kensington and down Fulham Road via Chelsea, just as an alternative to her usual King's Road route. She was enjoying the ride in the warm air until she noticed the distinctive arched steel veranda of the Chelsea and Westminster Hospital coming-up on her left. Her conscience gnawed at her. Billy McBride was in there. She was still debating whether she'd see Billy tonight when the bike almost turned itself into Limerston Street, which bordered the hospital. Decision made.

The narrow street offered the only real chance of a parking spot. She didn't fancy the hospital's underground car park – she knew from visiting a friend who had been a patient there recently that it was claustrophobic and difficult to exit – particularly at peak visiting times.

She quickly navigated through the Porsches and Jaguars parked on the Kensington street, finally squeezing her bike into a half-spot in a car park adjacent to the hospital grounds. A fabulous, shiny black Triumph Rocket III motorcycle occupied an adjoining parking space. The bike made Allie's Yamaha look like a child's plaything. She'd really fancied one of the Triumphs until she'd checked its weight; she was strong, but her slight frame would never have allowed her to manage the bulk of the bike if she dropped it at the traffic lights – or worse. Looking again at the big bike, she made a promise to herself to hit the gym during the coming summer. Her promotion might add enough into her budget to put it within easier reach. She wasn't one to give up easily. Motorbikes made sense in this part of London, avoiding peak-time congestion charges being a major advantage – *although it's after 6:00 p.m. now anyway*, she reminded herself.

Cramming her jacket and helmet into the leather panniers, she made her way back around to Fulham Road and to hospital reception. She was directed to the nurses' station on level three where an ancient nurse ushered her to room twelve. She raised her hand to knock but a feeling of dread froze her. She felt its pressure like a heavy black cloak. Opening the door now seemed like a very bad idea. A nurse shuffled down the corridor towards her. Embarrassed, she forced herself to knock twice and go in. Billy was alone and trying to figure out how to work the remote control for the wall-mounted television.

'I'll fix it for you, Billy.'

'Ah, I'm so glad you've come,' he said without looking at her.

'*Are you?*' Her voice was too shrill.

He twisted to face her. She was shocked to see he'd turned into an old man. There was almost no trace left of the corpulent, outgoing Billy she'd tolerated for so long. His alarmingly sunken face matched the grey of the bedding and she was sure he had less hair than when she'd last seen him – hardly more than a week ago. His eyes were jaundiced orbs protruding from a seemingly shrivelled skull. He drew his lips far enough back in an attempted smile, displaying the smashed-off front tooth she'd noticed so often. She could never fathom why he hadn't had that fixed years ago.

'You're a good looking girl, Allie.'

What is this? she wondered as she put up her hand in protest. *What drugs are they giving him?*

'Hang on,' he said, 'don't worry. I haven't gone all strange on you.'

She relaxed a little, managing a smile for him despite the clinging cold of the room. *Don't they ever turn the heaters on?*

'Allie, I wanted you to come see me for a reason. Let me say first that I don't feel sorry for myself, and I am not looking for pity. You should know that anyway. But I do know that I've disappointed you.'

'Billy—'

'Shut-up for a second, girl. Let me finish!'

She sighed. That was more like the old Billy. He composed himself and motioned to her to come around to the other side of the bed.

'Grab yourself a chair. And close those bloody blinds. That fucking neon sign over the road blinks at me all night.' He waited until she was seated. He hesitated again for a moment, seemingly lost for words. 'I've been waiting for days to talk to you – you'd think I'd be organized by now, wouldn't you?'

Allie smiled and nodded.

'Okay, here we go. You've been successful, Allie.' He waved his hand to forestall any comment she might make. 'You're good looking, educated, but above all, you are *genuinely* smart. No doubt about that.'

She said nothing. This speech from him was a real surprise given their differences of opinion on most things.

'And it seems to me you have the two things you think I lost a long time ago – integrity and compassion.'

He twitched and looked at the blinds as though something was about to burst through them. 'Allie, there's something very wrong out there. Not just morons and drug heads – I mean *very* wrong. Something beyond us. Something untouchable and . . . *new*.' He coughed violently, his face momentarily reddening before draining to the colour of putty. He worked his rheumy gaze back to her. 'I know this sounds strange, but I can't shake the feeling that something terrible is about to happen. Things are . . . *changing*.'

Allie still said nothing, but her brain fizzed. *What's he saying here? Billy is genuinely affected,* she realized. *This isn't his usual bullshit. On the other hand, perhaps his treatment is . . .*

'I know wha' you're thinking, girl. Let me tell you this – I haven't taken any medication for four days. I wanted to be clear-headed for you.' He stared at her unblinkingly as if willing her to understand – to grasp the significance of what he was saying. He finally looked away and scanned the room – the frightened rabbit expecting the fox to pounce from the shadows.

Allie reached for his hand but he jerked and retched, making a sound like a buzz saw. She jumped up to help him. He was heaving and sobbing. She felt tears in her own eyes. Billy was clearly in trouble, perhaps mentally as well as physically. She put her arms around him.

'Billy, you must take whatever medication they give you. You absolutely cannot risk your health! Your wife and family need you. You *must* do everything they tell you to do to get well.'

He laughed and coughed at the same time. 'Oh, Allie,' he rasped, staring at her through crazed eyes. 'There's no getting well for me!'

'Please stop this, Billy!' Her tears were brimming now. She cared about him more than she'd realized.

He sat up abruptly, staring somewhere near the ceiling. 'Accept him.'

She hadn't quite caught his low tone. He'd said it so differently, quietly, like they were chatting over coffee.

'Pardon me?'

'Accept him.'

'Who?'

He coughed hard. Black-red blood spouted from his mouth, coating the bedding, the floor, and Allie. Air hissed from his throat. She heard herself yell as she ran for help.

It was an hour and a half before Allie felt she could leave the hospital. A tall unflappable Indian doctor hadn't hesitated in pronouncing Billy McBride dead. Billie's distraught wife and two of his three sons arrived within an hour of his death. The third son, a banker, was in transit from Paris and couldn't be reached.

His homecoming will be morbid, she thought idly. She'd rung DS Carr, who'd been understandably upset, and planned to call her friends when she got home. She borrowed a blue-green smock from the old nurse who had also promised to dispose of her blood-spattered shirt. Allie was tired. Screw the Spanish restaurant; a JD and Coke and an early night were about all she was up for now. She said a quiet farewell to Billy's wife who struck her as a slightly put-upon type; her slumped shoulders and square figure suggesting a largely joyless life. But she was stoic and that was impressive given what she must be thinking about the shape her future would probably assume. Allie knew from experience that Suzie McBride's real grief would bite in a few days, just when she thought she was coming to terms with her husband's death.

She pushed through the double glass doors of the hospital, taking an involuntary step backwards as a vicious wind slammed into her chest. This hadn't been forecast and the triple glazing of the hospital windows had masked the change from her. Nor was respite from the wind available around the corner in Limerston Street. Garbage bins were blowing over, spilling waves of foul-smelling liquids. A large advertising hoarding above where she'd parked her bike flapped wildly. 'Great,' she said aloud, 'what next? Rain?'

The big Rocket III motorcycle she'd been so pleased to park next to had gone, as had most of the cars from a couple of hours ago. Fast-food wrappers and paper cups from nearby cafés skated across the narrow street, whipping around her ankles before cartwheeling away. She stooped to retrieve her helmet from the left storage pannier on the bike. The advertising hording was wrenched from its mounting. It missed her by an inch. It smashed itself to a hundred pieces on the hard asphalt a yard in front of her and she realized her helmet had saved her before she'd even put it on. 'Jesus H Christ!' she yelled to no one. She stared at the remains of the sign as paper, metal and sheeting were torn from it and dashed against the brick walls and ornate iron fences of the exclusive villas across the street. Debris was piling up fast.

Exhaling slowly, she decided to get the hell out of there. She turned back to her bike. A feather sat on the seat. It was bright white and about twelve inches long. It was just sitting there – *despite the howling wind*. It hadn't been there a moment ago, she was sure. Picking it up, she ran her index finger along its trailing edge and a mild electric current ran from her fingers to her feet. It was not unpleasant. Doing it again brought the same result. Almost giggling, she looked around to see if anyone had witnessed her private little pleasure.

She put the feather back on the seat, so she could wrestle her tight leather jacket back on. The feather didn't move. *Curious*, she thought, supposing it must be an aerodynamic thing. Stowing it in an inside pocket, she donned her helmet and stirred the bike into gear. Things were getting weird. It was definitely time to get home.

Chapter Three

DCS Ellen Carr stood at the window of her airy city apartment, wine in hand, looking out to the west. The full-length windows spanning the width of her apartment afforded her an unsurpassed view of the dome of St Paul's Cathedral, which dominated the London skyline even at night. She changed her focus as she caught her own reflection in the tinted glass. She self-consciously smoothed her skirt, noticing again the unwanted bulges at the hips. Recently she'd resorted to telling herself that, being well above average height, she could carry a little extra weight better than most. But the reflection didn't lie. At fifty, she was exercising too little, drinking too much, and relying on her blaze of strawberry-blonde hair to carry the day. It wasn't working. She sighed and hoped her partner, Janice Finlay, a barrister with high-rolling London law firm, Cranston Lock, and who now sat cross-legged on the low couch behind her, hadn't noticed. She wrestled her thoughts back to her job, and in particular Billy McBride, about whose sudden death she'd been advised just minutes earlier.

'Billy was an irascible old sod, you know,' Ellen said. 'He had a thirst like an Iraqi bricklayer as well. Lord he could chuck it down.'

Finlay laughed despite the sombre mood since the news of his demise.

'Where *do* you get these sayings?'

Carr let the remark pass. She knew exactly where she got them – mainly from the working class underpaid stooges who worked for her. *A good bunch,* she thought, *but not a lot of talent.* Too many of them were like Billy McBride – just wanting to get paid and go home half-liquored so they could face their dumpy wives and feign interest in the kids. But Billy had been all right once. She was old enough to remember when he'd cut a reasonable figure in uniform. It was his promotion to CID that had done him in. She remembered too that the Hungerford massacre back in 1987 had worried him deeply. There had been too many bodies, too much emotion. There was only so much you could take in this job – everybody knew there was a use-by date – the trick was knowing when to look at your label. She turned back towards her partner who was pouring another Sauvignon Blanc for herself.

'Maybe it's time I gave this game away, Janice.'

'You're not planning on dying on me too now, are you?'

Carr smiled despite her melancholia. 'No, but the future belongs to the kids. Smart kids like St. Clair.' Despite her concerns about her weight in contrast to Janice's forty-something, stick-thin corporate look proclaiming an admirable dietary discipline, her willpower failed her again. She held her glass out for a refill. 'You know St. Clair read at Trinity College?'

Janice was impressed. 'Well, well, my Alma Mater. She's no slouch then.'

This was said as a matter of fact. Cambridge grads were not destined to become waitresses or coppers pounding the beat.

'Why is she slogging it out through the ranks of the CID then?'

'Because she believes in it – how rare is *that*?' Ellen waved her hand holding the wine, spilling some on the tiled floor. 'She told me that at her job interview, and you know what? She convinced me absolutely. I believed her then, and I still do.'

A light bulb went off for Janice.

'She's nothing to do with Professor David St. Clair by any chance?'

Ellen nodded and smiled. 'Well done. Yes, he's her father.'

'Aha,' Janice chuckled. 'No wonder she's bright then, Ellen. Hang on to her. David's a bit of a whiz really. Very impressive.'

Ellen nodded. 'He is. Here's another snippet for you. Her mother is Suzie Whiteman.'

'Whiteman . . . not the children's author?'

'The very same.'

Janice clapped her hands. 'My niece loves her books – has about four of them, I think. Pretty sombre stuff for kids, I would have thought, but Sophie absolutely devours them. I don't mind them myself to be honest.'

They each retreated to their private thoughts.

Carr broke the silence, not wanting to change the topic. 'Her family's high profile has been a bit of millstone for Allie, actually.'

Janice pulled herself back from her own ruminations.

'How so?'

'Her workmates got wind of it early on in her career, and she cops the whole silver-spoon thing pretty hard.'

'Character building stuff I'd imagine.'

Carr thought about that. It shouldn't still be an issue for Allie, but it was. It wasn't helped by the fact that either of her parents could pop up on television, radio or in a bookstore at any given moment.

Janice broke in, 'It must have been a hell of day for her today. Promoted with all the euphoria that goes with that one moment, then watching her old boss die in front of her the next.'

Ellen nodded, a far-away look in her eyes.

'True. She'll have mixed emotions about today, that's for sure. By all accounts, they didn't like each other much, Allie and Billy. They got results, but we knew it was her work. Billy couldn't solve a child's riddle in the end. Too busy propping up the bar at that bloody pub over the road from his office.'

Janice didn't really fancy another tirade about Billy's alcoholism.

'How do you think St. Clair will go as a DCI?' Ellen sat beside her, putting her glass on the low coffee table.

'Good question. She'll need to find a way to work with people a little better, there's no doubt about that. She's a bit of a lone wolf and some see that as arrogance, but I don't think it's that at all. In fact, I know that she hasn't told them she graduated top of the class through the Crime Academy. Mind you, it'll come out in the newsletter next week, so she's in for some more fun and games. She's the best and brightest to ever come out of the High Potential Development Scheme, and that's good news and bad news for her. The bulk of our long-serving personnel still think the whole notion of "accelerated development" is an elitist wank and that good, honest coppers – the ones who have been doing it tough on the streets for decades – are being ridden over in favor of these bright young things.'

Janice pulled a face. 'Well, they *are*. Aren't they? Isn't St. Clair a prime example of the teacher's pet queue jumper?

Carr shrugged her shoulders and waved her hand towards the city. 'We desperately need management talent, Janny, and this is the best way to get it – at least in my view. In St. Clair's case, she has her chance to show them all what she's got. If she messes up this opportunity, the high-potential scheme will probably go down the drain with her.'

They sat in companionable silence for a minute, but Finlay could see Carr's mind was still whirring away on work issues.

'Okay, spit it out, Ellen. Let's have your final thoughts on the matter.'

Carr smiled and rested her hand on Finlay's thigh.

'Sorry, but it's worrying me. It's important. No, *vital* that she succeed. St. Clair simply *must* prevail.' She looked at Finlay then gazed out of the big window, watching a jetliner slowly sink towards Heathrow Airport. 'Otherwise, early retirement will definitely be on my agenda.'

Janice Finlay ostensibly examined the thin meniscus of wine clinging to the inside of her glass, but in fact she was very deep in thought. Carr hadn't just said that it was important St. Clair succeeded. She had used the term prevail. And *that* was interesting.

Allie hit the light switch, simultaneously cramming her riding gear into the tiny hall closet with her left foot, forcing the door shut to keep it in. She scanned the galley kitchen for the Jack Daniels.

She found the three-quarters-full bottle nestled by her collection of Italian recipe books. She remembered she'd left it there when she'd last had a drink – a week ago when Carr had privately given her the nod that she'd succeed Billy as detective chief inspector, at least in an acting capacity. It had been a pleasant, solitary evening during which she'd allowed herself to bathe in the satisfaction of having made the grade.

She smiled at the recollection. She also remembered managing just two shots of the JD over two hours before falling asleep by 9:00 p.m. A big drinker she was not.

Kicking off her boots she padded, glass in hand, to her sofa by the window, flicking on the sound system as she passed. She dropped on to the soft leather as Nora Jones whispered the intro to *Come Away With Me*. Allie gulped her drink and shivered. Her eyes watered at the strength of the drink. She closed them and revisited the terrible scene at the hospital. She shivered again.

Poor Billy's last words came back to her. They were bizarre and disturbing. What had rattled him so much that he'd risk not taking his medications just so he could tell her about his fears? And why her? Surely there were people closer to him who he could have confided in?

Despite their dysfunctional working relationship, she had definitely learned things from Billy, at least in the early days.

And now he'd alluded to something else beyond normal crime, if there was such a thing. He was troubled by something nastier, *darker*.

'Accept him,' Billy had said at the last. Perhaps he'd been hallucinating, thinking he was actually talking to God or whomever he defaulted to in a crisis. But somehow that didn't feel quite right either. She looked at her watch. It was late and she really should call her friends. She sighed as she thought about the next day's priorities. She'd have to go in to work early to brief the rest of the team about Billy first thing. She threw down another gulp at that thought. The funeral would be held on Friday, she supposed. That was three trying days away.

Fixing another drink, but with less space-wasting ice this time, she settled down, her head nestled back on the largest of the sofa's loose cushions. The strange bike-adhering white feather drifted into her mind, but before she could explore that bizarre little cameo appearance, her eyes closed again. It had been a draining twelve hours.

*

4:15 a.m.

She bounded off the sofa like a gymnast, spilling the remains of her drink on the wool rug. Staring stupidly at her watch, she cursed herself. She'd completely forgotten to ring Greg and Phoebe, her friends from BTP she'd be meeting tomorrow . . . no, today! *'Goddamn it!'* Her head swivelled as an email pinged on her laptop. She picked up the empty glass, stalked over and pounded the key to open the message.

Better watch that language – he'll get pissed off.

'What the . . .?'

She spun around as if to catch someone hiding in the room.

Long pure-white feathers cascaded down the walls, covering the sofa, the mat, the coffee table – the entire living room. It was a blizzard of white. The fine dust from the feathers caught in her throat. The room filled and the feathers were now waist deep. Panic took hold as she tried to wade to the door, but the feathers were like thick snow. Her leg hit something hard and unseen under the blanket of feathers and she felt herself falling.

The feathers rose up to claim her as she fell through them, plummeting towards a dark door. After an eternity, she landed on something familiar. She felt around tentatively, unable to see, her eyes swollen and streaming from the fine dust. Her hands moved across a coarse material, then some piping. Her sofa? Frantically clawing at the cushions, she fell to the floor, jolting herself awake.

Clambering to her knees, she rolled back up on to the sofa, sweat making her top stick to her. She realized she'd just experienced her first true nightmare. Restless now, she swung her legs off the seat cushion and walked to her shuttered window. She peered left through the white-painted slats to the street corner. Barely a hundred yards away the River Thames was being sucked east towards Kent and the North Sea. She raised her eyes to the sky. The sun would be up soon. Taking a few deep breaths and stretching, she decided to revive herself with a cup of Earl Grey tea and some sourdough toast. Perhaps she'd go for an early run along the Thames' embankment. That might clear her scrambled brain before heading in early to work.

Thirty minutes later, she closed the front door of her flat, set her stopwatch, and ran past the rows of identical Victorian orange-brick terrace houses and chest-high fences toward Rotherwood Road, then on to the embankment. This was a run she enjoyed, but had trouble finding time for. At least her nightmare had given her *that*.

Her mood lightened. Running always did that for her. In fact, any physical activity worked that magic. Her chosen line of work was all consuming, and there had been little time even for karate, a sport she had embraced as a ten-year-old and still loved. She had reached instructor level years ago and was now supposedly studying and training for her third-degree black belt, but the last six months had seen that all slip. Relationships too had suffered over the past few years. Beyond the very occasional and, in retrospect, ill-considered one-night stands, there had been no regular male presence in her life, apart from her father.

She conceded that she didn't suffer fools gladly and so many of the boys/men who showed an interest in her seemed to her to be somehow a bit lame, wimpy, or just plain silly. She'd often thought her expectations might just be too damned high. Her decision to pursue a career in criminal investigation had alienated her from her university friends, many of whom were now well established in law firms and medical practices and earning three times her salary.

Of course, there had been quiet, intelligent Alan from Trinity. He'd tried valiantly to keep their relationship going beyond its one year on-and-off-again life; but if nothing else, the timing was bad. University ended and his career dictated that he find work in the wilds of Scotland, farming and studying his beloved trout. They'd emailed and rung each other for a while, but it was just too hard and she was already busy carving out a career in a tough world. To be honest, she'd been finding Alan more than a little boring at times. *Trout* for God's sake! The prospect of spending the rest of her life listening to wild-eyed stories about *Salmo trutta's* spawning cycle somehow failed to light her fire.

The monotony and rhythm of the run worked its endorphin-driven magic. Her mind rid itself of the confusion of the past day and her thoughts roamed freely, landing on her father and his reaction to her choosing a career in CID.

He hadn't been disappointed, he claimed, but she could see then and even now, that something worried him about her work. She never could put her finger on it, despite good-naturedly interrogating him about it occasionally over the years. Her mother, Susan, had always been supportive, but again, there was a level of *concern* there that she could not quite fathom. She wondered if it was because she didn't have a job as a high-powered lawyer. Still, she'd earned the law degree, with first-class honours, so her mother had half her wish.

She remembered she was to go to her parents' home for a drink and dinner that night to celebrate her promotion. She wondered wryly who her mother had arranged to prepare the meal. Suzie Whiteman couldn't boil an egg.

She was working up a fair sweat now, even though it was still dim and cool. It had been a good summer so far, which had made last night's strong winds so out of character. There were no signs of any damage this morning that she could see. The Hammersmith Bridge came into view and she checked her time as she always did at this point. She was much slower than normal. No surprise there. That mental promise from last night to hit the gym would have to be honoured.

She heard someone running up behind her and moved to the right of the track to let him pass. The footsteps were heavy, so she assumed it was a man. She figured he must be much fitter than she was – he was really travelling. The footsteps kept coming and were now appreciably louder. So loud now that he must be on top of her! In a last-second manoeuver, she stepped on to the grassy verge. Nobody came past. She was alone.

Allie stood there in disbelief, dumbly looking up and down the track, even across the river. Thoughts returned of her near miss with the advertising hoarding. 'Easy, girl,' she said to herself. 'Don't get spooked.' Checking the time, she decided to run back home in any case. It was time to focus on the grizzly job at hand this morning – informing her team that Billy McBride had passed away. Below that, the excitement of taking the reins of command still bubbled away. It would be a big day, moving offices thrown in for good measure. As she ran, she listened for footsteps other than her own and ran a little bit faster because of it. She was unnerved. The footsteps had seemed very real.

Detective Sergeant Rachel Strauss arrived at her office much earlier than usual. It was only 7:00 a.m., but she had given up on sleep at 4:00 a.m. She had the place almost to herself and headed for the tearoom. She filled a jug with water, ferreted out the instant coffee, and sniffed the milk. She needed a caffeine hit. Minutes later and cradling the cup to warm her hands, she wandered down the corridor towards the common area on to which most of the CID offices fronted. The emptiness hummed.

She stopped outside Billy McBride's office. Anger immediately rose at the thought of Allison St. Clair occupying it later that morning. Billy had been a joke, she knew that, but of all people to succeed him, why did it have to be *her*? Little Miss Over-Educated, oh, so attractive Allie-fucking-St. Clair, the poster girl for the Met. She was destined to become the youngest superintendent in the history of British policing, according to the latest scuttlebutt. *Spare me,* she thought.

She wondered why she'd ever thought she could have competed with St. Clair. Presumably, St. Clair had political connections through her big-time father and more money than you could poke a Versace label at. St. Clair's Putney apartment, to which Rachel used to be regularly invited, was worth way more than Rachel's parents' house in East Cheam – and they had worked hard their whole lives to finally clear their mortgage. Putting Rachel and her brother Damian through university had all but broken them. Their expectations of her still weighed her down. At some point in her sleepless night, she had resolved that this was just round one with St. Clair.

She slumped into her swivel chair behind the featureless wood and metal desk and picked up the file on the investigation to which Billy had assigned her only a week ago, the morning of the start of his health troubles. Once again Allie invaded her thoughts. Even though south Londoner Billy clearly didn't relate to the privileged St. Clair, he still gave her the best cases – the eye-catching ones, while she, Rachel, was chasing petty thieves operating in and around tube stations. At least Billy and the boys still gave St. Clair a hard time – that was *something*.

Hearing footsteps, she looked up. It was DC Peter Banks.

'You're in early, Rache. Mess the bed did we?'

'Get stuffed, Banks.'

Banks clutched his chest, the bulbous rolls of fat around his waist wobbling like jelly. He laughed.

'Ouch! Rapier-like reply there, DS Strauss. Have another coffee and try again in twenty minutes.'

She was in no mood for Banks' smart-arsery this morning. Her humour was blackening by the minute.

Chapter Four

Allie booted the little black Yamaha over Putney Bridge and up the King's Road. There was no need to bother about Fulham Road at this early hour, and in truth, she didn't want to pass the Chelsea Hospital again. Not for a long while. She had a good clear run, with traffic only thickening around 7:30. She swung through Hobart Place, Buckingham Gate and into Petty France. She parked her bike, entered the Yard building and a minute later came up beside DC Mathew Connors who was waiting at the lifts.

'Good morning, Al . . . DCI St. Clair,' he said, clearly uncomfortable with her new rank.

'Oh please, Matt – that sounds so weird.' She laughed.

He smiled back. 'The big day, eh? Feeling different . . . nervous?'

She hesitated before answering. Nervous? She couldn't admit to that.

'Well, certainly *different* anyway. Unfortunately, the day is also tinged with more than a little sadness.'

She saw his concerned look.

'I'll explain shortly,' she added.

They stopped at level five. Walking to her office, she was greeted by random staff as they shuffled to their desks. Her co-workers offered a few more congratulatory remarks, which she graciously accepted. Rachel Strauss didn't acknowledge Allie's friendly, 'Good morning,' as she passed by her office. Noticing this, Allie decided to speak to Rachel later that morning. Best to jump on it early.

The balance of Allie's team and the support staff trickled in, and by 8:15 a.m. it looked like everyone was in. Allie asked her inherited PA, Margaret Daly, to gather everyone in the meeting room at 8:30 a.m. She spent the next few minutes sorting files for the move and gathering her thoughts about Billy.

There was a hubbub in the meeting room as she approached it, including someone, probably Banks, saying he thought that there should at least have been some sausage rolls and little pies on offer. *Normally, there would be,* she thought.

She greeted everyone again with the standard, 'Good morning,' and stopped in her tracks as they replied in unison with an obviously rehearsed, 'Good morning, ma'am!'

There was no getting past this, she realized. Things had changed, but she smiled warmly and rolled her eyes theatrically.

Surveying the room, she saw that the same people as yesterday were there and she wondered what they thought she was about to say.

'I wish I could start today on a positive note, but alas, it's not to be.'

Puzzled looks greeted her words and she got straight to the point.

'I'm very sad to inform you all that Billy McBride passed away at approximately 7:00 p.m. last night.'

The reaction was as she'd expected. There were expressions of surprise, sadness and one or two of the long-time employees were clearly very upset. Surprisingly to Allie, none of her core team appeared to take it too hard – at least that she could see.

'I'm aware that some of you have known Billy for a long time and if anyone feels they need time to deal with this, I leave it to you to do as you see fit. You have my support and sympathies.' No one came forward or expressed a desire to leave the room.

'I don't want to go on about it, but I can tell you he died suddenly and with virtually no suffering.'

There was silence.

'Just so you know,' she continued, 'DS Carr is aware of the situation, and I imagine funeral arrangements will be announced later today. I'll organize a wreath from us and flowers for Billy's widow, Suzie.'

'How do you know?'

Allie looked to the side of the room to see Rachel Strauss gesturing towards her.

'Sorry . . . how do I know . . . what?'

'That he didn't suffer,' she replied, the nasty edge to her voice evident to all. 'I mean, you weren't exactly *close* were you? Socially, *universes* apart, wouldn't you say?'

There it is, Allie thought. Okay, she'd deal with this right now. Electricity crackled in the room.

'Rachel, I think everybody knows Billy and I had our differences – it's not exactly news. It is regrettable and something I personally feel considerable remorse about.'

'*Really*?' Rachel barked. 'But you haven't answered my question yet.'

Adrenalin surged through Allie's veins, carrying a boatload of pent-up anger with it. Her natural inclination was to let her have both barrels. This was inappropriate and untimely behaviour from Strauss, but she had to resist the obvious bait.

She eyeballed Rachel, delaying a response for nearly five seconds, until she saw her flush bright crimson. Only then did she speak – slowly and calmly.

'I can see that Billy's sudden passing has upset you, Rachel, and I fully understand that. If, unlike the rest of the team, you feel you need to take a break for an hour or even go home, *feel free to do so now.*'

She waited, along with everyone else in the room, for Rachel to respond. Rachel said and did nothing, however, except remain crimson.

Allie allowed herself to be sidetracked no longer and returned to the subject at hand. 'Despite this awful development, we all have a busy day ahead. Once again, I'm sorry to be the bearer of such sad news.'

No one shuffled or looked away now.

'I'd planned to at least begin a series of one-on-one interviews with you, as is our normal procedure when a senior management change occurs, but under the circumstances, let's leave that for tomorrow. Thank you, everyone.'

Turning to leave, Allie brushed against DCS Carr, whom she now realized must have been standing behind her, watching the show.

'Good morning, ma'am,' Allie managed, despite her lingering annoyance with Strauss.

Ellen Carr smiled and suggested Allie walk with her to the cafeteria downstairs.

They walked in silence, beginning the lift descent to the first floor a minute later.

'I suggested we go for a walk rather than talk in your office, Allie, because it may have looked to the others as though you were copping a bollocking.'

'I appreciate that courtesy, ma'am.'

They ordered coffees and walked to the table Allie expected – Carr's favourite spot, which overlooked Broadway from just above the building's main entrance.

Carr didn't speak again for a couple of minutes and Allie wondered what was coming next. *First morning on the new job and in trouble already*, she thought.

'Well done in there, by the way. Nasty little scenario on two fronts,' Carr finally said.

Allie couldn't deny she was relieved.

Carr continued, 'Strauss was out of line there – I was approaching the door to the room and heard her performance.'

Allie blew a stream of air and flicked back a lock of dark hair.

'And I thought it was my evil eye that had turned her crimson,' she said.

Carr laughed. 'Oh you did that all right. She was staring at you like a rabbit caught in the headlights. I doubt she even knew I was there.'

Allie had to smile despite the tension of the morning.

'Well, I hope never to have another exchange like that with her – at least not in public.'

Carr caught the 'not in public' qualifier and frowned.

'I couldn't agree more, Allie. You need to sort this problem out before it becomes a monster.'

'Absolutely,' Allie broke in. 'I plan to talk with her privately at the first opportunity – perhaps even later today.'

'Glad to hear it. Let me know how it goes.' It was an order.

For the next ten minutes they discussed Billy and the events at the hospital the night before. Carr finally drained her coffee and suggested it was time to get on with things, but not before reminding Allie that over the slightly longer term, building a strong cohesive team was her core challenge. The message wasn't lost on Allie, particularly in the context of the morning's theatrics.

Allie enlisted the help of two administration staff and completed her move into Billy's glass-encased office by 11:45 a.m. It offered a different perspective on the CID operations centre. From her new desk, she could see the length of the general office and, apart from the little IT nook off to the side by the fire escape, she could see all twenty occupants of the section – or at least their desks. She'd catch up with the office supervisor and go over all the resources issues later. She called a meeting for 3:00

p.m. to review all active cases and the issue of DC Rachel Strauss floated back to the front of her mind. It had been hovering all morning of course. She checked her watch; she had about an hour before catching her friends for lunch. *Time to do it*, she decided. She rang the head of human resources, then DS Strauss.

Allie figured that Rachel had been expecting the call from her, but perhaps not quite so soon. Rachel had crossed the line earlier and she'd know that Allie wouldn't be able to let it go. In truth, no DCI worth his or her salt could have ignored her outburst. Rachel had been curt on the phone, arriving at her door fifteen minutes later.

'Take a seat, Rachel,' Allie said, waving at the narrow vinyl-covered chair she'd placed in front of her desk moments earlier. From her reaction, it was clear Rachel had not anticipated there being a human resources representative present.

'You know Trevor, I assume?' Allie asked her.

Rachel looked at him and offered a faltering smile. Trevor Bailey was a thirty-year veteran of the Met and had interviewed Rachel four years ago when she'd first applied to be a detective. He was as plump as ever and had lost even more of his wispy silver hair.

'Yes, of course. Hello, Trevor.'

'DS Strauss.'

Trevor was usually a jovial type despite his job description, but today he showed no hint of cheer. Strauss knew she was in trouble.

Allie studied Strauss and was a little disappointed in what she saw. Rachel had been attractive in a healthy, buxom, outdoorsy way only a few years ago. But hardness lurked about her now – her hair was cut thin and bleached, her eyebrows pencilled in unnecessarily. Thin lines radiated from the corners of eyes which narrowed over dark circles her heavy make-up failed to mask.

'Rachel, I'll get to the point: I cannot and *will not* accept the type of behaviour you exhibited this morning.'

Rachel was taken aback by the aggression, but replied nonetheless. 'May I ask what behaviour that is . . . exactly?'

Allie realized she was still angry with Rachel and made a huge effort to control it. She wanted this conversation to be short.

'Okay, you know very well what I'm talking about – your sullenness towards me, your refusal to communicate in a normal, effective way and that bitter outburst this morning – you must realize I can't abide it.'

Rachel stared back at her.

'Look, whatever personal views you may hold about me are beyond my control and are yours to hold. However, I believe you to be an intelligent and effective operative and I will give you every opportunity to shine and progress your career. It would be an abrogation of my duties to ignore your insubordinate remarks – particularly those made publicly.'

Strauss said nothing. Allie pressed on.

'Do you understand that the open animosity you display towards me is unprofessional, could undermine our effectiveness as a unit, and is demeaning to you personally?'

Rachel Strauss looked as though she'd crawl into a hole if God opened one up for her. Big tears glistened in her eyes. The best she could manage was a nod.

Allie and Trevor glanced at each other. Allie continued, but in a softer tone.

'Rachel, if there are issues you'd prefer to discuss with Trevor, or if you feel you need to talk to a counsellor, just say so. I'll understand and support that.'

Again, there was no response.

'Something has to change or we'll have an insurmountable problem.'

Allie thought she caught a 'You can go fuck yourself' look pass across Strauss's face, but her reply belied that.

'I understand,' Strauss said quietly. 'But I'd like a transfer to another division.'

Allie jumped on the comment hard. 'You're not getting one, Rachel. That's not the answer. I'm not transferring my problem from here to someone else.'

'It's not all about *you*, Allison, and how *you* look.' Strauss pouted. It was an answer a child might have given.

Allie thought quickly. If she pursued Strauss's infantile reaction, this conversation would never end, plus Strauss would end up out of the force – such was the road she was starting to travel. Despite Strauss's animosity, she'd been a close friend once; she was a damn good cop and they were in short supply. Allie threw her a lifeline, simply by ignoring her outburst. She hoped Trevor Bailey would do the same.

'What's it to be, Rache? Can you see yourself buckling down and applying yourself in a positive way to your job?'

Strauss squirmed in her chair, her inner conflict obvious. She held a half-smile.

'Yes, DCI St. Clair, I believe I can.'

'Starting now?'

'Yes, starting now.'

'All right,' Allie said. 'I'm personally very glad to hear it. I'll discuss this issue further with Trevor and make a note in your file about your favourable response.'

Rachel nodded.

'Thank you, Rachel. I know this isn't fun, but I hope you understand the reasons for it.'

Rachel nodded, more at Trevor than Allie, then left the office. She didn't return to her desk, preferring instead to go to the restroom.

Allie looked at Trevor.

'What do you think . . .?'

'Dunno,' said Trevor, with stunning insight. 'You're not exactly her pin-up girl, are you?'

Allie had to admit he was right on that score.

Trevor went on to suggest there be a further performance review for Rachel in six weeks. Allie readily agreed, glad to get the difficult business over with.

She was late for lunch.

*

Rachel wasn't just upset by the meeting with St. Clair; she was incensed. How *dare* she drag HR into this! Now her record was besmirched, all over what she considered to be home truths that St. Clair had been too thin-skinned to handle.

Rachel had always thought that she and Billy had been good mates over the years. Sure, Billy was over the hill, but he'd treated her all right and they'd had the odd drink together. She knew Billy was uncomfortable around St. Clair. He'd never said much, but it was obvious that they weren't close. So how would *St. Clair* know how he died? It was pure PR veneer from her – pretending to have an intimate connection to his last hours. St. Clair had become smug and superior over the past year, and it was going to be a nightmare working at the Met with her in charge of the unit. She examined herself in the restroom mirror and decided her little burst of tears hadn't made her look too puffy. *Good*, she thought. *Don't want her to think I'm still bothered.* It was, after all, still only round one.

Chapter Five

The Feathers Inn was only a hundred yards from her office but, approaching the building, Allie wondered why on earth she'd chosen that location for lunch. It was great by all accounts and a historic eatery, but she'd simply never thought of it before. A text message blipped. She reached for her phone, sure that Greg and Phoebe were wondering where she was. The message read: *Great pub The Feathers, a personal favourite - Michael.*

She stood still, scanning the immediate area. No one was taking an inordinate interest in her. She checked the message and knew there would be no reply number. *How can that be?* IT stuff wasn't her forte. She was worried. This was amounting to electronic stalking, if there was such a thing – harassment at the very least.

She dodged a plumber's smoky van which wheezed across her path. The façade of the Feathers Inn, with its bright row of flowers atop the veranda, red woodwork and dark wooden door, came into view. It was British charm at its best. The huge white bird sculpture above the flower boxes took her eye as she entered the warm, polished wood interior of the inn. *In all*, she thought, *an inviting place.*

Greg and Phoebe stood and clapped as Allie approached their table.

'Hail, the conquering heroine!' Greg Johansen proclaimed, waving thin arms in the air. 'The youngest DC—'

'Shut up, for God's sake, Greg!' Allie laughed. Phoebe was in hysterics as well, her bright-red lips surrendering the battle to contain her big, gapped teeth as she laughed loudly, throwing her head back, her frizzy brown hair shaking like a shrubbery in a breeze. Phoebe Kite was the flower child her mother would have loved to have been.

The three friends hugged. Phoebe offered her heartfelt congratulations and Greg, in gestures Allie and Phoebe knew well, adjusted his tie probably for the twentieth time that day and tried in vain to smooth down his little spike of errant black hair in the front. Also, as expected, he quickly turned the conversation to the serious matter of beer.

'Er . . . I can't do that, matey,' Allie said, touching his arm.

Not missing a beat, he laughed and called for three orange juices, specifying they be doubles.

They spent the next forty minutes chatting about her promotion, their own respective hopes, and the disappointments they'd endured thus far, all the while demolishing a classy platter-style lunch.

Greg left to answer a call of nature and Phoebe, in typical style, leaned over and nudged Allie.

'Check out the hottie in the corner.' She nodded to Allie's left. Allie thought everyone in the room would have noticed Phoebe's theatrical, eye-rolling performance. Subtlety was not her strong suit. Allie paused for a moment, coolly sipping again at her orange juice, then followed Phoebe's gaze. She saw a guy, maybe late thirties, with longish, thick, dark hair and a shadow of stubble gracing a firm jawline. He wore a tan jacket, blue open-neck shirt and darker blue jeans. He was absorbed in stirring sugar into his coffee.

She turned back to the enthusiastic Phoebe. 'Bit eighties isn't he?'

'*Jesus*, you're hard to please, aren't you?' Phoebe shook her shrubbery in feigned disgust. 'I don't know, Allie. If George-effing-Clooney walked through the door, you'd say he was too short or too tall or too old.'

Allie laughed and looked over again at Phoebe's fancy. He glanced up at that moment, meeting her gaze. She lost her grip on her orange juice, but somehow managed to guide it down to the table, not without a thump. An electric current vibrated to her bones.

She had grunted involuntarily and Phoebe hadn't missed it. 'Well now, was that a reaction or *what*?'

Allie flushed bright red and knew it. She deliberately dropped her napkin, pausing a moment under the table to regain her composure. *Whoa!*

Phoebe was still smiling when Allie finally resurfaced. Greg re-joined them and Phoebe grabbed his arm and started to blab, but stopped abruptly when she caught Allie's gigantic warning look. Phoebe got it – a blind beggar would have understood – and she adroitly, albeit reluctantly, changed the subject.

The conversation relaxed and ranged through the usual topics, but Allie noticed Phoebe's regular, knowing looks. She wasn't going to let this go without a fight. Allie was on her hook.

They ordered coffee and Allie, rocking back in her chair, announced that she really liked the Feathers Inn.

'Can't imagine why I suddenly thought of it,' Allie said, taking the opportunity to glance over again towards Eighties Man. He'd gone. *Funny*, she thought with more than a tinge of disappointment, *I didn't notice him leave*.

The memory of the white feather in the storm and her nightmare about drowning in feathers flooded back . . . and now she was in the Feathers Inn. *Feathers! How could I not have connected them?* She must have worn a strange expression because Phoebe leaned over and asked if she was okay.

Allie laughed and said she was fine – going completely bonkers, of course – but other than that, 'All good.' They agreed the Feathers Inn would make a great local for them.

Allie realized she'd also not yet mentioned the freaky text messages she was getting. Maybe it was because there was the off chance one of them was behind some sort of joke. After all, they'd all played silly pranks on each other over the many years they'd been friends. In truth, however, the messages were playing on her mind. She decided to fess up.

Even as she told them, she could see they genuinely had no knowledge of the messages. In fact, Greg and

Phoebe expressed great concern. 'These things could be nasty,' they said. Once the conversation about the texts had run its course, the mood lightened again and Allie raved about the fabulous bird sculpture above the Feathers' veranda.

'I must have walked past this place a hundred times, but never noticed it before.'

Laughing, her friends exchanged puzzled looks.

'Sculpture?'

'See, you haven't noticed it either! I'll show you on the way out – it's gorgeous!'

They paid their respective bills and, weaving through the still well-populated inn, emerged under the veranda by the road. They stepped out during a break in the traffic so Allie could point out the sculpture.

It was no surprise to Greg and Phoebe that there wasn't one.

After the goodbyes with Greg and Phoebe and vague promises of catching up early the following week, Allie walked quickly back to her office, scanning left and right just in case she could spot her phantom text buddy. She was worried. The episode with the sculpture was just too much. She'd laughed it off at the time, but this was serious. Her heart had pounded like a hammer when she'd looked up to discover she'd merely imagined the sculpture. It had seemed so real to her, yet it didn't exist – *couldn't have existed*.

She hurried through the Met offices and closed her office door behind her. She wondered again about what the hell her subconscious preoccupation with feathers, and now birds, was all about. Her phone bleeped again – another text message. She stared at the phone like it was a bomb and decided to take it to the IT guys downstairs to see what they could make of the crazy messages – *if they're really there*, she caught herself thinking. Finally she weakened and read the message. It was from her sister, Jo. Thank God!

What time is dinner at home tonight? Need a lift?

The girls always called their parents' house 'home', even though they were both well settled in their own apartments. Jo and her husband, Marcus, owned a place in Clapham, not that far from Allie. They'd been furiously renovating, so any meal they didn't have to prepare would be welcome. Allie confirmed the 7:30 p.m. kick-off for dinner and accepted their offer of a ride to the St. Clair house in upscale Belgravia. She suggested a pickup at 7:00 p.m.

Arthur Wendell clicked the lock on his brown leather satchel and closed the door to his Earl's Court taxation consultancy and accountancy practice. He had but four clients: one large organization and the rest private clients – those, he personally liked. He was financially comfortable, as a result.

It was 5:00 p.m. precisely. And it was Wednesday; his personal treat night. Walking for exactly seven and a half minutes, he arrived at the heavy wooden door of the Black Crow Hotel, which had perched menacingly on the corner of Earl's Court Road and Frankston Gardens in Chelsea for a hundred years. He saw barmaid Sarah Blascombe glance up from the job he knew she hated most: cleaning beer glasses. She acknowledged his arrival with the usual nod. Arthur Wendell sat at his regular, little round table, set for one, beside the staircase, and awaited the arrival of his Young's Ramrod Special Bitter. He knew Sarah would abide by the Wednesday night ritual and would already be pouring his beer for him. Once more he allowed himself the thought that she would one day make someone a nice wife. She knew men and understood the value of anticipation and ritual. His eyes wandered to her neckline as she momentarily bent low over the counter. He averted his eyes – she would think he was some sort of pervert if she caught him staring at her milky cleavage. He pushed the troublesome thoughts from his head and checked his watch. He was pleased to note all was progressing according to his treat-night timetable.

Sarah put a nice frothy head on the Young's, looked over at Arthur and smiled. *There he is*, she thought, *regular as clockwork. Dressed, as always, in the same black trousers, a brown waistcoat over a white buttoned-to-the-neck shirt, no tie, and fawn coat. Funny little beige man*, she thought. He'd order the cod and chips and then, as an afterthought, politely ask whether he might trouble her for some extra tartar sauce, no matter how much had already been supplied.

It was always *exactly* the same routine. She'd worked at the Crow since leaving secondary school after the accident. She loved it there. Its warm atmosphere and generally nice, chatty clientele suited her and, best of all, her father managed the pub – for nearly seven years.

Arthur was the most regular of regulars in a pub which had built a profitable family of customers.

The Crow had saved Sarah from seriously having to look for work when she left school – a task she'd found terrifying in prospect. Her father had come to the rescue and she hadn't yet found a reason to leave. She'd 'inherited' Arthur when she started waitressing, serving him very nearly every Wednesday evening since, absences through holidays and illnesses excepted. He was, in her view, a nice middle-aged, slightly lonely man – although she had once caught him furtively eyeing her blonde hair and fuller figure. But that was okay; it went with job and the uniform *was* stupidly tight.

It seemed to her that over the years, he had changed very little – maybe a little thicker around the middle, but his thin hair had never really lightened and his bespectacled face looked pretty much the same as time had worn on. If pressed, she'd put him at about fifty, but she'd have said that seven years ago as well. Above all, he was unfailingly courteous and seemed appreciative of her bouncy, friendly service. She could ask for no more.

Arthur enjoyed his fish and chips with extra sauce, paid the bill in cash, neatly folded his napkin, gathered his satchel, and smiled his thanks at Sarah. He left the hotel and turned right on to Earl's Court Road towards Watson's Newsagents, where he would buy a copy of the latest *Electronics Monthly*. Before settling on accountancy as a career and discovering the brilliant symmetry of numbers, he'd been mad keen as a kid to work in electronics. He loved the gadgetry and the magic of electricity. It illuminated the world, but there was an ever-present danger which you ignored at your peril. It was misunderstood. But his father had been adamant – accountancy and a life in business it would be. That was when his father was home. Most of the time he was left with his mother and her . . . games. In a fit of pique when he wouldn't get back into bed with her, she'd smashed his major electronics project which would have shown the other kids at school he was somebody with *talent*.

He shrugged off the memory and wiped the sheen of sweat from his forehead with his immaculately ironed handkerchief. He had to catch the 179 bus to Notting Hill Gate at 6:20 p.m. Tonight he would also indulge his other passion. He would clean the upholstery on his light-blue classic 1965 Mercedes 230S saloon – the one with the fin tail. He loved it when the rich upholstery shone. There wasn't a mark on it or the body, and he'd owned it for nearly twenty years. He drove it once a month from Notting Hill to Richmond Park and back. He always made himself a picnic lunch of home-baked bread, Dutch cheeses, pickles and a thermos of instant coffee. He hated that stuff they made in cafés.

He greeted the girl behind the shop counter with a warm hello. She returned his smile as he moved to the magazine racks. He hadn't seen the girl before – he'd have to ask her name. It was nice to know the people with whom you regularly dealt. Arthur thought it just made life . . . nicer. He rifled through the magazines as if he might buy something other than the electronics magazine, but of course he bought it again. Turning from the racks, he walked slightly to his left to check his hair before leaving the shop. That troublesome little cowlick might need some plastering down. He knew it would be the only mirror he'd have a chance to look into before boarding the bus. He harboured a more-than-slight hope that Francine Higgins, a recently widowed, forty-something woman who lived on his street, might just be catching the 179 home tonight as well. He fronted the mirror and stared into the black, dead eyes of a winged monster.

Arthur Wendell regained consciousness at the third stinging slap. He looked around wide-eyed before focusing on an earnest young face framed by black, curly hair no more than a foot from his own.

'Are you okay?' the young man enquired. 'You've been out for about a minute – we were about to call an ambulance!'

Arthur looked again at him, then *through* him. He jerked involuntarily and tried to scramble to his feet.

'Take it easy, my man,' another, deeper voice said. 'We have work to do.'

Arthur turned to see who had spoken, but there was only the young man and an elderly woman crouching unsteadily beside him. With their help, he struggled to his feet. He heard his glasses break underfoot. Groaning, he bent down to pick up the shattered remnants. He realized with another jolt that he could see perfectly well without them. He turned the broken frames over in his hand and peered at them. Every minute detail was revealed to him – the tiny screws, the etching on the side 'made in China', even a tiny initial 'H' on the screw heads.

'Yes, thank you,' he finally replied to the helpful young man. 'I'm . . . *we're fine.*'

Arthur Wendell didn't catch the 179 bus to Notting Hill. He lingered at the bus stop and disinterestedly watched as Francine Higgins boarded. Her tight skirt and furtive look over her shoulder should have had his adrenaline pulsing. But not now. Francine might have been made of cardboard for all he cared. Another filled his brain. *Consumed him.* He had to have her – that was what she was there for. He knew it. He now understood what she'd been thinking; it was so clear now! She'd been put there for him – *a gift* – and he'd nearly missed it! She was *the one*! He almost physically cringed as he thought how utterly stupid and insensitive it was of him not to have sensed her feelings.

He laughed loudly, startling a young mother so much she shepherded her child further away from him as they walked past. *Careful Arthur* the voice said. He'd have to watch himself. He must behave normally. Mousey Arthur Wendell would remain his cover, oh yes. But it would be hard to camouflage his animal self, his new magnetism. Women would be drawn to him; it was going to be embarrassing! He knew he'd have to try to stay bland, but the juices coursing through him prickled against the sides of his veins and pulsed through his fingertips. He felt hyper-alive, in charge and abso-fucking-lutely unbreakable!

He jogged back to the Black Crow Hotel. A raging thirst, unlike any he could remember, gnawed at his throat. There was a lot that was different about him now. He felt confident, *stronger*. He breasted the bar and waited for Sarah to reappear. She managed this section. She'd come; he was sure. He jiggled the little golden bell, something he would never normally do. He waited. But it wasn't Sarah who finally came. It was bored, condescending Jilly, or Julie, with her gothic black hair and bright-red lipstick. She didn't serve him; she confronted him. She raised her eyebrows – the minimum effort from her was the best he would ever get. Another wafer-thin girl also came to fetch some glasses from under the bar. Where the hell was Sarah?

Any port in a storm, Arthur, the inner voice said. It was a cool voice, even-toned, lacking emotion, with no inflection or accent that he could discern – just a new voice in his head. He asked for a pint of dark. The girl didn't acknowledge his request, just turned to the tap and poured. *So rude.* The new girl at the far end of the bar organized the glasses into a rack and looked over at the girl pouring his drink.

'What time d'ya finish, Georgie?'

Georgie, that's right, Arthur thought.

Georgie looked at her watch and replied that she'd be off in about fifteen minutes, 'Once I get rid of this lot.' He heard her shout back. Obviously, she was referring to him and the old couple who were just finishing their meal at the small, oblong table by the window

'This lot,' Arthur noted. Charming.

Looking somewhere in the middle distance over his right shoulder, she plonked the heavy base of the glass on the towelling bar runner, the dark ale barely staying within the confines of the glass. There was no please or thank you, just a statement of fact, 'Three quid.' His eyes slowly travelled the length of her as she waited for him to fish out the money.

He took in her showy, sequined top which clung like a wet thing to her upper body, her too-perky breasts cantilevering at a ridiculous angle, and the skin-tight pink jeans which stopped prematurely above her ankles.

Something squirmed in his brain. He became slightly disoriented, his vision blurring and shifting. For a panicky moment he thought he might lose his balance. He gripped the rounded wooden moulding of the bar's edge for support. A trickle of sweat ran between his shoulder blades, its warmth enveloping each pore of his skin as gravity pulled it to the base of his spine. He heard himself pant. As suddenly as he'd lost it, his balance returned, as did his super-vision.

Again, he marvelled at its laser-like clarity. Sarah's inexplicable absence no longer bothered him. He smiled at the way he could now do that – just redirect his thinking and apply himself completely to a new target. Everything else in the room receded to the background as the rest of his senses joined the game. They became almost painfully sensitive – *amplified.* He stared at the barmaid who was still standing there as if in a dream. He could hear her faint breathing with its wheezy hint of a restricted airway. Yes, he could smell the cigarettes now, too. His eyes zeroed in on her troweled-on make-up and heavy black eye shadow. He could see the blobs of black on the ends of each eyelash and the teeny-tiny crow's feet around her eyes. She wasn't as young as she made out. He looked in an almost detached way at her arched, plucked eyebrows and the thick, stubbly line which betrayed the track of the originals.

Georgie was probably not her real name, more like *Georgeta*. He followed the line of tiny blackheads running the length of her nose and saw, with a little amusement, how they concentrated in a little dark patch at the turned-up point. *Not a good look, Georgeta*. He saw that her make-up didn't quite mask her failure to scrub the rest of her face, either that morning or maybe as long ago as last week. Her nostrils had minute broken veins inside the curve where they joined her thin lips. She either had a cold or liked the odd snort of cocaine.

He felt his nose involuntarily crinkle as the odour of too many sticky roll-ons and sickly-sweet discount perfumes reached him. There were about four different scents layered in there. He noticed, with a little thrill, that she had a red welt on her neck, only partly masked by a shiny mock-silver necklace. She'd earned that cheap trinket, no doubt as payment from her latest 'boyfriend' for services rendered. *Even the boyfriend was cheap,* Arthur thought. He knew her now, knew who and *what* she was. God knows he could probably X-ray her if he wanted to. He liked this new supercharged Arthur. He didn't know how or why, but he was transforming. He could feel himself crackling with energy and *power*. It even felt to him as though he could feel his hair growing.

'Very cool,' he said.

'Huh?' Georgie said, staring at him with a 'what th' fuck?' expression.

How long had he been taking his inventory of the girl? It felt like minutes, but it couldn't have been. Time had somehow stretched for him. *Even cooler.*

He was too excited to speak. His blood turned to hot champagne. He slapped the three pounds on the bar without looking at her again. He didn't need to. Every detail of her was imprinted on a chart in his head. He could fold it, turn it around, change the colours and it just sat there – *the Georgie file* – ready for him to access any time he chose. And that would be very soon. He knew now what he was going to do and where. Had Georgie bothered to take an interest in her customers, she might have seen him drain the glass in two gulps, then abruptly leave. She might also have stopped him slipping the heavy-bottomed beer glass into his jacket pocket.

Chapter Six

Allie and Jo whooped at the sight of the caterer's van parked in the driveway of their parents' home. Of course that's how their mother had prepared Allie's congratulatory dinner! Kensington Katering – perfect!

Marcus trotted out the old joke, 'What do Belgravia women make for dinner?'

'Reservations!' Allie and Jo chorused. Allie's father and mother met them at the door and were effusive in their praise for Allie's promotion to detective chief inspector.

They were genuinely pleased for her, she could see that, although she was a little disappointed they hadn't seen fit to invite her brother, Robert. Apparently, the wounds still ran deep. Inside, the requisite bottle of Bollinger was cracked and Kensington Katering tiptoed efficiently around the cavernous dining room as the evening progressed. It had been a little while since Allie had been back to the house in which she'd grown up. Little had changed. The white stucco home looked pretty much like all the rest around the Chester Square area. It was old, as was her family, and it reeked of money, ditto her family. Her father drove a spanking new Aston Martin Vantage and her mother, Suzie, had just told her she'd placed an order for a smart new Audi TT. Allie didn't ask what had happened to her only slightly older one. She'd probably wrapped it around a tree in a drunken stupor. Suzie Whiteman, successful author of the acclaimed Celtic Cross series for young adults, was a lush of Churchillian proportions.

After the award-winning dinner, the catering staff politely thanked and paid, Allie's father motioned for her to join him in the drawing room. It amused Allie that they had such a thing as a drawing room – she'd thought of it as a playroom for so long. Jo and Marcus looked at each other, wondering what the secrecy was about. Suzie slipped away to the bathroom.

Allie and her father sat roughly opposite in the huge rounded brown leather chairs she'd loved as a child. They still smelled rich, although grey spidery cracks wound their way through them, testament to years of use and neglect. Snuggling into the chair brought fond recollections of long, dark winter days when she'd stoke the fire and read until her eyes hurt. She scanned the books in the room, another childhood habit. The heavy oaken shelves occupied an entire wall and faced the ornate rosewood desk by the curtained window. The shelves groaned under the weight of a thousand books – mostly historical tomes about the British Isles, although she spotted one about Normandy. There were huge, ancient-looking Bibles, mysterious leather-bound books with faded engraving and, in the corner, and surprisingly, there was some modern fiction. She was amazed to see *The Da Vinci Code* crammed next to a book about Faeries. She smiled to herself. Even the venerable Professor St. Clair wasn't immune to a great bit of escapism. It was the room in which Allie had always felt most comfortable as a child. But at this moment, it seemed slightly different to her. She thought she remembered it being bigger than it now appeared. The perspective of children often distorted reality.

David St. Clair was an impressive man – even Allie could see that. He was tall, silver-haired and good-looking in that St. Clair way. Allie looked a lot like him; everybody said that, apart from the height. She was the same, average stature as her mother. There had been rumours in past years of female undergraduates finding Professor St. Clair very appealing indeed, but nothing ever seemed to come of it, at least that Allie was aware of. His voice was his chief asset though: deep, relaxed and cultured – he'd sounded authoritative on radio and it hadn't been long before television executives had noticed. His Celtic Myths and Legends series for BBC2 had been a huge hit. 'You're on your way, Allison,' he said, raising his brandy in salute.

'Thanks, Dad,' she replied. 'It seems so.'

'How's life generally, though? Are you happy with . . . everything?'

She knew what he was alluding to. As with all fathers, he was concerned that, at thirty, she hadn't found a partner or made babies.

'Yes, all good,' she said, trying to head off an inquisition.

He hesitated a moment. *Here it comes,* Allie thought, *something's on his mind.*

'You know you can always move back here if you were inclined, don't you?'

This was such surprise that she didn't quite know how to respond.

'What's brought this on?'

He smiled and swirled his brandy. 'Nothing, really. I just wanted you to know that if life was to become a bit tough or threatening, you're always welcome here.'

'Well, thank you, but I guess I've never thought about it. Are you worried about me for some reason?'

David St. Clair looked hard at her and she felt a little alarm going off.

'I am, to tell you the truth. And I'm not going to explain quite why, mysterious as that sounds.'

'It *does* sound mysterious. Now you're starting to worry me,' she laughed. 'What's going on?'

'Let me ask you this,' he said. 'Have you been contacted by anybody recently? Has anybody new come into your life . . .?'

'No, I've not met anyone new . . . there's no time for that at present. You basically just asked me that a few moments ago, didn't you?'

He got up out of his big chair and walked to the bookshelf, scanning a section about head high and to his left. He took down a pale volume and placed it on the desk.

'It was a slightly different question, Allison.' He smiled. 'So you're saying that apart from the wonderful promotion, life goes on to your satisfaction?'

'Yes, absolutely. If you're worried about my breaking up with Alan, don't be. It was never—'

He chuckled and told her it was nothing to do with Trout Boy. They both smiled at that. He asked whether she'd seen his interview on BBC4 about the Glastonbury Tor sightings.

'Sorry, I didn't. When was this?'

'Monday night. That airhead, Roseanne Palmer, called me to talk about new lights seen orbiting St. Michael's Tower.'

'Really? Anything to it?'

He looked closely at her. 'There just might be. I played down the sightings, of course, but you never know.'

Allie was intrigued. She remembered the Tor very well – it had played a big part in her childhood. She'd spent many summer days climbing that funny bump in the landscape. She remembered an old farmer guy down there shooing her off his property as well. He'd been fierce; unreasonably so, she'd thought at the time. She'd only brushed one of his roses, but he'd gone off his head at her.

In fact, something about the Tor had freaked her out a bit once back then and the family had cut short the visit as a consequence. The St. Clairs had visited the Tor many, many times while her father was doing his PhD in ancient Celtic history. Her brother, Robert, had come to hate the place though.

'You never know?' she persisted. 'What do you mean exactly?'

'The chief detective coming out in you, is it?' His tanned face cracked into a broad smile.

'Absolutely! Give.'

'No great theories here, Allison, but these sightings are consistent with those reported in the 1940's and way back beyond that as well.'

'Weren't they put down to bombers returning from raids over Dresden at the time?'

'Good memory,' he said, clearly pleased with her. 'They were ascribed to aircraft, but I have to tell you, I don't agree with that. There were obviously no aircraft about when the lights were first recorded in 461.'

'So, what are you suggesting . . . that something truly weird is going on?

'I think—' He was interrupted by hoots of laughter from the living room. Allie's mother burst into the room, giggling loudly. She'd had a champagne or three.

'Allie! You must see this!'

She was holding a battered green photo album, open at the centre. Allie could see photographs plastered over the pages at random angles.

'Check this one out,' her mother said, pointing to one of the smaller photos on the right page.

Smiling, Allie studied the photo. It was a birthday party shot with a highly decorated cake, displaying a big '10'. It showed Allie sitting at an old outdoor furniture setting, perhaps at the back of a hotel. She remembered now. It had been a pub, but where? She saw that her mum and dad, Jo and Robert were huddled behind her for the photo and her childhood best friend, Isabelle, leaned on her right shoulder.

Everyone wore outrageous hats and Allie had on her silly photo face – all teeth and crinkly eyes. Pub patrons were looking on and some were obviously singing happy birthday to her. Seeing Isabelle was sobering. She'd died not long after the photo had been taken. A water skier had run her over while she was swimming with Allie in a lake not far from Glastonbury.

'Whose idea was it to drag all this out?' she asked Jo.

'Mum's. I couldn't stop her. Look at your face!'

Allie couldn't help laughing. She peered more closely at the photo. Her laughter died on her lips. She studied the photo for a long minute, unaware that everyone else in the room had fallen silent.

It was unmistakable. The tall, dark man in the photograph, the one standing off to the side and definitely not singing with the other strangers, was the man she had seen earlier that day, stirring his coffee at a table at the Feathers Inn.

His daughter's reaction to the photo wasn't lost on David St. Clair. In fact, the album had been introduced into the evening at his bidding. His wife had played her part well, digging out the album right on cue. David St. Clair had understood Suzie's reluctance to be involved, but he was confident she'd understand what had to be done and why. He knew now, without any trace of doubt, that his daughter's life was about to change into something unimaginable to her, but he couldn't tell her, at least not yet. There were rules to be observed and he dared not break them. He had already run it too close.

Allie was about to tell everyone what she'd discovered when something stopped her. Something *strong*. Instead, she pretended to study the photo until she regained her composure and was able to summon her happy face.

'Funny stuff!' she proclaimed.

'God, you had me going there for a minute!' said Jo. 'What was all that silence about?'

Allie laughed it off and said she hadn't seen a photo of poor Isabelle for a long time and it had brought back sad memories. This was accepted with understanding looks and everyone drifted back to the living room, except Allie and her father. Allie explained to her mother that she'd be there in a minute.

Once they were alone, she looked pointedly at her father, but he immediately held up his hand, walked to the desk, and picked up the book he'd previously plucked from the bookshelf.

'Don't say anything, Allison. Just read this, okay?'

'Okay? You *know* who I saw, don't you?'

'I know *what* you saw, yes. We can't speak of it, not yet, anyway.'

Something stirred in her subconscious. She knew something about this, but couldn't quite put her finger on it.

'Tell me this, then, if you can. Where was the photo taken?'

It was a smart question – just the one he'd been hoping for.

'Glastonbury.'

Jo and Marcus dropped Allie back at her Putney flat. It was 11:45 p.m. She'd hardly spoken during the drive from Belgravia. She was tired, but that wasn't the reason for her near silence. The conversation she'd had with her father kept pinging off the walls of her brain. Questions ate away at her about Glastonbury and that man in the photo. She hadn't recognized him at the Feathers Inn, but she sure as hell had been jolted by his gaze. She must have met him all those years ago at the birthday party – and clearly he'd been involved in their lives in some way – but there was something else to it, she was sure.

The big question was how come he looked exactly the same at the Feathers – he should be twenty years older than he'd been when the photo was taken, but her fleeting look at him earlier that day suggested he hadn't aged a day. She felt in her handbag for the book her father had given her. She hadn't mentioned it to her sister. Again, this seemed a secret subject, one strictly between her and her father, yet he hadn't actually asked her not to say anything.

She bid farewell to Jo and Marcus, promising to ring them about lunch on Sunday. She grappled with the two locks on her front door, the deadlock sticking a little. She rushed, eager to get inside and check out the book. She hadn't had the chance to even read the title. Throwing her light switch, she made for the couch, reading the book title as she went. *The Promise of Maewyn Succat*.

She looked inside and saw it had been self-published by her father in 1982 – a year after her birth. There was no printer's name or acknowledgements of any kind. Simply a one-line foreword written by her father:

This book is dedicated to the St. Clair family, past, present and future. The burden of responsibility remains. David St. Clair, August 16, 1982.

Bit short and sweet, she thought. It was unlike her father not to take the opportunity to write something expansive. *The burden of responsibility remains? Let's not take ourselves* too *seriously*, she thought. There was a further note at the bottom of the same page, a quote: *Vinculum infinitas.* She'd have to look up vinculum, but infinitas obviously meant forever.

The first page was headed *461 A.D.* Interesting, the same year her father had just mentioned as the year the Glastonbury lights had first been recorded. She flipped through the book. It wasn't written in her father's usual style. It was sparse and clipped, lacking the flowery language he normally employed. She realized she hadn't read anything of her father's for years. The little book was barely a hundred pages and she noticed there were a lot of scribbled asides and hand-drawn maps. An elaborate sketch of the Tor took up an entire page.

The ring tone on her mobile phone startled her. She quickly grabbed the little phone out of her cavernous handbag, the display alerting her that the call was from Police Operations.

She identified herself, then listened intently. She made a couple of notes, answered a question, and hung up, staring at the floor for a moment, digesting the information she'd been given. The body of a young woman had been found in a lane off Earl's Court Road. The PC said that the scene of crime team had been dispatched. The PC had hesitated and then said that according to the initial report, there were aspects of the scene that were 'disturbing'. Allie assumed this meant beyond the ordinary. They were all disturbing in her book.

Operations had asked whom DCI St. Clair would like to attend the scene. She advised that Detective Constable Mathew Connors was on call. Allie had written down the exact address of the crime scene and decided to check it out as well, even though it was after midnight. Earl's Court wasn't far from her apartment – maybe fifteen minutes, maybe less at this time of night.

Excitement and dread coursed through her in equal measure. She trusted DC Connors, but didn't want the first case on her watch to be mishandled. She cursed that she hadn't arranged to bring a pool car home. It was a perk of the new job, but she'd forgotten about it when she'd talked to the guy from administration earlier that day. She threw her father's book on top of her desk and looked out her window as she ran for her motorcycle gear. It was raining.

Chapter Seven

Earl's Court
Thursday 12:20 a.m.

Twenty-six-year-old DC Mathew Connors made a sound like a fur seal as his beef curry from earlier in the evening involuntarily heaved from his stomach, splattering down into the darkness of a drain hole. The murder at 21 King's Lane was unlike any he'd seen. He'd greeted the grim-faced SOCO moments earlier with a cheery, 'Good evening,' and immediately regretted it. Sergeant George Houghton had been ashen-faced and Mathew knew he had attended many, many crime scenes in his thirty-something years on the force. George had wordlessly led Mathew down the winding lane, pointed to the corner, and walked away.

Sweating and heaving, Mathew now knew why George hadn't lingered. Wiping his mouth with his now sodden, stained handkerchief, he backed away from the scene. He ducked under the blue and white barrier tape and hurried back out into the steady rain. He reached the point where the lane intersected with Earl's Court Road, across from the normally busy tube station. He needed to breathe cold, wet air and regain control. Images from the lane raged through his brain. He looked up, startled, as DCI St. Clair coasted her motorbike to a halt beside him. He hadn't expected her.

The rain fell heavier. Allie St. Clair manoeuvred her bike under the canopy provided by the now closed Chinese restaurant bordering the lane. Fixing the stand and stowing her helmet, she peered down the length of the cobbled-stoned lane to the arc lights at the end. She looked at Mathew Connors, who had not spoken.

'That bad, eh?'

He retched again. 'Christ almighty,' he squeaked St. Clair felt the stirrings of real concern now. Connors was young, but he was an experienced officer. She decided to abandon any further attempt at conversation.

She approached the tape, but was intercepted by Sergeant Houghton, his right arm extended towards her. 'Are you sure you want to go down there, girly?'

Girly?

Fortunately, Allie knew George well and he'd always called her that. It had ceased to be offensive years ago, particularly after they'd worked on a number of cases in which George had proven a compassionate competent officer. He was, at base, a kind man who had no pretensions to advancement and no time for 'yuppy bullshit' as he called it. He was old-school; honest and a complete chauvinist, as were most of his contemporaries.

'I have to look, George. Connors is badly shaken . . . I guess you noticed that?'

'He has every reason,' George said, looking away. 'It's the worst I've seen. Can't say any more than that. We've got a complete maniac at work here.'

Allie nodded her understanding and bent under the tape which George finally lifted for her. At first, she could see nothing as she rounded the elbow bend and looked into the darkened corner of the lane. She peered hard at the space, trying to make some sense of it. Three rusted drums, overflowing with garbage and some crushed and empty boxes of plastic take-away containers – presumably refuse from the restaurant on the corner, stood to one side. Rags and general detritus awaiting collection from the city's garbage men lay strewn across the rough surface of the lane. She lifted her gaze. Her breathing stopped.

Above head height and against the chipped, red brick wall which formed the end of the lane, below a blue tarpaulin which had been erected as a temporary shelter against the cold rain, a dark-haired, naked girl had been crucified.

Allie jumped as a voice behind her offered her a torch. George.

The shrinking little girl inside her almost pushed it away; she didn't want to look at the bad thing on the wall. Wordlessly, she took the torch and, after a deep breath, flicked it on. The torchlight gave the scene a macabre, jaundiced glow. She slowly moved the beam over the body.

Revulsion and pity coursed through her in equal measure. The girl had been crudely gutted. Her entrails hung out of her belly cavity in pink and blue lumps, a liquid glistening on their surface. Thick, sticky blood swirled over the wall behind her and a trickle from a ragged wound in her groin formed a black pool at her feet.

The girl's too-black hair hung in sodden spaghetti strands framing her pinched, bloodless face. Black, weeping eye sockets stared uncomprehendingly out at the squalid surroundings. Allie involuntarily stepped back a pace, looking behind her as she heard glass crunch under foot. She steadied the torch once again on the girl and it hit the red glossy lipstick smeared exaggeratedly over lips stretched around a mouth locked forever in a rictus scream.

No tongue could be seen. Allie breathed fast and shallow, her body's defence against rising bile. The torch flickered, then came back on, illuminating the girl's thin, pale arms that had been spread – pulled to dislocation – to mimic the classic crucifixion pose. Fat, rusty metal spikes protruded from a line of jagged holes in her upper arms and chest, pinning and suspending her near the top of the brick wall. Her feet were lashed together with dark twine.

Allie stood staring, her mind still fighting an almost overwhelming urge to run out of the lane. She forced herself to stay, calming slightly after a minute, her thoughts finding order. Water dripped from the tarpaulin, which struggled to hold the incessant rain at bay. Slowly, she noticed little things about the horrific scene – the things so often overlooked on first examination, particularly when a complete horror show took centre stage. The girl still wore a silver necklace, but a line on her left wrist betrayed the recent presence of a watch.

Carefully, Allie picked her way around old fruit boxes and crumpled cans. Up close to the suspended body, there was not yet the strong odour of decay. Peering at the girl's left side, she confirmed what she had expected to see: a stab wound. Directly under the feet hanging a metre off the ground, a half-full bottle of wine stood, its label turned to the wall. Another biblical symbol.

Something pricked at the periphery of her senses. She played the light from the torch into the dark corners and down the adjacent cobbled lane to where it abutted a tall, concrete office building. Something pushed against her skin, something she couldn't see.

Two metallic sounds from the other end of the lane told her that the team from Forensic Services had arrived. She was fortunate to have had an unfettered first look at the scene, but it was time for her to leave them to it. They would not take kindly to her possibly contaminating the crime scene. Turning, she glanced back at the suspended body. The girl lunged off the wall, arms now free of the ropes, a low, gurgling scream issuing from her throat. Allie reeled back. A slapping, sucking sound, like boots being pulled from deep, wet mud filled the air. A foul, suffocating odour assaulted her. Arms flailing, she fell backwards, trying to scream and panicking because she could not. She hit the cobblestones hard, her hands and arms instinctively trying to cover her vital organs. But there was no attack. Allie lay on her back, panting, the rain running in rivulets down her face. George Houghton was yelling and running down the lane toward her, his boots throwing water up into the rain.

Allie was lifted to her feet. She was shaking badly. She felt her wet back where rainwater had invaded her leathers. A cut on her hand stung. Stepping back from a worried George Houghton, she stumbled, then straightened, nodding her thanks. She headed back to the comforting lights of the relative normalcy on the corner. The lane closed on her like a coffin. She quickened her step.

DC Mathew Connors was briefing the forensics team at the head of the lane. She saw he at least had recovered his composure. Allie heard him say, 'Here she comes now.' She didn't recognize any of the team and didn't think she needed to tell them anything – they'd do their best work unhindered and would deliver their report later that morning. She beckoned Connors over to her. He broke immediately from them.

'You okay now?' she asked, looking at him closely.

Embarrassed, he confirmed that he was now in control.

He was as white as a sheet, hardly in control, but he'd have to deal with it.

'Have any witnesses presented themselve to you by any chance?' Allie asked, still shivering inwardly.

'No, not a one. It's very quiet here.'

'We'll need bodies on the streets first thing, then. Are you okay to stay here with George . . Sergeant Houghton, for a little bit?'

Connors confirmed that he could, not that he had any choice, of course.

'All right, we'll talk later. Thanks, Mathew.'

Connors watched as St. Clair walked toward Sergeant Houghton. He would comment later to the team that she was ice cool and hadn't even blinked at seeing the carnage down the lane. 'Ice in her veins,' he would say.

St. Clair sought out George Houghton for a quiet chat, leading him under the veranda, out of the rain.

'Did you notice anything when you got here, George? Any cars leave, anybody hanging around? You know the drill.'

'No, didn't see nobody.' He jerked his thumb toward the restaurant behind him.

'Mr Lin from the Golden Bamboo called it in at eleven oh-five and we were here by eleven ten. Other than a very agitated Chinese restaurateur and his diners, there was no one about at all.'

'Who's *we*?'

Houghton pointed out a short, thickset officer with an outstandingly large nose. He was scribbling on a notepad.

'PC Crowley and I. Ken Crowley, do you know him?'

She replied that she didn't and asked George if he'd noticed whether Connors had interviewed Mr Lin before she arrived. George Houghton looked uncomfortable.

'Spit it out, George. I know Mathew is badly shaken . . . I'm not too flash myself.'

He smiled apologetically. 'No, I haven't actually seen him do that, Allie.'

She smiled her thanks and suggested he try to stay warm. Moving away from the crime scene she flipped open her mobile phone. She called Mathew Connors even though he was only yards away. He answered on the first ring, looking over at her as he did so.

'Ma'am?'

'Mathew, I'll be interested to talk to you later this morning about your interview with Mr Lin and what follow-up we can do with his staff and customers. How about 9:30 a.m.?'

He threw his head back and then waved a placatory hand.

'Sorry, ma'am. Yes, yes of course. I'll go straight up to your office?'

'That'll be fine. Thanks, Mathew.'

She knew he'd gotten the message and that he was chastising himself for not getting to Mr Lin earlier. She saw him hurry toward the restaurant owner as she snapped her phone shut.

Reaching her bike, she glanced across the road. A big black Triumph motorcycle was parked facing slightly in to the gutter. She didn't think it had been there when she arrived, but the rain had been heavy then too. She walked over to it, making a note of the registration number. There was no sign of the owner, but she was almost sure it was the bike she'd admired at the Chelsea Hospital last night.

Her mobile phone chirped announcing a text message. *No, I am not the killer, so don't be afraid. It has begun. I'll be outside your house in thirty minutes. Michael*

Of course, it was the mysterious Michael. Who else? She looked around and saw no one, but decided to up the ante. She typed: *Why don't we just meet here, now?*

His reply was instantaneous. *That's not my bike, Allie. Wait there as long as you like, but I'll be at your house in thirty minutes*

A million questions flashed through her mind. This was bizarre. If he wasn't here somewhere, how did he know she was standing by a motorcycle? But the strangest thing was, she already knew deep down that he wasn't the killer. And she knew with absolute certainty what he'd look like when they met.

Arthur Wendell curled into a foetal ball in his tiny tiled bathroom. He didn't want to live a minute longer. He knew what he'd done earlier that night. The girl's desperate pleading was still competing in his head with his own moaning. Clamping his hands over his eyes, he tried to shut out the images. But it was not to be. His mind watched the movie reel as the scene replayed itself again and again for him. He saw himself standing above her, almost *hovering,* as she begged for her life, her eyeballs having already been nonchalantly flicked over the high wall. He watched as he calmly bent down and ripped out her long tongue with a pair of electrician's pliers, the muscles attaching her tongue to the back of her throat coming away with a crisp *pop.*

He convulsed at the vision. He saw again how she'd vomited great gouts of blood as she gurgled and clutched at her throat. He saw his own impassive face, but yet, not *his* face. It was as if an image had superimposed itself on him. Arthur thrashed about in his bathroom, desperate to put an end to the images. But the scene continued on in living colour. The girl, *Georgie,* now lay on her back writhing and gargling blood, finally exposing her bare stomach to him. He saw himself calmly look over at the restaurant with its lantern lights and chattering diners. They only had to glance up from their Char Siu for a moment to pick him and the girl out of the gloom in the lane. But no one did. He saw the filleting knife appear in his hand – God only knew where he'd gotten it from – and watched as it approached her alabaster white abdomen. Arthur Wendell, Chartered Public Accountant and Tax Advisor, vomited into his shiny white hand basin.

Chapter Eight

Donning her helmet and glancing back at the now brightly illuminated lane, Allie mounted her bike, turned the key to start, and promptly stalled the engine. She knew without looking that everyone had noticed. As calmly as she could, she started the bike successfully and described a graceful arc in the street, sweeping past the black Triumph and accelerating south on Earl's Court Road.

Mercifully, the rain had eased enough for her to throw back the dark visor on her helmet. She knew she shouldn't do it, but she felt claustrophobic with the heavy polymer barrier across her face. She wanted to feel cold air on her skin, subconsciously hoping it would cleanse her mind of the frightful images from the lane. The road was slick and shiny. A mist formed. She came out of the corner of Earl's Court Road, flicked her indicator on and worked the throttle hard, eager to get home and see how this crazy meeting would play out.

The bike shot out from under her like a wet piece of soap. At once she was airborne, hurtling toward the ripsaw surface of the road. She watched almost in slow motion as the old Yamaha clattered in a shower of sparks toward a parked car. She noticed dreamily that it was a white Ford Focus. She looked down at the black gleaming road rushing up to meet her, powerless to act. She hit the road hard, face first. She felt her body jackknife at the impact. There was a moment's silence, then a kaleidoscope of lights and colours, followed by a mind-numbing collision – her right side slammed against a concrete and metal lamp post. She heard a canon shot a split second later, realizing it was her helmet smacking with incredible force against the unyielding structure. The rain hissed.

She listened from afar to the bike's motor screaming as it lay on its side, still in gear, the throttle jammed against an unknown object – maybe a wall – she didn't know, couldn't turn her head to see.

She was propped up in an awkward sitting position, her back against the lamp post, her legs splayed out at impossible angles. She finally managed to screw her head round and gaze in a detached way at her bike. She had to turn that bloody motor off; it was really annoying. She simply stood, walked over, squeezed the clutch handle and turned the ignition key. The engine died. Silence trilled in her ears. There was no traffic and she was glad. Looking down at herself, she wondered how she had stood up. Her legs must be barely attached. Her leathers were ripped to shreds and her jacket had no left elbow. Her visor had been smashed off, the remains strewn in a jagged trail down the road. She remembered now how she had hit the road face first and had thought before she even hit the lamp post how she'd probably need plastic surgery to sew her face back on.

Distracted, she peered at the road, stupidly expecting to see her face sitting there. *What a night*, she thought. Sighing, she effortlessly picked the bike up and wrenched the handlebars back into square. Had there been a witness to this, they'd have been amazed at the feat of strength this broken and bleeding being had just displayed. She noticed her hand trembling, then felt the tremble vibrate out to her limbs. Shivering set in. Reality hit as the shock of the accident moved to another level. Shivering gave way to an uncontrollable, force-ten shaking. Unconsciously, she propped the bike on its amazingly still-functioning stand and sat abruptly down on the wet road. Somewhere amid the shaking, she knew she had to screw up the courage to check herself out in the bike mirrors and call an ambulance.

She knew in a moment of clarity that in all probability, she looked like she'd slid face first down a cheese grater. She presumed that shock was anaesthetizing her, masking her true condition. Another text message came in. She decided to look at it – anything to delay looking in a mirror. She stood and fished in what was left of her pocket, surprised that the phone was still in one piece and working. She squinted through the heavy rain at the short message.

Bummer. Get back on your bike and get home as fast as you can. You're okay . . . this time.

Well now, she thought. I'm okay, am I, Mr Know-It-All? Let's just see. With that, she bobbed down so she could look squarely into the damaged mirror on the side of the bike nearest her, the rain so heavy now that it bounced off the road, speckling and distorting the image in the mirror. She lifted her helmet off and took the plunge; taking a long, hard look. She still had two eyes, a nose and a jaw. *A great start*, she thought with huge relief. She smiled at her reflection and noted that she still had teeth – the nice white even ones that Rachel hated. She smiled a little more broadly at that thought.

She swept aside her dark hair, now plastered to her forehead by the rain, and took the time to assess her legs and arms. She could see no blood through the holes which rent her leathers. She windmilled her arms and kicked her legs in a comical rendition of her usual karate training moves. No problem. In fact, she concluded, she didn't have a scratch and could feel no particular pain at all. The thought that she might be dreaming crossed her mind. A vicious wind tore down through the buildings, hurling horizontal bullets of rain at her. It was a frigid, stinging reminder that she was firmly rooted in reality, as frightening as that had now become.

Twenty blurred and uncomfortable minutes later, Allie crossed Putney Bridge, less than a kilometre from her home. She was cold, very wet, unbearably tired, and amazed her battered motorbike had not only started, but had also run like a dream. The rain and gale-force winds had been unrelenting and the sheer effort of staying upright on her bike was exhausting. Despite this, she felt her pulse quicken. She wondered whether this Michael would show up and whether she was being a complete idiot in meeting this guy alone in the middle of the night. Of course, she knew she was. But if he turned out to be the guy from the photo and the Feathers Inn, there was a mystery to be uncovered. Plus she felt no danger from this man and that was something she could not explain even to herself.

She slowed and scanned the narrow street ahead as best she could in the heavy rain – the narrow beam from her headlight barely carrying fifty feet. As much as she could determine, the curving row of identical terrace houses stretching before her contained nothing out of the ordinary, just the normal parade of expensive cars parked on either side, most of which she recognized as those belonging to fellow residents. Bringing her motorbike to a halt directly outside her own front door, she paused with the engine still running, just in case. Not one light glowed from any of the houses on the street. Rainwater thudded on her helmet in a great lump, dislodged from the tree that guarded her apartment. There was no movement on the darkened street.

Dismounting and turning the engine off, she kicked down the stand and walked quickly, swinging open her iron gate, still listening and watching. Unlocking the door, she heard a great whoosh of wind behind her. She worried the worsening storm would cause the tree to fall against her apartment.

'Do I have to stay out in this rain much longer?'

The deep voice was close to her ear. She yelped and jumped. She instinctively spun low into a defensive stance, anticipating an attack. For the second time that night, she'd prepared for non-existent violence. She stayed low in the crouch for a few seconds, then slowly straightened as she saw her would-be attacker standing across the street, arms folded, his broad smile visible even through the rain.

'Well?' he asked quietly. Yet she heard him as if he was right next to her.

She stared at him. He was very tall, hatless, and his wet, dark hair was swept back over his ears to his collar. He wore a long unbuttoned black coat, which partially covered a light shirt and denims. He was the man from the Feathers Inn, all right.

'What's my name, then?' she yelled, already questioning why she'd asked that. It was a lame attempt to convey her caution to him, she supposed. She was tired, after a ll.

'Allison St. Clair, daughter of David.' This was said matter-of-factly, no humour, no sarcasm.

'All right,' Allie said. 'Where were you in May 1991?'

'Which day?' He was mocking her now.

'The twenty-second.'

He put his finger to his lips, striking an exaggerated thinking pose.

'Let's see,' he replied thoughtfully. 'I went to a funny little village . . . Glastonbury, as I recall, to the local fair. I bought a child's book in the morning and in the afternoon I went to a pub and then, let me think . . . I was invited to a birthday party. Yes, that's right – yours.'

'What was the name of the book?' Allie felt a smile beginning, despite the horrors of the night.

'It was called, *If You Don't Open Your Bloody Door and Let Me Out of the Rain, I'm Going to Break it Down.*' He spread his arms, palms up. 'At least, I think that was it.'

'That'll do,' she said crisply. 'Come on then, *Michael*, let's get this nonsense over with.'

Allie pushed open her door, kicking the unopened mail her downstairs neighbour consistently refused to pick up, changed keys, and opened the door to her upstairs apartment. She trudged up her ridiculously narrow flight of stairs, leaving him to follow, too tired now to be worried or alarmed. Her life had just turned completely crazy. She'd seen things tonight she'd never forget, she was wet, and her leathers smelled like a wet dog.

She heard him close the doors downstairs as she threw her helmet down on her sofa. The helmet shattered into a hundred pieces. She stared at it as realization struck. Its strength – its integrity – had been totally compromised by the impact with the road and the lamp post. She wondered how it had remained intact for the journey home.

She checked herself in the living room mirror and recoiled. Her face was okay, nothing had fallen off, but her clothing was in ruins and covered in blood. *Blood from where?* She performed a little pirouette and checked herself out again, just in case she'd been in shock back at Earl's Court Road. But there were no cuts or abrasions, just the ragged holes in her leathers, including a huge one which revealed most of her left buttock.

'Fetching,' he said quietly.

She spun around to face him and the electric shock went through her again. She sat heavily on the sofa, crunching pieces of her helmet. She put her head between her hands and wept. Exhaustion, horror, shock and embarrassment – it was all too much.

After a minute or so, she heard clanking noises from her galley kitchen. *Christ*, she thought, *he's putting the kettle on. I don't believe this. Any of it.*

'Milk with no sugar, right?'

'Right,' she heard herself say. She was too wrecked now to care how he knew.

She stared at her wrist, realizing she'd lost her watch in the accident. Robert had given it to her on her twentieth birthday. She asked what time it was.

'2011.'

'Funny. About 3:00 a.m.?'

She looked over and saw him check the clock on the microwave.

'Yep, ten past.'

'Jesus,' she said. 'I have to get up in three hours.'

'You're already up.'

He came back into the living room and sat a steaming cup of tea on her low table, directly on the wooden surface. She reached over and moved it to the circular Balinese coaster.

'Ah,' he said, stepping back into the shadows in a corner of the room. 'So that's what it's for.'

'That's what it's for. You can sit if you like,' Allie said, gesturing to one of the lounge chairs. 'You don't have to stand.' Allie looked at him again. This time, the electric current was gentler. She coped without dropping anything. He was even taller than she'd first thought, maybe 6"7' in the old measure, maybe taller. Even in shadow enough light caught his angular face to suggest classic good looks. But his age was utterly indeterminable. He could be twenty eight or forty, yet he must be much older. She just couldn't pin it down.

'What are we doing here . . . Michael? *Do* I call you Michael?' she added, the bizarre aspect to all this still very much on her mind.

He smiled and she fumbled the teacup again. 'You can, yes,' he said.

'Can what?'

He frowned. 'You can call me Michael, if you wish.'

Allie shifted uncomfortably in her seat; somewhere in her consciousness there was an understanding that the conversation they were about to have was going to be life changing. She still could not fathom why she'd allowed a complete stranger into her home – one who could well be a threat to her – and wasn't feeling any sense of danger. She was sure she was safe and decided to push for answers.

'So what's this all about – the text messages, the impressive knowing-all-things act, and . . .' She stopped the question in mid-stream and simply looked at him. *She knew this man.* A weakness flooded through her, like her batteries were suddenly drained. 'Michael,' she said more gently, 'help me out here, please. What's going on?'

He was distracted by the clatter of the rain at the window and the shadows cast by the wildly swaying tree outside. Allie wondered if he was undecided about something or just being careful about his choice of words. He looked out the window, up and down the street, before answering.

'You're right to be worried about what is about to be said.' He looked over his shoulder at her. 'And about what now has to happen.'

She sat still, waiting for the explanation.

'I know you are wondering who I am and how it can be that I appear in that birthday party photo from all those years ago, among other things, of course.'

She nodded.

'You will have gathered that I know your father . . . yes?' He raised an eyebrow.

'Yes. We had a chat about you earlier this evening. Well, kind of.'

He smiled. 'Kind of, eh? He didn't say too much, then?'

'No, he mentioned there being "rules".'

He swivelled on his heels, looking out of the window once more.

'Ah, yes, the rules. The *eternal* rules. He is correct, of course,' he said, clasping his hands behind his back like a prosecuting attorney. 'I have taken your plea for help, as in "Michael help me out here, please", as your genuine desire for me to help you. Am I correct?'

She screwed up her face. 'Sure, yes, I guess.'

He held up his hand, cutting her off. 'Okay, that's fine. Weird isn't it? But it's part of the rules. You have to ask for my help before I can offer it, technically. Even though you've already had it, of course.'

'I have? When?'

'Tonight, or rather, this morning.'

Allie scoffed. 'I could have done with it half an hour ago when my bike went out from under me!'

A trace of annoyance crossed his face. He pointed at the mirror.

'Take a look at yourself if you doubt me.'

'I didn't mean to suggest I doubted you . . . I just—'

He pointed again at the large mirror. 'Look.'

Allie's jaw tightened. 'I did when I arrived.'

'Did you just?' There was a definite edge to his voice now. 'Have a look at what the accident *really* did to you.' He waived his hand toward the mirror in polite invitation – an usher at the cinema.

Sighing, she stood and moved toward the mirror. Her face gazed back at her, not unexpectedly. Everything was fine and she breathed a sigh of relief. She studied herself. She had dark smudges under her eyes and her hair was a wet nest, but apart from that . . . she stared as something began to change. The reflection twisted.

'Don't take your eyes off the mirror,' he advised.

She would have given anything to do just that. She was transfixed as she saw her nose morph into a short piece of jagged, twisted gristle and her left cheek fall away to reveal a semi-circle of shattered, grinning teeth. There was no left ear. Her mouth, from the right side up to the eye, looked like it had been sandblasted by a madman, and her skull was flattened and bloodied across the top. She'd been scalped then melted by fire.

She was crying now, but unable to take her eyes off her destroyed self.

'Do you want to know about the back of your head and your left arm . . . or should I say, *the places where they used to be?*'

Allie could not answer. She stood, tears distorting the mirror image. She couldn't move.

'Enough,' Michael announced. The horrors faded from view. She was whole again. She slowly turned to look at him.

'How could you do this to me?' Her voice was a frail whimper.

Michael waved a hand dismissively. 'What you saw was what you did to yourself, Allie, until I repaired you.'

She nodded weakly and slumped back on to the sofa. She stared up at him. He was closer now. He looked profoundly sad and weary – a look which could only be worn by someone who is tired and has had their heart ripped out by the roots.

She asked the inevitable question, the one to which her father had alluded. She could put it off no longer.

'What exactly are you, Michael?' Something stirred in her memory, images of her brother, feathers, no, *wings* and . . . Glastonbury Tor.

Michael looked at her steadily before answering. 'You're going to have the devil's own job accepting the reality of this, Allie, but here goes. I am in fact, the Archangel Mikal, Lord Protector of the Realms of Heaven and Earth – the Viceroy of Heaven, in a nutshell.'

Allie burst into laughter. 'Oh, c'mon! The Archangel Michael? You? A good-looking magician or hypnotist maybe, but . . . *really?*'

Michael smiled then chuckled. 'Well, I told you you'd have trouble accepting me.'

Billy McBride's words roared back to her. 'Accept him!' he had said. The smile faded from her face. This was what Billy had been on about. She looked at Michael again and thought about her father, the strange things to which he'd alluded, the photo from twenty years ago and the whole deal with the feathers and tonight's horrific accident.

'Don't forget the advertising hoarding from the Chelsea Hospital,' he reminded. 'It only missed you by an inch, as I recall.'

For the second time that night, Allie trembled. She wondered why on earth she'd laughed out loud. Exhaustion. But this *was* happening. It was no dream. This was real and he probably was who he said he was.

She sat again on the sofa, staring at the floor, not yet ready to engage in further conversation. She was limp, her grip on reality tenuous. Something from her childhood kept nagging at her, urging her to accept the incredible information he'd revealed to her. Angels, a concept she had utterly rejected and about which she now recalled arguing with her father many years ago, had come back to haunt her, perhaps literally. Now she understood the passion with which her father had defended his argument that they existed. Finally, she looked up at Michael. He stood over her; not smiling, not scowling.

'I suppose when I've rested and composed myself, I'll have a million questions. One of which will be, "You mean there actually is a Heaven and the whole God thing is real?" And another biggie will be, "Why are you here, now, with me?" But if you don't mind, I just need sleep. I've had a hell of a night and I just can't think any more.'

'That's exactly what you've had, Allie. A Hell of a night, but you didn't know it.'

'What do you mean?' she said, her face crumpled like that of an inquisitive child.

'You need sleep as you say, so I'll not bother you too much more. But you need to know this: the murder that was committed tonight is much more than it seems That is why I am here. If we do not find the murderer quickly, there will be consequences which do not bear thinking about, for you, me – every living soul.'

Allie was dead tired and in no shape to assimilate any more information, especially on the universal scale to which he was now elevating the conversation.

'Okay, fine,' she said flatly. 'You're welcome to sleep on the couch if you like.' She turned and walked towards her bedroom, then stopped and turned back to him.

'What do you mean "we" have to find the murderer? That's *my* job.'

Michael took two steps toward her, his face a mask. For the first time she saw his eyes clearly, they were a colour she'd never seen before. Sort of green, sort of blue, sort of a lot of colours, perhaps all of them. He spoke as if was in charge of, well, everything.

'Without me or my representative to guide and protect you, you will never apprehend him. And you will die in the attempt, along with thousands of others. Do you understand that?'

She nodded, still in a daze.

'You are not dealing with human intellect on this one. This is not some psycho who just forgot to take his little blue pills this morning. This *thing* is chaos – the betrayer of all things – if you want me to get all biblical. If you prefer, it is elemental evil – the yin to the yang of Heaven and light, fundamental antimatter made *live*.'

He stared hard at her, *through her*, reaching into her thoughts.

'He is known in human literature as The Destroyer – Belhor.'

'Belhor?'

Michael sighed and walked to the mirror, where he stood staring into it.

'Belhor, Belial, Mechembuchus, call him what you will, he has been known by many names over time.' He turned from the mirror, the weary look she saw before plainly evident. 'Cut the cake anyway you like, but you are about to confront one of the four Crown Princes of Hell.'

She stumbled, saving herself from falling only by grasping the mantelpiece. He made no move towards her. She noted he just stood there in that crazy, long black trench coat.

'Get some sleep,' he said at last. 'I'll wake you in three hours.'

She had no strength for further argument or questions; they would have to wait. Smiling weakly at him, she shuffled to the kitchen, drank some water, and bellyflopped into bed. She was asleep within seconds.

Michael walked back to the window, watching again as the rain hammered at it. He understood Allie's reaction and had expected it. She was exhausted, for a start. But he knew she had neither grasped the significance of what he'd told her, nor the enormity of the task before her. The reality was that he could not apprehend the demon without her and she could not hope to survive more than a day without his protection.

Allie would have many questions when she awoke, some of which he could answer, some he could not – unfortunately, there were still rules to be observed. In fact, he knew they were immutable *laws* that governed the ways in which a being such as he could interact with humans. He turned off the lights and backed into the darkest corner of the room where the streetlights did not penetrate. He would stand there, vigilant, until 7:00 a.m., at which time he'd awaken Allie from her dreams before plunging her into a nightmare from which she might never recover. He had no choice of course. *Vinculum infinitas.* A deal was a deal.

Chapter Nine

Thursday, 6:00 a.m.

For Arthur Wendell, the morning couldn't have come quickly enough. The darkness had been overpowering, suffocating. He hated it, yet he craved it. He showered, shaved and put on a fresh pair of beige trousers and a crisp white shirt. He buffed his brown loafers and selected a bright tie, then discarded it. No tie today. At 10:00 a.m., he was to meet with Paula Armstrong, the good-looking woman from *La Mode* magazine for whom he'd completed income tax returns for the past three years. He'd been recommended to her from another client of his, Jackie Bransden, a local girl who worked in the make-up department attached to the magazine's photographic studio. He liked Paula and she was unfailingly courteous, a trait he admired and valued.

Why don't you gut her while you're at it? the voice asked. Arthur hit the floor, shouting and covering his ears.

C'mon, you can have her as well. Before or after – she'll love it either way. You know she will. It's you, after all. You know how women crave you!

Arthur felt himself go rock hard. His thinking twisted in on itself. *That's right*, he thought, *they* do *love me. Georgie would have done anything for me last night. In fact, she did!* Funny how he seemed to forget. He stroked himself and thought about how she'd begged him to stop. *God, what a feeling!* He remembered the lane, the Chinese restaurant, and what he'd done to her.

One thing leads to another, Arthur. You know how it goes. We're going to have such fun!

Arthur felt himself grow. The electricity coursed through him again. *What a day ahead*, he thought. *What a day!* He didn't bother about eggs for breakfast; he scrambled for the big red bus, instead.

Mathew Connors was ill. He couldn't imagine ever wanting to eat again. He'd barely slept, and the fact that his brain had gone into neutral at the crime scene in the early hours of the morning worried him. He'd been a detective constable for two years now and he'd never seen anything like the carnage in that Earl's Court lane. It had not only sickened him, but frightened him as well. He went over the events for the hundredth time, admonishing himself yet again for failing to interview Mr Lin. How could he not have done that? DCI St. Clair had been generous with him; he knew that. Rachel Strauss and some of the others at the Met were scathing of St. Clair's appointment, mocking her public school accent and self-possession, but he felt she'd shown over the two years of his tenure that she was clearly the star performer. He'd had no problems with her promotion, but he knew she would be tested by the crew.

Well, let's see how they react to the news that an unfortunate girl was crucified and ripped apart, barely twenty feet from a brightly lit restaurant. He wondered how St. Clair would handle the investigation. Certainly, she'd been ice cool and professional at the crime scene. He didn't know how she did it. He reached into his refrigerator for the orange juice, thinking that perhaps he could just handle a small glass of it.

She's not that fucking fabulous, you know.

Mathew spun around, expecting a man to be standing in his kitchen. Not seeing anyone, he ran into his living room. There was no one. He leaned on the doorjamb, his pulse galloping. He was hallucinating, he reasoned – overtired and imagining things.

You fancy her, don't you?

Connors spun around again, staring blankly into his tiny kitchen. *The voice had been right there!*

He stared at the door to his toilet, which was a few feet further down the hall. He crept slowly towards it, looking for any sign of movement from under the door. He flung it open, instinctively lowering himself into a crouch. An empty cubicle stared back at him. Letting out a half-chuckle, he decided he was overwrought. He'd use the toilet while he was there.

Closing the door behind him and flicking the latch, he fumbled with the fly on his navy-blue trousers. He was breathing hard, his pulse elevated, a film of sweat on his back. He rolled his shoulders and neck in discomfort, catching his reflection in the small mirror above the narrow porcelain washbasin.

DC Mathew Connors, rugby player and occasional pub bouncer, screamed like a schoolgirl.

Thursday 7:00 a.m.

Allie was deeply asleep until the noise woke her; a hissing, crackling sound. She wrestled the heavy cover off her bed and took a step towards her door, realizing only then what the sound was. Frying bacon. She could smell eggs now, too. A confusion of thoughts and images bombarded her. Michael, the hideous murder, the revelations, and incredible claims from the early hours of the morning – all of it flooded back. Was it all real? The bacon and eggs suggested it was. He was still here. She sank back on the bed and cradled her head in her hands – it was becoming a habit.

She peeked out of her window. The rain had finally stopped, but it was still dark. She looked down at herself, at her white singlet top and pink pyjama bottoms, the ones with the strange Japanese cartoon characters who had huge eyes and all looked like Astro Boy. She couldn't remember changing into them last night.

She creaked open her bedroom door. Michael stood at the stove. He said, 'Good morning,' without looking up. She ducked back behind the door. She had to get past him to the bathroom so she could take a shower. Fossicking in the wardrobe, she found a faded blue dressing gown. It had been her mother's and she'd never had occasion to wear it. Holding it up, she saw it was all out threadbare, with no cord, but it would have to do.

She wrapped it around herself and strode out through the kitchen, swishing past him, blurting out a brisk, 'Good morning,' as she went.

'How do you like your eggs?' he asked, as she swung the bathroom door shut.

Without thinking, she yelled back the old joke, 'Fertilized!'

She was mortified when she realized what she'd said and leant back against the door, her hands covering her face. What had she been thinking?

He chuckled. 'Would you settle for fried, easy-over?'

'Yes! Yes. I meant . . . that.'

Not wanting to think about her gaffe any further, she jumped into the shower and turned the tap on hard, wondering as she did what 'easy-over' meant. It sounded very American.

Ten minutes later, she emerged from the bathroom to find him tucking into his own eggs and bacon – a mountain of it, in fact. This surprised her. She'd assumed maybe he didn't need normal sustenance.

'Man's gotta eat,' he suddenly said.

'So it seems,' she replied a little sarcastically. 'Have you turned American overnight or something?'

'Why, why, why . . . no, ma'am I-I don't believe so . . .' It was classic, bumbling James Stewart and she laughed.

'Not bad, not bad,' she conceded.

'I'm surprised you know James Stewart,' he said. 'He was a big star when I was here . . . in the forties.'

He went on to explain that, over the years, he had spent so much time in the States that he had to watch the language thing. She thought that was reasonable, except for the part of her brain that kept telling her he was not of this world and she was basically having breakfast with a spirit, or an alien, or as he claimed, an Archangel. *The* Archangel, no less. They ate in silence – her head full of cosmic questions about Michael and the investigation ahead.

'Have you thought about our chat from early this morning? he asked, right on cue.

She simply nodded and kept eating, not wanting to look at him. She was just hanging on to reality. He said nothing more for a minute or so.

'Go on,' he said. 'Ask.'

She nodded again, a mouthful of egg and toast delaying her response. 'Michael,' she finally managed, wiping her lips on a serviette, 'I have so many questions that we'd be here all day. Basically, I'm not sure I can accept any of this . . . *craziness*.'

'Yes you can,' he said quietly. 'You know you can. You just can't rationalize it, like you try to rationalize everything else.'

'Is that so?'

'I'm sure of it. I've been around a while. I know stuff.'

There it is again, Allie thought, *the casual, idiomatic speech, the almost ridiculously normal conversation that you'd expect between two friends – except one of them is a Master of the Universe*.

'Look,' she said, pointing her fork at him. 'My head is swimming with the appalling sights of last night and I have to go soon and coordinate an investigation into a crime that will sicken everyone I speak to this morning and probably the *nation*, once the media gets hold of it. I'm really pretty busy just keeping my own sanity.'

'I can see that,' he said, perhaps a little tersely.

Allie got up from the table, carrying her clean plate to the sink. 'Maybe we can talk about this later tonight?' she asked, trying to lighten the mood again.

'Oh sure,' he said, rocking back in his chair. 'We can do that. I'll just potter about the antique shops in Portobello Road today, shall I? Maybe grab a coffee or two – maybe even lunch at Christies? Shall I catch you about 7:00 p.m. for drinks? Would that be okay, *poppet*?'

Allie froze at the sink, afraid to look around.

'You *have* to handle this, Allie,' he continued. 'There is no choice here – it doesn't work to your timetable, or mine for that matter. Yes, we'll talk about it later tonight, but after that, the talking is *done*. You have to trust me, as I have to trust you. Do you at least understand that?'

She spun round, her fear taking second place to annoyance. 'Don't talk to me like I'm a moron. You expect me to believe and completely take on board this fantastic story of Heaven and Earth and your pre-eminent role within it all, oh, and at the same time, understand I'm somehow pivotal to the outcome of some cosmic fucking game between goblins and Angels?' She held up her hand at him. 'I know it's not goblins – don't start on that! To use one of your beloved Americanisms, give me a freakin' break here!'

He stood up now, impossibly tall in the cramped room. 'Give you a break, eh? No. No break. You have a responsibility, St. Clair – no ifs or buts. You drop the ball here, the whole system fails. You think I'm here on holiday? That I have nothing better to do with my time? Do you want to see a million stinking corpses just like the one you can't get out of your head from last night? This is not about—'

He stopped in mid-sentence, whirled around, and stalked out of the kitchen, leaving her standing there open-mouthed and shaking. *Now what*? she wondered. She could hear him in the living room, his breathing loud, ragged and deep. He was angry, no doubt about that. She hadn't expected this from him, although what she *did* expect, she didn't know either.

His footsteps echoed on the timber floor as he returned to the kitchen. She braced herself. He poked his head around the corner like a child checking to see if the coast was clear.

'It occurs to me,' he said reasonably, 'that you don't know who you are.'

Allie frowned. 'What do you mean?'

'I have made certain assumptions about what you know about yourself and your family's past. It seems David has not apprised you of the situation. Correct?'

Allie's pulse quickened. *Here it comes*, she thought. Maybe deep down, she did know something.

'Assuming you mean David, my father, and not King David,' she said a little cheekily, but noting there was no reaction. 'We had a chat earlier last night . . . I told you that, and you certainly laid some very heavy information down last night yourself. Beyond that, he has not said anything about me specifically, it was more about *you*. Oh, he gave me a book to read, but I was interrupted by the small matter of a hideous crime, one I'm being paid to solve, by the way.'

She fought a rising annoyance and looked pointedly at her watch. She really had to get to work.

'Ah,' he said simply. 'I see. You really are in the dark, so to speak.'

'It seems so,' Allie said. 'I have to leave in about one minute. Care to enlighten me?'

'I'd rather not, just now, anyway,' he said. 'This isn't the time for a history lesson.'

Allie could only agree. 'True. I have to go, Michael – I'm sorry.'

He looked at her and again she saw the sad, timeless smile. 'Meet me at the Feathers Inn at 1:00 p.m., if you can. You will want to by then anyway.'

She sighed and told him the day was going to be chaotic and it wouldn't be a good look for her to go off for a leisurely lunch in the middle of the investigation – impossible, in fact.

Michael nodded his understanding.

'Okay, leave it for now. We better get you to work.'

She felt the tug immediately – something drawing her towards him. It was almost as if there was a glow about him at that moment.

'How do you mean?' she asked. 'I'll ride my . . .'

'I don't think so, Allison. C'mon, get your things together and I'll take you.'

All manner of possibilities ran through her mind as she fished for her bits and pieces. She heard him clomp down the stairs to wait for her by the front door. The blindingly obvious question finally occurred to her. She couldn't believe she hadn't thought of it before. Shouldn't he have . . . *wings*? Wasn't that what the feathers were all about? Was he going to *fly* her to work? Her heart beat like a hammer as she descended the stairs.

'Yes, I have, and no, I'm not,' he said matter-of-factly.

'You're reading my thoughts?' she blurted, stopping in mid-step.

'You already know that, Allie – I have been for days. But don't worry, I'm not reading everyone's, just yours.'

She was still huffing and puffing when he opened the door to reveal her motorbike at the roadside. Her mouth dropped open. Her bike was simply a pile of twisted metal, rubber and wire, smothered in thick, sticky wine-red blood that even the lashing rain couldn't wash away.

It was the blood that got through to her. She looked up at Michael.

'Remember?' he said quietly. 'I think you're still in shock, Allie.'

She knew now that he was right. She now really believed that he was whom he claimed to be and that he had saved her. She should be smeared all over south-west London.

He was about to put his hand on her shoulder, but she saw that he stopped himself. She wanted him to comfort her and was disappointed when he didn't. She suddenly felt small, vulnerable, and afraid of what might actually be.

They turned left toward the river and walked in silence for a minute or so until they came to his motorbike. It was parked between two Mercedes saloons near the embankment. Allie stopped and stared at the black bike. Beautiful though it was, she was reluctant to get on, the memory of last night's horrific accident now raging through her brain. Oblivious to this, Michael pulled out a petite helmet from a big black leather pannier and handed it to her.

He started the bike and looked questioningly at her.

'Aren't you wearing a helmet?' she asked weakly, as she climbed aboard, conquering her numbing fear.

He smirked and said something about being confident that he'd be okay. They roared off, Allie with another question forming – *how does an angel get to buy a motorbike or learn to ride one, for that matter?* She shook her helmeted head in disbelief. Maybe she really should have married what's-his-name and gone trout tickling in Scotland.

'Use the phone to get hold of me,' Michael said as he dropped Allie at the corner of Petty France and Broadway, as she'd asked.

'How? I don't have your number. Oh, wait a minute . . . you don't have one!'

He just flapped his hand at her. 'Just push "talk" or the green button or whatever you have – I'll be on it.'

She resisted asking how that could possibly be and just smiled at him. He smiled back, which was nice.

Everybody was happy. Now she just had a major murder investigation to coordinate. Michael went to shove off, but turned to her as she walked away.

'Remember,' he said, 'your murderer may be a man, but his mind is not his own.'

The conversation she'd had with Michael about Belhor the Destroyer, or whatever his name was, had not been lost on her. The trouble was, at the rational level, she just couldn't come to grips with the supposed supernatural elements to all this, but at the same time, there was no denying the events of last night and the tangible evidence provided by her shredded clothes and mangled, blood-stained bike. There was nothing surreal about that.

She was lucky to be alive. And there was still the lingering feeling that none of this was really foreign to her – she seemed to *know* how it all worked. *This strange inner knowledge explains*, she supposed, *why I don't feel compelled to bombard him with questions about who and what he is, how he got here, how my family is involved and a thousand other things.* She would demand answers at some stage, but for now, she reckoned she had enough on her plate.

Allie saw that her suggestion to Michael that the media would be all over the murder investigation had been right. A huge gaggle of journalists, cameramen and hangers-on waited outside the New Scotland Yard offices. She hoped to slip by the pack while they waited for DCS Carr or Commander Whitcombe to appear and answer their sensationalist questions. But she was wrong – they were there for her. She rounded the corner and a young black man immediately pointed at her. She groaned as twenty heads turned her way. Cameramen pounded the pavement towards her.

Oh shit, she thought. *How do they know I'm handling the investigation?* Clearly, they'd already been tipped off from the inside. Connors. DC Mathew Connors – had to be.

She couldn't turn and run, but the thought did cross her mind. She decided to brazen it out and quickened her pace towards them. She hit the pack before they came to a halt and slipped past half of them in an instant. She continued walking and nearly got out the other side before a microphone appeared under her nose, then another. She was encircled just ten yards from the front door of the Yard.

'Detective Chief Inspector, what can you tell us about the Earl's Court Crucifixion?'

There it was. Already branded and packaged up, ready for the 6:00 p.m. horror show that was the evening news. *Christ*, she thought ironically, *the media is really something.*

The sheer weight of numbers brought her to a halt. She had to reply, there was no getting around it. Plus, she didn't want to run from them like a cheesy loan shark caught on an exposé program.

She held her hand up and was surprised that the pack fell silent. She recalled her media training and looked at one camera, regardless from where or whom the questions might be asked. She chose a BBC camera and looked down the glass barrel.

'Officers attended a crime scene last night in the Earl's Court area. Suffice it to say, it will be a major investigation.'

A voice from her left side said, 'That much is obvious, DI St. Clair. Is it true a young girl was brutally murdered and strung up like Christ?'

Allie paused for a long time before answering.

'What *is* true is that prematurely releasing any detail of what might have occurred last night has the potential to prejudice any investigation and cause significant emotional stress to the girl's family.'

She knew as soon as she said it that she'd made a mistake – a really stupid one.

The pack shouted as one, 'So it was a *girl* who was murdered!'

Sweat pooled in the small of her back.

'It is clear that there is significant speculation already and it would be counterproductive to fuel that. It is simply too early to release any details. However, as is policy, we will hold a media conference at the earliest practicable time and furnish you with as many details at that time as we are able. Thank you.'

With that, she turned and strode for the glass doors of the main entrance to New Scotland Yard and safety. She pushed through them quickly, leaving the media shouting and jostling in her wake. Already a dread gnawed at her – she shouldn't have spoken to them at all.

Riding the lift to her floor, she tried to compose herself. She figured she'd go insane if her life didn't calm down soon. The lift doors opened to reveal

Commander Whitcombe and DCS Carr standing there, obviously waiting to descend to the ground floor.

'Good morning, ma'am,' Allie offered, also nodding at Whitcombe.

Carr wasn't happy. 'Allie, you should have called me early this morning about the Earls' Court situation. Now we have to go and front a media pack that is demanding to talk to . . . somebody.'

The blood drained from Allie's face. Carr and Whitcombe pushed into the lift before she had a chance to speak.

The doors closed. She felt Carr staring at her. 'Aren't you getting out here?'

'No, I—'

'Quick, Allie. I have to speak to the media now.' Carr pushed the 'open' button to let Allie exit the lift.

'Ma'am, I already have.'

Carr stared at her. 'Already have . . . *what*?'

Allie could see Carr had made the connection, despite the question. She just needed confirmation.

'Spoken to the media, ma'am. I was surrounded as I entered the building.'

Carr looked past Allie for a moment, clearly a device she used to control her anger.

After what seemed an eternity to Allie, Carr apologized to Commander Whitcombe, who hadn't uttered a word, and suggested she see him in his office in a few minutes. He stormed from the lift, taking long strides down the corridor.

Allie and Carr stood there together, watching him walk away. Neither spoke. Carr still had her finger on the 'open' button.

Allie looked at her. 'Your office?'

'My office,' Carr confirmed.

It took three days to walk to Carr's office, or so it seemed to Allie. She heard every footfall as if it were thunder, every breath Carr took along the way as a hurricane. Her senses were heightened beyond belief. She could feel the heat of Carr's anger and hear her pulse pounding. They arrived and Carr slowly closed the door and sat with exaggerated slowness in her black leather chair. She made no offer to Allie for her to sit.

'Is this how it's going to be, Allie?' Her voice was unnaturally calm. 'Every five minutes we end up in my office because we have a problem? First, it was Strauss, now it's the media. You've been on the job one bloody day. *One!'* The unnatural calm had evaporated.

9:57 a.m.

Paula Armstrong pushed through the frosted-glass door and climbed the narrow stairs to Arthur Wendell's BizTax Ltd. She hesitated at the dark-stained door for a moment, checking she had all the information she needed for him to complete her tax return. Satisfied that her bulky valise was packed full of the requisite receipts and documentation, she lightly rapped her knuckles on the door. A scuffling and scraping sound came from inside before the door was unlocked. She was reminded that, on a previous visit, she'd wondered why he locked the door. He was a funny little man and he certainly seemed to have his share of eccentricities.

The door swung open and Arthur greeted her – more enthusiastically than he usually did, she thought. He ushered her to a faded swivel chair and as he did so, she noticed that he looked a little younger than she remembered; and taller, if she wasn't mistaken. He locked the office door again, walked around and sat as he normally did at his wide grey pressed-steel desk, self-consciously fiddling with the desk blotter and pencils before looking up. She was immediately struck by his coal-black eyes – another thing she'd not noticed before. They were almost Mediterranean. In all, she decided, Arthur was a better-looking man than she recalled from their previous meetings. She fiddled with the collar of her blouse and smoothed down her red skirt.

'You have something for me?' he asked.

Inexplicably, she blushed before pushing the bulky valise toward him.

He reached for it, brushing her hand. She looked quickly up at him and saw that he was staring openly at her.

She could not believe she had just agreed to meet Arthur Wendell for lunch. The old Paula Armstrong just didn't do that. She felt a little tingle as she left his office and hurried off down Cornwall Street, past the famous row of funny little Edwardian boutiques, and towards the multi-story car park which housed her little silver MX-5 roadster. She would call her beautician shortly – there were 'things' that needed to be attended to: hair, nails, waxing, God forbid. She'd pop back in to work for a few minutes, but her staff at *La Mode* would just have to go it alone for the remainder of the morning. She had until 1:00 p.m., at which time she'd meet Arthur on the corner of Tottenham Court Road and Oxford Street, not far from her offices in St. Giles Road. He'd said he'd book 'somewhere special' for them. She loved surprises and the little girl inside her was already having a good time.

The half-hour it had taken Arthur to check her tax information and complete the necessary online work had gone by in a blur. There was something about him that seemed to interrupt her thoughts – obscuring her normal caution. She'd agreed to meet him without question, knowing how disappointed she'd have been had they not at least had another appointment.

She realized how much she'd been hoping for more when he coolly asked her out. She'd nearly jumped in his lap, she realized, but instead of being embarrassed, she felt . . . excited. She'd jump in his lap a bit later today, all right, she found herself thinking. *What the hell? What on earth has come over me?* she wondered. She nearly laughed out loud as she reached her car, threw in her heavy valise, and roared down the ramps to the pay station.

She checked her reflection in the rear-view mirror even as she sped down the narrow ramps from level four. Her hair *definitely* needed attention. Damn, why hadn't she had it done last week? She knew why, of course. There'd been no one in her life to dress up for in the past six months. Eric had left her in a blaze of self-recrimination over his newly-discovered 'gayness' and while he left her well provided for, with money and property courtesy of his flourishing real estate business, he'd caused her much embarrassment socially, to the extent that she could no longer stand the sideways looks from people she'd considered friends. Hence, the last few months had been simply miserable for her. Well, she'd not put on weight – worry had seen to that – and the girls at the office said she still looked like the pretty cover girl she'd been twenty years ago. Her legs were still great, and after her hair was 're-blonded' this afternoon, well, who knew? Maybe the dark, lonely days of the past six months were about to be put behind her.

Chapter Ten

10:35 a.m.

Allie finally slid out from under DCS Carr's office door after the biggest bollocking she'd ever had in her life. Her father's annoyance long ago when she'd crashed her scooter against his brand-new (purchased that day) Mercedes 300SL now seemed positively benign in retrospect. Allie had never seen Carr blow a gasket like that before – and she'd seen her with her fuse well and truly lit.

Still reeling, on a whim, she texted: *So where were u then, Angel?*

The reply appeared immediately: *Hey, that's one scary woman.*

DC Connors caught her wry smile. 'Something funny?'

The humour went out of it for Allie then and there. She checked her watch. 'Okay, sorry, Mathew. I'm running late for our meeting. Got your file together?' She led him to her office and waved a hand for him to sit at the chair pulled up at her desk, not the soft lounge chairs reserved for informal chats.

She asked him what he'd gleaned from Mr Lin, the owner of the Golden Bamboo restaurant. Connors flipped open his thin manila folder, carefully picking his way through to a particular piece of white A4 paper, on which Allie could see three blocks of handwritten text.

'Mr Yeow Chin Lin has owned the Golden Bamboo for nine years . . .'

Allie listened, albeit distractedly, while Connors ran through his report. There was nothing remarkable in it and she said so. She was still perturbed by the thought that Connors might have leaked information to the media about the case. Why he might do that, she couldn't imagine, but decided not to raise it for the moment.

It seemed Mr Lin from the Golden Bamboo restaurant hadn't seen or heard anything prior to discovering the body, when he carted out an empty oil drum and threw it in the corner of the lane at about 11:20 p.m. It had been a quiet night, presumably because of the inclement weather, and the last customers – a middle-age couple – had left at about 10:30 p.m. Mr Lin claimed he and two staff had packed up and cleaned the kitchen, and Mr Lin had been the last person at the restaurant.

Allie studied Mathew for a moment, noting the dark circles under his eyes and his pasty face. He was near done-in. She quietly asked if he'd personally checked the kitchen at the restaurant.

Mathew was clearly surprised by the question. 'No, I didn't. Do you think I should have?'

'How do you know Lin cleaned the kitchen? Just because he said so?'

Mathew looked uncomfortable and said he'd had no reason to doubt Mr Lin.

'The girl didn't murder herself, Mathew. What, our Chinese brethren don't commit murder?'

He flushed. Allie sighed and looked away. She was tired as well and probably irritable because of it but, by any measure, this was hardly an impressive start from Connors. She didn't think Mr Lin had committed the murder either, but assumption was the mother of all cock-ups. Theoretically, Lin could have murdered the girl after the last customers had left, then called the police. It was highly unlikely, but there had been time, so who could rule it out at this point? She changed tack.

'Have you secured copies of all the credit card transactions, then?' she asked, her slight exasperation unmasked.

Relieved, Connors said he had and that they were currently being sorted by another officer.

'All right, get someone on the phones as soon as you can. We need to talk to every customer from last night. How many transactions are there?'

'Twenty two.'

'Not unmanageable – that's good. Does Mr Lin know any of the customers personally?'

Connors looked down at the floor. 'Sorry, I didn't ask. I assumed he didn't, I suppose.'

There it was again – assumption and maybe a little racism lurking under it. What the hell was wrong with him? Connors was a better detective than this. Yes, he was tired, but even last night he'd failed to interview Mr Lin immediately.

'Did you look at any of the names on the receipts? Quite apart from anybody else, Chinese people eat at Chinese restaurants – that's why the restaurants were established in the first place. Besides, he may have many friends – Chinese or not – who support his restaurant. I could see last night that he was an outgoing type, he'll know something about most of his customers.'

Connors simply nodded. Allie rocked back in her chair and looked at him. Something was badly amiss here.

'Mathew, what's the problem? Is everything all right?'

He looked stunned by the question, but recognized that she was giving him a chance to explain his lack of performance. It was a gift under the circumstances. 'Al . . .' He hesitated. 'DCI St. Clair, I don't quite know. I saw that girl and I just stopped thinking, I guess. I've never seen such . . . sick brutality. God almighty, it's inhuman!'

Inhuman. Yes, she thought, *according to Michael, that's* exactly *what it is.* What to do about Connors though? He wanted to be assigned to the case, but was buckling at the knees already. Clearly, he hadn't conquered his revulsion from last night.

'I understand. And I agree, it's a shocking thing for anyone to witness. What she must have endured doesn't bear thinking about. But we *do* have to think about it. And thoroughly – every grizzly, evil, bloody aspect of it.

That's our job and you know it as well as I do,' she repeated the mantra she'd used on herself.

'Yes, of course.' Connors fiddled with his collar and shifted in his seat.

'You still want to run with it?' Allie asked the question, but was unsure what she wanted the answer to be. Either way, it could represent a problem. Her previous confidence in him had plummeted in the space of ten minutes. Connors nodded; he still wanted in.

'Let's get hold of the forensic report first and take it from there,' she said finally. 'Please ask everyone to convene in the conference room in thirty minutes.'

She watched Connors stumble from her office and made a decision. She would involve herself directly in this case. She alone knew what they were really up against – or thought she did.

Margaret Daly delivered the forensic report to Allie a couple of minutes after Connors left the office. Allie asked her to distribute copies to DCs Banks, Connors, and Wilkinson and, with some hesitation, added DS Strauss to the list. She also asked Daly to make sure everyone knew to gather in the conference room – the Green Room as it was known – at 11:00 a.m. It was already getting late – the briefing should already have been completed. Allie was keen to see the pathologist's report, which she knew would not be available for another hour.

The forensic report from the crime scene was comprehensive, as she had come to expect from Forensic Services, and contained about thirty A4 pages and as many photographs. The events of the previous night rushed back into her thoughts, including the moment when she could have sworn the girl had flown at her. It had seemed absolutely real.

She felt the prickle of sweat on her back as she remembered her horror. She also remembered the sound of breaking glass. She suddenly wondered where Michael was at that moment and looked at her phone, half expecting him to text her. But it remained silent. Perhaps he really had gone to Portobello Road to browse the antique shops as he'd threatened. His petulance still surprised her. He was a strange . . . man . . . thing, all right. She shook her head as if to purge it of an unwanted intrusion, like a dog shaking a flea from its ear. *The whole supernatural aspect is just too much*, she thought for the umpteenth time.

She quickly read the report, which covered the technical details of the scene, a broad description of the injuries to the young woman, and physical evidence on site: the wine bottle, scraps of clothing, shoes and blood. No murder weapon had been identified; nor had the victim, for that matter. Only one set of DNA had been found – presumably the young woman's – but it wasn't matched on file. Somebody's parents or boyfriend weren't too worried about her whereabouts either; no missing persons report had been filed that morning.

If the forensic report was a bit dry, the photographs made up for it. The photographer – a Mr Everett Blight in this case – had done a good job in the atrocious, wet conditions, perhaps too good. The brightly lit colour images were profoundly disturbing and Allie unconsciously put her hand to her mouth. By the third photograph her eyes had misted over. Her breath came again in short bursts as images from last night merged with those in front of her. Even the smell burst back, causing her to dry-retch noisily. Margaret Daly's head jerked up outside her glass-panelled office. Jumping to her feet, Allie spun and, parting the thin venetian blinds, opened her tiny window. She looked out of her office window, down towards Broadway.

The Feathers Inn stood right in her line of sight. Breathing slowly, she brought herself under control again. She turned from the window and half-lowered herself into her chair before straightening again and turning back to the window. Something wasn't right. She pulled the braided cord, hoisted the blinds to the top of the window, and stared out on to the streets again. She saw it immediately – the colour of everything was . . . different. There was a grey pallor to the sky and a similar washed-out look to the buildings; even the cars moving along Broadway. She looked through St. Anne's Gate towards St James' Park, which abutted the Mall and Buckingham Palace. Even through the narrow lane and archway, she could see the pale trees and the faded stonework of the once-tan palace. It all looked like a sun-damaged impressionist painting. The light had changed. Colour blindness sprang to mind. Surely it couldn't happen just like that.

She turned back to face the office. Margaret stood in her doorway, a deeply concerned look directed at her. But it wasn't *exactly* Margaret.

Allie stared at her long enough for the middle-aged woman to fidget uncomfortably. 'Ma'am?' Margaret finally breathed. 'Is everything all right?'

Allie snapped out of her sepia-coloured zone and refocused on the hunched figure before her. She looked normal enough now, but a moment ago she could have sworn Margaret had red blotches on her throat, eyes that seemed to have shrunken to pinpricks and hair that had three distinct colours to it: brown, orange and grey. Very grey. It was as if she'd glimpsed the unadorned Margaret, devoid of make-up, artificial hair colour and pride. Allie had seen a frightened, grey rabbit desperately trying to disguise its real self. And she could smell her fear.

Allie finally managed a laugh. 'Sorry, Margaret. I was deep in thought!'

Margaret sighed and manufactured a half-smile in return. Allie had clearly frightened her. Margaret was all but backing out of the room.

'Don't suppose you could rustle up a cup of tea and a biscuit, by any chance?'

This broke the spell and Margaret returned to her safety zone. Allie *saw* it happen. Once again, the colours in the room paled. Margaret's skin faded to a cool blue around her neck and her face regained a pink hue. Allie watched as the pupils in her eyes returned to normal size as blood returned through the minute spider web of veins surrounding the pupils. Her hair remained multi-coloured though – it looked embarrassingly bad to Allie. Funny, she'd never noticed it before. Allie quickly shifted her gaze in case she spooked Margaret again by staring too hard at her.

To her relief, Margaret simply uttered a cheery, 'Right you are,' and scuttled off towards the tearoom.

Allie fell back into her high-back chair and exhaled hard. *What was* that *about?* she wondered. She looked down between her outstretched fingers at the old desk she'd inherited from Billy McBride and decided to concentrate on it to see what might happen. Sure enough, after a couple of seconds, the fibres in the wood leapt out at her. She could clearly see ink marks, graphite ridges from lead pencils, old phone numbers that had been unsuccessfully erased, stains – ones she hoped were just the result of spilt coffee and tea – fragments of paper lodged in the minute crevices in the wood grain and scratches – hundreds of tiny scratches. She unfocused her gaze and everything returned to normal – colours, light, everything. She looked again at the desk and saw nothing of her previous vision. She pinched her nose high up and squeezed her eyes shut for a moment, hard enough to make them water. *Weird* was all her inner monologue could offer.

It hit her then that something was missing. The photographs – there was something about the photographs. She reached for the huge manila envelope and emptied the contents out on to her desk. There were nineteen 10"×12" photos in all. She suspended her revulsion as best she could and carefully studied each one.

Margaret arrived with the tea and a mountain of chocolate-coated biscuits. Allie smiled as she saw the feast appear on the corner of her desk. Chocolate biscuits were not the normal morning tea fare. Margaret had made a special effort; clearly, she had a stash of 'special' biscuits and Allie made a mental note to remember that. She thanked Margaret without taking her eyes from the photos, mostly because she was afraid she'd now see Margaret in digital Technicolor and they'd both freak out.

She checked her watch; there were just ten minutes until the briefing. Her first run through the photos revealed nothing, but she was certain she was missing something. She had previously made notes about the crime scene she would run through with her team, but that wasn't what was bothering her. On photo six, she felt herself tense again at the persistent memory of the girl lurching off the wall at her and realized with a jolt that it was a message. The photo was important; this she grasped. It was almost as if the girl was trying to tell her that. The photo; why was it important? What was it showing her? What was *Georgie* trying to show her?

She shivered, clasping her hand to her mouth in an involuntary effort to hold herself still. She cast her mind back to King's Lane. She saw again the cold, hard rain, the hopelessly inadequate blue tarp the uniformed officers had erected, the huge frame of George Houghton standing against the lights, the rubbish strewn across the lane and the stinking drums of used cooking oil. Her mind walked her up to the dead end and she saw herself standing, torch in hand, staring up at the eviscerated girl spiked to the wall. *The wall. That's it!* She had it now. She distinctly remembered big circles or sweeps of blood on the old red bricks behind the girl, but the photos didn't show them. She pored through them quickly again, just to make sure, but there was nothing – just red-brown bricks.

She hadn't imagined the blood, of that she was certain. *Georgie* knew too; she *felt* that. She looked for the photographer's contact details on the bottom of the report and scribbled down his phone number. She'd ring him after the briefing. It was show time in the Green Room and she quickly stood to gather her files. She froze as she put her hand on the door handle to swing it open. *Who the hell was Georgie?*

The morning galloped in an adrenalin-fuelled rush for Arthur. Paula Armstrong's sinewy, athletic legs filled his thoughts to the extent that he abandoned his regular work. Profit and loss statements, balance sheets and tax returns could not compete for his headspace. At 10:50 a.m., he locked his office door and set off for the tube station. There was still plenty of time to prepare for today's 'lunch'.

He already knew exactly where he'd take her – in every sense. But he needed some tools to make the occasion the special one he imagined for both of them. Paula was smart and attractive, so the lunch should be structured appropriately. His inner 'friend' suggested an army surplus store in Soho – Manny's near Greek Street – as the one that might carry just the implements he needed.

He bounded effortlessly down the time-blackened steps of the Earl's Court tube station, not bothering to scan the signs for the line that would take him to Tottenham Court Road, a stone's throw from Greek Street and the meeting point with Paula. He already knew he'd have to backtrack to his home station at Notting Hill Gate, then change to the Central Line for the trip through Marble Arch, Bond Street and Oxford Circus. He knew this part of the Monopoly board very well. This was his territory. It was important to organize things with certain symmetry – a congruence of time and purpose to achieve the desired outcome efficiently. Everything should line up, just like numbers. Nothing should stray from a column or appear twice or be added more than once. There was an order to be observed and accounting provided the perfect metaphor for his life.

His friend was organized too, he was pleased to note. Suggesting Manny's was a masterstroke. They were becoming a great team and they would be remembered, like Batman and Robin, Bonnie and Clyde – or maybe even Posh and Becks! He nearly fell over laughing at his own joke.

Steady there, Artie, the voice cautioned. *Don't draw attention to yourself.*

Suitably chastised, Arthur shuffled on to the train with a dozen others and found a seat opposite a teenage boy. The boy was staring at him, mocking. He didn't like it.

'What's up, pimples?' Arthur said recklessly.

The boy hurriedly returned his gaze to his Nintendo game.

That's better, Arthur thought, *a little respect – maybe a little fear thrown in, as well. Fucking teenagers these* days – rude little self-centred pricks and all with the latest gizmos and baggy-arsed jeans hanging down past their knees. Who the hell was going to run the country in twenty years – these pasty-faced little faggots? Hardly. Calming himself, he sat and let the rhythm of the train work its magic. His friend was quiet. The idea of a partnership kept popping into his head. He started running through great duos of the past to whom he and his friend would one day be compared. He realized that his friend hadn't given him his name. Should he ask him, he wondered?

Mr Black, the voice intoned.

Mr Black? Arthur rolled that one around his head for a while, waiting for inspiration. Black and Arthur? Nope, didn't sound right. Wendell and Black? Hmm . . . not bad, but it sounded like a firm of solicitors. Something was missing. We need a memorable name, like Starsky and Hutch or Harley and Rose or Frankie Lee and Judas Priest. They were the best of friends too, of course.

You're losing focus, Arthur.

He knew it, but a great name was important, damn it. He gazed out of the train window, thinking hard. A name. Something to be known by . . . to stand for something. In frustration he turned away from the window, his eye catching the advertising banners which had been strategically placed above the seats to hook and persuade.

A brand, that's what it was all about these days! Marketing and branding . . . like having to deliver a quality product at a competitive price, time after time, no matter where, no matter when. He and his friend needed a company name and a positioning statement that encapsulated the ethos of their company. That was it. They would brand their work, almost like an art gallery, for that was what he . . . A sharp pain shot through his brain. Okay, *they*, would create the art, but it had to be within defined limits. Like accounting, it had to add up to something and be whole, self-contained and recognizable as quality work, time after time.

It came to him at last. *Paint it Black. That's what we'll call themselves. That's how the world will know us. Paint it Black.*

Already copyrighted, Arthur – The Rolling Stones, remember?

Shit, that's right. Okay, okay . . . Painted Black – past tense, already happened by the time the bodies are found. It's like 'Design by Franco' or 'Lifestyle by Bernanchi'.

I like it, Arthur. You're on to something.

Yes! Arthur lurched in his seat. Just like the first one – Georgie – the message had been there for anyone who cared to see. Layering, messages. Messages to the people.

Just for her, actually, Mr Black interrupted.

Who?

Never you mind, Arthur – just someone we'll meet soon.

'Wha'ever,' Arthur said loudly, rolling his eyes, feeling sixteen and full of pent-up energy.

He looked again at the boy across from him. His check shirt askew, silly black cap perched too far back on his head and faded black trousers all but covering his worn tennis shoes. The boy, sensing something, suddenly looked up at him, the Nintendo forgotten.

Arthur reached across the aisle and touched him lightly on the knee.

'Painted Black,' he said flatly. 'What do you think . . . catchy?'

11:00 a.m.

The Green Room was occupied by three pink-faced and expectant detectives – those to whom DCI St. Clair had asked the full forensic and photographic reports to be sent. Jamaican-born DC Jacinta Wilkinson, whom Allie had decided should also be included, mainly because her predecessor had pointedly excluded her from such meetings in the past, was also in attendance. She was disappointed Strauss turned her head away as she entered the room. *The feud continues*, she noted with an inward sigh. The room was small, too brightly lit and sparsely furnished. The large whiteboard dominated the wall opposite the entrance, a desk with a projector immediately in front of it. Heavy dark-green curtains blocked light from the western window and a low wooden bench, enlivened by a bright green Formica top, ran full-length below it. The Green Room was aptly named.

Allie strode to the whiteboard and slipped six photos from the crime scene up under the catch-all clip at the top. Gasps preceded her move to face the four detectives.

'I know,' she said as she turned. 'It's—' She stopped speaking as she saw the ashen faces of her team. She paused for a moment longer, then pointed at their folders.

'Have you not already looked at these?'

All four shook their heads. 'Dear me,' she said almost to herself. 'I'm sorry, but we simply do not have time to catch our breath here. Presumably, none of you have read the forensic report, either?'

There was more shaking of heads. Allie looked at her watch and sighed loud enough for them to catch her slight frustration.

'Okay, please sit now and we'll go through it. Henry Gladstone from Pathology and profiler Jillian Groenewagen will be here shortly.' She gestured towards Connors.

'Mathew will kick things off. I visited the scene also, and I'll add anything I think is germane.' She saw Strauss look at Banks, her eyebrows theatrically raised.

'*Relevant*, then, Rachel,' Allie added flatly. Strauss squirmed in her seat, but sat up as Connors cleared his throat.

During the next fifteen minutes, Connors ran through his observations; the interview with Mr Lin from the Golden Bamboo; comments from the uniformed officers who attended the scene; and what steps he was taking to follow up on the previous night's customers from the restaurant. Banks asked a couple of questions and Jacinta Wilkinson queried whether residents in the area had already been interviewed.

'No,' Allie interrupted with a thin smile. 'That's going to be your job, Jacinta.' Wilkinson smiled back and nodded. 'Also,' Allie added, 'check with anybody at the Earl's Court tube station who might have been about late last night. It's right across the road. You might also start the ball rolling on getting some posters up on the platforms as well. We'll work on the wording after this briefing.'

Allie looked at the four members of her team and took a deep breath. 'There's no getting around it any longer, I'm afraid. I'm going to have to throw these photos up on the screen. She looked out through the doorway towards the common area.

'I see Gladstone and Groenewagen have arrived.' Waving them in, she completed quick introductions and asked Gladstone to address her detectives.

Allie had worked with Forensic Pathologist Henry Gladstone before, as had all but Connors from her team. Henry was experienced, thorough and, mercifully, to the point. He was conspicuously tired from what had turned into an all-night examination and autopsy, and it showed. His skin was pasty and his normally flashing eyes were dull and hooded. Allie suspected that the nature of the wounds inflicted on the girl had also shocked and saddened him.

Sounding more resigned than normal, he postulated that the woman was about thirty three years old and confirmed she had very poor dental hygiene, a general rash over her upper body, and slightly deformed feet – possibly from wearing ill-fitting shoes from a very early age. There was deathly silence in the room as he detailed her injuries. He described her evisceration, the way in which he believed the eyeballs had been levered from the sockets and the gaping gouge at the very back of the girl's throat where her tongue had been torn straight out.

Gladstone spoke about the sharp, narrow wound in the girl's left side and the torn fingernails and bloodied fingers on both hands. The girl's thin dyed-black hair had been ripped out in clumps from the nape of the neck and her kneecaps were severely grazed. She had, of course, been roughly sexually assaulted anally, but the mutilation to her pelvic region precluded any thorough vaginal examination. Allie saw Rachel Strauss's hand fly to her mouth at this point, and Jacinta Wilkinson squirmed uncomfortably.

Gladstone went on to note the unusual finding that the tendons at the back of the girl's knees had been severed, as had those at her wrists. Gladstone completed his report by advising that analysis of her hair dye, make-up, etc. would not be available until after lunch. Allie doubted lunch would be on anyone's agenda today.

She took a very deep breath, smiled almost apologetically at Henry Gladstone, thanked him, and invited questions about his report. There were none. He smiled at Allie, then left the room without a backwards glance.

With mounting concern, Allie immediately brought Doctor Jillian Groenewagen to the front of the room. She hoped the psychological profile would prove insightful and stimulate her team to engage more fully, but wondered whether it might not be totally off-beam, given Michael's claims. She ticked herself off as soon as the thought crossed her mind. They were not *claims*; she would have to accept Michael without question, including the situation he'd presented to her. She shrugged her shoulders and Groenewagen noticed.

'Are you ready for me to begin, DCI?'

Allie waved her hand as a go-ahead.

Jillian Groenewagen was almost embarrassingly long-faced and thin. She had fuse-wire hair and ridiculous – at least in Allie's view – speckled horn-rimmed glasses that even Elton John would reject. If Groenewagen was shooting for a look that was equine, eccentric, academic, and more than a little scary, she was grouping her shots nicely. In her high, toneless voice, she outlined the type of person she felt they should be looking for. Ten minutes later, Allie privately decided that, despite her annoying mannerisms, Jill Groenewagen had run a reasonable 'by the book' argument. She also knew, however, that in all probability 'Groener' was completely wrong. She threw open the discussion.

'So there were have it, right from the horse's—' She quickly changed tack. 'The, er . . . Doctor Groenewagen's perspective.'

If Allie's red face was heating the room, Groenewagen's glacial stare was cooling it fast. Banks guffawed.

Allie jumped in with a question while firing her own lethal glance at Banks.

'So, Doctor, in a nutcase . . . *sorry* nutshell, so to speak.' another breathy snigger from Banks, 'we are possibly dealing with a homicidal maniac with a God or religious phobia, who was abused as a child, possibly by a priest, and whose father, if he had one, was most likely an extremely violent man. Yes?'

'Yes.' More ice from Groenewagen.

Allie pressed on. 'Any guesses . . . theories on ethnicity, age and perhaps intelligence and profession?'

Groenewagen thawed a little, adjusted her glasses upward and turned to face the four detectives.

'Definitely white male, women don't do this and aren't strong enough, anyway. Age? I'd say early twenties, and intelligence . . . definitely high. It's impossible to guess an occupation, but he's probably working beneath his capabilities, possibly as a storeman or transport operator, something like that. He's strong though, very strong, so again, he's somebody who probably lifts heavy things regularly.'

'Or works out a lot,' said Connors.

'Possibly,' Groenewagen agreed.

'Not sure about that,' Allie countered. 'I think he might be very shy, damaged goods if you will, and that makes him unlikely to join groups or workout publicly, like in a gym.'

'He might have a home gym,' offered Wilkinson.

Allie nodded and agreed that anything was possible. 'Of course,' she added, 'we don't yet know if we're dealing with just one person. I've got the boys in the back room chasing up CCTV footage. I know there were at least two cameras near the restaurant. Hopefully we'll have something very soon.'

Allie thanked Doctor Groenewagen who, to Allie's relief, even shook her hand. She was also pleased to see that the slight interlude of manic giggling among her team had subsided. It had been a safety valve reaction to the horrors they'd just been exposed to and there was nothing else for it but to ignore it and press on. Her mobile phone declared a text message had arrived. She snatched at it a little too quickly. It was, of course, from Michael.

Don't pin your hopes on video footage.

She saw quizzical looks go around among the team and shoved the phone back in her pocket.

She looked hard at her group and immediately wished she hadn't. The crazy colours came back. Wilkinson glowed crimson from head to foot. Connors had what Allie assumed was a nervous green tinge. Banks, she now saw, dyed his hair brown – there was an underlying carroty hue evident – and Strauss was stony blue.

She looked at the floor to allow the tableau to fade. It did. She wondered again if she was losing her sanity. Again, her phone pinged. She knew it would be Michael telling her she wasn't insane. Even that knowledge was a strange comfort. She realized she was drawing strength from him and that was a little revelation. Turning to the whiteboard, she spoke to the four detectives, doling out instructions in an almost staccato fashion. It was time to get the operation motoring and she left no one in any doubt about it.

She asked Connors and Strauss to team up and doorknock the immediate area of the murder and told Banks to complete the task of running down the Golden Bamboo customers from last night and interview them.

She didn't add that it was the job Connors had been originally assigned.

'Wouldn't it be better if I did that?' Connors bleated.

Allie ignored him. In her view, he was lucky to still be on the case, let alone complaining. She asked Wilkinson to stay on the CCTV trail and stay behind for a moment to confirm the poster wording for the tube station and general area posters, plus radio and TV bulletins. Wishing them good luck, she suggested they reconvene at 6:00 p.m.

'What are *you* going to be doing?' Allie didn't need to look around to know it was Strauss. She turned and answered her evenly. 'As a matter of fact, I'm going back to the crime scene.' She glanced at her watch.

'I expect to run into you and Connors in and around the area fairly shortly.'

She eyeballed them all again. 'I'm open to suggestions at all times, you know. This is not the Allie St. Clair show.' She realized she had said this purely for Strauss's benefit and mentally kicked herself. 'Obviously, my approach is going to be different to Billy's and I guess we're all going to have to adjust in some way. The last twenty four hours has been horrendous – Billy's passing, this heinous crime – and to some, my appointment as your DCI might also qualify in that regard. It's a lot to take in, believe me, I understand that.'

There was no discernible reaction from any of the detectives. She wondered whether Billy had also felt this strange isolation. What was amazing to her was the immediacy with which her colleagues seemed to have separated her from member of the team to part of the establishment. Most of them had worked, laughed and drunk with her for nearly five years, and apart from the falling-out with Rachel, it had been enjoyable and, at least from her point of view, there had been genuine camaraderie. She admitted the possibility with a sinking feeling that she would never again experience that.

In any case, it was time for everyone to get moving, so she wrapped things up. 'Okay, let's go. Please touch base if anything significant turns up.' Despite the lack of reaction from the team, she smiled and again wished them good luck.

She watched her young murder investigation team file out of the Green Room door and again noted there was no particular urgency to their movements. There should have been. They were the youngest MIT at the Met and they were on trial as much as she. She sighed again and shook her head. She'd been waiting for someone, *anyone*, to ask the obvious question during the briefing, namely, 'Were any fingerprints taken from the scene, either the victim's or the murderer's?' Very, very basic stuff, yet no one had asked.

The fact was, there was one set of fingerprints all over the crime scene, but there was no record of them on the HOLMES system. The murderer wasn't known to the police. It was all in the report. She checked her watch. It was 11:32 a.m. She started back to her office, now planning to ring the scene of crime photographer, Everett something or other. Those photos of the wall in King's Lane were *wrong*.

Everett Blight struggled to comprehend what the female voice on the end of his telephone line was saying. He knew why. It was the only thing he *could* understand. He'd snorted a line of coke longer than a McDonald's queue about four hours ago and now he felt like death. His eyes were streaming and his nose felt like it had been infused with lemon juice. It was a nice, cultured voice on the line though, that much he comprehended. Quite sexy, really. His senses were rousing themselves. Not only hope raised its head.

'I'm sorry,' he managed at last. '*Who* is this?'

'Detective Chief Inspector St. Clair.'

'*Christ*,' he said to himself. Or did he say it out loud? He couldn't be sure. He sat up straighter in his bed. 'Yes, Inspector, umm, what can I help you with?'

He heard the exasperation in the voice.

'Last night's crime scene photos, from Earl's Court . . . You *did* take them, did you not?'

Now he understood. His brain was clearing fast. 'Sorry, yes. Indeed I did, Inspector. You should have them, I dropped them at—'

'Yes, I have them, Mr Blight.' He liked the formal mode of address. It was rare.

'Great, so what is it that I can do for you?'

'I visited the scene last night, Mr Blight. My memory of a couple of things isn't reflected in the photos,' she paused, 'strange as that sounds.'

'No, no,' Blight blurted, even though he thought it sounded bloody strange.

'Can I ask a favour of you, Mr Blight?'

He figured that voice could ask him anything, but he'd still be charging.

'Yes, of course, Inspector.'

'Could you meet me at the crime scene in about half an hour and bring an infrared filter and appropriate film with you?'

Now this is unusual on two counts, Blight thought. First, nobody ever asked for infrared shots during the day and secondly, here was a cop who knew something about photography. *What next?* he thought, although mild panic nibbled at the edge of his brain. He hoped her real enquiry wasn't about another aspect of his business.

I'm coming with you, the text message announced. Allie wasn't entirely surprised by it. She figured Michael wasn't going to twiddle his thumbs all day. *What the hell*, she thought as she typed her reply; this whole thing was just getting weirder by the minute.

I'll be in a black Vauxhall, she typed. *Meet me near the corner of Broadway and Tothill Street, outside the adult shop*. Despite the seriousness of the morning, she smiled to herself.

His reply, as usual, was instantaneous. *Cute. Okay, ten minutes.*

Ten minutes was cutting it fine, but doable. She asked Margaret Daly to quickly organize a pool car for her then called Wilkinson and asked her to progress the work with the communications department without her and work up a draft treatment for the posters and TV stuff which she would have to look at later. She grabbed her bag and headed off to the lifts for her journey to the basement car park. How she would ever explain Michael's presence to anyone else, she didn't yet know, but she'd take the risk. Superintendent Carr walked out of her office, narrowly avoiding a collision with St. Clair. They fell into step as they walked to the lifts. This wasn't St. Clair's ideal scenario. The inevitable question came.

'Is the investigation underway?' There was no note of friendliness that Allie could discern.

'Yes, ma'am. I'm just going back to the crime scene now for a second look, and to coordinate some local enquiries.'

Carr nodded. 'Any early clue as to the victim's identity, or the perpetrator's for that matter?'

'None yet, ma'am. The victim was badly—'

'Yes, I heard,' Carr interrupted. 'Not from *you,* I might add, but I heard.' Allie exhaled heavily. Carr noticed. 'Too much to ask was it?'

Allie stopped in her tracks. 'Sorry, ma'am?'

Carr stopped as well and faced Allie squarely, speaking slowly, as if to a child. 'Is it too much to ask that I be briefed on significant aspects of the case?'

Allie slowed her speech down too and took a step towards Carr, her fatigue leading her to a retaliatory response she might not otherwise have mounted. A flicker of hesitation crossed her features before 'Sod it' won the day.

'Ma'am, I'm very sorry I got in the way of your media interview this morning. I know how important it was to you. It won't happen again. But as for the case, information to enable the briefing and plan to be put into operation had only just come to hand. My team, to whom I have assigned various duties, has only left the building in the last five minutes. They are well aware of the importance and urgency with which they are to discharge their duties and the need to report in as per my instructions.'

Carr flushed and stepped back. Anyone who had heard St. Clair's response and who had an ear for such things would have realized Carr had just been told in the classiest of ways to basically fuck off and let St. Clair do her job.

'Right, the, er . . . best time to get me will be after 2:00 p.m. I have meetings till then,' she stammered.

'2:15 p.m. it is, then, ma'am. Hopefully, I'll be ringing you much earlier with some news!' she said brightly over her shoulder as she continued on to the lift.

Detective Chief Superintendent Ellen Carr stood and watched the lift doors retreat at precisely the right time to allow St. Clair to walk straight in. They stared at each other for as long as it took for the doors to close again. She hoped the two administration staff who passed her in the corridor at that point couldn't hear her elevated heartbeat; it was thumping jackhammer loud because of what she'd just seen. She glanced behind her and noted that the couple hadn't broken stride. *Good, they didn't notice.*

She exhaled a long, slow breath and decided a cup of tea was just the thing. She allowed herself a small smile as she headed for the amenities room. The last time she'd seen eyes change from green to that unique flame red had been more than twenty years ago.

Steven Bannister

Chapter Eleven

The black Vauxhall saloon was brand new and St. Clair breathed in that peculiar smell that only emanates from hot-off-the-production-line cars; that heady mixture of leather, rubber and maybe silicone? It was the only thing cars had over motorbikes, she conceded. But bikes had their own allure. Exhaust fumes weren't half bad.

She swung the car right out of Broadway on to Tothill Street and spotted Michael immediately. He was trying to stand inconspicuously in front of the adult shop entrance, but failing. He was not easily camouflaged. She pulled to the curb, holding up a car behind her. Michael sprinted the ten yards to the car, his black coat flapping wildly. He vaulted into the passenger seat, slamming the door as he did so. Allie hit the accelerator hard and gave a wave to the gentleman driving the low car behind her. She looked again in her rear-view mirror – was the man yelling at her?

'Everything okay?' Michael asked.

'Cloth-cap man back there obviously didn't like me pulling over for you. He's going butchers back there.'

'Butchers?'

Allie laughed. 'Sorry, butcher's hook – *crook*. She noticed his lingering no comprende expression.

'He's rather annoyed,' she said finally in her best Belgravia. 'One hopes he will regain his composure without undue delay.' She shot him a twinkly smile.

'Right,' said Michael, half-turning in his seat and eyeballing a wizened old man in an even older green Jaguar soft-top.

'Shall I kill him to get him off our tail?'

'Would you mind?' she replied coolly, glancing at Michael. 'He really is tiresome.'

'The boys are already on it.'

She looked across at him and saw he wasn't smiling. A mild panic rippled through her. 'Michael, you do know I was only—'

He laughed. It was a deep, rumbling sound, full of genuine amusement. She liked the sound of it a lot.

Arthur Wendell disembarked from the tube at Tottenham Court Road, as did the pimply faced kid he'd so comprehensively spooked earlier. Just for devilment he followed the kid too closely down the corridors and towards the stairs to the Oxford Street exit. The kid eventually broke into a stumbling run and that was enough for Arthur. Job done. With a laugh, he branched off for the Tottenham Court Road exit. He touched his Oyster card at the ticket barrier and it obligingly allowed him to emerge into the pale spring-summer sun. It wasn't yet midday; *there's still plenty of time*, he reasoned.

'Yer havin' a party, mate?'

Arthur spun round and looked down to see a filthy legless man in what had once been a cream coat, selling a 'social' magazine. According to the cover, the girl on the front was in need of something.

'Are you talking to me?' Arthur asked, noticing the man was unshaven and had wedged himself into the corner of the tube station building where two stone walls met. The man had set up shop on a tartan rug, a stock of magazines protruding from a large black leather bag.

'I asked if you was havin' a party.'

'A party? Why would you ask me that?'

The man laughed, the mucus in his lungs bubbling like a pot of hot custard. He pointed at Arthur's legs.

'Cos' if you was, I reckon ya could invite yer trousers down!'

Again, the liquid laughter. Arthur looked down at himself.

'What on earth are—' He cut short his question as he saw at once what the magazine seller was on about. His trousers sat above his ankles by some margin. *I've grown, maybe as much as two inches! Jesus!*

Jesus has nothing to do with it, Mr Black said. *That's down to me and I'll thank you to remember it.*

Arthur walked quickly away from the legless man, the laughter echoing behind him. He found a shop-front window and studied himself in the reflection.

What else have you done for me, Black? Arthur saw immediately that his hair was just a little thicker than it had been even an hour ago. A wave of excitement flowed through him. He studied every inch of himself as best he could. Nothing else seemed different.

Better find a clothing shop, eh? Can't meet the scrumptious Paula looking like I'm wearing my little brother's clothes now, can I?

Arthur didn't have to look far. Across the road stood a bright new men's clothing store, almost as if it had been created for him. Three minutes later, he was immersed in racks of expensive trousers, jackets and shirts with the attentive Thomas hovering like a hummingbird around him. Arthur had flashed his credit card as he walked in and Thomas had dropped the seventy-something gentlemen he'd been serving like a tired old boyfriend.

Allie saw Michael twitch. Something had grabbed his attention.

They'd only travelled a hundred yards in the clogged traffic and were still in the St. James' park precinct. She glanced enquiringly at him.

'He's here,' Michael said calmly. Allie returned her gaze to the road; cars were moving again.

'I hadn't realized there was any doubt,' she said.

'No, no doubt. I mean he's active right now, on a mission.'

'Mission?'

'He's hunting again.'

'You can feel that?'

'Oh yes. I can feel him, Allie. I just can't *find* him.'

She turned the wheel right, the car gliding on to Victoria Street. Her stomach churned at the thought of another victim possibly hacked to pieces.

'That's my job, right? To find him.'

Michael took some dark wraparound sunglasses from his coat pocket and put them on.

'Right. That's the deal – has *always* been the deal.'

'Always?'

'Read the book your father gave you. I told you. It's all in there.' He stared straight ahead.

'Well,' Allie said, 'this is turning into a newsy little conversation.'

Michael smiled and peered at her over the top of his glasses like a college professor might.

'We aren't going to get too many more opportunities to run through this stuff, Allison.'

She chewed this over. No, of course they weren't. The last day had been complete chaos.

'Yes,' Michael said, interrupting her thoughts, 'chaos is the word. Things are looking black.'

She looked quizzically at him, inviting an explanation.

'That's what he normally calls himself – Mr Black or Chaos. Pick one. Remember, I mentioned this to you after your motorcycle accident. Presumably this time around it's no different.'

Again, she picked up the weariness in his tone. She accelerated as she found some clearer road behind Victoria Station at Belgravia, quite near Chester Square and her parents' home. She thought she might change the subject for a moment.

'There's a lovely church quite near . . .'

'Yes, I know,' Michael interrupted. 'St. Michael's.'

Allie felt herself redden. Of course, *St Michael's.* Incredibly, she'd not made the connection. The church actually backed on to her parents' house on the corner of the square.

She saw him look over at her, a slight smile on his lips. 'There are thousands of St. Michael's and related churches around the world. It's very . . . *nice*.'

It was her turn to smile. 'Nice? I'll say! Thousands of churches all built to honour you? *Very* nice indeed.'

'I've earned it.'

'Of course,' she blurted. 'I'm sorry, I didn't mean to suggest . . .'

'For heaven's sake, relax, Allie.' Michael laughed. 'I've been around a while, I don't offend that easily!'

They drove in companionable silence until she turned the car into Old Brompton Road. They weren't far from the scene of the previous evening's carnage. Her stomach tightened. She noticed he was jigging his right leg slightly.

'Are you,' she groped for the word, '*worried* about this?'

He answered without hesitation, 'Yes. And so should you. You need to be careful here.'

'Right. By the way, I've asked the contract photographer from last night to meet me here. I'm keen to get some more photos of certain aspects of the scene.'

Michael lifted an eyebrow.

She ploughed on. 'I felt the photos didn't quite show everything I expected.'

'Interesting,' was all he said.

The crime scene was clearly visible from some distance up Earl's Court Road. Two police vans blocked King's Lane and the blue and white SOC tape flapped wildly in the strengthening wind. Allie brought the black car to a halt two hundred yards away.

'This is as far as you go, Michael. I'm sorry.' She held up her hand to forestall his protest. 'How exactly could I explain your presence, do you imagine? A consultant? My brother? You see the problem.

The expected protest didn't come. 'I don't need to see it, Allie. You're the detective.'

She stared at him. 'That's it? No argument?'

'Nope. Well, that is unless you felt something at the scene last night, then that's a different matter.'

Allie turned the engine off. 'Like what?'

'You tell me,' he countered. 'Did you feel anything beyond utter revulsion?'

She narrowed her eyes at him. 'You *know* I did, don't you?'

Michael sighed. 'Not exactly . . . well, yes. Tell me.'

She told him about the dead girl screaming off the wall at her and of crashing to the ground as if she'd been pushed. He opened the car door. 'I'm coming with you. Make up any story you want.'

Allie was dismayed to see Sergeant George Houghton was still at the crime scene. 'George!' she yelled, waving to him as she approached. 'What in God's name are you still doing here?'

Houghton blew gently on the surface of a takeaway coffee. A volcanic amount of steam rose from it. He looked up and tried an exhausted smile.

'Hey, girly. You can't have had much sleep your little self!'

'Ha, not a lot, but at least I've been home for breakfast and a shower.'

George was studying Michael. 'George, this is Michael. He's . . . assisting me with some thoughts on the murder.'

Houghton stuck out a hand the size of a plate. Michael didn't take it. Houghton glanced at Allie before lowering his hand. Allie merely shrugged her shoulders.

'So, Michael,' said George, forcing himself to be polite after the handshake rebuff. 'You're a profiler are you?'

'I have some thoughts on what we're dealing with,' Michael replied.

'So do I, son,' George growled. 'A fucking . . . sorry, a sodding psychopath, that's what.'

Michael agreed and asked if he might just have a wander around. George lifted the tape, but barred his way with an outstretched arm.

'You know not to touch anything don't you . . . Michael?' It was phrased as a question, but it wasn't. George Houghton wasn't staying up all night to have this nancy boy profiler screw it up.

'I do,' Michael said pleasantly and walked directly down the lane.

George raised his eyebrows at Allie. 'Don't ask,' she said with a dismissive wave.

She looked south along the road and saw Banks and Strauss pushing through the front gate of a small cottage with no garden or trees in the front yard. She shook her head. George noticed.

'What's up?' he asked.

She pointed towards the two detectives. 'I'd have liked those two to doorknock separately, not go around like a couple of kids selling biscuits.'

He looked at them. 'Yes,' he said. 'They don't relish this foot-slogging stuff, do they?'

Allie guessed they had grizzled to him earlier. 'It seems not.' She looked again at him and asked him for a second time why he was still on duty.

He looked about furtively and just said that he sensed that things weren't quite *right* and he felt an obligation to hang around. Allie assured him that she understood and he could go now and be confident the scene would be locked after.

George made to walk off, but hesitated. 'How are you, Allie? After last night, I mean.' He smiled. 'You were flat on your arse at one point, I seem to recall.'

'I was!' She chuckled until the details came back. 'I felt a revulsion and sorrow I've never felt before.' She didn't quite know why she told him that, but it seemed the thing to do.

'You'd be a sociopath if it didn't bowl you over,' said George. 'By the way, any joy on an identification of the victim?'

She told him there wasn't and that no one had been reported missing either.

'Probably a druggy, poor little thing,' George said. Allie explained that no drugs of any consequence were present in her blood, what there was left of it.

'Well then, somebody's boyfriend or parents don't give a toss about her then, do they?'

They were interrupted by a male voice enquiring after an Inspector St. Clair. Allie turned to see a tubby, short man with unruly orange hair. He was about forty, buckling under the weight of two enormous black cameras strung about his neck and a large grey bag hoisted over his left shoulder.

'Mr Blight,' Allie said, holding out her hand. 'Thanks for coming.'

George took the opportunity to bid farewell to Allie. He nodded curtly at Blight – he remembered him from the early hours of the morning – they were never going to hit it off. Allie pointed at the larger of the two cameras. 'Is this the infrared one?'

Everett Blight reached for the camera and cradled it in his hands, a little too lovingly for Allie's liking. She didn't like where his thoughts might be going.

'Detective St. Clair, if ever—'

'Forget about it, Mr Blight. Many have tried, all have failed. Come with me.' She led him down the lane, fighting her own internal battle to remain calm. Blight, she noted, seemed not to have any trouble.

Allie studied the red-brick wall and saw the photos were true to reality, there was nothing written on it. She endured a moment of doubt, then asked him to take some infrared shots right along the length of it. She saw again the Victorian-era metal security spikes, noting how they had been bent over at right angles to allow the woman to be impaled.

'May I ask why?' Everett said in his most obsequious tone.

Allie was momentarily startled. She'd been lost in thought. 'Sorry?'

Blight presented his best smile, seemingly unaware of the effect his yellow teeth might have at close quarters.

'Just asking why you want infrared photos of the wall. I mean, it's just a wall.'

'Humour me, if you will, Mr Blight.' She gestured towards the wall, then handed him her card.

'I won't hold you up.'

Allie gazed around the scene as Blight fiddled with bits of equipment, then checked the light and a thousand other little things. In the moments she'd spoken with him, Allie had once again had the benefit of a magnified view. She saw the redness around his nostrils, the dark capillaries under his eyes, the broken veins on the bridge of his nose, and the scaly skin around his eyebrows. Mr Everett Blight, Allie decided, should eat more vegetables and ingest a little less cocaine.

'There's a bag over this fence.'

The voice was right in her ear. She spun round to realize Michael had done it to her again. He was waving to her from a distance down an adjacent connecting lane.

'I'll be back in a minute, Mr Blight,' she said and started down toward Michael. Everett Blight lowered his camera and watched her walk away. He licked his lips and made a purring sound. 'What a stunner,' he said, not quite to himself.

And way out of your league, Ginger, a voice in his ear advised. He smacked himself in the temple with his camera lens as he whirled to see who had spoken. There was no one there.

The bag was name brand and shiny blue with silver clasp and thin shoulder strap. Allie donned clingy plastic gloves and extracted the bag from under a pile of fast-food containers and soiled plastic bags. Someone had dumped refuse from a nearby food store on the bag, presumably without noticing it was there. She could only wonder how Michael had found it.

The important thing was that it was chock full of female belongings. No attempt had been made to scatter or pilfer the contents. She tensed as her hand closed around the little purse. She fumbled with the clasp. Michael stood quietly by, scanning the neighbourhood, every inch a guardian.

Allie finally snapped open the purse and took out a driver's license from among the credit cards, bubblegum wrappers, and soggy tissues. The name leapt out at her. Georgeta Konstanzo. *Georgie.* Tears stung Allie's eyes. Georgie – so it *was* her. Despite the fact that the dead girl had seemingly attacked her in the lane the night before, she knew it wasn't Georgie's doing. It was that *thing* out there, and it was reaching for her; she knew it now with absolute certainty.

She turned and looked at the sky, the rooftops around her and the trees now swaying in a stronger wind. She felt herself lifted above the level of the lane – floating on a sky hook; a vibrating, low humming in her ears. She saw across the city in a black and white tableau – the gothic Houses of Parliament; Nelson's column towering above The Strand; Temple Church sandwiched into the concrete and glass business district; and Ludgate Hill, the highest point in London, crowned by St Paul's' Cathedral, its dome contrasting brilliant white against a rapidly darkening sky. And she alone saw the abomination on it – the crouching black grinning thing perched on a balcony rail beneath the highest point. She could see and *smell* it. She spoke in a guttural voice not her own, 'Bring it on, Black. Bring it on.' Its misshapen head with its protruding mouth and bulging white eyes turned towards her. Michael grabbed her, shook her, and ran her up the lane. Her legs pumped on autopilot, her mind still in the sky, her hands still clutching the bright blue bag.

They approached Everett Blight who seemed not to notice their distress, babbling something about the photos he'd taken. Michael held his finger up as they brushed past.

'Just email the photos.'

Michael hustled Allie into the car and told her to drive. She didn't respond. He roared at her with a scurr that turned heads on the street. She snapped out of her reverie and gripped the wheel with clammy hands. She looked helplessly at Michael. 'Drive, now!' he yelled.

And drive she did. She pulled straight out into traffic without looking, miraculously missing a BMW estate by inches. She pointed the standard issue black Vauxhall saloon down Earl's Court Road and floored the accelerator.

Allie slowly regained control and focus as she drove. The thrumming noise in her head abated and her thoughts cleared. They approached a major intersection. She looked questioningly at Michael.

'Don't go anywhere near your home,' he said. 'Just drive.'

Just driving, she turned right and then right again, heading vaguely west, towards Hammersmith.

'Why am I doing this?' she finally asked.

'Because you saw each other.'

'So?'

He looked at her with a sad expression. '*So*, he has found you.'

Allie braked hard, pulling the car into a bus stop, scaring the life out of a grey-haired cyclist.

'Wait a second, I'm confused here. *He found me?* I thought we . . . *you* were looking for *him*!

'Let's get a coffee.'

'Coffee? You want coffee? Fine, let's do that. No drama at all. I'll just drive leisurely until I see a suitable, intimate place.' She swerved back into the traffic.

Michael pointed up the road. 'There's a good place up here on the left about a mile. Victor's, I think it's called. They have Ethiopian Yirgacheffe coffee beans.'

Allie shook her head in disbelief. She was losing her mind; she was now sure of it. God's big, tough general had his favourite little coffee shop. Victor's – how sweet. Never mind that she now knew the victim's identity and hadn't yet called it in. She hadn't even properly examined the contents of Georgeta's bag.

Ten minutes later, they were seated at a wonky little wooden table jammed into a corner next to a bookshelf stuffed with 1970s era books. *Fabulous*, Allie thought,

Victor's is in its own time warp. They both ordered double-shot flat whites.

'Right,' Allie said. 'Now we've got the all-important coffees on the way, may I ask what on earth, or maybe what the *hell* is going on? What are we doing here?'

Michael leaned back in his chair, surveyed the tatty little café, then looked back at Allie.

'We're here because it's crowded and you need a break and some answers. You're overwrought, over-stimulated, and overcome by what you're experiencing.'

'I'm over all this. You're right about that! Go on.'

'In a crowd like this,' Michael said, again looking across the room, 'he can't see you, at least not easily. I don't want him to get into your brain. My job is hard enough without him filling your head with paranoia.'

'He'll do that?'

'Of course, particularly now that you've spoken to him.'

Allie paused. 'I did?'

'You went into another zone there for a while. You actually threatened him.'

Allie shook her head. 'I remember seeing him, but not saying anything!'

'Trust me, you did.'

The waiter arrived with two coffees in fat round cups. They waited for him to leave, then each took a thoughtful sip. Allie figured that as long as they were here for five minutes, she'd push him for more information. 'This rollercoaster of the last thirty six hours has been rough. I'm seriously short on sleep and maybe even a little grumpy.'

'You think?' he chimed in.

Allie ignored the barb. 'Let me get this straight. This thing, Bellhop—'

'Belhor – *Mr Black*, if you like,' Michael advised.

'All right, yes, *Mr Black* is at large from,' she waved at the sky generally, 'wherever, and you need to capture him and the only way you can do that is if I find the murderer whom he inhabits. Correct?'

'Correct.'

She sat back in her chair. 'But I've seen Mr Black – he's sitting on top of St. Paul's. Can't you just go and get him?' Michael drained his coffee and signalled the waiter for another.

'Okay, first, let's not keep using his name – his radar is pinging like a battleship as we speak. Secondly, he was not just sitting there. What you saw was his effigy – what he symbolizes to you. That's been sitting there for three days waiting for you to get on the wavelength. It was bait, Allie.'

'And I mindlessly took it.'

'Well . . . yes, you did.'

'Shit.'

Michael smiled. 'Perhaps *mindlessly* is a bit harsh, don't beat yourself up about it. I confess, I did it once years ago – actually, it was a thousand years ago. Hopefully, we all learn from our mistakes. What's happening is that your senses, the ones you were born with but have never used, are awakening. He's just been waiting for you.'

They stared at each other for a long minute before Allie spoke.

'You said to me the night we met that you realized I didn't know who I was. That didn't make any sense at the time, but there are definite shadows across areas of my life, I see that now. There's something nagging at me, but I can't grasp it. Why is that? Do you know?'

He looked directly at her and a trickle of electricity bit her again.

'No, I don't. I'm sorry. I don't have all the answers, and the ones I do have, I can't yet give you.'

Allie pushed her serviette away in frustration. She looked at her watch.

'I have to call in the information about Georgeta now. I'll be seriously derelict in my duty if I don't.'

Detective Constable Jacinta Wilkinson took the call from DCI St. Clair at 12:53 p.m. She took down the details of Georgeta Konstanzo's address to run through the databank and confirmed to Allie that CCTV footage from the King's Lane area from the previous night was now available for viewing. Wilkinson advised there were three sets of footage, two from cameras owned and operated by a security company and one from a London City Council camera mounted on the far side of Earl's Court Road. Allie said she'd return to headquarters to view it and added that it hadn't yet been established that the blue bag belonging to Georgeta Konstanzo was in fact that of the victim. They might just have found a bag unconnected to the murder, so caution should be exercised when contacting or visiting her home address – a bedsit in Shepherd's Bush, West London. Wilkinson spun in her chair to find Strauss standing virtually on top of her. 'Oops, sorry, Sergeant,' she said. 'I thought you were still out in the field.'

'Did you? That was St. Clair on the phone, presumably?'

'Yes, she found a woman's bag, possibly belonging to the victim. I'm about to check whether we have any record of her.'

Strauss put her hand out. 'Give the name and address to me. I'll do that.'

Wilkinson hesitated a moment. 'I'm happy to do it.'

'It's no problem at all,' Strauss insisted. 'Just give it me. It'll only take five minutes.'

Reluctantly, Wilkinson surrendered the piece of paper. She turned back to her desk. She had flushed in anger and didn't want Strauss to see. She heard Strauss walk quickly to a computer terminal across the room and thought briefly about texting Allie about the intervention. Everybody knew they didn't get on and it was affecting them all one way or another, but maybe texting Allie was crossing a line of sorts. Besides, Strauss could be pretty scary at times.

Chapter Twelve

The Arthur Wendell that emerged from Spenser's Clothing on Tottenham Court Road looked appreciably younger and taller than the one who had trudged to his Earl's Court office to start his normal working week just four days ago. Any casual observer would see a fit individual, perhaps in his early forties, well dressed and with a spring in his step – a successful, attractive man with places to go and people to see.

Smokin' now, Artie! Lookin' good! Good enough to snare an editor wouldn't you say?

Arthur heard the voice, but he was troubled. Despite his outward appearance of confidence, he'd been reminded of who he really was in the mirror at Spenser's. The black head staring back at him, its unblinking dead eyes fixed above a lupine, crooked smile. He'd shrunk from it, but had been transfixed at the same time. It wasn't who he wanted to be, but it was so . . . *forceful.* It had a way of making him want what *it* wanted. But he wasn't a murderer. The thing, *Mr Black,* was. He didn't want to hurt the lovely Paula. She didn't deserve it. No one did. He'd stared at the pavement as he walked and now looked up to see a red double-decker bus pulling to the kerb towards him.

He decided to throw himself under it right then and there. With a rush, he felt this was the answer. He could end this and at least save Paula. The bus drew near, just ten yards away and still travelling fast. He launched himself towards its wheels. If he could just get under those huge tires . . .

But in reality, he didn't move. In fact, he never broke stride. The bus slid past and he barely acknowledged it. He walked on. He'd started to think about that girl, Georgeta, at the last second. *Why did she have to be such a slut? Why had she been so rude? And that filthy make-up! How could they employ a slag like that? Sarah's nice, not at all like greasy Georgeta. You never know with women. They might look all right, but underneath, where they really live, who knows what they do, what they think? Like Paula, with her strong legs and bouncy tits, what's she really doing with them at that magazine? She's the same as Georgeta, classed-up a bit, a more polished turd, nothing more than that. It's all bullshit. She'll reject me in the end like all the rest. But I'll get in first. She'll be beggin' for it . . . when she gets it.*

Arthur twitched as Mr Black's voice boomed again. '*Heheheheh . . . Nice to have you back, my man. I thought I'd lost you there for a second.*'

Photographer Everett Blight thought DCI St. Clair to be arrogant and dismissive. She'd rushed past him in King's Lane with her advisor or boyfriend or whatever he was, without a word. *She might look good*, he thought, *but she isn't my type – too damn smart by half.* Anyway, she should have stopped and looked at the photos. They were amazing. He'd really wanted to show her how clever he'd been in capturing the artwork on the brick wall at the end of the lane. And in daylight! She obviously knew a bit about photography, so she might have appreciated his talent.

Placing the big camera down on a wooden bench affixed to the restaurant wall, he reached for the more compact model he'd used last night and clicked on 'review'. As horrifying as the murder scene had been, the photos were damn good. He scrolled through a half-dozen to luxuriate in his talent. He'd be sure to get more contract work from the Met after they saw these. Perhaps they already had. He stopped randomly on a photo and magnified it to check the resolution. The girl's ravaged face stared back at him through huge, weeping eye sockets. He winced at the ragged mouth and lewd lipstick, then hurriedly moved the focus of the image to her legs. He could just make out something on her left ankle. He increased the magnification to maximum. He could now see it was a tiny tattoo. He hadn't noticed it last night – of course, he'd been slightly under the weather in every sense. The tattoo was of a dolphin, leaping from a tiny stylized wave. Coldness gripped him.

He knew that tattoo. Staggering backwards, he squeezed his eyes hard shut. How could he have not picked it out last night? The girl . . . he knew her, had photographed her just a week ago at the club. He'd even asked her out for God's sake! It was Georgie. Feisty, sexy Georgie. She'd loved the camera and, with a soft lens to disguise her poor skin, it loved her, every stark naked inch of her. Now she was dead – *slaughtered* – and he hadn't even realized it was her. *Holy fuck* . . . Mr Riley was going to be *so* pissed off.

The corner of Oxford Street and Tottenham Court Road was chaotic. The tube station was wrapped in plastic, like every second building in London, presumably some major repairs were underway. The impending Olympic Games had everybody sprucing up any building that might conceivably be filmed as part of the 'Postcards from the Olympics' television vignettes. They'd be flashed around the world to two-hundred-million, sports-hungry and, hopefully for London City Council, travel-hungry viewers.

Buses, cars, bikes and myopic pedestrians all vied for the same restricted strips of pavement. Arthur checked his watch and cursed. He was on time to meet Paula, but he'd dallied too long at the menswear store. He hadn't made it to Manny's Army Disposals for his supplies, nor had he booked anywhere for lunch as he'd promised Paula. He'd allowed himself to be caught up in an adrenaline-filled little space and now he'd have to wing it. At least Greek Street and Soho Square were only a stone's throw back behind the tube station and he had an enormous wad in his trousers. He laughed aloud. 'An enormous wad of *cash*, my friend, not . . .'

I get it, Arthur, Mr Black said wearily. *Pay attention, now, she's standing over there in front of the theatre.*

Paula had spotted the man on the opposite corner. On her second well-disguised appraisal, she'd confirmed it was Arthur. She marvelled at how good he looked! She thanked her new blue-tinted contact lenses for being able to see across the road at all. A week ago, he'd have been a camel-coloured blur. She looked away again, preferring that he see her and make the first move. She didn't want to seem too keen. She didn't have to wait long. Out of the corner of her eye, she could see him talking to someone. Was he on the phone? He was certainly laughing. At last, he looked over at her. It struck her, momentarily, as being odd. He'd zeroed in on her like a laser sight after having previously looked everywhere but at her. Excitement, nonetheless, tickled her. She was pleased to see him wave and trot to the crossing.

Arthur thought Paula looked fabulous. Slim and shimmering in a green skirt and white top; her hair, slightly blonder than he remembered, was swept coquettishly around her face. She was a stylish pixie waiting to grant his every wish. He thought she looked thirty, but he knew her to be forty three. His own pulse galloped. Goddamn, she was a fine specimen, but where the hell was he going to take her? The traffic lights changed and he joined a large crowd, many of whom were surging towards the Dominion Theatre, no doubt. Arthur looked up at the huge billboard and a s ow smile crept across his face. There was an afternoon showing of Ben Elton's Queen Show that everyone was raving about. *Hmmm, maybe later, that might be an option.* Plans were made to be modified, improved and then implemented with a minimum of fuss. He sang quietly to himself as he shuffled along with the crowd. 'Big disgrace, blood on your face . . .'

'Hi there, Arthur.' Paula rushed to him and kissed him on the cheek. It was an encouraging start. He greeted her with equal enthusiasm.

'Paula! You look . . . delicious.'

Allie St. Clair figured they could be back at New Scotland Yard by 1:30 p.m. if she took the right route. They were no further out of Westminster than West Brompton, so the King's Road would do the job. It would take half an hour at best. She was keen – in a professional way, as she imagined all of her team were – to see the CCTV footage from the Earl's Court scene. She rang Wilkinson and asked her to assemble everybody who was available in the media room at 1:45 and perhaps organize sandwiches from the canteen. She was uncommonly hungry now, as well as tired.

Wilkinson advised that Strauss and Banks were already back and she hadn't yet heard from Connors. Allie heard her hesitate.

'Is something bothering you, Jacinta?' The phone reception dropped out for a moment, but she caught '. . . the address off me so I couldn't follow up.'

'I'm sorry, repeat that, please,' Allie said loudly. Michael glanced at her.

The phone's reception dropped out completely. Allie stared at the phone as if to admonish it.

'Problem?' Michael asked.

'I don't know. Jacinta, one of my detectives, seems ruffled by something. We'll be there soon, in any case.

Which, of course, means,' she added, looking at him, 'you'd better hop out somewhere soon.'

Michael was relaxed. 'The bike is near Queen Anne's Gate. Anywhere near there is good.'

She still hadn't had an answer from him about her safety. She decided to let it go, although dropping him off would leave her vulnerable.

'I'll be around, you'll be all right,' he said calmly.

Allie pounded her hands on the steering wheel. 'Stop doing that! My thoughts are my own, surely!'

'Surely, they are, yes,' he said. 'At least, they certainly should be, I agree. And they will be . . . later.'

She threw him a confused look. 'Later? What does that mean exactly?'

'It means afterward or anon. Look it up.'

Exasperated as she was, she guffawed. 'All right smart ar . . . er . . . Michael. Will I see you later, at home?'

'I don't see why not,' he said. 'What will we eat?'

Allie was about to tell him they'd have whatever he cooked, but thought better of it. She glanced at him to see if he'd picked that up. There was no sign of it. 'Tell you what, there's a new fish and chip shop just opened up on Lower Richmond Road, near my flat. We'll get something from there.'

'I don't like fish and chips.' He said it like a five-year-old boy.

'Oh, for God's sake, why not?'

'They give me a terrible haddock.'

Allie nearly ran off the road. 'That is a *terrible* joke!' But she was laughing just the same.

She dropped him off where Birdcage Walk intersected with Queen Anne's Gate. She continued the short distance to the Yard. Her phone rang. It was Connors.

'Ma'am, have you heard from Strauss?' He sounded edgy.

'I believe she's here at headquarters, Mathew. I'm just arriving myself.'

'She's okay, then?'

Allie frowned. 'As far as I know; Jacinta said she was at her desk. Is there a problem?'

'No, no, I just haven't been able to contact her since we split up earlier, that's all.'

''What time was that?'

'About two hours ago. She said we should separate to do the door knocking.

'Quite right,' Allie interrupted.

'Yes,' he went on, 'of course, but she . . . look, it's nothing. Just so long as she's okay.'

Allie was reminded again how high-strung Connors could be. Still, he was right. They should have closer and more regular communications than this morning's effort. She was coming up in the lift and was about to hit her floor.

'Right, where are you now and what are your plans for the next few hours?'

She heard him hesitate. 'There's still plenty to do here . . .' She lost his voice for a moment due to loud jackhammering and traffic noise at his end. '. . . be an hour or so, just another street to doorknock, then back to headquarters.'

'No luck yet, obviously?'

'No, it's amazing to me, but no one has seen or heard any damn thing.'

Allie stepped through the lift door as it opened. She heard Mathew trying again to yell over some loud background noise. It sounded as though he said something like, 'See you later.' The line went dead.

Allie rang off, a slight concern lingering about Connor's work ethic.

Banks spoke from behind. 'Ma'am, the CCTV footage is ready to roll in the media room, if you're ready?'

'Great, thanks.' She looked around the room, noting that Strauss and Wilkinson were there, absorbed in their respective tasks.

'Grab those two, would you please, Pete,' Allie said, jerking her thumb towards the centre of the room. 'We should all view the footage.'

The windowless media room was compact but it nonetheless housed two staff and a huge control panel which featured the latest Avid video editing suite software. There were, after all, nearly two million cameras in the UK and no one really knew just how many in London itself, but it was arguably the most watched city in the world. But, strangely enough, there were disproportionately fewer cameras in the Chelsea, Kensington and Earl's Court areas.

Allie greeted the two staff and asked them to roll the footage. The balance of her team stood beside her, peering at the square Sony monitor. The footage was black and white and opened with a scene of the lane, shot from the camera she'd seen mounted on the corner of the Chinese restaurant.

'This is from camera one,' advised 'Smiley' Lang, who was the senior of the two media room staff.

'How many camera views do you have altogether?' Strauss asked.

'Just two, but this is the best one.'

Allie wondered what best meant. *Most graphic? Clearest?*

'Here we go,' Lang said, leaning forward in his high-backed chair.

They watched in rapt attention as the previously empty lane was subjected to the incredibly heavy rainfall from the previous night. 'Great,' someone said.

A man and woman appeared at the left of the picture. Allie knew from her visit to the scene that they must have entered via the connecting lane from Hesper Mews. The woman had already been dispossessed of the blue handbag. Despite the rain, the images were clear – they were close to the camera. The woman, *Georgie,* tottered into frame wearing very high-heeled shoes. She appeared to be naked from the waist down.

Wilkinson frowned. 'Is she . . .?

'No,' Strauss said quickly, 'I think, *I hope*, she's wearing tight skin-coloured knickers.'

'Oh, right.' Wilkinson still wore a horrified expression.

The man in the video was about average height and wearing a light-coloured jacket and a baseball cap. There was a logo on it that would bear further scrutiny. He was carrying a small black bag in his right hand while ushering the woman to the end of the lane forcefully with his left. He was a strong man; that much was obvious.

He looked at the camera. Smiley stopped the footage. They all stared at the man's face. Or, at least, at the place it should have been. There was nothing there. Puzzled looks were exchanged. 'What th'?' Banks said. 'Can you zoom in?'

Smiley zoomed in. For a few seconds, there was just the sound of breathing in the tiny room as they grappled with what they were seeing. Or *not* seeing. There was just a black smudge where a face should be.

'Well,' Banks said, 'it doesn't look like a mask.'

'Okay,' Allie said at last, 'keep going.'

The film moved forward. The man shifted his attention from the camera, then looked over his shoulder at something else out of shot. He walked the girl another three steps and checked the camera again. He turned to face the brightly lit restaurant.

'He's stage-managing this,' Allie said quietly.

'Okay, folks,' Lang announced. 'From here on in, Brett and I are out of here. I'll start the tape rolling again, but that's it – neither of us wants to watch this again.' He looked at St. Clair. She knew he was asking permission to leave, but at the same time, he was brooking no objection.

'Will it roll on to camera two?' Allie asked, tacitly giving him the okay to scoot.

'It will. Thanks, ma'am.' A relieved Brett pushed the green button to resume playback. The two operators hurried from the room. What followed was a horror show the likes of which no one in the room would ever forget. They were transfixed as the man dropped the bag on the cobbles of the lane, turned his attention back to the woman, reached into his jacket pocket, and pulled out a pair of pliers.

'Oh, no!' Jacinta Wilkinson moaned and turned away from the screen, her hand covering her eyes. St. Clair, Banks and Strauss watched intently as he pulled the woman roughly towards him and shoved the hand gripping the pliers deep into her mouth. What looked like white shards of teeth fell to the ground. Her head was bent back at a crazy angle as he suddenly jerked away from her, the pliers emerging with a long lump of wriggling, dripping flesh – like a calf's liver only narrower – pinned between the pincers.

Gouts of dark blood welled from the girl's mouth as she sank to the ground. He opened the bag and delicately placed the tongue and a tendril of attached stringy matter into it. From then on, it was a systematic, psychotic ritual. From the ripping of the girl's shiny top, the slicing of her knee and wrist tendons, to the gouging and *throwing* of the eyeballs, and the final blind, flailing attempts by the girl to have her life spared – it was a frenzied, visceral attack; a demonstration of inhuman ferocity and intent that simply stunned and sickened the detectives.

Footage from camera two rolled on relentlessly to show the whole panorama from a perspective just north of the first camera. But it added neither fresh clues nor any relief from sixteen minutes of hell.

The screen faded to black, then to vertical, colour-spectrum lines. No one moved, spoke or dared look anyone else in the eye. Self-control teetered on the edge of collapse.

Allie finally chanced a look across the room at Strauss – she could see her just on the other side of Banks. Thick tears ran down her face. Banks was visibly shaken as well. Immediately next to Allie, Wilkinson looked to be in shock and she put her arm around her. Still no one spoke.

Rachel Strauss's voice eventually smashed the silence. 'No one,' she said, her voice unnaturally constricted with emotion, 'should *ever* have to endure something like . . . *that*.' She spat out the final word of the sentence, her voice breaking.

It was an obvious thing to say, but it echoed what they were all thinking. The photos they'd viewed earlier had been bad enough, but witnessing the woman begging for her life, then the remorseless carnage that followed had left them all with a churning dread in their stomachs and hearts. There was nothing anyone could add to Strauss's sentiment.

'Take a break, everyone,' Allie said, shepherding Wilkinson out of the room. Allie deposited Wilkinson in her chair in the main office and called Margaret Daly aside. Daly looked at Wilkinson and knew immediately what Allie was about to ask.

'Leave it to me, ma'am. I'll see that she's okay.'

Allie thanked her and said she'd catch up with Jacinta a little later. Falling into her office chair, she rubbed her itching eyes and opened them to see a blurry Banks about to knock on her door.

'Ma'am, are you, you know . . .?

She smiled. 'Yes, Peter, I'm fine. Thank you.' She waved her hand towards the media room. 'At least as much as anyone can be after viewing that . . .'

Banks nodded and pulled a face. 'You look terrible, ma'am. Sorry, but you do.'

'Oh, I don't doubt it. Been burning the midnight oil a bit. Events haven't confined themselves to the day shift this week have they?'

Banks offered a thin smile. 'No, they haven't. Anything I can do?'

She sat back in her chair and blew out a long breath. She looked at Banks – all six feet three of him. His belly hung down below his belt line, his food-stained shirt in no way camouflaging hips that overflowed his trousers like overcooked dough.

'You can catch the murderer, book him, and shout us all a beer by 6:00 p.m., if you would,' Allie said.

He laughed, the first real laugh anyone had probably heard in the office for a few days. Heads turned. 'Hmmm, that's a tall order. Might have to make it 7:00 p.m., if that's okay?'

'Done.'

Allie glanced down at her computer screen and saw that an email had come in from the photographer, Everett Blight. She looked back at Banks, who seemed to be expecting more conversation.

'How are you doing with rounding up the customers from the Golden Bamboo? Just about finished?'

'I'm starting the interviews shortly. I have a complete list now. I'm going out with Strauss to Ms Konstanzo's address. Rachel is going to advise her parents, assuming they lived with her, and conduct an interview.'

Allie had to work hard to maintain her composure. That wasn't Strauss's job.

'When's she leaving?'

'Any minute, I think.'

'Send Rachel in, please,' she added. 'And Peter, just requisition a car and start the interviews with the customers yourself. Leave a copy of the list here as well. Thanks.'

Banks left the office, exhaling a long breath. Allie saw him beckon Strauss over and tell her something. She saw Strauss smile grimly, straighten her back and walk purposefully towards her.

'Grab a car, Rachel,' she said as Strauss reached her door. 'You and I are going to visit Georgie's place. How about I meet you in the garage in ten minutes?' She looked back at her keyboard and resumed typing. Strauss stood for a long moment before finally acknowledging the order and leaving the office. Allie printed off the address and shoved it in her bag. She advised Wilkinson where she and Strauss were headed and said they'd be back by 6:00 p.m., maybe a little later, and for Wilkinson to hold the rest of the team there for a briefing. This business with Strauss was going to get sorted one way or the other.

*

Being granted the best table at Michelin-star rated Il Forno restaurant near Oxford Circus had been far easier than Arthur had anticipated, although, being nearly mid-afternoon helped. Paula Armstrong hadn't realized he'd failed to make a reservation. Palming the maître d' a fifty-pound note had facilitated a seamless, satisfying transaction, one that Arthur had previously never contemplated. He'd entered a new realm and he immediately felt comfortable in it. Wine was ordered, entrées were chosen, and conversation flowed easily. The afternoon meandered along and Arthur marvelled at Paula's wit and erudition. He came to understand how she'd become one of the top women's magazine editors in Britain. There was a sharp mind there, he could see that. He really could *see* it. More importantly, though, for him, she was clean – no heavy make-up, no ladled-on antiperspirant, no bloodshot eyes. She had looked after herself for him. *And those legs, Lord above!*

Below, you mean.

Arthur jumped at the voice. Sometimes he forgot Mr Black listened to him. Paula looked up from her meal and smiled; a line of perfect teeth dazzling him.

'Are you okay?' Her voice was soft, intimate, caring. She was letting him know she was interested.

Laughing it off, he raised his glass of St. Henri and proposed a toast. Giggling, she touched her glass to his. He looked her in the eyes and smiled. Had Paula Armstrong been just a little more sober and a little less carried away by this newfound romance, something deep within her, some ancient survival mechanism – the thing that sensed danger in the night while you were asleep – might just have spotted the predator.

Allie strode towards the pool car parked in the underground garage. Strauss already had the motor running. Allie opened the passenger door, threw her bag on the floor, and started to buckle herself in. Strauss accelerated away before she'd finished.

Allie looked across at her and saw a determined face staring out over the wheel. She was hunched, tense.

'You know the Shepherd's Bush area, Rachel?' Allie asked.

'A little better than you might, I imagine, ma'am.'

There it is, Allie thought, *the little jibe*. People of wealth and privilege don't frequent the Bush. That was the message.

'Is it near Sloane Square?' Allie asked with wide-eyed innocence. Strauss didn't react, she just drove. Allie watched the build-up of traffic. It was now 3:15 p.m. – no way could they get back by 6:00, but there was no time to waste. It would be a long day. As if reading her thoughts, her mobile phone pinged. It was DCS Carr.

'Allie?'

'Yes, ma'am?'

'I just viewed the CCTV footage. This is . . .' there was a long pause '*monstrous!* I hope you'll be very careful.'

'Thank you, ma'am. I, *we* will. I'm travelling with DS Strauss to the victim's address. According to records, it's a bedsit in Shepherd's Bush. We've had no luck in finding parents or next-of-kin. There are no Kostanzos listed in the telephone directory.'

'I see. Strauss, eh?' Allie glanced at Rachel to see if she'd heard her name. It seemed not.

'Yes, ma'am. We hope to back by maybe 6:30 p.m., if you would like to attend the briefing?'

'I'll do that. Watch yourselves.'

Allie flipped her phone shut and told Strauss that Carr had said to take care. Strauss raised her eyebrows.

'That's rare.'

Allie nodded. 'It is. The footage got to her, I guess.'

'*You* handled it all right, I noticed,' Strauss said, although not in a complimentary way. The inference was clear – Allie was cold. She waited while they negotiated a roundabout near Hammersmith and straightened out on to the A40. Shepherd's Bush was a little way yet.

'Depends what you call handling it, doesn't it? I'm not paid to fall about sobbing, I have to think.'

Strauss acted surprised. 'Of course! Yes, you'd be paid *even more* as a DCI wouldn't you? I'd forgotten that!'

Allie opened her mouth to speak, but shut it again. There was no point rising to that bait. It seemed traps were being set everywhere for her. They travelled in silence for the balance of the journey, pulling up outside number 45 Erskine Road. It was just two hundred yards from Wormwood Scrubs prison.

'Great,' Strauss said. 'The clink on one side and the Queens Park Rangers football ground on the other. Welcome to Hell.'

'Welcome to Hell, indeed.'

Strauss jerked her head around to look at Allie. They stared at each other a moment longer before St. Clair opened her door and got out. She stood on the pavement, arching and stretching her back to iron out the kinks. She appraised number 45. It was the worst house in a street which spoke more of middle class than not. *Too close to the A40*, Allie thought, *but there you go*. It wasn't a bedsit at all, as records had suggested. This was a little grander than that; not quite a young lawyer's pad, but not bad. It would depend on what the inside looked like. They still had no idea what Georgie had done for a living. There had been no clue in her handbag.

Strauss knocked at the door. There were bars on the window and rubbish flowing over the dustbin. A faded blue curtain hung inside the glass-panelled door to exclude any view of the inside of the flat. A scratched, poorly maintained bicycle was jammed in between the fence and the corner of the house. Strauss raised her hand to knock again, but the door swung open.

A young man stood peering out into the light. Naked to the waist, he wore red and white striped pyjama bottoms. He lifted a hand to his long, dishevelled brown hair and squinted at his visitors. Seeing two women standing there, he straightened visibly, eyes widening further as he realized they were police.

'Hi. What can I do for you, Officers?'

He was well spoken. *Not from around here*, Allie assumed. She held up her warrant card for his inspection. 'DCI St. Clair and DS Strauss. May we come in?'

Conscious of his state of dress, the young man made a lame attempt to cover his chest as he stepped aside.

'And you are?' Strauss asked.

'Jeremy Watts.' His voice was thick; clearly he'd only just woken.

'Does Georgeta Konstanzo live here?' Allie asked without further preamble.

'Who? No, there's only . . . *Georgie,* you mean?' Realization hit. 'Georgie Stanton?'

'Yes,' said Allie, 'I imagine that's who we mean.'

'She's not home, I don't think. I haven't heard her,' he said, looking vaguely toward the stained ceiling.

'You live with her?'

'Yes. Well, no, not in the sense you mean! She lives in the upstairs room. My room is here,' he said, pointing to his left.

'When do you expect her home?' asked Strauss.

Jeremy, with the smooth chest, laughed. 'Who knows? Georgie works crazy hours.'

'And what's your story, Mr Watts?' Allie asked pleasantly. 'Are you a student or do you work? It is rather late in the day to still be in your . . . jammies, is it not?'

'I work at the TV studio at the end of the street,' he said, pointing to the big brown brick block to the east of them. Allie glanced back at the studios; they were well known. Some of Britain's most popular television shows were filmed there.

'Doing?'

'Post-production. That means—'

'I know what it means, Mr Watts, thank you.'

He blushed; even his chest reddened. 'Sorry, most people don't have a clue.'

'Indeed,' Allie replied. 'One of the great mysteries of television, second only to how some of the vacuous young tartlets ever get on there in the first place.'

Jeremy Watts' smile was uncertain. 'I guess.'

Allie turned her attention to the house and moved toward the stairs.

'DS Strauss will ask you some further questions while I look around upstairs. Do you want to put a T-shirt or something on?'

'No, I'm okay.'

'Put one on, Mr Watts,' Allie insisted. She glanced at Strauss, who clearly wasn't bothered at all by the young man's attire, or lack of it.

Georgie's room at the top of the stairs was, by any measure Allie could apply, a pigsty. It was small, multi-coloured, hideously decorated, and airless. It stank of alcohol and God knew what. Careful not to touch anything, Allie picked her way across rumpled clothes strewn about the floor, along with chocolate wrappers, empty flavoured-milk containers, photo magazines and, not unexpectedly at this stage, condoms of varying sizes, colours . . . and flavours.

'Jesus, girl,' Allie muttered, 'what were you thinking?'

She shook a thin plastic glove out of her pocket, blew it open and put it on her right hand. She pulled open a bedside drawer. More of the same debris was crammed in, plus some CDs, an iPod, beer coasters and assorted receipts. Allie would have someone go through all that tomorrow. Moving to the dark wooden wardrobe, she gingerly opened the door. It was stuffed with clothes of all types – thousands of pounds worth. She gently poked at some as she moved along the rack. Most of the clothes were gaudy, flashy and common – take your pick. She found herself thinking less and less of unfortunate Georgie. She flung aside some clothes to look into the wardrobe proper. She reeled back, tripping over clothes and falling hard to the floor. Georgie stood there, staring at her from the back of the wardrobe.

Allie's heart tried to leap out of her chest. She levered herself to her feet, backing away from the wardrobe.

'It's just a poster, *ma'am.*'

Allie flinched. Strauss had come up the stairs and was standing behind her.

Blood still pounding in her brain, she fought hard to control her breathing, even managing a strangled laugh of sorts. She looked hard at the wardrobe. A full-length poster of a near-naked posing Georgie was pinned to the back wall.

'Sure is. Tripped over all these damn clothes and shoes.'

Strauss remained impassive. 'So I see.'

Allie smoothed her clothes and stepped closer to the poster, examining it closely. Georgie had been attractive, no doubt about that; but for Allie, the image of the decimated face from King's Lane stubbornly imposed itself on the poster. She shook her head, noticing a logo in the bottom right corner of the poster as she did so. It featured an inverted camera and the stylized profile of a woman's breast. *InCamera Photographics* was printed below it. She made a note in her iPhone diary.

'Okay, let's get the boys in to have a look at the place.' She turned to face Strauss. 'Did you glean anything interesting from Blue Lagoon Boy?'

Strauss's mouth twitched into a half-smile at that. 'Yes, Georgie apparently works . . . *worked* at the Black Crow Hotel in Earl's Court.'

Allie's face screwed up in thought. 'The Black Crow, why does that ring a bell? Georgie was what, a barmaid?'

'Yes.'

Allie made a sweeping gesture toward the clothes in the wardrobe. 'She didn't buy all this on a barmaid's wages. She was into something else.'

Strauss agreed and suggested the crazy hours might be a clue to something grubbier. Allie thanked the still-bewildered Jeremy Watts and noticed he was a little less bewildered when Strauss said something to him as she passed.

On the way back to the Yard, Strauss reported that, to the best of young Jeremy's knowledge, Georgie had no parents or other family in London, nor was he aware of anyone hanging about her.

'But,' Strauss said, 'he doesn't know much at all about her. She keeps to herself, according to him.'

Allie considered this. 'He's about what, eighteen?' Strauss advised he was twenty.

'Okay, *twenty*, lives downstairs from a girl most men would consider red hot and he doesn't know *anything* about her? Is he gay?'

Strauss blushed. 'Definitely not.'

Allie smiled despite their history. 'Well, I bow to your superior knowledge.

It was Strauss's turn to gaze out the window.

The long lunch at Il Forno passed in a light-hearted haze. In Paula Armstrong's opinion, the pasta had been perfect, the veal cooked to melting point and the Tiramisu, 'To die for'. She hadn't had so much fun in years and it was obvious. Arthur had been charming, funny and, most importantly, he had that little element of danger about him that she found irresistible. She couldn't believe she'd overlooked him for two years and she told him so in terms she only used when she was liquored-up.

'You're hot, you know, Arthur,' she slurred slightly. 'Totally hot! How come I never noticed you before?' Arthur smiled like an indulgent father, or as you might imagine a spider would, once he had the fly in the web.

'I think the Devil's got into you, Paula. You're seeing with new eyes. I know I am.'

He beamed at her and she laughed again. She looked at her watch – it was 4:00 p.m.

'Well, I should put some sort of appearance in at work. The girls are working on a tight deadline for this week's edition.'

'I have an idea,' Arthur cut in quickly. 'Have you seen the show on at the Dominion? They have a five o'clock showing. We could catch that and it would put us back on the streets at, well, now let me see . . . time for dinner!'

Paula clapped her hands with delight. 'Now *that* is evil. And you reckon the Devil's got into *me*?'

Allie's phone bleeped. It was Michael. She shielded the phone from Strauss and read the message.

He's about to kill.

She typed back a message. *Where? Any clues at all?*

She waited a few minutes, but there was no reply. She knew Strauss had noticed her agitation, so she dialled headquarters and asked Jacinta Wilkinson whether anything was going on and whether Connors had returned. Wilkinson replied that all was quiet, she hadn't heard from Connors, but Banks had phoned in and was on his way to interview one of the customers from the Golden Bamboo.

'Have you rung Connors?' Allie asked.

'No, ma'am. Should I?'

Allie confirmed that indeed she should and that she'd like to be informed of his whereabouts as soon as possible.

'DS Strauss and I will be about half an hour, Jacinta. Who is Peter going to interview from last night, by the way?'

There was a small delay while Wilkinson consulted her list. 'A Mr Raymond Riley.'

Allie looked sharply at Strauss, then back at the road.

'What's his address?'

'I don't have it, ma'am, but I think Pete said he was going to Chelsea.'

Allie cupped her hand over the phone and told Strauss to pull over as soon as she could. 'Jacinta, listen carefully. Phone Peter right now and tell him that under *no* circumstances should he interview Mr Riley and that he should return to headquarters immediately. Got that?'

The concern in Wilkinson's voice was obvious, but she confirmed her understanding without further questions and rang off.

Rachel had brought the car to a standstill.

'Are we talking about *the* Ray Riley?' she asked. 'The Ray Riley who runs half the nasty stuff in London and is under investigation for just about everything?'

Allie nodded, also noting her phone must be very loud.

'*The* Ray Riley. Pretty sure he lives in Chelsea. God, the last thing I want is Peter walking into his den and asking questions. We'll have every law firm in London on our doorstep by dinner time.'

Strauss murmured her agreement. 'What are you going to do?'

'Good question. Maybe just think about that for a moment.'

Strauss pulled back into the line of traffic and Allie now stared intently out of the passenger-side window. The spring sun was high in the sky again, but clouds darkened the horizon. Michael's message resonated. *He's about to kill.* Allie had so many questions for Michael. *How could he know that a murder was about to be committed? Why can't he see where and to whom?*

It was 5:15 p.m., technically forty five minutes until the briefing. If Michael was right, and she had to believe he was, there was no time to slack off. Two murders would make things super-hot.

'Rache . . . I'd like us to swing by the pub where Georgeta worked, the Black Crow.'

'Bit late, isn't it?' she said, pointedly flexing the arm with her watch.

'It is, but I think it's important to chase down as much information as we can as fast as we can or this one.'

Strauss laughed harshly. 'Going to make a name for yourself right from the outset, eh, *ma'am*?'

Allie swung to face her, but time suddenly slowed. She looked at Strauss as she drove, but it was as if a shield of semi-transparent liquid floated between them. She could see Strauss gripping the black steering wheel as if she could squeeze the life out of it. Red colours radiated off her, only partly diffused by the silicone-like curtain. Strauss's white-hot anger thumped at the curtain like a living battering ram. And something else was there, but she couldn't quite grasp it. Strauss's thoughts suddenly boomed at her as if broadcast from an unseen stage. *Jeremy. Jeremy Watts.*

The curtain lifted for Allie as Strauss looked back at her. She calmed herself, pausing for a few moments before speaking.

'Rachel, apart from the obvious reasons related to this investigation, he's a kid. Don't go there.'

Strauss flinched. Allie knew that at least part of the target had been hit.

'*What?*' Strauss all but yelled. 'What are you talking about?'

'You were going to ring him tonight and see if he was interested in a drink. I'm just saying *don't*, that's all.'

Strauss jerked her gaze back to the road, fortunately, in time to take the turnoff that would take them into Chelsea.

'I don't know what on earth—'

Allie lazily waved her hand in the direction of the road. 'Spare me the bullshit, Rache, just drive.'

Arthur and the still-excited Paula Armstrong took their seats at the very back of the darkened theatre. Arthur had promised they'd go to a special bar he knew after the matinee performance and then to Gaucho – the Argentine restaurant in Piccadilly. Paula had squealed with delight. Gaucho was so hard to get into and she marvelled at the way Arthur could so easily arrange these things. They settled into their seats as the opening chords of the show rang out. Paula reached for his hand, deliberately brushing his inner thigh as she did so. Arthur smiled back and softly took her hand, although he was fearful the revulsion he felt for her now could be seen by others – but the nearest people were thirty feet in front of them. He looked at his watch in the gloomy light. In fifteen minutes, he'd excuse himself and leave the theatre for no more than twenty minutes, but that would be enough.

Arthur's enjoyment of the show was interrupted precisely fifteen minutes later by a voice he now knew well.

Time to go, Arthur. Let's do this.

He leant over to Paula and explained that he'd just remembered he had to ring a client at 5:30 p.m. and that he might be fifteen or so minutes, but she shouldn't

Fade to Black

worry. She squeezed his hand and said, 'Missing you already.'

Holy Whore-Mother, Arthur, the voice said. *You're sure done a job on her.*

Arthur Wendell exited the theatre and ran to catch the lights across Tottenham Court Road. Turning right, he hurried down to Soho Square and Greek Street.

Did you know Casanova used to live here, many years ago?

Arthur parted a reply to the effect that no, he didn't know that.

Knew him well, Mr Black said. *Malleable he was – very open to new ideas and Lord, what charm! He had young girls and bo—*

A white delivery van dipped to a halt just two feet from where Arthur stood in the middle of the road, its horn screaming at him.

Arthur! Take it easy, man. No need to run. Manny's is close. I know it, I've been here before. There's plenty of time.

Arthur glared at the driver and completed his crossing.

Manny's is just here on the right . . . See it?

He saw the military-style sign and felt himself relax with anticipation. Its warmth ran through him.

That's better – enjoy the moment. By the way, we might need some help on this one, Arthur. I've arranged for you to meet someone; he's standing outside Manny's now.

'Whoa,' Arthur said, coming to a sudden halt. 'This is *my* show!'

159

'Ha . . . I like that, Arthur – 'show' in every sense, eh? Absolutely, you're in charge, never doubt that. But this is a complex job which calls for strength and dexterity beyond the abilities even of someone as gifted as you. Trust me, I won't steer you wrong. Here he is now. Oh, great, I see he already has some supplies for you. Now be nice, you'll like him.

Arthur tentatively extended his hand toward the man. He was rewarded with a firm, no-nonsense handshake. They stared at each other and knew within moments they could work together. They felt they already knew each other, understood each other without the need for words. The team was now three.

Chapter Thirteen

Strauss brought the car to a halt in Berkeley Gardens – the little street running at right angles to Earl's Court Road on the corner of which stood the Black Crow. Allie hesitated as she walked around the corner to the main entrance of the hotel. The Black Crow, *black feathers*. There was something about the place she fundamentally did not like, despite it looking so much like the Feathers in St James' Park. It was somehow *wrong*.

Strauss pushed past Allie and breasted the front door, brushing past the menu stand and walking up to the highly polished oak bar. Allie lingered by the front door, noting that the licensee was one Ronald Blascombe. *Well, well*, she thought, *'Rabbit' Blascombe*. She mentally conjured his file. He'd been implicated in a number of minor scams over the past three or four years, but never convicted. Quite well thought of by the boys that drank here – she reminded herself to check with them – but he danced on the margins of the law just the same

She saw Strauss present her ID to a thin, young bar attendant, then read a noticeboard to her left filled with local notices, ads and the like.

'Hmmm . . .' Allie murmured as she walked up behind her. 'There's a lot of "remedial massage" places nearby, aren't there? This must be a very, *very* sporty neighbourhood.'

Strauss made a weird noise. Allie was reminded that she hadn't heard that snorty laugh for a long time. They wandered the bar area of the Black Crow, waiting for the licensee to appear. The pub was nicely appointed with a lot of warm English timbers, dining nooks, separate tables, and a substantial stone fireplace on the back wall. Allie picked up a menu from the bar and scanned the specials' board.

'Quite reasonable prices here, Rachel. Says here they do the best spotted dick in Britain.'

Strauss made a face. 'Nothing to do with the massage parlours in the area, I hope.'

Ronald Blascombe burst through the slatted wooden doors behind the bar. Scanning the room, his eyes locked on to Allie.

'Are you looking for me?' he said, a flicker of recognition in his eyes. Allie studied him for a moment. He was pleasant-faced, but had put on about a stone since she'd seen him last. She put out her hand as he approached.

'Yes, Mr Blascombe. DCI St. Clair.'

'Of course. DCI now, eh? Well done, you. I've not seen you since you were a PC up in Islington.'

'Good memory, sir, that would be right. How's your daughter, by the way?'

Rachel Strauss looked from one to the other.

'She's fine now, thank you, Inspector. In fact she works for me now – here.' He inclined his head towards the bar. Allie nodded and suggested they find a quiet spot for a chat. Allie introduced DS Strauss.

'Anything wrong, Inspector?' Blascombe asked, again ignoring Strauss. 'I mean, I'm not aware of anything . . . and I'm pretty busy. One of our staff has just decided to take the day off or something.'

Allie held up her hand. 'Would that be Georgie?'

Blascombe sat slowly in the chair opposite Allie. 'It would.' He looked at Allie, then to Strauss and back. 'What's happened?'

'She's dead, Mr Blascombe,' Strauss said bluntly. Allie shot her a filthy look.

Rabbit Blascombe lowered his head into his hands. He didn't speak for a minute. Allie put her finger up, warning Strauss not to say anything.

Eventually, he looked up. 'Drugs?'

'Actually, no, it wasn't,' Allie said softly. 'She was murdered last night. Not far from here.'

Blascombe rocked back in his seat. His eyes misted over. 'God in Heaven! Why? Do you know who did it?'

Allie's phone bleeped, but she couldn't very well look at it now. She dreaded what the message might say. Blascombe spoke again. 'The police, the tape near the tube station this morning – that was for Georgie?'

Allie nodded slowly. She looked at Strauss, who stared intently at Blascombe, *as she should*, Allie thought. He was a suspect at this point, no doubt about that, but Allie wasn't getting any strange vibe or noting any weird colours as she had come to expect. All she could sense was genuine compassion.

'Mr Blascombe, we know it's going to get busy here very shortly, but we do need to ask you some questions.'

'Yes, of course. Just let me tell Sarah and warn everyone I'll be out of action for a few minutes.' They watched him pass his hand over his forehead as he walked quickly towards the kitchen.

Strauss rounded on Allie. 'You're being very nice to him, aren't you?'

Once again, Strauss's lack of respect for a superior officer was on display. Allie walked her over to the far corner of the large room. Customers were dribbling in, filling some of the tables.

'First off, he's just lost an employee, and secondly, don't speak to me like that, particularly in public. You know better than that. Air your grievances when we're back in the car.' Strauss, to Allie's surprise, looked shocked, then apologized.

'Right,' Allie said. 'He is a suspect, *obviously*, as is everyone else here. I want you to start talking to Rabbit and get the names and details of his employees, when he last saw Georgie, all the usual stuff. I want to look around for a minute or so, then I'll take over for a bit. Let's get this initial chat over with and be out of here by 6:00 p.m., yes?'

Strauss agreed and sat at the table to await Blascombe's return. Allie wandered deeper into the pub, rounding the far corner of the bar. The pub was larger than it appeared from the outside. She entered another dining area, which backed on to a pleasant courtyard decorated with potted plants and brick paving.

Looking across the bar from her vantage point, she could see into the kitchen through a serving hatch. Rabbit Blascombe, in profile, was talking to a blonde girl who was covering her face, crying. She recognized her immediately as Sarah, the same girl she'd attended five years ago at the scene of the horrific car accident in North London. Her mother had been killed and Rabbit Blascombe, who had been driving, had suffered extensive injuries to his legs. Sarah, in her final year of school, completely freaked out like no one Allie had seen before. The sight of her mother's headless body had turned young Sarah into a jabbering mess. The drug-addled driver of a huge Toyota four-wheel drive had been trying to evade pursuing police officers when he'd hurtled through the intersection near The Angel in Islington, against the lights, and slammed into the Blascombe's Ford Mondeo. It had been no contest. The superior weight of the four-wheel drive had crushed the barely mid-sized Mondeo like a soft drink's can.

Allie stepped through the glass-panelled French doors that opened on to the courtyard. A smattering of self-important young executives were already enjoying drinks in the area, which was bathed in the last of the afternoon sunlight. She continued through the courtyard into a small adjoining car park. Rounding the corner of the brick building, she paused. Four very expensive cars were parked there: two Mercedes, both black; a large BMW saloon; and what she imagined was a Hummer – a ridiculously large military-style vehicle which barely fit in the car park.

A fifth car wheeled in at that moment. Allie stepped back behind a potted bamboo, her curiosity piqued. It was a huge silver Bentley with completely blacked-out windows. Immediately the car pulled to a halt. The driver got out and walked towards the rear of the vehicle. He was a hard man, if ever she'd seen one. Tall and broad-shouldered with a very short haircut and wraparound sunglasses, he exuded menace. He chewed gum and was looking everywhere but at the door handle towards which his hand now reached. Allie shrank back against the wall. The driver stood back to allow his passenger to exit.

Allie knew the face instantly – the sharp nose, mean set to the mouth, and the shaved head. She couldn't see the gold earring with the diamond inset, but she knew it was there. Nearly as tall as the driver, Ray Riley unfolded himself from the leather seats and waited for his fellow passenger to emerge. A slim, young man stumbled from the car. His sunglasses were pushed up into the tangle of his bleached blond hair revealing eyes which looked as though they'd been bought in a jumble sale. He was smashed out of his brain, belligerent and not happy about being asked to leave the comfort of the soft leather upholstery. The driver ushered them to a steep set of steel stairs that lead to rooms above the Black Crow. Allie watched the young man with interest. He looked vaguely familiar. He was dressed like a refugee from 1970s Portobello Road – tight blue jeans with ragged edges and a sleeveless hippy top fringed with sheepskin. Allie took her iPhone from her jacket pocket and snapped a quick pic, then retreated. It was 5:40 p.m., time to return to headquarters. She retraced her steps to the main dining room, where Strauss was in earnest conversation with Blascombe. They both turned at her arrival. Allie took an empty chair, saying nothing. Strauss resumed her questioning, looking at her watch as she did so.

'So, you say Georgie worked for you for about two years?'

'Yes,' Blascombe confirmed. 'I can check that, if you need exact dates.'

'Thank you, yes.' Strauss made a note on her pad before continuing. 'What sort of employee was she? Conscientious, punctual . . . what?'

Blascombe hesitated. 'Not the greatest, to be honest. She was a bit moody and seemed very tired a lot of the time. But, by and large, she did her job.'

Allie cleared her throat and moved a salt cellar on the table away from her.

'How did she get on with the customers – any trouble there?'

'Some of 'em loved her,' Blascombe said 'They thought she was sexy. She flirted with some, but could be rude at times, especially if she was tired.'

'Why do you think she was so tired?' Allie asked.

Blascombe put his palms up. 'Fuc . . . *buggered* if I know. But she did slump around on occasions.'

'Did you talk to her about it?' Strauss asked.

'I did, once – she bloody near bit me head off, as I recall. She said what she did in her private life was nothing to do with me.'

Allie frowned. 'Interesting. You weren't actually asking her what she did in her private life, were you?'

'No, just got sick of her moods. Other staff had complained that she was, well, bitchy. But that was only sometimes, mind. She was okay, generally.'

'Did Sarah complain?' Allie asked, moving her seat forward on the slate floor.

Blascombe sat up straight. 'Whoa now, I know where you're going with this!'

'We are not "going" anywhere, Mr Blascombe, other than back to the office in a moment,' Allie said evenly. She handed him her card.

'Contact me if anything else occurs to you – things like any customers who might have had a grudge against her, other staff with whom she might have been involved, that type of thing.'

Allie looked at Strauss. 'I'm sure Detective Sergeant Strauss has covered that territory with you already?'

'Yes,' Strauss said, 'I have.'

'We'll come back tomorrow and talk to your staff in any case, Mr Blascombe. Please ask them all to be here.' Strauss handed her a list of staff. Allie put out her hand and thanked him for his time. He shook it and smiled uncertainly.

'Nobody here is involved in this, Inspector. I am absolutely certain of it.'

'How about the boys upstairs?'

Strauss jerked her head around in surprise. Blascombe froze and said nothing.

'Mr Blascombe?' Allie persisted.

'Upstairs?' Blascombe finally stuttered. Allie sat back in her chair and pointed a finger skyward.

'Yes, *upstairs*, as in just about directly above us.' Blascombe looked furtively out towards the courtyard. Another car arrived.

'Look,' he said, 'not here, *not now*, all right?'

Allie abruptly rose from the table and told Strauss to wait in the car. Strauss made to protest, but backed away from Allie's glare. She turned and left the room. Allie nodded towards the bar.

'Go to the kitchen, now. I'll follow you in one minute.'

Blascombe hustled back out of the main bar and into the kitchen. She phoned DC Wilkinson and advised she and Strauss would be late and the briefing would be held closer to 7:00 p.m. She heard Wilkinson groan under her breath.

'I know,' Allie said, 'but, Jacinta . . . this is important.'

Blascombe was waiting for her by the chip fryer. He put chips in as soon as Allie entered the room. The bubbling hiss was sufficient to interfere with any interested ears.

'Give,' Allie said without preamble.

'Look,' he blurted, 'it's nothing to do with me. They rent the room by the month and hold meetings every now and then. We supply food and ask no questions.'

'Do you know who "they" are?' She saw a pained expression come over his face.

'Please don't ask me that.'

Allie considered this for a moment. 'All right, tell me this, have you seen a young man with long, fluffy blond hair, like a hippy, go upstairs?'

Blascombe frowned. 'No, I don't think so. It's usually just—'

'Just *who*?'

'I think you already know, Inspector.'

Allie smiled ruefully. 'I'm just giving you the chance to cooperate. Is it the same mob every time?'

'Usually.' Blascombe glanced out of the kitchen serving hatch. 'Christ,' he said, 'one of 'em's here now to order some food.' Allie peered through the server. It was Hard-Man Driver from the car park.

'So I see.'

Sarah burst into the kitchen. 'Dad! I'm not serving those horrible—'

She stopped short at seeing Allie. Her red-rimmed eyes widened.

'I remember you, you're—'

'Shhhh,' Blascombe said. 'Keep it down.'

'Sarah,' Allie said, 'was Georgie involved with those guys?' She inclined her head towards the upstairs room. Sarah looked at her father for reassurance. He nodded.

'Well, I don't really know. I saw her talk to one of them a few weeks back and he . . .'

'He what?'

She looked at her father again before answering.

'He patted her bum as she walked away.'

'How did she take that?'

'She looked annoyed, but I think it was a bit of an act really. But you never know with Georgie.'

Allie chose her words carefully. 'Do you think Georgie might have been a working girl, if you know what I mean?'

A moment's confusion passed over Sarah's face before she smiled in a slightly embarrassed way and brushed a loose strand of hair from her forehead.

'You know, it had crossed my mind, but I'm not sure. Maybe.'

'Christ almighty!' Rabbit Blascombe exploded. 'You might have mentioned this to me before now, Sarah!'

Arthur Wendell and his friend emerged from Manny's Army Disposals after just five minutes. Arthur had found exactly the right tool for the job.

What did I tell you, Arthur? Manny has the goods, doesn't he? It was Mr Black's voice.

'Manny's a horrible man,' Arthur said, 'a complete creep.'

And you're not? Mr Black asked in a light-hearted way.

'Not like him, no. I . . . *we* have purpose and a . . . mission. Manny is a greasy rat of a thing.'

You're absolutely right about that, Arthur.

The man walking beside Arthur smiled. 'You can hear this conversation?' Arthur asked, not masking his surprise.

'Sure can. It's very entertaining – a good prelude to events.'

They neared the Dominion Theatre. 'Okay,' Arthur said, 'you buy yourself a ticket. I'll wait just inside the big doors to the stalls.' The man turned without further ado and approached the box office.

Arthur watched as an argument ensued between the man and the box office attendant.

'What's he doing?' Arthur said to himself and, by default, to Mr Black.

He knows what he's up to, don't worry about that. Mr Black's voice chimed. *He's just establishing himself as the man who arrived late and couldn't possibly have had time to be involved in anything. He'll buy a ticket for the front stalls as well.*

'I didn't think of that.'

He's good, Arthur.

Clutching his plastic bag to his chest, Arthur moved into the darkened theatre, waiting behind the large wooden doors. He could just see Paula if he stood on tiptoes. He noted no one was sitting anywhere near her. *Excellent.*

His new friend appeared beside him. They waited a moment while his eyes adjusted to the lack of light.

'Is that her?' his friend asked, pointing to Paula. For a moment, Arthur didn't want to answer. Panic and guilt overwhelmed him. He felt his heart galloping and sweat beading on his forehead.

His friend nudged him. 'Well?'

Arthur looked at lovely, trusting Paula, patiently waiting for him to return and be the man she thought was going to turn her life around. Bile rose in his throat. *How can I even contemplate this?* He looked around frantically, something inside looking for salvation in any form.

Show time, my soldier, my main man. Show time.

Mr Black's voice was fatherly, encouraging, warm. Black understood he was nervous. Arthur had been like that when he'd tried to play football as a boy. Crossing the white line was the big problem; the rest took care of itself. He didn't want to let the voice – Mr Black – down, or his new friend. They had a bond, a *commitment*.

He smiled at the man beside him and, rustling the plastic bag slightly, pulled out the NATO-approved, stainless steel, thirty-inch commando saw with its 'unique eight-strand design guaranteed to saw through plastic, wood, rubber and bone'. It featured round steel handgrips at each end so you could loop the serrated wire around the target material and pull with both hands. Didn't everybody have one for cutting through that problem leg of lamb or stubborn piece of pork? He turned to his new friend.

'Got the powder ready?'

Friend held up the cake-mix-sized pack.

'Show time!' Arthur said, imagining he looked just like Betelgeuse.

Arthur approached Paula and smiled like a spider as he sat down beside her. She leaned in towards him.

'Everything okay?' she cooed. 'You were such a long time!'

Arthur glanced over her shoulder. New Friend had sat directly behind her, as planned.

*

Allie St. Clair was driven away from the Black Crow by a privately seething DS Strauss, who considered she'd been asked to go and sit in the car like an errant child while the grown-ups had a chat. Allie knew they were on the brink of a new dimension in the case beyond that which she already knew to be otherworldly – the realm of the hard men; a moral wasteland to be entered only as a last resort.

It was hard to ignore Strauss's anger.

'Are you interested in knowing who was upstairs, Detective Sergeant Strauss, or would you like another five minutes to complete the entire ten-step sulking program?' Allie asked with an innocent look. Strauss looked over at her. A small smile pulled at the corners of her mouth.

'Yes, Detective Inspector St. Clair, I would indeed be interested in knowing.'

'Excellent, DS Strauss. Let me tell you that his initials are R.R.'

Strauss needed no further hints. 'You are fucking joking! *Ray Riley* was there?'

'Just ten feet above your pouting head.'

Strauss shook her head in disbelief. 'But wasn't Banks going to see him at his home in Chelsea?'

'That's the thing,' Allie said. 'Banks would have completely wasted his time. I'll be interested to know what arrangements he thought he'd made to interview Riley.'

'Holy hell.' A nervous laugh escaped from Strauss. 'This is getting seriouser and seriouser.'

Allie smiled at the corruption of 'curiouser and curiouser'. Lewis Carroll would be apoplectic. But Rachel had nailed the personal parallel. Allie herself had been plunged into a different world, one with a new reality or dimension which only she could experience. *Allison's Adventures in Wonderland* indeed. Or was it *Through the Looking Glass*?

'So,' Rachel said, continuing her focus, 'we have Diamond Ray Riley at both the Golden Bamboo and the Black Crow.'

'Yes. Too much of a coincidence, is it not?'

'What are you thinking, then?' Strauss asked. At least Rachel was initiating conversation; that was a big step forward.

Allie fiddled with the hairpin which held her thick hair in check.

'I'm thinking we're in a world of pain here. If Riley *is* involved in Georgie's murder, I'll have to clear any contact with him with Carr. They might even try and take the case off us.'

'No!' Rachel thumped the steering wheel. 'We can nail this!'

Allie sighed. 'I said they might *try.*' Her phoned bleeped yet again. This time she checked it.

They've killed again

Allie slumped in her seat. Strauss noticed and asked what was wrong.

'I just have a horrible feeling the worst is yet to come, Rachel.' Had Strauss not been driving, she would have seen the glistening in Allie's eyes. Allie looked again at the message and pondered the use of the plural:

they've killed again. Presumably, Michael meant the murderer and his inner demon?

Connors had completed his task. It had been worse than he'd anticipated. His new life would take much more planning and he would have to be *so* careful. Checking his watch, he saw it was 6:30 p.m. He'd been out of contact with head office for five and a half hours! Sweat stuck his shirt to his back and his hands shook. The feeling of light-headedness would surely abate soon. He wondered if it would affect him like this every time. Driving was still a problem, but he had no choice. If he wasn't back at headquarters soon, serious questions would be asked. He tried to jog across the busy road, but his legs failed him. He slowed his pace. After all, it was just a couple of minutes back to where he'd parked his car.

Chapter Fourteen

6:45 p.m.

DC Jacinta Wilkinson saw Allie St. Clair and Rachel Strauss emerge from the elevator. She grabbed the messages that had come in for Allie and prepared to greet her. The fact that St. Clair and Strauss had arrived together was interesting. Normally, they wouldn't have been seen dead in each other's company. She saw Allie striding towards her and held out the phone messages.

'Ma'am, there are three messages from your mother.'

Allie stopped and spun around. 'Three? How did she sound?'

Wilkinson squirmed and Allie saw it. That could only mean one thing – Suzie Whiteman was drunk. Allie took the messages, thanked Wilkinson and asked that everyone assemble in the briefing room.

'Please ring Superintendent Carr and ask if I can have a word first.'

Allie continued on to her office. She couldn't yet ring her mother. She opened her emails, immediately spotting the one from photographer Everett Blight. It had a short message and four attached images. The message was self-serving drivel, so she opened the first attachment and printed it out. It showed what she hoped it would – great swirls of paint of some sort on the brick walls of the Earl's Court Lane. She made the image as large as she could and peered at it.

'You wanted to see me?' DCS Carr stood in her doorway.

'Yes, ma'am. Sorry, I was just on my way. You might like to come around and check this out.' Carr obliged and they talked about what the images might mean. Allie then briefed Carr about Ray Riley and his connection to the murder scene and the Black Crow Hotel. Carr was thoughtful about the new information. 'Perhaps someone's sending him a message. I don't see Diamond Ray as actually committing a murder like this. Not his style. Maybe he's upset someone. But what's the connection between him and this Georgeta? Surely he wasn't banging a common barmaid?'

Allie left that alone, stood and picked more copies off her printer. They exited Allie's office and walked into the briefing room together.

Allie saw Connors seated in the front row. She made a mental note to follow up on just where he'd been. Pecking away at the back of her brain was the feeling that, at any moment, another murder would be reported – if Michael was right. She turned her phone off before he responded to that thought.

I'm right, his voice boomed in her ear. *I just use the phone so I don't scare you. The gloves are off now.*

She flinched at his unexpected communication and saw Carr looking quizzically at her. She brushed some imaginary lint from her sleeve, cleared her throat, and addressed her team. She ran through the information they had and asked Banks and Connors to add anything they had turned up. Banks spoke up. 'Inspector, may I ask—'

'Hold that thought please, Peter,' Allie said, knowing full well he was about to query why he'd been called off Mr Raymond Riley of Chelsea. She turned on the overhead projector and threw Everett Blight's weird infrared photo of the crime scene on to the white screen. There was the initial intake of breath and Allie saw everyone lean forward to study the scribble on the wall behind the suspended body of Georgeta Konstanzo.

'I asked the crime scene photographer to take an infrared photo of the scene and the images you see have come to light, literally.'

Judging by their rapt attention, she had no doubt that, finally, her team was fully engaged with the case. *Hallelujah.*

'Does it say *Chase*?' Banks asked. 'Does this nut bag want to lead us in a merry dance, is that it?' Connors disagreed and suggested it was just nonsense. Wilkinson thought the lettering spelt *Chaps*, as did Strauss.

'We,' Allie said, gesturing toward Carr, 'think it says, *Chaos*.' Allie, of course, *knew* it said *Chaos*. If nothing else, it validated everything Michael had said.

'So what do you make of that?' Carr asked the team.

'Well,' Connors piped up, 'he's created chaos and he's naming it.'

'Not bad,' Allie said. 'He's created or is he *creating* . . . as in, there will be more?'

Connors shrugged. 'I think,' Allie said, 'there's a number 2 embedded here as well. She traced a sweeping line through the word 'Chaos'. 'See it?'

After a moment, all heads nodded. Yes, they agreed. There was a barely discernible number there. Strauss walked to the image, but addressed her question to Allie.

'What made you think there was more here than the first photos showed and, moreover, why did you choose to have an infrared photo taken?' It was the question Allie had been hoping to avoid. She wasn't surprised that Strauss had tumbled to it. Despite their differences, Allie still considered her to be, by far, the brightest member of the team.

Careful, Allie, Michael's voice cautioned.

She hesitated a moment, then launched into her explanation.

'In an overall sense, what we have here, in my view at least, is a biblical tableau – a parody of the crucifixion. I think we all see that – the arms akimbo, the posture of the body, the wound in the side, the bottle of red wine below the body depicting the current Holy Grail bloodline idea, and the removal of the eyes and tongue, denoting blind faith and the inability to bear false witness. I was expecting to see a reference to a psalm or similar, but there was nothing. I just felt there had to be more, it was half a message.'

'But why infrared?' Strauss again.

'Couldn't think of anything else, to be honest. What would the alternative have been? Lemon juice, as in the old invisible writing? The question for us is, how the devil has it been done? Because I certainly don't know.

I'll be asking forensics to go back and look at the wall, in any case.'

'Incredible,' said Banks. 'Absolutely incredible. Great thinking.' Everyone agreed, including Carr.

'The thing is,' Allie said, 'what does it tell us? That its murder number two and we've missed one? Or that perhaps two people are involved?' As she said this, she realized that of course that was it. Two people – duality. Man and temptation, working towards a common destructive goal. That's what it meant.

'Or God and the Devil – good and evil – the two sides of man,' she continued.

'Deep,' said Banks.

Allie laughed. 'It is. In any case, we have a religious zealot or very troubled soul, about whom we have no idea, no evidence, and no trace.'

Carr raised her eyebrows at Allie. She took it as the signal to feed the team the latest info.

'Except,' she said with just a hint of theatrical flourish, 'for this afternoon's events.'

Bright eyes shone up at her. This was more like it. She invited Rachel to summarize what they'd learned from the visit to Georgeta's house in Shepherd's Bush and the quick drop in at the Black Crow. Rachel left until last the revelation that the notorious Diamond Ray Riley might be involved.

'You see, Peter, I just couldn't let you tackle Ray Riley at that point in the investigation.'

'Just as well you stopped me.' He laughed. 'I had no idea who he was!'

Allie studied Banks for a moment. 'You might just tell me how you were going to see him, anyway. Presumably you hadn't rung for an appointment?'

'I certainly did. His "secretary" said he was in and would be happy to see me.'

'That's interesting,' Allie said, looking at the others. 'He was at the Black Crow at 5:30 p.m. That's a little distance from his home, but I suppose *not that far,* as the crow flies.' Banks groaned at the lame pun.

Allie dug her mobile phone out of her bag and clicked it back on. 'Does anybody know who this is?' She flicked up the photo of the young man from the Crow car park. She handed it to Connors first. He had no idea, nor did Banks, who passed the phone to Wilkinson.

'You're kidding, right?' she said with huge smile. 'C'mon, you're having us on, yeah?'

'Er . . . no, not all,' Allie said. 'You know him?'

'Like, yes! He's only the biggest thing in pop music at the moment! Jase Britt!'

No one had heard of him. Wilkinson was incredulous.

'C'mon! The *Britain's Got Talent* winner, Jase Britt! He's gorgeous!'

Allie laughed. 'I'll take your word for it. He didn't look too gorgeous a couple of hours ago, I can tell you. The boy's got a substance problem.'

'No, no way!' Wilkinson said. 'He's a devout Christian – "wholesome as", as they say.'

Allie saw a bright pink light all around Wilkinson. It was so fierce she wondered if anyone else could see it. Wilkinson was a child at heart – a sweet, warm person who, it now seemed, was heavily into Christianity. She probably had no long-term place in the police force. Allie knew she could never cope with what lay before them. Allie and Carr exchanged looks. Allie suspected Carr had come to the same conclusion. Jase Britt's appearance now made sense. Riley was chasing music industry money.

'Okay, everyone,' Allie announced, 'it's been a long day and tomorrow is looking very challenging. Mathew, I'll talk to you in the morning about how it went today, say 8:00 a.m.?' Connors confirmed the arrangement with a curt nod and left the room. Allie and Superintendent Carr lingered while everyone filed out. Carr turned to her. 'So basically, you're thinking Ray Riley is mixed up in this somewhere along the line.' It wasn't a question.

Allie zipped up her satchel. 'It's all we've got and it makes sense. Quite how it fits together is a question for tomorrow, of course. Are you comfortable with me interviewing Mr Riley or would you also like to be involved?'

'An informal interview you mean?'

'Absolutely. As casual as I can make it, I don't want lawyers involved!'

Carr patted her on the shoulder. 'That's the way to do it. It's all yours. I've got his mobile phone number if you want it.'

Allie's eyebrows shot up. 'Well, that's handy!'

Carr walked with her to the door. 'Mr Riley has had numerous conversations with us over the years. In the end, he gave it to us voluntarily, told us it would save us all a lot of time.'

'What a thoughtful sweetheart he is,' Allie said without smiling.

'I'll text it to you. I'm off to meet . . . someone for dinner.'

'Nice. Thank you, ma'am. I'll see you in the morning.' Carr waved over her shoulder and made for her office. It was late and Allie was undeniably hungry. She thought of Michael and he answered, his voice reverberating in her head so loudly it was hard to believe no one else could hear. *Were you listening to that? she thought.*

Only the last part, when she mentioned this Riley character. He's a bad man, then?

He's the worst – prostitution, porn, extortion, car theft – his mob is in to everything.

You still want fish and chips?

You don't like them, as you so plainly pointed out earlier.

I was just kidding. I'll get 'em. I'm starving. See you in what, an hour?

About that, she replied silently to him as she walked out on to Broadway, the cold wind slapping against her face. *I'm taking the Tube, so I might be a bit earlier.*

Fine, keep the channel open.

Hoisting her heavy, black handbag over her shoulder, Allie walked the short distance to the St. James' Park tube station, hesitating momentarily as she walked past a cosy coffee and pastry place in the shopping section. She'd not seen it before. Approaching the turnstiles, she glanced at a group of youths huddled together by the wall. They were reading a girlie magazine. The shortest one lifted the magazine to turn the page. Allie paused, a man running into the back of her before brusquely pushing past. She stared at the magazine a moment before walking over to them.

'Hi, guys. Want to sell that magazine by any chance?'

They all stepped forward.

'Why?' asked the short guy with the faded beanie. 'Are you in it?' They all laughed and ogled her.

'No, but I know someone who is. Say, ten quid?'

'Ten? Sure, it's your money, sister.' Allie handed over a tenner and Short Guy held out the magazine, but hung on to it as she grasped it.

'Are we going to play games now?' she asked.

'The thought crossed my mind,' he leered. She stepped a little closer.

'Then uncross it.'

Short Guy blinked and let go of the magazine. 'Hey, that's freaky! How did you do that?'

She didn't stop to ask what the hell he was talking about. She walked away quickly through the turnstiles before stepping on to the escalator to the District Line which led to Putney Bridge. Looking back, she saw Short Guy pointing at his eyes and staggering about exaggeratedly. She just made the train to Putney, even securing a seat, which was rare at this time of night. Normally, the kids with the backwards caps claimed them all. She unfolded the magazine and looked at the front cover. No doubt about it, it was Georgie. Spread-eagled Georgie also adorned pages twenty and twenty one. *Stupid girl, look what's happened to you*. The pages of the magazine suddenly turned over, as if a breeze whistled through the carriage. Allie clamped her hand on the newly turned page. She glanced up at the people sitting opposite her.

The executive with the brown briefcase on his lap smiled crookedly at her. She returned her attention to the page. There were advertisements for all kinds of adult services – massage, bondage and associated leather accessories, vacuum cleaners, which brought a puzzled frown to her forehead, and a plethora of customized toys. In the bottom right corner was an ad for InCamera Photographics and a phone number. Allie recalled the name from the poster in Georgie's wardrobe. She swiped her phone and rang the mobile number listed. After the fourth ring, as she was about to hang up, it was answered with a bored, 'Hello.'

'Is this InCamera Photographics?' Allie realized she'd affected a less educated tone than she normally used. She glanced again at the man sitting opposite her as the train pulled in to the first stop – Victoria Station.

'Yes, yes it is. Looking for work, darlin'?' The voice was rough with a smoker's wheeze underpinning it.

She'd learnt earlier that her phone was loud and noticed the entire row opposite her was now deeply interested in her conversation, especially two skinheads near the end of the carriage.

'Could be,' she said. 'Where's your studio?'

'It can be wherever you like, my dear.' He was a creep and there was something else; his voice sounded familiar.

'Who is this?' she asked suddenly.

The voice went cold. 'Does it matter?'

'It does to me.'

'You give me your number and I'll ring you back, okay?' Allie knew her number was blocked from him.

'I'd prefer to know who's . . . capturing me.' Allie blushed under the gaze of her fellow passengers. She thought about holding up her police ID to remove all the smirking.

'No, I think we'll leave it there,' he said and rang off.

That voice, she knew it. The older man across from her leaned forward and pointed at the magazine.

'You might like to close it, dear,' he said softly. 'I doubt the lady next to me really wants to look at *Gobber* magazine.'

Exiting Putney Bridge tube station, Allie dodged across the pedestrian crossing outside the entrance and paused to take a free *Evening Standard*, expressly because her photo was plastered all over the front page. She walked slowly towards the pedestrian underpass, which featured stylized motifs of rowers. Putney, after all, was where the Oxford and Cambridge Boat Race started and was the source of so many jibes from workmates about how they supposed she'd be catching up with all her Cambridge mates for Pimm's on the embankment.

She stopped midway in the tunnel and glared at the headline: DOLLYBIRD DCI ON THE HUNT! She groaned out loud. She felt for her phone, more than half-expecting Superintendent Carr to already be on the line. She looked at her watch and realized she'd missed the television news. Who knew what they were running? Almost under her breath, she groaned again. '*God!*'

'He won't help you, sweetie.'

She looked up to see a man standing at the end of the short tunnel. He was silhouetted in the half-light, but she recognized him. He was one of the multiple-pierced skinheads from the train. She turned and saw what she expected, the other one walking up behind her. She looked past him and saw that she was alone. Her delay back at the station while she picked up the copy of the *Standard* had been her undoing.

'Why should I need help?' She continued to walk towards him.

He held up a nasty knife, big enough for her to see its length even in the poor light. 'Because of this little baby.'

Her training kicked in. She wasn't going to show fear to this lowlife.

'I'll bet it's the longest thing you've got by a mile.' She slowed as she drew near him. He was stocky, stinky and angry. She was getting used to seeing the colours around people and his red glow was very bright at the crotch. This was about rape. '*Gobber* magazine got you all hot and bothered has it, shorty?' she asked, holding it up. 'You have to take sex from the unwilling – the *repulsed* in this case, do you? Nobody offers it I guess . . . huh?'

'Fuck you.'

'I don't think so. Not today.'

She heard the heavy footsteps of the guy behind her quicken. Stocky Man made his run now too. She pivoted to the side of the tunnel, her back against the tiles, her arms up at the ready. But their attack never came. They were both backing away, looking at the far end of the tunnel. She turned her head and saw the enormous man who filled the tunnel entrance.

He hadn't spoken and she hadn't heard his approach, but her attackers had. He walked slowly towards them, totally ignoring her, his footfalls resonating in the tiled tunnel. It was Michael; she saw that now. But he'd changed. An ice-blue light radiated from him, but she knew he was angry. Her attackers stood transfixed as he walked right up to them. He calmly moved to a position directly in front of them; his arms, which were hanging loosely by his sides, were only a few inches from them. He spoke now; a rolling thunder of a voice, magnified even more by the hard surfaces of the tunnel. His words came from a language she didn't know, but they unmistakably formed a question. Her would-be attackers seemed to melt into the concrete pavement on which they stood. He asked the question again and she discerned a greater insistence in it. As frightened as the skinheads were, they didn't speak. Suddenly, Michael's arms flashed forward. He now had both of them by the genitals. Neither of them had time to move or even flinch. Allie stood there, barely daring to breathe.

The knife clanged to the floor. Michael repeated the question. Allie jumped a little as they answered in unison . . . *in the same obscure language.* It was a short answer and he was obviously not happy with it. He spoke again, different words this time. She saw them wince in pain and buckle slightly at the knees.

She saw that Michael did not stoop as they sank to the ground. His arms, in the fading light, seemed to grow longer. She looked again at him; he was huge, bigger than he'd been this morning. She didn't feel completely safe herself. They started babbling again, in that strange tongue. Their talking abruptly stopped. There was a slight pause, a low grunt, then a wet, popping sound. They screamed, long and loud. It turned into a piercing shriek that seemed to go on forever. She covered her ears and closed her eyes for a moment. The noise cut off like a power plug had been pulled. She heard a sighing, followed by a liquid splashing on the pavement. She risked a look. Michael just stood there looking at her. In his arms hung two limp bat-like creatures, still clad in jeans and cut-off jackets. Thin, leathery arms hung from their clothes. Identical, narrow stoat-like faces with embedded steel rings stared sightlessly at her; a thick, translucent drool hung from each mouth.

Without speaking, Michael trudged towards the end of the tunnel, a bat-thing grasped in each hand. Allie followed him from a distance. She saw him enter Bishop's Park garden at the end of the tunnel. He walked in a heavy, measured way across the manicured grass, through the lovingly tended rose beds to the public walkway, which bordered the low stone wall which held back the Thames. He looked up at the road, at the point at which it crossed the Putney Bridge, then back up river towards Craven Cottage –Fulham FC's football stadium. He flung the two shrivelled bodies far out into the river's strengthening ebb tide. She came up beside him, staring out on to the river.

'A mistake, do you think?' he said in the voice she'd come to think of as his normal one, '. . . to throw them in the river?'

Allie hunched her shoulders. 'I don't know. Assuming those things float, I guess they'll wash up and be found by somebody. I can see the photos in the papers now. But maybe it has to be that way.'

He turned to her and smiled. 'Only you see them for what they are.'

Allie's eyes widened. 'Michael, that means I've just watched you needlessly murder two men whose bodies will be discovered sometime tomorrow! I'm supposed to be okay with this? My God,' she said, putting her hand to her mouth. 'I'm an accessory to murder!'

'Calm down,' Michael said as he strode towards the steps that led up to the roadway. 'They're not *human*, Allie! They don't have ID or mothers or a school record or even a failed driving test. They *appear* human, granted, but that won't last. They are transients in every sense. They'll be sludge in an hour. C'mon, let's eat.'

Allie calmed herself by gazing out on to the turgid river, the brown water gathering momentum as the tide raced eastward to greet the grey North Sea.

'How did you know about my failed driving test?'

'Word got about.'

'Is that so? Well, speaking of word getting about, have you realized that their master now knows where we both are?'

'I have considered it, yes,' he said, quickening his pace, causing her to trot to stay abreast. 'These things are just mischief makers. They've been here all along.'

Allie wondered how long 'all along' actually was.

'They are . . .' Michael continued with disdain, 'mere irritants, rats in the greater scheme.'

Allie felt relief and confusion at the same time. 'So these nameless things just wander around creating a nuisance like assault, rape and so on?'

'They do. And what's more, there are more of them all the time.'

'Why is that?' she asked, a trail of white breath swirling from her in the now still, cold night air.

'They breed like squirrels.'

'Rabbits, you mean?'

'Yes. Rabbits.'

Her phone rang, sounding like an air-raid siren in the quiet night. She remembered she hadn't returned her mother's calls and groaned as she saw it was her phoning . . . again. *There's nothing like a reality check*, she thought. What followed was a ten-minute conversation in which Allie contributed virtually nothing. Her mother was coherent, but emotional and was really just ringing to see if Allie was all right. She'd seen her on the television news and was 'worried' about her. She was nearing her home when her mother asked a strange question.

'He's there, isn't he?'

'Who?'

'*Him.* You know who I mean.' Goosebumps ran up Allie's spine as she looked at Michael walking beside her.

'Spell it out, Mum, please. I'm not quite following you.'

'That . . . *Michael*. You know him now, don't you?'

Allie floundered for an answer, surprised that her mother even knew about Michael, but finally just said, 'Yes.'

Her mother was silent for a moment. 'So it's begun, has it?'

Allie heard the resignation in her voice and sought to reassure her. 'Mum, don't worry.'

'He gave you that damn book didn't he? Your father – he gave it to you the other night, didn't he?'

Allie shook her head in irritation. 'Are you okay, Mum? I mean, you're very wound up!'

There was another pause. 'Allie, I'm worried. No, I'm terrified. We didn't know you were the one. If we'd known, Robert would—'

'Robert? What's he got to do with this? Is he all right?' She glanced again at Michael who seemed not to be listening.

Her mother laughed. 'All right? Robert? You know he's not *all right*, Allison! Let me tell you what he's been doing today – sitting in his wheelchair in front of that bloody computer writing his music 'blog' . . . the same thing he does for twelve hours *every* goddamn day!'

Allie and Michael had reached her front door and she was rummaging in her bag for the keys. 'No, Mum, I meant, nothing's happened to him, has it?' She was concerned, but tiring of this angst.

'Not since that time, no. He's the same.'

'Look, Mum, I've got to go. Can I phone you or see you tomorrow night perhaps? Will Dad be around then?'

'Oh yes, he'll be here I expect. He's been waiting to hear from you for days I gather.'

Allie let that go. 'Say, seven o'clock then? I'll come straight around from the office if I can.'

Suzie Whiteman simply said, 'Dinner will be ready,' and hung up.

They walked into the tiny kitchen and Allie reached for the Jack Daniel's. Michael ducked his head to avoid the doorframe. She was sure he hadn't had to do that before.

She looked questioningly at him. 'Drink?'

'Never.'

'Not allowed?'

'Clouds my perception.'

'Mine too, hopefully.'

'Don't have more than one, Allie.'

'Why?' she asked, putting the ice cube tray back in the freezer.

'Your phone's going to ring and you know why.'

'My mother again?' she asked flippantly.

'No.' He was looking serious.

'It's going to be even rougher tonight, isn't it?'

'Sorry, but yes, it is.' Allie thought he looked very tired and said so. He shrugged as they walked into the living room, sitting opposite each other.

'There are problems elsewhere – big problems.' He rubbed his face with both hands.

She waved her drink at him. 'Elsewhere *being?*'

'Everywhere, really. It's all a bit much.'

A bit much? For him? Isn't he invincible and indestructible?

'I wish,' he said, reading her thoughts. He smiled for the first time that evening. She gulped more of the JD and coke.

'Thank you, by the way,' she said, raising her glass to him. 'I might have been in trouble back there under the bridge, for a moment.'

'*Might* have?' he snorted. 'I'd be fishing pieces of you out of the river by now.'

'I can handle myself,' she said, lifting her chin a little higher.

'Yeah? How long since you went to karate class? Hmmm?'

'A while, but I have a black belt.'

'Against those little turds, a black gun would be handier.'

She took a clinking sip of her whiskey. 'Okay then, what exactly are they, apart from some kind of weird rats, that is?'

He thought for a moment. 'Let's just call them Black Santa's little helpers.'

'Helpers as in . . .?'

'Not well-intentioned individuals, shall we say. Their aims run counter to those society would consider to be in line with accepted norms.'

'Evil little insurrectionists, perhaps?'

'Your education has not been wasted.'

She studied him for a moment – his tired eyes with a smudge of blue-grey under them, the weary tilt of his shoulders.

'Do you ever sleep, Michael?'

'Only when I'm here, otherwise it's irrelevant.'

'Here, meaning on Earth?' It sounded bizarre to her even as she said it.

'In a sense, yes. But in a way, I never leave either. My life, my *realm* if you like, centres on this place, but not always as you might perceive it.'

Allie sat the glass, which now only contained half-melted ice cubes, on the long coffee table. 'You mean like another dimension? I loved *Twilight Zone,* you know.'

'Exactly like that. You know I can't say much, Allie.'

'Ah yes,' she nodded. 'The *rules*, right?'

This elicited a thin smile from him. 'The ever-present rules, yes.'

'They frustrate you a bit, don't they?'

He stood and stretched, his flat palms resting on the pressed-tin ceiling. 'You know it!'

'I'm having another drink,' she said, swirling the cubes in the glass. 'Don't care what you say.'

She sprang off the couch and walked down the narrow hall. But that's as far as she got. Her feet wouldn't move her into the kitchen.

She slumped against the doorframe. 'Are you doing that?'

'Nope. You are. That funny little thing you have is taking over.'

'What funny little thing?'

'Your conscience.'

'Cute.'

'No. Very true. I'm really hungry by the way.'

She came back to the living room and waved her hands expansively toward the ceiling.

'It surprises me that you eat, given that you move between *realms*.'

'It takes a lot of calories to do that you know.'

She laughed. 'Well, I guess it does. Do you eat in *other places*?'

'Like restaurants you mean? Sure.'

Allie clamped her hands on her hips. '*Other realms*, you know what I meant!'

Michael put his hands to his lips, the cosmic sign for shut up.

Allie froze. They stood there looking at each other but his concentration was clearly elsewhere. After a minute, he relaxed.

'That was close,' he said, settling back into his chair. He caught her questioning look. 'He was looking for us.'

'Us? Not just me?' Allie asked. He reached over and pulled a roller blind shut, then two more.

'Us. He's trying to avoid me and engage with you. Anyway, food. C'mon now, are we going to eat?'

Chapter Fifteen

Checking the theatre between sessions was a pain, but Robbie Davies did it anyway. Show business was in his veins, and if starting work as a ticket collector/usher gave him an opportunity to brush with real actors and maybe even get a part in a production, then that was just fine. Only last week he'd made a cup of tea for Ben Elton. Ben Elton! The man was a comic genius full of nervous energy and chatter. He'd nearly asked for his autograph, but shyness had overcome him – again.

He worked his way back from the front of the theatre, putting sticky chocolate wrappers and wet plastic cups into the canvas sack he dragged behind him. He looked towards the back of the theatre and cursed. Two people were still sitting at the back. It was hard to see – the light was always dim up there. Nearly every session, somebody tried to stay on to see the next show or worse, engage in clandestine sex before they went back to their workplace and pretended not to know each other.

The two just seemed to be sitting there looking at the stage as if they expected a personal encore from the cast. *Nutters*. Striding toward them, he clicked on the big black torch he always carried on his belt clip. It wasn't that dark, but hang it, it reinforced his authority; it put the plebs off a bit as well. He walked to within twenty feet of the couple. There was no acknowledgement from them.

'I'm sorry, folks, but you'll—' He stopped in mid-step and mid-sentence. He slowly sank to the floor. A sickly, sweet smell wafted his way. His throat closed up as he tried to yell for help. But, as if in a nightmare, all he could do was squeak. He bashed the torch against the floor repeatedly, not looking anywhere near the couple seated three rows from him. Finally, his voice came back. He made a sound like a wounded animal at first, but he kept trying. Tears rained down his face. Finally, he heard a scream erupt, then another, and another.

The JD and coke relaxed Allie enough for her to let her thoughts drift. She ran a bath while Michael went to get fish and chips. She smiled, then shuddered at two disparate thoughts. The Lord Protector of the Universe was buying her fish and chips, even though he admitted he didn't like eating fish. If her life hadn't recently turned into a carnival of the occult, she could have convinced herself that there was some normalcy here and they were just two friends messing about. On the other hand, he was a *being* from God knew where and had just crushed the life out of two evil vampire-bat things right in front of her. Maybe this was all a complete delusion and she was actually strapped down in a padded cell for the insane in a brick building far away.

Even though the new chippie was only a few hundred yards from her house, she knew it would take him a while. The last time she'd walked past The Plaice on a Thursday night, there'd been a line stretching out of the door and down the road. He'd be forty five minutes at least. Turning off the bath taps, she remembered the book her father had asked her to read and about which her mother had been so upset earlier. She did a crouching, nudie run into the living room and grabbed it off the corner of the dining table. She locked the bathroom door, frothed up the pink bubble-bath liquid in the almost-too-hot water and sank gingerly into it. Heaven. She reached for the small book and noticed a white feather sandwiched between two pages. Was Michael telling her to read that page in particular? She suspected he was.

Forty minutes later, the bliss of the soothing, hot bath had been obliterated by the revelations contained in the book. She pulled on her dressing gown to the rattle of the key in the front door, the fiddling with the lock in the second door, then heavy footsteps on the stairs. She was seated at the dining table as Michael thumped on to the landing.

'They are making a fortune in that joint!' he exclaimed. 'There must have been thirty people . . .'

She looked at him through red-rimmed eyes. He sat the food on the table and pulled up a chair across from her.

'The world just changed for you, didn't it?' he asked softly.

She nodded and pushed the book at him. 'Tell me this isn't true.'

He picked it up and thumbed a couple of pages. 'It's true, Allie. I won't say sorry, because that's just the way it is.'

'Bloody hell,' was all she could say. 'My life thus far has just been a prelude to *this*?'

He threw open the big parcel of food. 'Have some chips.'

'Screw the chips, Michael!' she yelled, slapping her hand on the table.

'Have some chips,' he said again, in exactly the same tone.

'What on earth is wrong with you?' she shouted.

'Shut up, Allie!' he seethed. '*He* will see you if you carry on like this. Deal with it! You have no choice, so let's eat and we'll talk later.'

She almost had to pinch herself to make sure this wasn't a dream. They were eating fish and chips and the world was caving in – unbelievable.

'It won't cave in,' he said in answer to her thoughts, shoving a huge piece of cod into his mouth. 'Not if we get it right.'

'I see. Oh, right then. Pass some chips would you?' she said, with a sweet smile.

She took a limp, greasy handful and threw it at him. He didn't react, just poked another chip into his mouth.

'Try throwing the cod,' he said. 'It's heavier and will stain my coat.'

She pushed back in her chair, huffing and puffing.

'You mean to say,' she said deliberately, 'that everything in that crappy little book is right? That *The Promise of Maewyn Succat* actually chronicles the story of St. Patrick, whose real name was Maewyn Succat? And that I'm directly descended from him and my name, St. Clair, is a corruption of Succat?

'Cool, huh?'

She stood, then just as quickly, sat again. 'And what's more, you *knew* him?'

'Yes. He was a brave and clever man – more than a man really – which you are discovering.'

'How old *are you,* Michael?'

'In human years or dog years?'

Again, despite the serious nature of the conversation, he was flippant. She couldn't help but smile slightly. 'Aardvark years, if you prefer. C'mon, how old?'

'About ten thousand years, as you would understand it. Not as "old as time" and all that garbage. We were asked to look after you lot after you had developed to a certain stage. Actually, maybe it's fifteen thousand years – I can't quite remember. It's an age thing.'

'Amazing. What moisturizer do you use?'

Michael roared with laughter. It was a sight to behold. Allie smiled broadly. Two could play this warped space-time game.

She waited a moment for him to compose himself. 'Dad wrote "Vinculum infinitas" in the preface to the book. Infinitas I get, but Vinculum?'

'That's the crux of it,' he said, throwing the fish and chip wrapper into the small bin by the table. 'Vinculum infinitas is why I am here and part of the reason you have no choice but to participate.'

'Well, what does—'

'Hold on,' he said, pushing his chair back and standing. He brushed himself down and looked steadily at the mirror before sitting again on the brown leather dining chair.

'It represents the commitment Maewyn made to me in 461 and that your family, that is, his descendants, have continued to uphold since that time. We needed someone we could trust implicitly here and your family has provided that resource without break for more than sixteen hundred years. You're not the only St. Clair family, but you are the one with whom we deal exclusively.'

'We?'

'It's not just me – the problems are bigger than that and I can't be everywhere, although I give it a shot.'

'You can be in more than one place at a time?'

'Not physically, but mentally, definitely. I have no choice, either.'

It was Allie's turn to stand, if only to break the tension. She hugged her dressing gown to her and moved to the centre of the small room. 'Let's go back a step,' she said, her hand up like a traffic policeman, which she had once been, on and off, for about six weeks. 'Why does a bargain you made with just one man bind his family for so long? Sainthood is merely a religious artifice – eventual saint or not, he was just a man, surely.'

Michael sighed. 'He was more than that, as I said a minute ago.' There was slight irritation in his voice. 'Much more – Maewyn was the progeny of beings who were more like me than not.'

'Beings?' Allie asked. 'You mean non-human? Not like those dog-bats, I hope!'

'No, non-human and yet not, is more like it. There are variations. You've heard all the nonsense about fallen angels fornicating with humans millions of years ago, etc.?'

'I have. I assumed it was all apocryphal.'

'It is. The stories going around are that in prehistoric times. Angels, also known as the Giants, succumbed to the temptations of human flesh and were cast out of heaven, blah, blah.'

'Not true then?' Allie asked, now completely intrigued and wondering still how she fit in to all this.

'Not true. Humans were basically apes back then. Think about it – who'd be interested?'

She did think about it – red monkey's bums and gums – and it didn't make a lot of sense.

'So all of that is a lie, then?'

'Well,' he hesitated, 'mostly, yes.'

'Whoa,' Allie interrupted. 'That's a big proviso there – *mostly . . .*?'

Her mobile phone rang. 'Not now!' she yelled in mock anger. She checked the screen; it was Phoebe. She gave Michael the one-minute sign and answered it. The phone went dead.

'Not now, Allie,' Michael said with a wan smile. 'Sorry.'

'Phoebes will think I just hung up on her. Thanks a lot.'

'You can ring her back soon. We have priorities.'

Allie sat on the leather couch. 'Okay, Michael, fair enough. Please continue.'

'Much, much later, there was an opening for my kind to interact with humans. There were reasons at the time that I can't go into now, but certain things had to evolve – medicine, technology, that type of thing. Humans were encouraged and led to pursue particular avenues of thought.

'Religion being one of them?'

'Definitely not. Religion was nothing to do with us and got up and running all by itself – human nature, you might say.

'To believe in something greater than ourselves, you mean?'

'Exactly. It's why churches are tall, cathedrals massive – it's all about making humans feel small and humble in the presence of a church-based higher power. It's marketing, basically.'

'Marketing. Well, that's good to know,' Allie said wearily. 'Very comforting to now find out that, for at least half of my life, I've believed in complete bullshit.'

Michael laughed. 'Not quite. The spiritual side of things is a little different. It's where we do intersect. Churches are mostly about power and money – nothing to do with me or my crew.'

'The obvious question, Michael, among many, I guess, is what about Jesus?'

Allie held her breath waiting for the answer. Deep within her, she wanted Jesus to be real. She was shaking.

'You're worried I'm going to say he didn't exist, aren't you? That it's all make-believe generated from an early form of Judean church?'

She nodded.

'Relax, he was real all right. He wasn't called Jesus and he lived in a slightly different place than is chronicled – there are reasons for that – but he was real. Even your major religions acknowledge that.'

'Was he one of your kind?' Allie ventured.

'No. He was the Son of God; everyone knows that.'

Ray Riley stalked about the faux wood-lined room, muffled sounds from the Black Crow's bar below filtering up through the floorboards. He pushed past his driver standing guard at the door and kicked over a curved coat stand.

'She was killed right outside a restaurant I was dining in? Fuck! How long do you think it will be before the Blue Meanies come knocking on my door?'

He threw a pen across the table and sat back down. 'And worse, I have to find out about it from that stinky photographer. Not one of you bothered to let me know.' He scanned the six other men at the table. 'You've got shit for brains, the lot of you! Why do I pay for information if I don't get it?'

Terry Burdon squirmed in his seat. He'd been with Ray Riley for twenty years and he was still scared of him. He'd seen him stick a fork in a waiter's eye because he was told the restaurant had run out of Pâté de

Foie Gras, plus he'd heard Capone had done that. He was like that, Ray, living the mobster dream. It was a nightmare for those around him, but he paid stupendous money. Burdon had been a delivery van driver before hooking up with Ray in the early days; now he was making two hundred thousand pounds a year, more if wet jobs were scheduled.

'We didn't know it was her, Ray,' he said carefully keeping his voice even. 'Don't even know if the coppers know it yet, either.'

'They do,' said Shoulders Blanchard, Ray's third-in-line. 'I got the call as we arrived here. They've even been out at her flat. That new bird, the posh one, went out there.'

'Really?' asked Riley. 'The new DCI at the Yard? What's her name? Sutcliffe?'

'St. Clair,' said a voice from down the end of the table. 'Allison St. Clair, the daughter of that professor who knows about Celtic history.'

'Well now, is that right?' Ray Riley looked at the man who'd spoken and a puzzled look crossed his face. 'Had a bit of work done lately, have you, mate? Had the old eyes done, maybe a hairpiece? What's going on, a mid-life crisis?'

'Nope, nothing like that. Clean living.' He smiled back at Riley.

'Well, I'm impressed. More of you should follow that example,' he said, looking around at the assembled team. 'Might make you all a bit smarter as well, who knows?' He laughed loudly at his own joke. 'Anyway, it's getting late and I'm hungry. It's time to get this month's financial report out of the way. He gestured toward the clean-living man. You right to go, Arthur?

Allie jumped at the fierce banging on her door. She must have drifted off on the couch for a moment. Michael was sitting on the opposite couch reading a magazine; *Gobber* magazine, in fact. Allie sprinted down the stairs to see what was going on. She threw open her door to the street.

'We can't raise you on your phone,' Rachel said bluntly.

'Christ,' Allie said, inwardly cursing Michael. 'I'm sorry. Ummm, come up . . .'

Rachel walked straight in and mounted the stairs two at a time. Allie followed as quickly as she could, given the constraints of her mangy dressing gown. She heard Rachel say, 'Oooh . . . hello!'

'Ah, Rache,' she said as she rounded the corner to the living room. 'This is—'

But Rachel was alone, flipping through *Gobber* magazine, a playful look on her face. 'Changing teams, are we?'

Allie relaxed. Michael was nowhere in sight, miraculously. She ignored Rachel's suggestion.

'What do you notice about it?' she asked.

Rachel closed the thin publication, looked at the cover, opened to the centrefold, then back to the cover. 'Hold on. That's *her*, isn't it? Georgie?'

'Yes. In fact, it says so if you look at the bottom right of the centrefold. "Georgie S". It calls her, *"Top bush from the Bush"*. Apparently, it's quite an honour.'

Rachel looked askance at her. 'How on earth did yo_ drop on to this?'

'Some scabby teenagers were reading it at the tube station. I walked right into her.'

Rachel looked thoughtful. 'Amazing.'

'What's up anyway, Rachel? Why the visit?' Allie was amused to see her close the magazine with a quick flourish.

'Another body's turned up. It's at the Dominion Theatre in Oxford Street this time. It's pretty bad and looks like it might be linked to Georgie's murder.'

Allie swept into her bedroom, throwing off her dressing gown. She collided with Michael, who was standing in her little work-in-progress en suite. She yelped and scrambled for the gown again. Rachel called up from the living room, asking if she was okay. 'Fine, no problem,' she yelled back, thinking that two days ago, Rachel couldn't have cared less about her welfare.

She glared at Michael who, holding his hands over his eyes and grinning, manoeuvred himself out of the tiny room and sat on the bed facing away from her, towards the window. Nothing was said by either of them.

Allie threw on slacks and a jacket and brushed her hair.

'I'll be back around ten o'clock, hopefully. Will you be here?' she asked Michael.

'I'll shadow you to the scene.'

'Why?'

'Allie, it must have occurred to you that, to find you, all the killer has to do is wait at the murder scene – you'll come to him.'

'In truth, that occurred to me at Earl's Court over coffee, Michael, but I have to do my job.'

He stood and looked directly at her. 'Fortunately or unfortunately, I think he – *it* wants more than you, so I'm hoping you'll be okay, but I'll be around just in case.'

Time was up. 'Gotta run, we'll talk later. You know the Dominion Theatre?'

He smiled and confirmed that he did. Allie found it an interesting smile and wondered for a brief moment what lay behind it.

Sarah Blascombe didn't want to take the plate of hot food up to the men meeting in the upstairs room. They were creeps. She knew that the man with the diamond ear stud was a bad, bad man. Her father had warned her to stay well clear of him. Still, they brought in good money to the Black Crow and she knew how precarious the finances were. She negotiated the steep, steel-framed external stairs and knocked on the door using her right foot. The freaky driver guy opened the door and, after staring at her chest for too long, he let her in. The men around the table all stopped their conversation while she bent over the table to place the heavy, steaming tray in the middle, between the bottles of wine. She hated this manoeuver; she knew where their eyes were.

She straightened up and noticed the man standing by the big whiteboard. There was what she took to be

financial information, numbers and columns scribbled
on the board and he had a black Texta pen in his hand.
She knew him, didn't she? He half-smiled at her and
looked away. She hurriedly left the room amid catcalls
and whistles from the men around the table. She
shouldered her way past the oaf at the door and slammed
it behind her.

'Please continue, Arthur,' Ray Riley instructed.
Arthur Wendell nodded and turned back to the
whiteboard on which he'd detailed the last three years'
trading figures of Riley's 'interests'.

'How much fucking longer do I have to listen to this
shit?' blurted Jase Britt, whose patience and attention
span had parted ways. He addressed his remarks to Ray
Riley. 'Is this dickhead going to bore us all fucking
night?' Britt flapped his hand at Arthur. Riley's men
stirred. Nobody spoke to Diamond Ray Riley like that.
But Riley was unfazed.

'Okay, okay, Jase, we'll do it now. Arthur, give it a
rest, buddy. We'll come back to it later.'

Britt looked at Arthur as he resumed his seat and
made a wanking motion with his hand. It was a big
mistake. Arthur's right hand shot across the table and
clamped itself around Britt's neck. He lifted him right
out of his seat and, swivelling round, pinned Britt hard
against the wood-panelled wall.

'Fucking hell!' yelled Riley. 'Somebody get Arthur
off him!'

Terry Burdon and big Joe Turner jumped up, trying
unsuccessfully to pry Arthur's hands off Britt. The slim,

young man added more colour to the scene by turning purple.

Easy, Arthur, not the time to tip your hand now, Mr Black said soothingly. *Show some leadership now, okay?*

Britt crashed to the floor as Arthur let him go.

'Jesus, Arthur,' Riley said. 'Where did *that* come from? Are you on the 'roids or something?'

Arthur straightened his tie and smoothed down his jacket. 'Something like that.'

Terry Burdon helped the coughing and gagging Jase Britt to his feet. Britt glared at Riley. 'You can forget our—'

Riley cut him off and cocked his finger at him. 'Don't be stupid, Jase, that's not an option, boy. Anyway,' Riley said, 'now is as good a time as any to announce my new venture.' Riley looked at his board members.

'You all know that I've got interests in media, publishing and pharmaceuticals.' He said this with a wink. 'As of last night, I – *we* are also in the entertainment business . . . not to be confused with our adult entertainment division, of course. I've formed a new company called Firestone Music and the first act we will be handling is . . .' He did a drum roll on the table and affected a ringmaster's tone. '. . . *the Christian answer to Justin Timberlake, Mr Jaaaase Britt!*'

Nobody spoke. Now they knew why the pesky kid was there. Terry Burdon looked around the room and sensed the danger. He jumped to his feet and applauded. 'Fantastic!' He clapped harder. The other men got the hint. One by one, they stood and applauded, even though absolutely none of them had ever heard of Britt. That wasn't the point. The master had spoken and acted. It was time to like the idea regardless of their private trepidations.

Riley beamed at them. Britt managed a lopsided smile himself. Arthur Wendell stood and applauded as well and Riley acknowledged his change of heart. Riley made a settling motion with his hands and they all sat again. Joe Turner put his hand up, like a schoolboy waiting to ask teacher a question.

'Joe?'

'You did say "Christian", didn't you? I mean, my hearin' ain't the best, but . . .'

Riley laughed. 'You heard right, Joe, despite those cauliflower ears.' This got a chuckle around the table 'Jase here is a genuine heartthrob and his market is the fifty six million, I'll repeat that, *fifty six fucking million* people who buy Christian music each year. And he'll be number one amongst them in a few months, especially after his competition win. He's signed exclusively with Firestone Music in return for a healthy fee and a supply of certain premium-grade essentials.' More smiles around the table.

Riley clapped his hands. 'And I've got a treat for all of you.' He reached into his jacket pocket and pulled out a thick envelope. 'Tickets to see Jase perform at the nation's biggest music event, Glastonbury Festival!' Lukewarm applause rippled around.

'Great,' Terry Burdon managed. 'When is it?'

'This weekend! Tomorrow, actually! How about that? I can count on all of you to be there.' Nobody heard an option in there. Arthur looked at Riley and then Britt, where his eyes remained. 'I'll be there,' he said coldly, 'you can count on that.' Riley smiled broadly. Britt wasn't so thrilled.

The Dominion Theatre was surrounded by police vans, blue and white tape, arc lights, ambulances and onlookers. Inconvenienced drivers honked horns and gave the finger to police. Allie and Rachel showed ID to the Scenes of Crime officer who told them they'd already established that the victim was a Ms Paula Armstrong, then led them into the now brightly lit theatre. A white-faced young PC took them over, showed them to the stalls, and pointed along row Y. They saw two people sitting side by side, roughly in the middle of the row. Allie and Rachel glanced at each other; nothing appeared out of the ordinary. Rachel led the way as they crabbed along the row to within fifteen feet of the couple when Rachel stopped and backed hard into Allie, bumping her forehead.

'Oh shit, Allie, look at this . . . *Christ!*'

Allie peeped around her as Rachel wasn't going any closer for anybody's money.

Sitting in seats Y23 and 24, respectively, were two halves of the same person. At first glance, the person in Y23 looked perfectly normal – a smartly dressed woman perhaps in her mid-thirties. Next to her was a cross-section, viewed from the inside, clearly displaying brain, teeth and internal organs, all neatly halved. She'd been

split down the middle from cranium to pelvis, perfectly
Both seats were blood-soaked, as was the floor, but the
victim's clothes were unstained and cut neatly in two. It
was a science experiment gone wrong – a three-
dimensional page from a medical journal.

Allie squeezed around Strauss who was nailed to the
spot. She crept to within a few feet, the tape around the
seats preventing her from approaching any closer. She
peered at the cutaway side of each half of the corpse. A
shiny, jelly-like substance coated both halves of the
body from head to crotch and a fine pale powder coated
the hair, the floor and surrounding seats. Allie surmised
it was a solidifying agent that had set the remaining
blood and was keeping the half-organs locked in place.
She thought fleetingly that it might be silicone, but more
likely gelatine – lots of it. She vaulted the seats in front
of the corpses and walked along the row until she could
see them from the other side. It was the same story.
Viewed from this angle, the woman's right side seemed
as untouched as her left. Rachel hadn't moved. Today's
CCTV footage of Georgie's slaughter plus this horror
had tripped her fuses.

Allie studied the paradoxical nature of the horror.
Could you have such a thing as clinical carnage? But
that's what it was. Cold, deliberate and methodically
planned – it had to have been. And all of it executed
noiselessly in the back of the theatre *during the show*?
Despite her own disgust at the scene, she didn't pick up
a residual feeling of terror. If she was right, the woman,
Paula, hadn't suffered an agonizing death. It had been
relatively quick. The atrocities had been perpetrated on

her lifeless body. The scene had obviously been designed as another message.

Allie sensed a heavy sadness, *regret*, hanging in the air. She knew at once it was Paula's emotional pain. Paula was telling her, without words, that she'd done something she wouldn't normally do – she had acted on a whim, let her loneliness and broken heart pierce her protective shell – and it had killed her. Paula's sense of the *injustice* of it all came through in waves as well. 'And just when you thought your life was taking a turn for the better,' Allie said, barely aloud. 'I'm so sorry, Paula.' She saw Rachel Strauss's head swivel to look at her. She started towards Allie. Returning her gaze to the split corpse, Allie saw it come into view, as she knew it would. The number three was emblazoned across the body halves and the seats behind.

She waved Rachel away and said she'd see her in the foyer of the theatre. She looked again at the macabre scene as she walked back down row X. Two halves of the same person – it represented duality. It was the same message: good and evil, side by side. The number three was puzzling. Again, it made no immediate sense. Another two might have, but not three. She approached the Scenes of Crime officer whom she'd seen on her arrival. Allie introduced herself to him and addressed him by name. Ken Crowley was surprised she remembered him.

'You attended the King's Lane crime scene last night, didn't you?'

'I did indeed, ma'am, with Sergeant Houghton.'

'George not working tonight?' Allie asked, hoping to put the nervous man at ease. In truth, she remembered him because of his enormous speckled nose.

'Ma'am, George suffered a heart attack earlier today I'm sorry, but we've been advised he passed away.'

Allie spun away from him; her grief immediate and debilitating. She stood with her back to Crowley for a long minute. Her thoughts whirled through her early years as a PC and the kindness George had always shown her, despite the silver spoon tag that had bedevilled her from the outset of her career. He had defended her in the squad room and, more than once, on the streets. Guilt swam through her as well; she hadn't seen enough of him in the past year, evidenced by the fact she'd had no idea he'd had heart trouble. She marshalled her self-control and turned back to Crowley.

'I'm sorry, PC Crowley. I wasn't aware of it. George was a dear colleague and friend.'

Crowley, she was surprised to see, was emotional. 'I understand, ma'am. I understand.'

'Do you know when the funeral is?' she asked.

'No, ma'am. Probably in three or four days, I should imagine.'

Allie took out her handkerchief and blew her nose. Crowley looked away. She hated blowing her nose in front of people and was glad of his sensitivity to it. It was such a stupid thing, really. She thanked Crowley and said she expected she'd see him at the funeral.

Rachel was talking on her phone and turned to her as she approached. From her expression, Allie could tell she'd noticed her red-rimmed eyes. She jumped on to the front foot to avoid a grilling from her.

'Let's find out what we can here and skedaddle. Has any media been sniffing about?'

'None that I've seen,' Rachel said.

'Have you got all the details from Crowley, time of discovery, etcetera?'

Strauss said she had, so Allie decided she'd leave for the evening. She was in danger of falling over. Lack of sleep was impairing her thoughts.

'Are you up to looking after things here?'

Rachel bristled. *'Am I up to it?'*

Without thinking, Allie put her hand on her shoulder. 'Rache, I meant are you not too tired or drained from today, that's all. You've seen a lot and there are others we can call in.' Strauss looked at the ground, as was becoming her habit.

'I'm fine. You don't have to be concerned on that score.'

Leaving Strauss in charge and with specific instructions about photographing the scene, she stepped out into the sharp night air, pulling the collar of her thin jacket up around her ears. She hoped Michael was around somewhere, as he'd said he would be. She really didn't want to run into any more of Black Santa's little helpers. Plus, she'd prefer a ride home, despite having to perch on the back of that big bike and freeze for twenty minutes. She heard his motorbike somewhere in the distance.

*

Allie and Michael got back to her Putney flat at 11:00 p.m. Allie was near exhaustion and said so. Michael nodded. 'Okay if I kip in the spare room or would you rather I went elsewhere?' he asked.

Allie flapped a weary hand. 'The spare room is fine. Just pull the sofa bed out. There's bedding in the wardrobe. I'll get it for you.'

'Don't bother,' said Michael. 'I'll be fine. See you in the morning.'

Allie trudged upstairs to her own bedroom, then back down to the bathroom, then back up. She swan-dived into bed and was asleep within seconds.

The water was deathly cold in the cave. She hadn't wanted to go in, but Robert had sneaked away from the party and she had seen him go. The cake had already been cut and people were talking, so she reckoned she wouldn't be missed for a while. How he knew there was a cave under the strange hill, she didn't know. You couldn't see it from the grassy field. He'd just parted some pink bushes at the base of the hill by a farmer's fence and crawled under them. He didn't know she'd followed him. At first, she'd bridled at the thought of following him into the narrow channel of water, but she reasoned she'd be okay. If he could do it, she could. She was a better swimmer, even though he was fourteen and she was just ten. Besides, it wasn't really swimming, more like wading.

The bottom was sandy and smooth, not at all like a muddy river. It felt quite nice. The water was clear and a tiny light seeped in from somewhere, so she could just see well enough to make out the weird carvings on the rock walls. They were scary. Creatures with cruel fangs and pointy wings and snakes – long, long snakes – had been chiselled along the entire length of the walls. Lots of them.

She slowed her pace. Maybe this wasn't such a good idea. If she listened hard, she could just hear him splashing away up front. Where was he going for goodness' sake? She looked back at the entrance. She could barely make it out above the tiny rock ledge, where the spindly roots from the bushes poked through. Her shorts, top and scuffs were still there. Lucky she'd put her bathers on that morning. She'd hoped to swim somewhere that day. This summer was 'Caribbean hot,' according to her father.

She gasped as something touched her ankle. She stood still for a moment. It didn't come back. A little fish? She nearly turned back, but at that moment, she heard voices. One was definitely Robert's, but the other was a man's voice, very deep and it echoed harshly off the walls. Somebody was not happy with Robert. The words were hard to make out because they were echoing so much, but after a moment, she learned how to distinguish the words. Robert was saying sorry about something. The big voice was saying it was dangerous and that he shouldn't have come down there.

She turned to go, frightened now that they would get into trouble. A terrible screeching pierced the air. She covered her ears with her hands, but even when the screeching stopped, she could still hear other sounds – little squeaks and giggles. She peered around her, but couldn't see anything. The noises were all in front of her, around a bend in the rocks. She saw shadows up ahead as she moved gingerly forward, more out of concern for Robert than curiosity.

Reaching the place where the cave changed direction and bent to her left, she could hear more plainly now. The squeaking and strange chuckling filled her ears. A huge shadow suddenly moved opposite her, obliterating her view of the motifs and symbols that adorned a big flat wall. She cowered against a jagged outcrop of rock, her own breathing now loud in her ears. She crouched, her supporting left hand flat against the boulder which concealed her. The boulder moved. She flung her hand away from it, frantically wiping a glistening stickiness on her bathing costume, a glow remaining across her chest.

Backing away from the rock, she saw it now for what it was: a writhing mass of motley skin, uncoiling. Stepping backwards into the light, she saw Robert about thirty feet away. He was standing in the shadow of a huge, dark two-legged creature, whose head was bent low towards his face. She gasped, stepped sideways, and fell into the water. Resurfacing, she looked up to see Robert and the creature turn towards her.

She saw that Robert was surrounded by small long-tailed animals with thin stripes running down their backs; their huge eyes shiny granite-black, and fixed on her. Some of them started a mad chattering, some jumped up and down, and others turned to the big creature as if waiting for instructions. Something strong wrenched her from the water and threw her hard on to *the rocky embankment. She felt a tearing in her shoulder. The thick, slow-moving uncoiling thing slid slowly past, its thick skin rasping against the rocky floor as it noiselessly slipped into the water inches from her outstretched legs. She never saw its head, just the spiny, speckled ridge which traced the line of its long backbone.*

Something stepped over her, a soft material brushing against her face and upper body. She looked back at Robert who stood transfixed by the new entrant. She knew the stranger was there to help her. She saw as he entered the light that he had long white silky bird's wings which hung down nearly to his knees. She knew instinctively what he was. The dark creature shrieked unbearably again and flung Robert somersaulting into the water with a sweep of its clawed hand. The feathered being ran hard at the dark thing, which backed away a pace, then drew itself to its full height. They clashed.

She saw the striped animals scatter, but some came straight for her. Robert was nowhere to be seen. She screamed for Robert, but he didn't come up. She screamed again and tried to run, but the stickiness on her hands was now under her feet. She realized it must have come from the big slithering thing, which she could now see glowing on the bottom of the narrow channel. She tried lifting her legs, but couldn't. The striped animals arrived with their sickening giggles and she could do nothing. Robert's name was being screamed from afar. The stripys pawed at her and dragged her . . .

'Allie! Wake up! *Allie!*'

She stared sightlessly for a moment until Michael's face crystallized in front of her.

'Allie,' he said more gently, 'snap out of it.'

He had hold of her by the shoulders. He lifted her to a sitting position and stared into her eyes as if he was looking for the rest of the dream.

'God,' she breathed as she slumped against him. Even in her befuddled state, she realized this was the first physical contact they'd had.

'I'm only touching your stripy pyjamas,' he said with a chuckle.

Stripys. She jerked and stared at him. 'What were those things?'

'What things? What are you talking about?'

'Those horrible, giggling little creatures, like those monkey things from Madagascar . . . *lemurs*, but different!'

Michael let go of her shoulders and stood by the bed 'It was your dream, Allie, not mine. I can't see dreams – they are in your subconscious.'

She saw a distant coldness come over him. He looked away with what soldiers call the thousand-yard stare.

Chapter Sixteen

The Green Room, New Scotland Yard
Friday, 9:15 a.m.

Detective Sergeant Rachel Strauss wrapped up her summary of the Dominion Theatre crime scene with the infrared photos of the halved body. The number three was clearly visible, as was the distress on the faces of DCs Connor, Wilkinson and Banks.

Allie St. Clair addressed them. 'The victim was a Miss Paula Armstrong, forty three, of 21 Chichester Close, Kensington. She was the successful and well-known editor of *La Mode*, which is a glossy design/lifestyle magazine for the well-heeled.' Strauss coughed loudly and Allie saw the smirks go around the team. She glanced at Carr who remained impassive. She ploughed on.

'She had no children and lived alone after the breakup of her eleven-year marriage to Mr Eric Leonardi, a middle-level property developer. We are yet to locate him or any next of kin, so therefore, cannot yet release any information to the media.'

She couldn't miss Carr's wry smile directed at her from the back of the room.

'This is the only photo we have of Ms Armstrong from our archives,' she said, throwing an image up on the big screen. 'It was taken, according to this note, five years ago at a press launch for a new lifestyle section for the magazine. On her left, you will note, among the many guests, is the former prime minister. *La Mode*'s offices are in Soho and I'll be visiting them in the next hour.'

Strauss pointed at the photo. 'She's attractive, so she'll have a boyfriend somewhere.'

'Or girlfriend,' Carr interrupted.

'Yes, of course – or girlfriend,' Strauss added.

Allie noted the wink from Carr. She picked up her file again and summarized from it.

'We don't yet have a list of phone calls from her mobile phone, which was in her bag, but it shouldn't be long.' She looked at her team then switched off the noisy data projector.

'We can all see that this murder is linked to that of Georgie Konstanzo from yesterday. The number three, which is clearly visible in the infrared photos—' her mind suddenly fizzed back to her dream from early that morning, the glow from the rock in the cave, '—is evidence enough of that.' Everyone nodded. 'So,' she continued, 'we have two brutal murders in two days, both with female victims, both with biblical overtones.'

'What overtones are there in this murder?' asked Strauss. 'I didn't see anything to indicate that.'

'And we have no real idea where to go next,' Banks chimed in. 'Is there anything from CCTV footage at the Dominion?'

Allie shook her head and shrugged. 'The Dominion doesn't have CCTV covering the foyer. For whatever reason, their security system only covers the backstage area and the external stage entrances and exits. Given that, we have no prime suspect. I'm inclined to exclude young Robbie the usher for the moment. He appears to be genuinely traumatised by his discovery of the body . . . and who wouldn't be? But, having said that, I think we have plenty to occupy ourselves with. Let's start with the biblical stuff. It may not be as overt as the first murder,' she said, once again noting Banks' raised eyebrows at the use of overt, 'but I think the splitting in half is a reference to good and evil, two sides of the one coin, denoting the duality of man, if you like. Anyone agree . . . or disagree?'

'I agree,' said Carr. Not surprisingly, everyone else suddenly did too. 'But what of the number three – what does it mean, given that yesterday's murder had the number two sprayed over it?'

Again, no one had any ideas, so Allie spoke up. 'Well, I've thought about this and unless there's an earlier victim out there who is yet to be discovered, I think it relates to the number of people involved in the crime.'

'Go on,' said Carr. Allie walked to the window and looked out at the gathering storm clouds.

'If you look at the second crime, you see the impossibility of it. I mean how could one person manage to subdue the victim, saw her in half vertically while pouring a solidifying agent all over her, prop her up in seats Y23 and 24 and exit the theatre, all in such a manner as to not alert one single person as to what was occurring? It's preposterous that one person could do that. The first murder, we saw, had one perpetrator. This second one has to involve at least two people.'

'Okay,' said Carr, 'Why the number three then?

Allie shrugged her shoulders. 'Unless anyone has a better idea, I'd say the murderer thinks he works with the devil and now they have a little helper.'

9:30 a.m.

Sweat drenched his pillow. All he could see was the ever-widening fissure in Paula's surprised face as it split down the middle. The commando saw was ruthless, carving a trench in soft tissue and bone with equal ease. The fine, powdered gelatine rained down on her, filling the gap in her being and thickening the blood around the jagged bone and the smooth cleft in her brain.

He'd had to push the saw to the left of her spine, as it took too much time sawing all the way down through bone, so he'd cheated a little with the consequence that the right half of her ended up a little wider than the left. He hoped his new assistant hadn't minded. The gelatine powder had gotten on his hands and mixed with his sweat to set as a clear lump on his pink knuckles.

He'd found fine slivers of bone in his bed. He supposed they must have gotten into his thickening hair at the theatre. He carefully arranged them in two halves on his bedside table. He decided he needed a little display case; he had a memento of Georgie in his bag as well. He wondered if his new friend had also taken souvenirs.

He reached for his mobile phone and swiped and dabbed at it until he got to the photos section. Pushing his sodden pillow up behind his back, he sat up, looking at his photo gallery. There were six pictures of Georgie and four of Paula. Paula had been really lovely.

She's twice as lovely now, Arthur.

He nodded. 'I guess,' he said, only half-acknowledging Mr Black's comment. He was still lost in thought as he scrolled through the photos.

She'd get into the theatre for half-price now, especially what's 'left' of her, wouldn't you say? Arthur?

The black humour lost on him, Arthur said, 'She was so nice . . . why did we have to do this? I've never had anything so beautiful in my life before and now . . . now I've destroyed it!'

He wailed in anguish, self-loathing a tidal wave. He tore at the bed sheets, then pounded them over and over. He was breathing hard when his mobile phone pinged loudly. He stared at it as if it was a hand grenade. A text message waited. He grabbed the phone and read the message:

Good job last night; thanks for your leadership

Arthur read it again. *Thanks for your leadership.* Yes, he'd noted the other man's deference to him at the theatre. He'd liked that; he had to admit. He supposed he did bring something special to situations; he had felt that quite strongly recently. No room for weakness in leaders. Look at Churchill – he was willing to sacrifice half of the colonies to ensure England's survival. *That* was leadership. People had to die for the greater good. At least he, Arthur, did things at the frontline. Not like MacArthur who never stepped on a foreign beach until the enemy had been reduced to a whimpering rabble.

No, he'd been in there at the Dominion theatre parrying and thrusting, showing the way. That was leadership, wasn't it? Leading by example meant never asking someone to do what you were not prepared to do yourself. He felt those self-inflating, feel-good endorphins flood through him again. His little crisis was over. He rolled his neck around on his shoulders and stretched his arms above his head. He let the relaxing muscles tingle. He was back in control. Perhaps it had been a little mid-death crisis. He chuckled.

That's it, Arthur, the voice said. *You have to see the funny side of this.*

La Mode magazine occupied the entire upstairs area above three shops on the corner of trendy Denmark Street and St. Giles High Street in what was loosely described as Soho. Allie knew the area well. She was reminded, as she walked with Connors towards the door of the magazine's office, that she'd bought her first guitar here with her father when she was fourteen years old. She remembered the tremor of excitement that ran through her that day. There had been so many music stores, all selling much the same type of instruments, but the prices had varied enormously.

Steven Bannister

'This is it,' Connors said, pushing at a narrow brown wooden door leading on to a steep staircase. A tiny arty plaque to the left of the door confirmed it to be *La Mode*. The fond memories of Denmark Street faded as Allie steeled herself for the task of telling Paula Armstrong's unsuspecting workmates of her untimely death.

An hour later, they left *La Mode*, feeling they had a strong lead. Once the shock of the announcement had subsided, two of Paula's workmates, Bridgette from the art studio and Jon from editorial, told of Paula's excitement at having suddenly been asked out to lunch. It had happened so fast that she'd rushed off in a complete flap to the hairdresser in the late morning, but hadn't been seen since. She'd not rung later, as promised, and the staff, who had been waiting for decisions on a range of issues, had been very annoyed. Those staff members now dealt with different emotions. It was clear to Allie that Paula had been a popular and respected leader at *La Mode*.

Connors had taken a note of the hairdresser's address and the two detectives headed off. The big revelation from the *La Mode* staff had been that it had been some sort of advisor or insurance guy who had gotten Paula into a hot sweat. St. Clair and Connors had Paula's home address and house keys from her handbag and Kensington was on the call list after the hairdressers, which was ironically named the Cutting Edge.

The gender non-specific Jasmine from Cutting Edge confirmed Paula's excitement of the previous morning. 'He was so dreamy; she couldn't believe it!' Jasmine's thin arms waved a little too enthusiastically.

'Why couldn't she believe it?' Connors asked.

'Well,' said Jasmine, sweeping ironed black hair aside with a flourish, 'apparently, she'd been going to this professional guy for advice for some time, but she suddenly saw him with fresh eyes, she said. She couldn't believe she hadn't picked up on it before.'

'Er . . . picked up on what, exactly?' Allie asked.

'His heat! Paula said he seemed taller and better looking than she'd remembered, and his eyes – Lord, she couldn't believe his smouldering Mediterranean eyes!' Jasmine was going into orbit and other customers were looking their way. Allie thought heat an odd word to use and smouldering eyes was straight from a Mills and Boon.

'So, he was of Middle-Eastern descent, then?' asked Connors.

'Hmmm, no, I don't think so.' Jasmine pouted. 'I think, at least my *impression* is, that she'd never noticed his eyes before, so no, I don't think he's a Paki or anything like that.'

Allie smiled at the indelicate nature of Jasmine's answers. Not so delicate either was the enormous, poorly concealed bulge in Jasmine's pants suit. Jasmine had some work to do to finalize the transition.

'So,' Allie said, 'you think he's in insurance or something? An advisor, I think you said?'

Jasmine struck an exaggerated thinking pose, left lip flung out to one side. 'Yes it was important to her at this time, anyway. Maybe he's a shrink?'

It was clear Jasmine was guessing. Allie asked if Jasmine had heard Paula mention a name, but it seemed she'd been careful not to reveal too much to anyone at *La Mode* or Cutting Edge. If you couldn't trust your hairdresser to keep a secret, who could you trust?

Allie felt they'd reached the end of the road with Jasmine, apart from the obvious question. 'Do you know where they were going for lunch?'

'No,' Jasmine answered without hesitation. 'He was going to surprise her.'

DC Mathew Connors drove towards Paula Armstrong's Kensington flat and St. Clair appeared to be deep in thought in the passenger seat, until she surprised him by asking where he'd got to the previous afternoon.

'What do you mean? I was knocking on doors in Earl's Court, as you know, ma'am.' It was a hurried, breathless answer, its implication not lost on Allie.

'Strauss said you disappeared off on your own early in the afternoon. She was back at headquarters by 4:00 p.m., but you weren't. Care to enlighten me?'

Connors flashed a look at her. 'Strauss, that is *DS* Strauss, had half the workload I did. I kept knocking on doors around the Earl's Court area and a little beyond until about 6:00 p.m., then I came in for your briefing. Simple as that.'

Allie brushed some lint from her trousers. 'Why didn't you report in?'

Connors exhaled a long breath. 'I'm sorry, ma'am, but I let my phone go dead and hadn't taken a backup radio. I completely forgot.'

Allie looked at him for a moment. 'Mathew, are you coping all right? We had a brief chat about this a day or so ago, you'll recall. It's been a long week, God knows but you seem flustered and a bit erratic, to be honest. What's going on?'

Connors shifted in his seat and pulled at his collar. *Careful Mathew, she's a smart one . . .* 'I haven't been sleeping very well, and I'm trying to work that out. I haven't been quite myself lately, for some reason.'

'Do you need a break?'

'A break? No, definitely not. I think I'd better stay on this horse or I won't get back on.' It was an interesting analogy. She didn't quite know what he meant, but didn't push him.

'I see. Let me know if you think you need to take recreation leave or seek some counselling.' He turned quickly towards her, but she put up her hand. 'Don't get upset. We all need help at times. This week we've all seen some utterly terrible things. We could all use a break. Anyway, let's leave it there, but please let me know if you decide I can help you.'

She saw Connors smile and turn his gaze to the rear-view mirror for a moment. Talk returned to the subject of Paula Armstrong.

DCS Carr sat in the deep leather chair opposite an unhappy Commander Bradley Whitcombe. Carr had been summoned and she'd not been surprised.

Whitcombe levelled his peregrine gaze at her. She knew this to be an old tactic of his. He no doubt felt that his rank and tall, patrician bearing had an intimidating affect. He swept a hand through his thick silver hair and leaned forward. It was a rehearsed move.

He held up two fingers, a gesture that could easily have been misinterpreted.

'There've been two brutal, ritualistic murders this week. Probably the worst we've seen in a decade, Ellen, and you're still putting your faith in this St. Clair kid?'

Carr let the silence hang for a few seconds, until she saw his gaze alter. 'Obviously, yes, sir.'

'Don't get cute here. You know what I'm driving at. Are you absolutely sure you want to continue up this path? I mean, I hear that no one has *any idea* who has done these things or why! And you've got this toffy kid running the investigation!'

'C'mon, Bradley,' Carr said evenly, deliberately using his first name. 'She's hardly a *kid* and don't forget, you were very happy to see her promoted to DS so early through the ranks a few years ago. You certainly enjoyed the public relations rub-off at the time.'

Whitcombe glared at her. 'Be that as it may, I've got media crawling over me again and I have absolutely nothing to tell them. Have we made *any* progress on either of these murders?'

Carr had had enough. 'It's been three goddamn days! What do you expect? The two crimes are obviously linked, so St. Clair's murder investigation team has to run with both. There's been precious little time, sir. And sod the media.'

'Great,' Whitcombe replied. 'Sod the media. Well, thank you indeed, DCS Carr, for that sage piece of advice. I'll call in our communications director, shall I, and apprise him of our new strategy?'

Carr leaned forward in her chair, the leather squeaking as she did so. 'St. Clair will do this, don't you worry. There might be many more experienced officers out there,' she waved her hand towards the window, 'but there's none smarter. What chance do you think Billy McBride would have had running parallel investigations on crimes like this? I'll tell you, he'd be in the fucking pub right now pissed to the gills, while St. Clair did it for him anyway!'

'Calm down, Ellen,' Whitcombe said. 'You're getting hysterical.'

'Hysterical my arse,' she said in a shrill voice. 'The killer, or *killers*, will be in custody by Monday – you have my word on it!'

Whitcombe laughed and stood up. 'Monday! Really? Well that's a change; one minute there's been no time, now, it'll all be fixed by Monday!' He made a play of looking at his wall calendar. 'So, let's be clear,' he said. 'Monday is, let's see . . .' He counted off on his fingers. 'One, two, *three* days from now. We'll reconvene here in my office at 4:00 p.m. Monday for the wrap-up media conference, shall we?'

Carr was boxed in. 'We shall,' she said. She abruptly stood and walked out.

That went well, Bradley. Those charm-school lessons really paid-off.

Ellen Carr threw a glance over her shoulder as she left Whitcombe's office and saw him shake his head and scowl at some unseen annoyance. She wondered fleetingly if the prick fell somewhere on the Asperger's spectrum.

*

Allie phoned DC Jacinta Wilkinson from the car and asked her to follow up on which company published *Gobber* magazine and who owned it.

'*Gobber* magazine?' Wilkinson asked; she'd never heard of it.

'Glad to hear it.' Allie saw Connors smile.

'Also, ask Rachel to follow up on a company called InCamera Photograpics. She'll recall the name from Shepherd's Bush. I want to know who the proprietor is as soon as possible, please.'

Allie had meant to get that little line of enquiry going earlier, but priorities were stacking up this morning. She still had no clear motive for the murders, other than the obvious biblical themes which were evident to all. The fact that there was direct demonic intervention was a bizarre concept that would see her laughed out of the Green Room at NSY. Alluding to the killers' delusional belief in demonic possession was as close as she could get to it at briefings.

So far, that had gained some level of acceptance, thanks to Carr's timely endorsement of the theory. But theory was one thing; finding the person or persons responsible was another and in reality, they had nothing but a blurred image on a CCTV tape. So far, the link between Paula and Georgie, other than the bleeding obvious – that they were both attractive females – eluded her.

'A penny for your thoughts, Chief Inspector?' Connors stared across the car at her.

'I'm not sure they're worth that much, Mathew.' She studied the streets as they approached Chelsea-Kensington. She thought of Ray Riley who, on reflection, was the one genuine thread they had. He'd been at the Chinese restaurant the night of Georgie's murder in the adjacent lane, and she'd seen him at the Black Crow where Georgie had worked. The trouble was, fifty people could bear witness that he didn't leave his table all night at the Golden Bamboo; not even for a pee. But, it was a connection. A thin one, but it was something. Her phone rang. It was Rachel Strauss.

'Good morning, Rachel.'

'Good . . . umm . . . hello, ma'am. I thought you'd like to know there's no listing for InCamera Photographics anywhere. It doesn't exist.'

'But we know it does, don't we?' Allie said, thinking back to her sprawling, tumbling act in Georgie's bedroom.

'We do.' Rachel replied. 'But it's not legally registered.'

'Hold on a moment,' Allie said and punched up her call history. 'See who owns this mobile number then – it's the one from the advertisement in Gobber.' She reeled off the number she'd rung from the tube the night before. 'I should have thought of it earlier Oh and, Rachel, take Jacinta with you when you can and see if you can find the restaurant where Paula Armstrong had lunch with her 'advisor' yesterday. We know it must be reasonably close to the New Oxford Street-Bedford Square area, otherwise Paula couldn't have made the afternoon matinee at the Dominion. Flash her photo around . . . you know the drill. Hopefully, you can find a credit card imprint somewhere. Thanks.'

Strauss rang off without further comment. Allie looked at the phone a moment, thinking that Strauss really needed some social re-engineering. Traffic was heavy and a weak sun was losing the battle with darkening clouds. They crawled past Knightsbridge toward Gloucester Road and the Royal College of Art, en route to Kensington Road. Allie's thoughts landed on her vivid dream, from which she'd been roughly awoken by Michael that morning. Some dream. She'd never before experienced one so *real*. Michael's strange reaction also worried her. He'd been defensive. She supposed her tiredness and the bizarre and disturbing events of the week were stimulating her subconscious. Her phone bleeped. It was Michael: *Check behind you. See anything?*

She twisted in her seat. She could see nothing behind the car, no suspicious vehicles following . . . nothing. Connors asked what was up.

'Not sure,' Allie said thoughtfully. 'Just a feeling.'

Connors checked his rear-view mirror. 'I can't see anything unusual.'

'Forget it,' Allie said. 'We can't be far away from Paula's flat, can we?'

Connors checked his GPS unit. 'Probably ten minutes away, it's just down left from here, past the National Dyslexic Teaching Centre.'

Allie looked at him. 'You're kidding.'

'Nope, that's where it is.'

'Is that according to your PGS unit?' she asked, smiling.

'Yes.' Clearly, the joke was lost on him. Her phone bleeped. *Funny.*

DCS Ellen Carr's mobile phone ringtone exploded into life – Dylan's *Knockin' on Heaven's Door*. It was her code ring for Janice.

'Hey,' she said.

'Hey yourself.' Janice laughed. 'What are you doing for lunch?'

Carr was surprised. It was a rare thing for them to be seen out during the day, rarer still for Janice to initiate it. 'Nothing. What have you got in mind?'

'You know our managing partner, Jason Lock, *Lockey*, don't you?'

'Yes,' Ellen confirmed. She'd met Lockey a couple of years ago. She hadn't liked him.

'Anyway,' Janice continued, 'he's hosting a lunch for our top clients at Alain Ducasse at the Dorchester. Are you interested in coming with me?'

'Alain Ducasse? That's got a heap of Michelin stars, hasn't it?'

'Three, in fact. You in or out?'

'In! What time?'

Janice laughed. 'Be there at 12:30. It'll go until 3:00 p.m., though. Get a cab and I'll see you there.'

'Done!' Carr hung up and looked at her watch – 11:05 a.m. She'd better check in with St. Clair before she scooted off to the Dorchester. A ripple of excitement ran through her.

*

Paula Armstrong's flat was simply magnificent. It boasted an unobstructed view of Kensington Square gardens and a peek down towards Thackeray Street. It boasted two bedrooms; a snug but luxuriously appointed kitchen; and a living room with pressed-tin ceilings and a bay window.

'Big bucks here,' said Connors.

'Yes,' Allie replied, choosing not to mention that she'd looked at a flat just three doors down herself, but Putney's wide-open space along the Thames had won her over. Her mother had been keen for her to buy in Kensington, as it was closer to the family home. She recalled that was the other reason she'd chosen Putney.

An unwashed breakfast bowl with a veneer of cornflakes clinging to the edges and a half-cup of cold tea sat on the kitchen bench. A huge, shiny retro-designed toaster, which looked as though it could lift off at any moment, sat beneath white overhead cupboards. Presumably Paula had come home to change for lunch after the visit to the hairdresser. This was confirmed by a look into the larger of the two bedrooms – the one Paula obviously slept in. Clothes were strewn over the bed, and scarves and shoes littered the floor – she'd left in a hurry. Allie stepped over the mess, thinking how different it was from the one she'd confronted at Georgie Konstanzo's flat in the Shepherd's Bush. Some messes were tolerable and understandable; some were not.

They spent the next hour searching Paula's flat for anything that might look relevant. Her laptop computer was password protected so that would have to be cracked by the IT boys. Allie noticed there were no photos of family or friends on the walls, desk or coffee table. That was unusual. They did find registration papers for a Mazda MX-5 sports car that must be parked somewhere in town, and various receipts and power bills. All in all, there was nothing unusual.

'Eureka!' Connors yelled. He backed out of a hall closet carrying a large black Expanda file marked 'insurances/finance'. They spread its contents on the dining table.

The mortgage for the flat was in the file, as were her life assurance papers and car and fire insurances. Allie was disappointed to note that they were all with different companies and nothing suggested she retained an insurance broker. Her previous year's tax return was there as was her contract renewal with *La Mode*.

'Interesting,' Allie said. 'She's only just had her contract renewed for a further three years. They must have valued her.'

Connors whistled at the salary printed in bold text. 'Makes my salary look sick,' he moaned.

'Mine too,' said Allie, missing his sceptical look. They rummaged about for another ten minutes until Allie called a halt. Paula had led an ordered, normal life. They were wasting their time. She sighed. 'Well, it's back to the Met, Mathew. There's nothing much here.'

She glanced out through the mesh curtains of the bay window on her way to the front door. Three men, wearing identical leathers and sitting astride identical Monza red motorbikes, sat outside the flat, their faces hidden behind shiny black helmets. They stared through the curtains at her. She moved two steps to her left. Their helmets swivelled in unison. Connors came up beside her.

'Well, well,' he said. 'What have we here?'

'Ducatis,' Allie said.

'I meant . . .'

'Trouble, Mathew, is the answer you are looking for – big trouble.'

Chapter Seventeen

Jason Lock, Lockey to his inner circle, was managing director of Cranston Lock and a consummate host. His law firm had grown from a team of three based in a third-rate shopping strip in London's outer circle, to a top-twenty-five Fleet Street firm with annual earnings of just under one hundred million pounds in just twenty years. Not bad for an orphaned kid who'd had more fistfights than hot dinners in his first fifteen years. But talent, raw intelligence and rat cunning had seen him blossom and gain scholarships to the best law schools. A certain sexual ambivalence hadn't hurt his chances along the way either, and he'd gained vital patronage from certain influential, middle-aged 'gentlemen' who valued discretion above all else. His dedication to honing his strong frame through rigorous physical training, culminating in a first in rowing from Oxford, had ensured welcome attention from predatory females and profitable relationships with senior legal benefactors.

Ellen Carr had to acknowledge that Jason Lock was an impressive individual. She could see why Janice was slightly in awe of him. He was warmth and charm itself – even inviting Ellen to sit beside him, which, with some hesitation, she did. Janice raised her eyebrows at her in a 'fancy that' way, chuckled and sat opposite her. The Alain Ducasse restaurant surpassed her expectations. The staff were attentive and thoughtful and the food, simply magnificent. Never one to really bother too much about wine, she was caught unawares when Jason Lock suddenly turned to her and, in a booming voice calculated to capture the attention of the entire coterie of guests, asked her opinion of the white wine. She was mortified and dropped her napkin, leaning in to Janice, hoping for help.

Janice caught on and whispered, sotto voce, '1967 Lessiere Frontignac – crisp, stylish.'

Her life saved, Ellen sat up and smiled at the guests. 'I always enjoy a crisp Frontignac. I've not seen the bottle, but I would hazard a guess that it's one of Paul Lessiere's . . . perhaps a '67?'

'Bravo, Ellen!' Lock cheered. He raised his glass. 'May more of our constabulary demonstrate style, sophistication and an appreciation of the finer things in life!'

The twelve guests arranged carefully around the table raised their glasses and smiled. Janice whispered, 'How did you know it was *Paul* Lessiere?'

'Aren't all Frenchmen called Paul?' Ellen replied through clenched teeth.

The main courses all arrived at precisely the same time, as one expects of a world-class restaurant, and conversation confined itself to muttered asides and little exaltations of praise for the food. Ellen was aware of Jason Lock's gaze. She cocked an eyebrow at him.

'Tell me, Ellen,' he said smoothly, 'how are you doing with these ghastly murders? The headlines are like something out of Whitechapel in the nineteenth century.' Carr set her fork down.

'Well, its early days, of course. Some crimes of this nature can take a year to solve – others a matter of weeks. Hopefully, it's more the latter than the former.'

'So, no leads then, eh?'

Carr smiled. 'I didn't say that. We're working lines of enquiry as hard as we can. We'll see what the next few days bring.'

'Aha,' Lock said, cupping his hands together. I sense that you're on to something!'

'Perhaps. The young murder investigation team s hard at it.'

Lock laughed. 'Are they now? Will that help?'

Carr realized she'd made a double entendre gaffe. She replied in true *Carry On* style. 'Well, it can't hurt, can it?'

Lock laughed loudly. 'No indeed. Well said!' She was relieved to return her attention to her swordfish; t really was superb. But Lock persisted. 'How's this young DCI of yours performing – the good-looking one – St. Clair?'

Carr now saw that she hadn't been seated next to Lockey for nothing. Once again, she lowered her fork. 'She's doing very well, in my opinion. I seem to get asked this a lot, in fact. It's a big test for her. Many DCI's who've spent thirty years on the force have never had to deal with crimes this confronting.'

Lock nodded his understanding. 'Of course, but she's not exactly cut out for the brutal stuff, is she? I mean she's a Sloane Ranger really – more used to fighting crowds in Harrods than in council estates.'

Carr decided she'd return to disliking Lock, her brief flirtation with the idea of liking him now abandoned. 'DCI St. Clair is the future of this city's policing, I can tell you right now. She's Cambridge educated, has a third-degree black belt in karate and mentally is as tough as they come – but she doesn't advertise any of that.'

'Is that so?' Lock asked, dabbing at his mouth with a silk napkin. 'I suppose she lives somewhere unprepossessing these days and dresses down as well?'

'No, in fact she lives in . . .' Carr stopped herself just in time. Her internal warning system was clanging away. '. . . quite nice surroundings really.'

Lock smiled slowly. 'Nice catch, Detective Chief Superintendent. Would you care for another drink?'

Allie eyeballed the motorcycle riders assembled on Kensington Avenue and they stared back. She saw a green glow emerging from them and looked at Connors to see if he'd noticed it. If he did, he said nothing. *Tricky*, she thought. Obviously, Michael had felt something when he'd texted her.

'What are we going to do?' asked a nervous Connors.

Allie looked at him. 'Do? We'll walk out, get into our car and go back to headquarters.'

Connors stared at the riders. 'But they're obviously waiting for us!'

'Well, let's not keep 'em waiting too long, then,' Allie said, reaching for the doorknob.

'Wait,' Connors blurted, a hand cupped to his ear. 'Listen!'

The thump of a big engine echoed down the square. A moment later, a massive man on an equally large black motorbike flashed into view. He rode straight at the three riders who were stuck in his path. Allie held her breath.

The riders looked at the big bike and, as one, realized they were under threat. They tried to manoeuver themselves into a position to evade the rider. But it was all for nothing.

They were stuck in a chorus line as the man on the bike flashed past and flung a long right arm out. It connected with the helmet of the first rider, knocking him into the second and then third. The riders and their bikes were knocked twenty feet sideways in a clattering, jarring jumble of machinery and men. Motors roared and died, except for the colossal black bike. It was now out of sight, but Allie and Connors heard it turn at the end of the street and begin its return, much slower this time.

'Holy shit!' Connors said. 'Have you ever seen anything like that?'

'He's coming back,' Allie said, knowing full well who it was. They watched as the bike came to a rumbling halt. The rider turned off the engine, dismounted and walked slowly over to the smoking jumble, his long black coat stretching to his boots.

'Let's get out there,' Connors said, making for the door.

'No,' Allie said, flinging her arm out. 'Wait.'

Connors frowned and returned to the window beside Allie. They watched as the big rider picked up a bike from the top of the pile and flung it thirty feet to his left.

Connors was ecstatic. '*Oh my God!* Look at that! Who is this guy?'

Allie didn't enlighten him. Bikes were heaved out of the way like child's toys to expose the three riders. The black rider picked them all up in one hand.

'That's impossible,' Connors breathed.

Allie felt a rising panic. *What's Michael going to do?* She saw him stop and look around at her. He'd heard. In response, he delicately removed the helmet from one of the riders with his right hand. Allie got the message. A rat-like face poked out of the motorcycle leathers. She looked at Connors – there was no reaction. Allie marshalled her thoughts and tried transmitting to him. *You can't kill them, Michael. Connors is a witness!*

He shrugged, then bashed their heads together like rag dolls and threw them on the grass. *Okay?*

Okay, she confirmed.

He walked to his bike and mounted. Connors bolted for the door. 'C'mon, Allie, get his registration number!'

Get out of here fast, Michael!

He waved. The big bike rocketed off its stand in an instant. Allie groaned. He'd forgotten to start the engine. The bike had just *gone.* She heard the engine finally start, but he was a hundred yards down the road. She made a show of sprinting out of the house towards Connors who stood confused in the centre of the street.

'Is it my imagination,' he said, scratching his head, 'or did that bike not make any—'

'Never mind that!' Allie barked. 'Let's see if these guys are all right. Ring an ambulance, Mathew.'

Once more, Detective Sergeant Rachel Strauss found herself pounding the beat – this time trying to locate the restaurant where Paula Armstrong and her lover boy had dined at lunchtime the day before. She and DC Wilkinson had split up and were taking different sides of Tottenham Court Road and Oxford Street near the Dominion Theatre. It was awkward trying to ask questions of restaurant staff – it was 1:15 p.m. and the lunch rush was on. *It's amazing*, she thought *how so many people can just piss off for lunch on a Friday*. She wondered how many would make it back to work. It would be nice to have a few drinks and take the afternoon off.

'Can I help you?' Rachel turned around to see the voice came from a tall, severe middle-aged woman. She held menus to her chest like armour plating and regarded her as if she were something just scraped from the footpath.

'Yes, I'm . . .'

'Do you have a reservation?'

'No, I'm from—'

'You can't just push your way in to a place like this, you know!' the woman spat out, turning away.

'Hey! Excuse me!' Rachel raised her voice. 'I don't think you understand. I'm—'

'Ronnie!' the woman yelled, flapping a hand in the air. 'Please *escort* this pushy trollop from the premises right now!' A mountainous, T-shirted gorilla with close-cropped blond hair lumbered towards Strauss.

'Whoa, whoa here!' she said in a raised voice, reaching for her warrant card.

Mountainous Man grabbed her upper arm and pulled it away from her pocket. 'No you don't, dearie; I don't know what you've got in there,' he said in a thick Belfast brogue.

Rachel was furious. 'I'm a police officer, paddy,' she said, wincing in pain. 'Let go now or there'll be real trouble.'

'Well now, of course you are,' he said. 'I'm an astronaut myself, but I work here just for the lunchtime banter. Now bugger off!' He shoved her out on to the street.

Furious, she phoned for Wilkinson. She'd have this fat Irish prick and the skinny maître d' on her own platter. Jacinta's phone rang out. Rachel looked back into the restaurant and up at the sign above the door – Il Forno. She tried Wilkinson again. Still, there was no answer. She looked across the road, hoping to spot her. Five minutes later, there was no sign of Wilkinson. *Sod it*, Strauss decided; she'd go it alone. Pulling out her warrant card, she marched back into the restaurant. Spotting Fat Paddy standing by the restrooms, she beckoned him over. He stormed towards her until he saw the warrant card thrust at him.

'Oh shit,' he said, putting a hand to his face.

'Get the skinny bitch back here, *now*,' Rachel demanded.

Arthur's father had always said, 'Luck was a fortune,' and he'd been right. He knew why he'd come back to Tottenham Court Road today. Paula. The time they'd had over lunch the day before was one of the best experiences of his life. She'd been warm, funny and attentive – he'd never known that before. He'd liked her very much. He now sat at a corner table by the window in a perky little café over the road from Il Forno. Paula had introduced him to macchiato coffee yesterday and he'd just ordered one from the woman who ran this café. He missed Paula. *Why did she have to go?*

The conversation at the counter seeped into his consciousness. A young woman was asking the café owner, Tippy, whether she'd noticed a woman wearing a green skirt and white top yesterday. She flashed a photo of Paula.

So, Arthur the game is afoot! his inner voice advised.

What are you now – Sherlock Holmes? Arthur barked inwardly.

Ooh, touchy today, are we? Like to spend some time, no wait . . . a long time in Wormwood Scrubs prison would we? Personally, I don't.

Arthur looked at the young woman asking the questions. A detective, no doubt. She turned and glanced at him, then at others in the small café. She had perfect coffee-coloured skin and, despite being a tad overweight for his liking, was attractive. He looked in the mirror behind the counter and saw her smile at Tippy. She had beautiful, straight white teeth. *All in all, very nice,* he decided. The police were raising the bar.

She could raise your bar all right, Arthur! In fact, if I'm not mistaken . . .

'Shut up!' he said, a*loud.* Jacinta Wilkinson whirled around to face him. Arthur hurriedly held up his phone. 'Sorry,' he said, hunching his shoulders in a gesture of helplessness. 'My girlfriend . . . she does go on about things!'

Jacinta studied him for a moment, then turned away.

She's picked up on you, Arthur, the voice warned. *She just memorized your face.*

Panic swept through him. *She focused on me intently,* he decided. Now she was being cool until she sneaked away and rang for backup. He looked across the street and saw her backup enter Il Forno. Shit! They were on to him.

Stay cool, my man. Stay cool, Mr Black soothed. *There's fun to be had here.*

Arthur watched the young detective shake hands with the smiling Tippy. *She's clinging to the café owner's hand for just a little bit too long,* he thought. *She's coming on to her! She's using her position as a trusted public employee to seduce women. That's just wrong! People have to have faith in the police, not have them abuse your trust . . .* like his mother had.

That's it, Arthur. You remember what she did to you – and you trusted her and loved her so much!

Arthur twitched in his seat. Something hot and prickly danced across his skin. He could see people for what they were. *This detective, with her arse too big for her pants and long black crinkly hair – it's all a trap. Carefully made-up and preened* bait. *They lull you into thinking they care for you, but it's just about using you!* He checked across the road; the other detective hadn't emerged from Il Forno.

He looked again at the dark detective. She was leaving the café. He made his mind up. 'Excuse me, Detective. I couldn't help but overhear your conversation. I think I might be able to help. Is there somewhere we can go for a chat?'

The uniformed boys finally arrived and carted Fat Paddy away. Strauss finished giving the scrawny maître d' a complete bollocking, but couldn't find anything to charge her with, despite her best efforts. Rudeness wouldn't quite cut it in court. Paddy would be released later, but at least she'd inconvenience the big bastard and maybe cause him to miss a few meals, which would be doing him a favour really.

She checked her phone to see if Jacinta had tried to ring during the commotion at Il Forno. There was no message. She tried her number again, but without success. She checked her watch – 3:00 p.m. *Where the hell is she?* They'd been supposed to meet at 1:30 for a bite of lunch. She rang the Met and got Margaret Daly.

'Hello, Margaret, Strauss here. Have you or anyone heard from DC Wilkinson in the last hour or so?' Daly said she'd check and put the phone down. Strauss paced up and down the pavement. She realized she was seriously worried; this wasn't like Wilkinson at all. If you could rely on anyone to be punctual and straight down the line, it was Jacinta. She might not have been the world's brightest cop, but she operated by the book. Daly came back on the line and said that no one had heard from her.

'Can you patch me through to DCI St. Clair, please?' Daly caught the urgency in her voice and transferred her to St. Clair's mobile number immediately. Allie came on the line; she was travelling and using the speaker on her phone.

'Ma'am, can you switch to private mode please?'

'Of course.' Then, after a moment's delay, she said, 'What's wrong, Rachel?' Concern was clearly evident in her voice.

'I don't want to be alarmist, ma'am, but DC Wilkinson isn't responding to my calls – hasn't for nearly two hours now.' Allie sat up straighter in the passenger seat. Connors noticed. 'You were canvassing the Dominion Theatre area, right?'

'Yes, ma'am. We split up our duties and Jacinta took the southern side of the street at about 12:30. I've not been able to raise her since about 1:30.' She hesitated before going on. 'I'm worried, Allie.'

The personal entreaty cut through. 'Right. Stay where you are. I'll organize a trace on her phone and get a team of uniforms there in ten minutes. Where should they meet you?'

'Right outside the Dominion, I guess,' Rachel said, looking about for any other obvious rendezvous point.

'Good. You coordinate the team and update me every thirty minutes.'

Rachel confirmed the arrangement and Allie thought she sounded fragile. She felt a stab of real worry, for reasons she couldn't even guess at. She phoned headquarters, even though they were only moments away, and organized the team and phone trace and asked that the information be conveyed directly to Strauss in the field. There was no time to waste.

Connors pulled the car into Broadway and down into the Met car park. Allie bounded up the stairs, leaving Connors waiting for the lift. She made straight for DCS Carr's office. She wasn't there and Margaret Daly didn't know where she was.

Allie ran her fingers through her hair and exhaled a long breath. What the hell was going on with people at the moment? First, Connors had done a disappearing act the day before; now, Jacinta and even Carr had done a bunk. There was nothing more she could do other than grab a sandwich from the canteen, then start writing up the incident at Kensington, although God only knew how she was going to explain it and the presence of the 'mysterious black rider'. She smiled at the recollection of his heroics – pretty damn impressive by any standards. But for now the problem of the horrible rat things would have to wait.

She walked to the canteen, grabbed a cup of tea, a 'salmonella roll', as the boys called them, and pinched a *Sun* newspaper from a spare table. Her own face stared out at her again from the newspaper. The headline read: MURDERS STACK UP FOR DCI DOLLY. She nearly threw the paper away. Her phone bleeped again. She checked it and noticed she must have missed an earlier call. She rang the message bank. It was the greasy Everett Blight wanting to know where to send his invoice for photography.

She stopped in mid bite and put the roll down. She played the message again, listening intently. That voice! It was the man she'd spoken to on the train last night. Everett Blight was InCamera Photographics, she was sure of it! She put her phone away and forced herself to take another bite of the roll and think about what she knew to be facts.

Georgie Konstanzo worked at the Black Crow Hotel. Ray Riley met with his band of goons at the Black Crow as well. At least one of Riley's men was familiar with Georgie, according to barmaid Sarah Blascombe. Riley had also been dining at the Golden Bamboo when Georgie was murdered, yet the CCTV showed it was obviously not Ray Riley on the film. Everett Blight had photographed the crime scene at Earl's Court, but had photographed Georgie previously for *Gobber* magazine. Hadn't he realized it was Georgie at Earl's Court? Or was he a terrific actor? Was there a connection between Riley and Blight . . . or Riley, Blight and Paula Armstrong for that matter?

Her thoughts turned to Jacinta Wilkinson. She'd been checking *Gobber* magazine's ownership and also the restaurant strip at Tottenham Court Road, but now she'd gone missing as well. Allie got up from the table and ran to her office. Startled clerks and officers jumped out of her way. She burst into her office's reception area and found Margaret Daly.

'Margaret, do you know what Jacinta found out about *Gobber* magazine, by any chance?' Daly was taken aback by Allie's brusqueness. 'No, no, sorry, she didn't say. But she was on the phone about it, I know that.'

Allie looked around. 'Where's Banks?'

Margaret looked blank. 'I don't know.' Allie smacked her palm on Daly's desk. 'Jesus H. Christ, what's going on here? Is every bastard out to lunch?'

'I'm back now, but thank you for asking.'

Allie spun around to see DCS Carr standing by the door. She turned back to Margaret Daly.

'Find DC Banks for me right now, please, Margaret.' Daly squeaked and scuttled away.

'Problem?' Carr asked, her senses picking up that all was not well, despite her two glasses of Paul Whatshisname's wine over lunch.

'Wilkinson is missing,' Allie said without preamble.

'Since when?' Carr asked.

'About 1:30 p.m.,' Allie replied. 'She's not answering calls and Strauss is very concerned.'

Carr was unimpressed. 'Two and a half hours isn't long. Are you sure you're not overreacting?'

'Yes,' Allie said flatly, turning her attention the returning Daly. 'Where is he?'

Daly looked at Carr, then back at Allie. 'He's coming now. He was in the . . . little boy's room.'

DC Peter Banks galumphed along the corridor towards them, his shirt hanging out of the back of his huge trousers. A little boy he was not.

'Peter,' she said immediately, 'do you happen to know what Jacinta found out about the publisher of *Gobber* magazine?'

Banks smiled and said, 'I wouldn't recommend *Gobber* for you to—'

Allie stepped towards him. '*Just answer the question, Peter!*'

He took an involuntary step back. 'Sorry, yes,' he stammered. 'It was published by err . . . Firebird . . . no, *Firestone* Publishing.'

'Firestone?' Allie repeated the name, looking at DCS Carr. 'Ring any bells to you?' Carr shook her head.

'Yes,' Banks said, managing a more relaxed tone. 'The owner is that Ray Riley guy you warned me off. Thank heavens that—'

'*Riley?*' Allie blurted. Banks took another step back. 'Right,' Allie said to Carr. 'Two people we have to talk to: Ray Riley and Everett Blight.'

'Remind me who Blight is again?' Carr asked Allie.

'He's a photographer. We use him as a freelance when we have to, but more importantly, he's the photographer who not only photographed Georgie Konstanzo's body at Earl's Court for us, but it turns out he had previously taken *gynaecological* shots of her for a *gentleman's* magazine, *Gobber,* which we now know is owned by none other than Diamond Ray Riley.'

Allie paused for breath. 'And get this – Ray Riley and his motley crew meet at the Black Crow Hotel in Chelsea, the pub Georgie worked at.'

Carr paced the floor. 'There are too many coincidences there, for sure. Are there any connections to Paula Armstrong?'

Allie shook her head. 'If there are, I can't see them yet.'

Carr accepted that. 'Who's going to talk to Riley . . . you?'

'It'll have to be, won't it?'

Her phone rang. It was Strauss. 'Any news?' Allie asked, still looking at Carr.

'Yes,' Strauss said, the urgency in her voice magnified over the phone. 'A café owner in Tottenham Court Road remembered Jacinta well. She spoke to her about two hours ago. A dark-haired man, who was dining at the café, asked to speak to Jacinta and they left together.'

'*They left together?* Was there any suggestion of coercion?'

'Not according to this woman from Tippys café. Jacinta and the man left after he paid his bill and they turned left out of the shop. She assumed they were heading further up Tottenham Court Road. We've asked up and down the road and no one recalls a particular man and woman walking or chatting.'

'Did she say anything about his eyes?' Allie suddenly asked.

'Yes, as a matter of fact she did mention them, very unusual for a pale-skinned guy. They were dark – almost black.'

'That's him, Rachel. I can feel it! Paula Armstrong's hairdresser mentioned that Paula Armstrong's new boyfriend had "smouldering Mediterranean eyes".'

A feeling of dread swept over her and she glanced again at Carr, who looked worried as well. Jacinta Wilkinson was in terrible danger. The connection to Paula Armstrong was there, but it wasn't to Blight or Riley. Allie lifted her game a gear.

'It's all hi-fi shops and car phones in that area isn't it?'

'In the immediate area of the theatre, yes,' Strauss affirmed.

Allie thought hard. Images of the area were flooding into her somehow. 'Try down that little street near Bedford Square . . . ummm . . . Morwell Street.' Another image flashed up on a big white screen that just seemed to materialize in her brain. 'No, wait . . . Have you tried the Bo Peep? It's a cute little eatery a bit further up on the corner of Bayley Street and Tottenham Court Road.'

'Yes,' Strauss confirmed. 'I went there myself.'

'Go back,' Allie said. 'There's something there.'

'Pardon? There's something there did you say?'

Allie realized how it must have sounded, but she *knew* Jacinta had been there. 'Humour me,' she said, trying to put smile in her voice. 'Try it again and look hard.'

'Interesting,' Carr said after Strauss had hung up. 'You know the area extraordinarily well.'

'I don't know it all,' Allie replied, walking briskly away toward her office.

Carr, Banks and Daly all looked at each other in puzzlement – a scene which at any other time might have been comical.

The bile rose in Jacinta Wilkinson's throat and slammed against the heavy linen gag. She tried to swallow it for fear the vomit would shoot up the back of her sinuses and block her nose. That would mean certain asphyxiation. She fought against the involuntary gag reflex, her body twisting from side to side in the confined space. Sweat ran down her forehead, stinging her eyes. She swallowed the hot vomit, shuddering as it slid back down, almost retching again, but halting it through sheer willpower.

She breathed heavily through her nose, searching for cold life-giving air, but it was warm and stale and didn't satisfy her heaving lungs. It was dark and unbearably hot in the box. She could only see the merest pinprick of light from what she imagined might be a faulty weld low down in the corner near her face. She kicked against the sides of the box. It was thin steel or tin. Her weld theory would be right, she assumed. A small victory. She knew she was in the boot of his vehicle – the noise was deafening and she felt every contour of the road as the car wove through traffic. She calmed herself and tried harder to regulate her breathing. She thanked God that sniffle she'd felt this morning hadn't turned into a head cold . . . yet. Her hands were tied too tightly behind her back and she felt them going numb. She thought of gangrene and redoubled her efforts to free them. The struggle only made her need for air more urgent and she snorted air through her nose as if it was cocaine.

Her breathing finally slowed enough to allow her to at least begin to listen to the sounds of the street; and to berate herself for being so stupid as to go with him to his car. He'd seemed so reasonable and *genuine*. She'd gone so willingly to the quiet café on the corner – the Bo Peep – and let him buy her coffee. She'd believed him absolutely when he'd said he'd felt so sorry for Paula Armstrong when he'd seen the story in the news and that he'd been so surprised when he saw her photograph to realize he'd seen her on the day of her death.

He'd said he couldn't sleep for worrying about what he'd seen and that he'd been so relieved that coincidence had put Jacinta in the café today. He just knew he had to come forward. *What bullshit!* And she'd fallen for it! She knew why. He was a reasonably good-looking man and he had something interesting about him. She'd *wanted* to believe it was safe to get into his car; it was a Mercedes after all. Well, she was in his Mercedes, all right. She felt the area behind her ear throbbing where he'd hit her with something very hard. Maybe a tyre wrench – she didn't know. Nor did she know how he'd got her into this tin coffin. That thought upset her. Why hadn't she contacted Rachel? She cursed herself again as worry set in. He was going to kill her, just like Paula Armstrong.

Images from the briefing Allie had given stormed back into her consciousness. They were too horrible to contemplate. She pushed them from her mind. She sobbed, but forced herself to stop because her sinuses started to fill immediately. *Please help me, God,* she prayed. She thought of her family and Mr Tomkins, her fat Cheshire cat, and Allie St. Clair. She felt an inner strength at the thought. She prayed for Allie to save her

She felt the car stop. The box slid forward and hit something metallic. She hoped it wasn't a shovel. Maybe stopped at traffic lights? She heard a door open, despite the motor still running. The door slammed with a heavy thunk and she felt the car dip slightly to one side. She heard muffled voices and a laugh. She listened hard as the car accelerated again. Two voices, both male. The words were indistinct, but her ears tuned out the road noise after a while. She deciphered the odd muffled word – particularly from the deeper voice on the passenger side of the car. She heard, or thought she heard, 'tomorrow' and 'rain' and maybe something about 'leadership,' but she couldn't be sure.

Chapter Eighteen

Allie St. Clair rifled through her emails until she found the one from DCS Carr containing Ray Riley's mobile number, then retrieved Everett Blight's number from her phone. It was a question of priorities – *Riley or Blight?* She decided to get DC Banks to locate Blight while she took Riley as arranged with Ellen Carr. She looked out through the glass panels of her office into the main operations area and the desk at which Jacinta Wilkinson normally sat. A cold tremor shook her. She knew Jacinta's chances were slim. A sudden claustrophobic pressure enfolded her lungs. *Good God,* she thought, *surely I'm not having a panic attack?* She rocked back in her chair and tried to take a deep breath. She couldn't. She heard a drumming, droning sound in her head, then a siren – a fire truck? Her breathing eased unexpectedly and she sat forward in her chair, the sounds gone. She shook her head, took a welcome, long breath and looked again to the ops area. Where was Connors? Anger stabbed at her. Had Connors not followed her in to the office an hour ago? Banks appeared in her doorway and knocked politely.

'Sorry about my babbling a bit before, ma'am, I hadn't realized what was at stake. And even if I had . . .'

Allie smiled thinly and told him to forget about it. 'You're up to speed with what's happening now, Pete? You heard me explain to the Super about Riley and Blight, etcetera?'

'Absolutely, ma'am.'

She reached across the desk, handing him Everett Blight's phone number. 'I'd like you to contact him now and ask him to come in to assist us with some questions. Can you do that?'

Banks sat up straighter. 'Of course.'

'Good. Tell him to come here and ask for you. I might be a while getting back, but make him wait, if you know what I mean.'

Banks smiled. 'I know what you mean.'

'Don't give him a drink or a ciggy or tell him why he's here. Direct lots of serious looks at him – you follow?'

'No problem.' Banks was enjoying this. 'When do you think you'll be back?'

'I don't know; it depends how things go with Riley. Do you know where Connors is, by the way?'

Banks shrugged his shoulders. 'No, I don't actually – haven't seen him since this morning.'

Ray Riley had been intrigued to receive a call from the famous DCI Dolly, as he entered it on his phone.

'You obviously read the funny papers, then, Mr Riley,' Allie quipped.

'When you're in them as much as I am, you do take an interest.'

'Mr Riley,' she said pleasantly, 'I wonder if we might catch up for a chat?'

'Certainly,' he said quickly. 'When do you have in mind?'

Allie laughed flirtatiously, even though her skin crawled. '*Now*, actually – if you could possibly make the time?'

Riley asked the obvious question. 'About anything in particular? I have a vast empire, you know,' he said with an equally friendly chuckle, but they were sparring.

'Oh, I know, Mr Riley.'

'Call me Ray, please, Chief Inspector. Listen, if you're at the Met, I'll swing by shortly. Do you know the Feathers Inn? I'll buy you a drink, how's that?'

The Feathers, of all places. Still, it was close and safe, in theory. She consulted her watch; it was 4:45 p.m. It struck her that she hadn't heard back from Strauss after she'd instructed her to revisit the Bo Beep café.

'How about 5:30 p.m., then, at the Feathers, as you suggest?'

'Fine, I look forward to it,' Ray Riley said and rang off. Allie wondered if this was a good idea.

Michael's voice floated across her consciousness. *Great idea. I'll be there.*

She smiled. *Thank you, much appreciated,* she thought back. *This telepathic communication could catch on* she thought. It saved time and money. She'd been wondering what he'd been up to after the

Kensington motorbike dust-up. At least he was around and that was good.

The Feathers Inn was humming. Corporate types spilled out on to the street and the hub from within suggested a big night ahead. Allie loved Friday nights; it seemed like a year since her last session at any pub, but in fact, it had only been a matter of weeks – less if you counted her weird little lunch with Phoebe and Greg. Phoebe! Lord, she hadn't rung her to apologize for the enforced hang up last night.

She skirted the menu board on the street and squirmed her way through a dozen or so men standing in the doorway – none of whom was in any hurry to get out of her way; she was, after all, just the sort of girl they all hoped to chat up. Diamond Ray Riley was in a booth halfway down the left-hand side, opposite the large wooden bar; a large, knobbly hand encircling an untouched pint of beer. He saw her and waved. Someone coughed nearby and she glanced sideways. Michael leaned against the bar, clutching a gigantic dark ale. She recalled his statement the other night that he couldn't or wouldn't drink alcohol. Interesting. She also noticed the man beside him. If she wasn't mistaken, and she rarely was, it was Riley's driver/bodyguard, who she'd noticed at the Black Crow the day before. He even still had his little John Lennon sunglasses on.

Riley stood at her arrival and made to kiss her on the cheek. She stuck out her hand at the end of a very stiff arm. Smiling, he shook it firmly. He waved John Lennon Glasses over and asked Allie what she'd like to drink. She asked for a Pimm's; he ordered a Dewar's single malt on ice to follow his beer. Riley clasped his hands on the dark oak table.

'Your photos don't do you justice, you know.'

'Seeing justice done is becoming rarer these days generally, don't you think?'

Riley laughed. 'Indeed it is. What can I do for you, Chief Inspector? Or may I call you Allison?'

'Only my parents call me Allison, mercifully,' she countered.

'You don't like it?' Riley asked, affecting surprise.

'Whenever I heard "Allison" it was usually accompanied by some kind of rebuke or worse – *advice.*'

'Ah yes, I see what you mean. "Raymond", in my case, was followed by a clip round the ear.'

'You weren't baptized Diamond then?'

Riley slapped the table. 'Now that *is* funny.'

Out of the corner of her eye, Allie saw Michael shake his head and look away.

'Speaking of funny,' Allie said, leaning a little closer to Riley, 'it's funny that you happened to be dining at the Golden Bamboo two nights ago when, right outside, a young girl was brutally murdered.'

The smile left Riley's face. 'You think *that*'s funny?'

'No, of course not,' Allie replied. 'The funny bit is actually that she worked at the Black Crow in Chelsea.'

Riley feigned ignorance well – probably due to a lifetime of practice.

'What's the Black Crow got to do with the price of eggs?'

'C'mon, it's where you meet regularly, *Ray*. And funnier still,' she said, making him wait while she took a slow sip on her Pimm's, 'she appeared in one of your magazines for discerning gentleman, why, just this week!' Allie popped her eyes in mock innocence.

Riley leaned way forward. 'You're very sexy when you do that.'

'What, slip slowly on the Pimm's or pop my eyes?'

'Take your pick.'

'I'll pass on that, but I think you might have taken your pick, Ray. Georgie was a special girl for you, wasn't she?'

Riley rocked back in his seat. 'You're fuckin' joking, aren't you, sister?' All signs of Mister Urbane were replaced by the Brixton street fighter. Allie saw Michael and Lennon Glasses both stand a little taller at the bar. 'What would I want with a scrubber like . . .'

'So you knew her, then?'

Riley wasn't drawn on that one. He smiled and took a sip of his scotch, the first time he'd touched it. Putting it back down on the square coaster he looked back at Allie with a lazy expression.

'Does Ellen Carr know you're talking to me?'

'Of course – her idea, in fact,' Allie said.

'Is that right? Well, well, she must rate you.'

Allie spread her hands on the table. 'Look, Ray, I don't think for a minute that you murdered Georgie Konstanzo; in fact, *I know* you didn't. But let me share something with you.' She leaned in towards him. 'I think someone close to you did.'

This time he was genuinely surprised. 'On what basis do you say that?'

Allie ran through the coincidences, including the Golden Bamboo, the Black Crow and the fact that Georgie posed for his magazines. She left out the bit where she'd been told that one of his men was familiar with Georgie. That would drop the Blascombes right in it. She hoped Riley might volunteer that information.

Riley was thoughtful. 'I read the initial police report on that murder,' he said, putting his hand palm up towards her. 'Never mind how I got it, but I can tell you, none of my boys did this. You have my word on it.'

Allie stared at him. 'I think you actually believe that to be true. But I think you're wrong and I really don't want to drag them all in and talk to them one by one. That would be boring and time consuming for everyone.' She let him stew on that one for a moment. 'Another small thing – you wouldn't happen to know where one of my detectives got to this afternoon?'

'What? One of your detectives . . . what *are* you talking about?'

'The detective in question went missing following up another incident this afternoon at about 12:30 and hasn't been seen since. You don't know anything about that, either?'

Riley smiled. 'Well, we're certainly covering some territory aren't we? If one of your operatives has got himself on to a bit of skirt and disappeared into a cheap hotel for the day, that's your problem. That is, unless he's in one of my establishments, then *he's* the one with the problem!'

Allie noted Riley's use of the word he – it was likely Riley knew nothing about Jacinta's disappearance. But it had been worth asking. Allie sipped her Pimm's and abruptly changed the subject. 'Tell me about Jase Britt.'

Riley was impressed. 'Well done you. That is very early breaking news. How did you know I was managing him? The ink is barely dry on the contract.'

'Word comes out of your organization pretty quickly.' She didn't feel the need to tell him that she'd personally seen him with Britt at the Black Crow. Her comment was a bluff, but it had its effect.

Riley was no poker player; his brow wrinkled with concern at the suggestion there might be a leak in his organization. But he recovered quickly. 'Yeah, right. It's probably already in the music press.'

'Do I take it, then, that you've suddenly got religion? Britt is big in the God-botherers market, as I understand it.'

Riley winked at her. 'I do some things religiously, Chief Inspector, but nothing you want to hear about . . . or do you?'

Allie made a big deal of getting the shivers.

'Well,' Riley said, draining his scotch and standing, 'it's been *interesting*, Chief Inspector St. Clair. You won't be talking to me again about these matters, will you?'

'Only if you ring me with information, and I hope you're a big enough man to do that if your faith in one of your men proved to be misplaced.'

'An interesting approach, I like that. Fair enough, if I believe one of my men is involved in some messy after-school activity, I'll deliver him to you.'

'In one piece, I trust?'

'Oh, I can't promise you *that*.' He smiled and shook her hand. 'It's a nasty world out there, Allison, be careful now.'

Allie smiled her brightest. 'You too, Ray.'

She watched Riley walk away and gesture to his minder, Lennon Glasses, to follow. As he pushed away from the bar to follow, he shoved Michael roughly. Michael pushed him back. Riley's minder stopped and turned back to Michael and said something Allie couldn't quite catch. Michael spoke quietly to him in return. Riley had stopped on his way to the door and was also watching the exchange. He looked over at Allie, shrugged his shoulders and smiled.

The inevitable happened, but not the inevitable Riley anticipated. Lennon Glasses threw a round-arm punch at Michael, then landed on his back at Riley's feet – ten feet from where he'd thrown the punch. It was as fast as that. Riley looked down at his man, then back at Michael, who stood nonchalantly at the bar. They remained staring at each other for perhaps ten seconds. Riley finally glanced at Allie, pointed a finger at Michael and said, 'He one of yours?'

She nodded. 'Everybody's, actually.'

Michael walked the hundred yards from the Feathers to New Scotland Yard with Allie. Commuters gushed in and out of St. James' Park tube station across the street and traffic was at its peak.

'Did you enjoy that little punch-up?' she asked with an impish grin.

'I did, as a matter of fact,' he said, smiling back.

Allie snorted. She looked at her watch and told him she had to interview Everett Blight and then was supposed to scoot around to her parents' home for a quick dinner. She intended coming back to the office afterwards; she wouldn't leave Jacinta hanging out there. Michael nodded and said he recalled her conversation with her mother from the previous night.

Allie stopped near the NSY revolving sign. 'This thing with Jacinta Wilkinson – it's *him* isn't it?'

Michael looked into the middle distance again. 'Yes, it is. I can feel his energy on this and something else . . . I think there's another person involved.'

Allie said, 'I'm sure of it.' She ran her hands through her hair, a sure sign of her frustration. 'Michael, I don't feel I'm doing enough for Jacinta. She might even be dead as we speak, God forbid. But I have nothing other than her last known location.' She looked up at him 'Are you sure there's nothing you can do to help me locate her?'

He shook his head. 'Y*ou* are the one making the running on this, not me. I can protect you until you find the human killers; only then is it up to me to see what I can do. That's how it has always worked.'

Allie looked back at the entrance to New Scotland Yard. 'I understand, disappointing as that is.' There was nothing more to be said on that subject it seemed. 'All right, let's see what tonight brings, then,' she said. 'See you later.'

She negotiated the glass doors of the NSY building and glanced back at Michael, who was still standing where she'd left him. She wondered what security might make of the huge dark-haired man in a long black coat who was pointedly staring at the nation's police headquarters. Best not to think about it, she decided, like so many recent events in her life.

Everett Blight stunk more than she remembered. The thought of drug-addled young girls being photographed naked and possibly fiddled with by this creep was repulsive. She now sat opposite him with Banks beside her, operating the digital recorder. This was an official interview and Allie wanted Blight to sweat, despite the odorous consequences for her and Peter. She let Banks handle the formalities and the initial questioning, until they got to the bit about InCamera Photographics.

'Tell me about this company of yours, Mr Blight. What is its primary purpose?'

Blight folded his arms across his chest. 'Art. It's about the creative side of me. Police photography and weddings are my bread and butter, but I like to let my artsy side free, occasionally.'

Allie nodded thoughtfully. 'Art. I see.' She reached down into her bag, straightened up and threw the issue of *Gobber* magazine across the table at Blight. Banks explained what had been tabled, for the record.

Blight stared at it. 'What's the matter, Mr Blight? Don't you want to touch an image of the dead girl, Georgie Konstanzo, *whom you knew*?'

'I didn't *know* her, not like that!'

'Not like *what* exactly?'

Blight shifted his weight on the seat, his eyes darting about the room. 'You know, I never touched her or anything.'

'Not even while she was high as a kite on her drug of choice?'

Blight laughed unexpectedly. 'Georgie? High? Never! She was much too . . .'

Allie raised her eyebrows. 'Please feel free to explain, Mr Blight. Much too?'

'Sorted,' Blight managed at last. 'Georgie was nobody's fool, I can tell you that. High and mighty she was, too good for any of—'

'Who, Mr Blight?'

'Never mind,' he said, twisting in his chair, his arms now firmly locked across his chest.

Well, well, too good for whom? Allie wondered. A thought struck her. 'Do you drink at the Black Crow in Chelsea, Mr Blight?'

'Occasionally. It's a good pub.'

Allie chanced her luck. 'You'd know Ray and the boys, then?'

Blight didn't answer. She repeated the question.

'Ray?' Blight shrugged.

Allie stood up and shouted at Blight, '*Yes, Ray Riley Mr Blight!* You drink with him and his boys, don't you? That's how you got the job with *Gobber* magazine, isn't it?'

DC Banks squirmed in his seat. Blight jumped and twitched. 'Okay, yes, I do drink with his crew. Everybody there does.'

'So you also knew Georgie as the barmaid. It was your idea to photograph her, wasn't it? What happened – did she knock you back one night? Where was it that you decided she had to die? At the Black Crow, or in your own love nest while you were photographing her . . . *artistically,* of course?'

'I never touched her!' Blight shouted. Allie could see the air around him was bright blue. He was telling the truth. He was no murderer and besides, they had the CCTV footage to prove it. Still, a good scare might flush something out.

There was no stopping Blight. 'Georgie would never look at someone like me. She could be very rude and what is it . . . *condescending,* if you were of no value to her. When I photographed her, she loved the camera, that's for sure. It was her ticket to fame, but I could have been a block of stone for all she noticed. Me and Georgie? Not in a million fucking years!'

Allie sat back in her chair, letting a silence develop. 'So,' she said at last, 'Georgie and who then? Ray Riley, Terry Burdon? Suppose you tell me.'

Blight looked even more edgy. 'I never saw her with any of Riley's crew. Big Joe pinched her arse once, and the next night she threw a beer all over him. He thought he was well in at first, but she could be a right bitch. Even the customers complained about her, according to Rabbit.'

'Ah yes,' Allie said, 'Mr Blascombe. Was *he* interested in her?'

Blight laughed. 'Not bloody likely. His virginal daughter with the big tits – sorry – keeps her eye well on him. Besides, he's not really the type. Bit of a family man is Rabbit.'

Banks looked at Allie questioningly. *He's right,* she thought, *this isn't going anywhere productive.* 'All right, Mr Blight,' Allie said, looking at the curiously old-fashioned clock on the wall above him, 'we'll leave it there at 7:12 p.m.'

Banks turned the recorder off. Blight asked if he was free to go.

'Yes, of course. Thank you for coming in at such short notice,' Allie said. Blight smiled and bobbed his head. 'Oh, one thing before you go, Mr Blight – when did you realize it was Georgie you were photographing at Earl's Court?

Blight's eyes misted over. 'Not until the following day, after you visited the crime scene with your big friend. I checked the photos on my camera and saw the little dolphin tattoo on her ankle. I didn't know before that – how could I? She was so—' he searched for the word, '—*butchered!*'

Allie returned to her office. It was time, in theory, to duck around to her parents' home for dinner, but Jacinta Wilkinson was her priority. She rang her mother and begged off. Her mother was predictably miffed, but it couldn't be helped.

She decided to ring Strauss and find out why she hadn't called in after visiting the Bo Peep café in Camden. After four rings, Strauss picked up her phone. A cacophony of sound bombarded Allie. It was the sound of a pub in full swing – live music, swearing, the works. Strauss was yelling into the phone, but Allie decided not to say anything and wait until Rachel saw who was on the line and found a quiet spot. It took a long time, but finally, Strauss's voice was audible and slurred – she was three sheets to the wind.

'Rachel? This is Allie St. Clair. Can you hear me?'

'Yep!'

'Rachel, I assume your visit to the Bo Beep Café wasn't productive?'

For a moment there was no reply. Then, 'Yes, sorry, Al . . . ma'am. We did find Jacinta's handbag, it was in the toilet, still on the bench. Can you believe that?'

'Why the hell didn't you let me know?'

Rachel was sobering up fast. 'Connors took it and said he'd advise you and give the bag back to Jacinta.'

'Connors? What was he doing out there?'

'You sent him to help coordinate the search for Jacinta, even though you'd told me *I* was in charge.' The rebuke from Strauss was obvious.

Allie couldn't mask her anger and confusion. 'Rachel, let's be clear – I did *not* send Connors to help you. The search out there was *your* operation. It still is, for God's sake!'

'But Jacinta was found safe and sound, ma'am,' Strauss said, panic rising in her voice. 'Wasn't she?'

Jacinta heard rain splatter on the boot-lid of the car. The air inside her box was hot now, but enough air seemed to get in. She'd heard nothing of the two men since the car stopped a long time ago, maybe an hour. She'd heard them both get out and slam their doors, but no footsteps. Tears moistened her eyes again, but she blinked them away, still terrified of her nose blocking up. Her throat definitely had a prickle in the back of it now.

What are they going to do with me? Where are Allie and my colleagues? Can't they track my phone? My phone! Of course, she didn't have it; otherwise, it would have rung. *What have they done with it? Have they kept it, but turned it off?* She could feel blood still trickling into her mouth from behind her ear. It should have stopped bleeding by now.

She wondered what time it was. She had no idea how long she'd been out, but she'd been able to see light before, of course. There was an odd smell in the car, like rotten vegetables, and it was getting stronger. A door slammed somewhere away from the car. She held her breath and listened. She heard a footstep, then another.

Both doors opened and the car bounced and dipped as two people got in. She heard the deeper voice ask how long the journey would take. The engine started, but she thought the muffled reply was, 'About three hours,' and then something about the rain. The car lurched and the gears crunched. She'd decided earlier he wasn't a good driver. Even though it was a Mercedes Benz, it was old – maybe 1960s. The car bounced and stopped. She heard the beeping of a pedestrian crossing and then a loud voice, someone outside on the street, and then more raised voices – Jamaicans, lots of them. She heard someone say something about hippies. She guessed she was in Notting Hill; a Jamaican stronghold for years. The car moved off, the thrumming of the tyres on the road drowning out the conversation from the front. Jacinta groaned. Three hours . . . to where?

*

Allie quickly dialled Jacinta Wilkinson's mobile phone number. If she was safe, why hadn't she been in contact? The number went straight to the message bank. She left a message for her. She then rang Mathew Connors' phone number. He answered immediately. She could hear a motor running and a hissing in the background.

'DC Connors, this is Chief Inspector St. Clair.' It was ridiculously formal, but the situation called for it and who knew where this was leading?

'Oh . . . yes, Ins . . . you?' The phone connection was terrible.

'Mathew, where are you?'

Static replied, then, 'Driving . . . able.'

'Mathew, I need you to pull over! I have to talk to you about this afternoon – *urgently.*'

The phone fell silent. 'Mathew?' The connection was dead. She punched in his phone number again, but it went straight to his message bank. 'Damn,' she said, barely managing to stay on the line to record a message for him to call back straightaway.

She threw her phone down on her desk and slumped forward in her chair, her elbows on the table. She rubbed her face hard. She was getting nowhere, fast. She couldn't sit any longer. Jumping up and flicking off her office lights, she strode to the window and stared out across the commercial zone, towards Westminster Abbey and the Houses of Parliament. It was raining hard. She could see a sheen of water coating Victoria Street and further on, Big Ben's clock face was smudged just enough by the horizontal rain to make it unreadable.

Standing in the dark, Jacinta's pain and desperation were palpable. Jacinta wasn't safe; Allie knew it with certainty. Someone, presumably Connors, had fed misinformation to Strauss about that. She'd flirted with the idea of putting out an alert to pick up Connors; but it would've been an overreaction. Something new was happening. 'Speak to me, Jacinta,' she pleaded aloud. Lightning lit up the city like a film set and the rain hurled itself at her window, running down in thick sheets, melting the symmetry of the cityscape into a crazy parody.

She stared defiantly at the rain, her face barely three inches from the cold glass. She was thinking so hard her brain hurt. Two horrible murders and Jacinta abducted, all in three days. And all she had were circumstantial links, at best, to Diamond Ray Riley. It wasn't enough.

The media was on it and she suspected Superintendent Carr was copping all sorts of grief from above. She was missing something. She punched at the window in frustration. The 'third day' played on her mind. *He rose again on the third day.* The number three had been sprayed all over Paula, then Jacinta abducted on the third day. But so what? Apart from the obvious biblical overtones, and she understood why that was, it made no sense. But there must be something in it. She'd been drawn into a game – Michael had made her aware of that. So, in this game, what were the rules?

Sharp hunger intruded on her thoughts, as it always did about six hours after her last meal. The metabolism that kept her so lean was also an inconvenience. If she didn't eat soon, her blood sugar would tumble and she'd be no use to Jacinta.

The menu at the Black Crow invaded her thoughts. She had to do something; standing in her office pontificating while Jacinta Wilkinson was in mortal danger wasn't an option. The Black Crow and its patrons were at the heart of this, she was sure. How it connected to Paula Armstrong, she couldn't yet see, but it was there. She pictured Michael in her mind's eye. *See you at the Black Crow in thirty minutes?*

Chapter Nineteen

The Crow was jumping. The four-piece band in the corner by the door rocked out a solid groove and Allie had to fight her way in through the door. A hand landed on her shoulder. She steeled herself for the inevitable slurred proposition. But it was Michael. He stood a good head above even the tallest in the crowd. He was hardly inconspicuous. She saw he still wore the long black coat, but had changed his shirt and jeans. She wondered where he had access to clothes.

'Stores in London sell them, you know,' he said with a smile.

'Can we eat?' she asked, pointing to where she knew the tables to be. He nodded and fell in behind her as she picked her way through the eclectic, gyrating crowd. Nobody bothered her on the journey to the lounge area and she reflected that it would be nice to have a permanent bodyguard who filled a doorway so adequately.

Miraculously, a couple got up from a little round wooden table as they approached. Grasping the back of the chair, she cocked an enquiring eyebrow at Michael.

'Nothing to do with me, just luck!' he laughed.

They chose their meals from the little laminated table menu, with Michael insisting there be hot chips involved. Allie pointed to the bar. 'You order over there,' she shouted over the band which had launched into their distorted version of Fleetwood Mac's *Rhiannon*.

He looked over at the four-deep crowd and winced. 'Don't they come to you?' he asked, his voice carrying to her easily despite the noise.

She just shook her head. 'This isn't Chez Nous, Michael.' He scowled and turned back to the bar. She wondered why they'd been shouting; he could read her thoughts anyway. She studied the crowd to her left, with half an eye out for Ray Riley's crew. She had to eat so it might as well be where she could possibly help Jacinta, she reassured herself.

'Well, well. DCI St. Clair!'

Allie turned to see Rachel Strauss swaying slightly against a young curly-haired guy, whom she immediately recognized as the one from Shepherd's Bush. She groaned. *Oh, Rachel.*

'Chief . . . *Allie*, do you remember Jeremy Watts?' Rachel asked, defiance radiating from her.

'Yes, of course.' Allie smiled as warmly as she could under the circumstances. She looked at Rachel. Despite the cold weather and the driving rain, she had on a very low-cut lightweight sleeveless black top and tight white stretchy jeans. She was out to get laid. Allie was in no doubt about that, nor, she suspected, were the two hundred other patrons of the Black Crow.

'Can I get you a drink?' Jeremy offered, seeing that Allie was sitting alone at the table.

'She's okay on that score,' Michael boomed as he came up behind them. Rachel and Jeremy openly gawped at him.

Rachel flushed bright red and said, 'Holy crap,' a little too loudly, as she took in the size and looks of the huge arrival. She looked open-mouthed at Allie.

'Where did you find *him*?'

Allie was surprised at how annoyed she was at Rachel's appalling manners, but that was countered by the tingle of pleasure she felt at Rachel's public acknowledgement of Michael's good looks. Rachel stuck out her hand toward Michael. 'Rachel Strauss. And you are?' Michael indicated the drinks he was carrying and apologized for not shaking hands. He nodded at Jeremy. Allie noticed Michael didn't introduce himself. This was awkward and just the type of thing she'd hoped to avoid. Mercifully, there were only two chairs.

'I had no idea that this was the pub you were in when I phoned earlier, Rachel.'

Rachel flapped a hand at her. 'No problem. I thought it looked okay when we . . .'

Allie was pleased Rachel had enough brain cells intact not to mention that she'd been here on official business. Plus, she figured, she'd probably seen the look on her face. 'Yes, it has a nice feel to it,' she lied. She still felt there was a darkness about it.

Rachel looked from Allie to Michael, then back again, obviously still waiting for an introduction.

'Sorry to bring up business, Rachel, but just quickly, who told you Jacinta was safe?'

The sound from the band drowned her out. Rachel held up her hands in a helpless gesture and smiled ruefully. It was no use; the volume had doubled. Rachel waved a full-on bye-bye at Michael and waved backhandedly at Allie as she and Jeremy turned for the dance floor. Apparently, the old standard *Nutbush City Limits* was too hard to resist. Jeremy smiled and looked again at Michael before following the hip-swinging Rachel to the dance floor.

'God,' Allie said to Michael, 'she'll be all over him like maggots on a carcass later on.'

'Nice analogy,' he acknowledged. 'But she'll be wasting her time.'

Allie frowned. 'Why do you say that?'

Michael took a swig of his lemon, lime and bitters. 'Gay as a Mardi Gras, that boy.'

Allie guffawed. 'You reckon?'

Michael nodded. 'Definitely.'

Allie shook her head in wonder, a small smile twitching her mouth. So Rachel had been wrong about young Jeremy after all. She was in for a disappointing evening. Allie looked round as the meals arrived. The waitress was Sarah Blascombe.

'Oh, hello,' Sarah said hesitantly, also looking at Michael. 'Out for a good time?'

'Hi, Sarah. No, not really, but one has to eat.'

Sarah smiled, lighting up her pleasant face. 'I guess one does.'

Allie said awkwardly, 'So how are you coping, staff wise, I mean?' She cursed inwardly at posing such a lame question.

Sarah straightened from delivering the meals and smoothed her skirt. 'Not too bad, a couple of my friends have rocked up to help.' She pointed to the kitchen. 'They're in there frying chips like there's no tomorrow.'

'Michael will be glad to hear that.' Allie smiled. Sarah looked directly at Michael and tucked a stray lock of hair back behind her ear. Allie decided to go for it. 'May I ask you a question?'

Sarah looked quickly about the room. 'I guess so, umm, we'll need to be quick.'

'Of course, 'Allie said, taken slightly by surprise and looking at Michael. 'Let's find a quiet corner.'

'No need,' Michael volunteered. 'I'll just duck to the tube.'

'The loo,' Allie corrected.

'Yes, *the loo*. Must have had one too many soda waters.' He laughed, quickly pivoted out of his chair and headed for the corner of the room.

'He's nice,' Sarah said, watching him leave. 'He's big, too.'

Allie didn't quite know how to answer that. 'Have a seat, Sarah. Tell me, have you seen anything more of Ray Riley and his lot in the last day or so?'

Sarah rolled her eyes theatrically. 'I think they've seen more of *me*, actually.'

'How do you mean?'

Sarah pointed at her uniform. 'These bloody things we have to wear are so tight and short – his men nearly have an org . . . er . . . a *convulsion* when I bring them their food.'

Allie nodded. 'I'll bet. Your *dad* makes you wear it?'

'Yep, says if I want to work here, I have to. He hates it of course, but it's good for business, apparently.'

'Hmmm, depends what type of business you're after. I think maybe you're getting it though, don't you?' Allie said with a wry smile.

Sarah looked embarrassed. 'Georgie looked better in this gear than me, and Jane, who works on Saturday nights, has her own band of followers – special T-shirts and all. It's amazing really.'

'Riley's men are real creeps then, are they?' Allie redirected.

'You said it. Mr Riley's actually not that bad. But the rest of them . . .' She shivered.

'It goes with the territory,' Allie said, taking a sizeable bite out of the shepherd's pie.

'Funny thing, though,' Sarah said. 'One of them isn't like that, but then I didn't know he was actually *one of them* until yesterday.'

'Come again?' Allie said, a jolt of electricity running through her.

'Old Arthur comes in every Wednesday night by himself at exactly the same time and has exactly the same meal and a pint of Young's, then toddles off to catch a bus, I think. He's been coming in for years.'

Allie cast a thoughtful look at Sarah. 'But you said he's one of Riley's men?'

'Well, he must be. I saw him talking to the group and writing on the whiteboard. But funny, though, he looked *different*.'

Michael arrived right on cue, standing by Sarah's chair. Irrationally, Allie thought he could probably see down Sarah's blouse. She shot him a look.

'How was he different, exactly, Sarah?'

'Well, you'll think I'm crackers, but he seemed younger and *taller* than he was even the day before! He even had more hair, but I'm sure it was him!'

Allie sat back in her chair. 'He was here Wednesday night?'

'Oh yes, as usual.'

'But you're saying you saw him here last night, Thursday, as well, yes?'

Sarah shifted uncomfortably on the chair. 'Yes, upstairs. It was about seven o'clock, I think. I've never seen him with that lot upstairs before.'

Allie glanced quickly at Michael. He was staring intently at Sarah.

'Sarah,' Allie said, levelling her hand at her, 'think hard now; what was he writing on the whiteboard?'

'Numbers, just numbers, like pound amounts in columns. I think he was saying something about "returns".'

'Returns?' Allie echoed. 'Like investment returns?'

'I don't know.' Sarah shrugged. 'Sorry. I'd better go,' she said, looking anxiously towards the bar.

'What's this Arthur character's last name?'

'Gosh!' Sarah said. 'You know, I've never asked him!'

'Do you think you could quickly ask your dad if he knows?'

'Of course, I'll just be a moment.' Allie thanked her and Michael nodded as Sarah gave him her broadest grin and sashayed away; at least that was how Allie saw it.

Allie and Michael looked at each other, but neither spoke. Sarah flounced back to their table a minute later. 'Wendell,' she announced proudly. 'Dad says it's Arthur Wendell. He's an accountant or something.'

Allie physically jumped. It fit what they knew about Paula Armstrong's new boyfriend. Some sort of advisor, someone had said. An accountant could be it.

Sarah departed for the kitchen after bestowing another blinding smile on Michael. 'I suppose you get that all the time?' Allie said in mock exasperation.

'Pretty much.' He tucked into his rapidly cooling chips, but not before smothering them in salt.

'Let's get out of here and go somewhere where I can hear myself think,' Allie said, pushing her chair from the table and standing. Michael poked another wad of chips into his mouth and followed. Outside the Black Crow there was the usual band of intrepid smokers and silly young girls milling around. At least in Chelsea, the girls wore expensive shoes and talked complete rubbish in cultured tones. The rain had stopped, but the gutters were swollen and the streets were a shiny black.

'Where's your car?' Michael asked.

'I didn't bother with a pool car,' Allie said a little defensively. 'I grabbed a taxi.'

Fishing her phone out of her bag, she told Michael she was googling Wendell.

'I'd like one of those,' Michael said. 'My old Motorola is a bit limited.'

But Allie wasn't listening. The first Wendell that came up on her search was a used car dealer in Kent. She specified Chelsea. Nothing came up. She tried Earl's Court. No result.

'Some big-time accountant,' she mumbled. 'Not even bloody listed. I'll have to ring headquarters.'

She dialled the first three digits, but stopped herself. Something Jasmine the androgynous hairdresser had said about Paula Armstrong niggled at her. Whomever Paula met with, it was important that she do so *at this time,* Jasmine had said.

Allie turned to Michael. 'What could be so important to Paula that she had to see an accountant *at this time?*

'You're asking me?' Michael asked.

'Aaargh.' Allie grumbled. 'I forget you're not of this world. How nice it must be not to have to worry about doing the laundry, buying food and doing your . . .'

She grabbed him by the arms. '*Doing your tax return!* Michael, its April – that's tax time in the UK! *That's* what Paula had to do *at this time!* Wendell is a sodding tax consultant!'

She punched at her phone again. This time Arthur Wendell came up as a tax consultant under the name of BizTax Ltd. Allie staggered back a pace. 'Michael, BizTax is the name I saw on Paula Armstrong's files when Connors and I went there today! I remember it because Connors was super-impressed by how much she earned!'

She studied the phone again. 'His office is listed as being in Earl's Court, but I'd say that's not far at all from here or from King's Lane, where Georgie was murdered. Michael, we're right on top of him!'

Michael nodded coolly and looked about. Allie saw him search the rooftops across the street.

'What?'

'Don't leave my side now, Allie, whatever you do.'

'Why now?' she asked, already suspecting she knew the answer.

'He'll come for you now.'

'Well, good!' she shouted. 'Let's have him then! So long as he comes to the party with Jacinta in tow, that's fine by me!'

He surprised her by smiling. 'Them's fightin' words, Ms St. Clair, but it ain't that simple.' He put his arm around her shoulders and walked her down the narrow lane beside the Black Crow. She felt the strength of his grip and the brick-hardness of his huge upper body.

'He'll come for you only when he's ready and it will be in his own peculiar way. It might be in twenty seconds or two days, but he's not going to give up your colleague in the meantime. To save her, you'll have to find her.'

She broke free of his grip and spun around to face him. 'It's been bugging me that you seem to know how he thinks, Michael. Why is that exactly?'

'We have time to debate this?' he asked, raising his voice. 'I would have thought your Jacinta's safety was paramount. Time's awastin', girl!'

Allie planted her hands on her hips. 'Michael, I'd better not be part of some damn game.'

Michael threw his hands in the air opening them to the heavens. 'We're all part of The Game, Allie – *that's all there is!*'

'What do you mean, "that's all there is"?'

Michael shook his head slowly and sighed. 'Look, it's not for you to worry about now. You're going to have to trust me. The Game is not what you probably think, but I'll tell you this, seeing as you're slow to catch on . . .'

She stared defiantly at him. A big saloon car came slowly by, a concerned look on the face of the blonde woman who stared at them from the passenger seat. Michael took her by the shoulders. 'I cannot rid the place of Belhor without you and you cannot even think about saving Jacinta or bringing this Arthur Wendell to justice without my protection.'

'I know that.'

'The rest, as the man said, will just have to wait.' He released her shoulders.

'*That's it*?'

'For now, yes.' Michael shrugged. 'Are we gonna catch the bad guys now or what?'

'Are you okay, dear?' The shrill voice came from the woman she'd noticed a moment ago in the passing car.

Allie stepped away from Michael and smiled at the woman. 'Yes, all good, but thank you!' Allie waved and the woman rolled up her window as the car accelerated away. Allie looked at Michael. Time was up. The rain came again.

Ten minutes later, Allie had received intelligence to suggest Wendell lived in Notting Hill. She authorized an assault team to apprehend him and, hopefully, find Jacinta. She advised that she'd go to Wendell's Earl's Court office address, seeing as she was nearby. She rang Ellen Carr and apprised her of developments.

Carr had been excited, but not as much as she should have been. Allie felt something else was preying on her mind. She looked again at the results of her Internet search. It had a phone number for BizTax Ltd. She rang it. The answering machine message said, 'Hello, thanks for phoning BizTax Limited. I'm Arthur Wendell. I am unable to come to the phone, so please leave your name . . .' It cut off before the message ended and she heard the beeps indicating recording had begun.

She hung up. At least she'd heard his voice. It struck her as totally innocuous – thin, slightly nasal and harmless. It told her nothing. Remembering Connors, she rang his number. There was still no answer. She hissed in frustration. There was no point ringing Strauss, she decided; she was in no shape to return to work.

Michael stood outside as Allie made her calls from a back room in the Black Crow, the misty rain beading on his woollen coat. Allie emerged from the hotel and spotted him. 'Do you have your bike nearby?' she asked.

He pointed further down the lane. 'Probably a hundred yards away.'

The ride to Earl's Court took just three wet minutes. They could have walked it. Allie clung to the tinier-than-they-should-have-been handgrips on the giant motorbike and was drenched before they reached Fulham Road. It struck her during the short journey that Georgie's murder, Ray Riley, and Arthur Wendell all had connections to the general Earl's Court/Kensington-Chelsea area. Paula Armstrong had been murdered in Camden, technically, but lived in Kensington; Ray Riley lived and operated around Chelsea. She recalled with a flinch that Billy McBride last drew breath in the Chelsea Hospital. It had all revolved around Arthur Wendell, his favourite boozer and his well-heeled local clientele.

According to the plastic plaque on the wall of the three-storey building, the BizTax office was on the first floor. The street door was locked of course. Michael merely turned the handle and pushed. The door sprang open, splinters of dark wood littering the linoleum-covered floor. They listened for a moment, but there was no sound from above. Allie placed her feet carefully upon each stair until she realized Michael was tramping about like a rhinoceros. Abandoning stealth, she found the appropriately branded glass-panelled door. It was locked. Michael opened it. A pattern was developing. She felt for the light switch and turned it on. They were standing in a shabby reception area. Two pale-yellow vinyl-covered chairs and a veneered coffee table, with three dog-eared magazines strewn on it, filled the tiny room.

They moved through to what had to be Arthur's office. Not unexpectedly for an accountant-type, rows of neatly stacked and labelled upright grey files lined tall wooden bookshelves. The central piece of the room was a huge battleship-grey steel desk. On it was a white phone, a desk blotter and a round glass paperweight.

One low plastic chair, presumably for clients, sat expectantly in front of the imposing desk, above which a light bulb hung from a long twisted cord. No photographs were featured in the office, save for a silver-framed photo of a blue Mercedes saloon parked outside a suburban apartment block, presumably Wendell's Notting Hill home.

Allie snapped a picture on her phone. What was surprising was the funny little collection of gizmos – battery-operated gadgets – lining the window ledge, filing cabinet tops and desk. They looked like the type of thing you'd expect to get for free from *Geek Monthly*. Allie noticed a neat stack of *Home Electronics* magazines on a low shelf. That explained it. She started as the grubby venetian blinds flapped loudly in response to a sudden wind. The window was open just an inch.

Allie moved to the bookshelves and immediately found Paula Armstrong's file, second along the top row after Armitage. She quickly scanned the other names, seeing Riley on one and making a mental note to revisit that sometime in the future. The rest of the names meant nothing to her. Opening the Armstrong file, she saw a wad of papers concerning Paula's latest tax return. April 4th was stamped on the first page; that was yesterday. She glanced up; Michael was looking right and left out of the window on to Hogarth Road. Opening the top drawer of the desk, she found Wendell's leather-clad appointments' diary, Paula's name clearly marked for 10:00 a.m. the day before. She was disappointed to see there was no record of a lunch venue. There were still ends to be tied up. She looked at her watch, wondering whether the assault team was hitting Wendell's residence.

Michael spoke for the first time since they had entered the offices. 'You don't expect the assault team to find anything, do you?'

'At Notting Hill? No. He'll be holding Jacinta somewhere else, if he hasn't already . . .' She let the inference hang. Michael didn't respond. He sat in the client's chair, or at least tried to. It was too small for him. He levered himself up again and pulled a face at Allie. 'His clients must have been midgets.'

'Mental midgets anyway,' she responded. 'Although Paula Armstrong was no dummy.'

'Look at this,' Michael said, holding out a folded cardboard brochure. 'It was in this waste basket,' he said, pointing behind the desk. Allie came around to the corner of the desk and took it from him. She opened it and stiffened.

'This is a gift voucher. There's a handwritten note that says "Enjoy the show, Arthur. You'll be seeing plenty of this guy!" It's signed Ray.'

'The obvious question is, what show?' Michael asked.

'One way to find out,' Allie said, reaching for her phone.

Ray Riley answered on the second ring. Allie heard the sound of a motor running and windscreen wiper blades thumping. 'Chief Inspector!' he said enthusiastically. 'What a nice surprise. Don't tell me you'd like to have a late dinner?'

'Nothing like that,' Allie said abruptly. 'Tell me, what show did you give Arthur Wendell tickets to?'

'Arthur Wendell? Don't know the man. Why—'

'Ray, there's no time for this, a woman's life is at stake. What show? Come on now!'

Riley got the message. 'Can't you guess? Who's the biggest new Christian talent going around at the moment? You know the answer, Allison.'

She smacked her forehead. 'Jase Britt,' she said. 'Of course! When's the show?'

'What's this all about?' Riley asked, his manner hardening. 'What's Arthur Wendell got to do with anything? And how do you know about the tickets?'

'I'm in his office now, Ray. We're looking for him. *When is the show?*'

'He'll be on his way to it now. He assured me he was going, despite his initial reservations about Jase. It's tonight at midnight. Surely you've read all the hype about the spooky midnight spiritual show he's putting on?'

'*Where is it, for Christ's sake?*'

'Okay, okay, take it easy. It's at the festival. Jase is the star turn.'

'The festival?' No bells rang for her.

'Jesus, you coppers need to get out more,' Riley snarled. 'I'm talking about the world's most famous festival. *Glastonbury.*'

It was 9:00 p.m.

She spent frantic minutes on the phone. Firstly, the assault team from Notting Hill reported that no one was home and nothing was out of the ordinary at Wendell's apartment. In fact, the young sergeant had said, it was, 'Well-ordered and clean.' There'd been no evidence linking Arthur Wendell to any crime, but there was a photo of him and a woman at what appeared to be a business function. Allie asked that the photo be emailed to her as soon as possible.

'No surprises there,' Allie said to Michael as she hung up and dialled again. This time she rang headquarters and asked that a helicopter be made ready. The transport operator just laughed. Flying in this weather *for any reason* was out of the question.

Allie phoned Superintendent Carr and briefed her on the situation. They agreed that Carr would alert Avon and Glastonbury police and send them a photo of Wendell and one of DC Jacinta Wilkinson. Allie undertook to forward her a picture of the blue Mercedes for distribution as well.

'I'll get down there as fast as I can,' Allie said to Carr.

'What? To Glastonbury? It's at least three hours, Allie,' she said. Then hesitantly added, 'We went to the festival last year, it was a nightmare getting there.'

'Well, ma'am, the traffic will be thinner at night and I'll just have to try. Jacinta is more than likely with this nutbag, so there's no choice.'

'Leave it to the locals and the festival police; they'll handle it,' Carr countered.

'Can't do that, ma'am. They don't know what they're dealing with. I'll phone you as soon as I can.' With that, Allie hung up.

'Got any spare leathers at home?' Michel said, walking towards the door.

They pulled out from her Putney home at 9:27 p.m. Michael had refuelled the Triumph while Allie had dried herself and changed. As Allie had mounted the bike, he'd simply said, 'We'll be there in ninety minutes. Hang on.' Allie remembered her own tumble on the wet street just two nights ago, but said nothing. This was going to be a wild ride. It was clear from the moment they blistered out on to Lower Richmond Road, heading south-west, that Michael wasn't going to worry about speed limits, other cars, pedestrians or road rules of any kind. Allie knew it was about a hundred miles to Glastonbury, she'd done the trip with her family many times as a child, but it had indeed taken three hours *or more* each time.

They whistled over the culvert bridge at the Marc Bolan Shrine near Putney Common at a hundred miles per hour, the wet road and fierce rain not bothering Michael at all.

I liked Marc Bolan, Michael's relaxed voice boomed in her head.

Never heard of him,' Allie thought back at him.

What, never heard of T-Rex?

Just kidding. Of course, I have. Get it On, *right?*

Correct. You have restored my faith. You know this was once a Roman road?

Are you my spiritual guide and travel guide now?

Someone has to teach you these things.

In fact, I did know that. My dad mentioned it every time we came down here. It's only thought to have been a Roman road, if you want to get pedantic.

It was *a Roman road, Allie – I know. I told your father that, but he won't believe it until he digs it up for himself. And where you live was mostly swamp, but there was a garrison there at one time. They'll discover all sorts of Roman artefacts around the area as soon as they start the big sewerage tunnel project.* Michael's comments about the tunnel were largely lost as the shock hit her again that Michael knew her father, quite well it seemed. She'd missed her opportunity to quiz him over dinner this evening, but she'd get back to it!

Nothing more was said as they thundered through Richmond, en route to Sunbury-on-Thames and the A3 motorway. The rain assaulted them. Each time Allie peered round from behind Michael at the road ahead, bullets of rain peppered her helmet. She wondered how he could possibly see.

I can't.

She kept her thoughts to a minimum for the next half hour. They hit the motorway just past Sunbury and Michael accelerated to maximum speed. The Triumph Rocket III lived up to its name. It was frighteningly quick in a straight line, rain or no rain. Allie prized her left hand from Michael's waist and sneaked a quick look at her watch. They'd made amazing progress, seventy miles in one hour.

There's a significant site on our right, Michael. It was her turn to play I Spy.

He could see nothing and said so.

Aha! And you call yourself a motorcycle man!

Among other things, yes. Okay, I give up . . .?

We just passed the Thruxton Circuit. Don't tell me you never heard of the Triumph Thruxton motorcycle?

Well, well, Michael responded, *I wondered why my old Triumph was called a Thruxton.*

'Rubbish!' Allie squealed. 'You never had one of those!'

Michael paused. *All right, I never had one, but I'll tell you what I do have.*

What?

About twenty motorcycles on an interception course about two miles ahead.

Allie leaned to the left. She saw a line of very fast moving lights just off to their left. There was no question, they would definitely cut across their bow.

Oh no, she groaned. *Ducatis again?*

Yep, more rats. They're taking their orders from him now. Can you hear them chattering?

Arthur Wendell heard Mr Black laugh in his head and wondered why. *Well, I'll tell you, good buddy,* Mr Black said. *About thirty miles behind us, an old friend of mine is about to meet a phalanx of the nastiest rodents I know.*

Arthur looked at his travelling companion, wondering whether he was picking up the voice as well. 'It's okay,' the man in the passenger seat said, nodding. 'I can hear him too.'

'How does this concern me?' Arthur asked his unseen mentor, his eyes firmly fixed on the wet road.

It concerns you, Arthur, because hi⁻ pillion passenger is none other than that tasty DCI St. Clair. They're coming for us, shipmate!

'Holy shit!' Arthur yelled, pulling the car dangerously to the left into long grass.

Arthur's passenger covered his face, obviously expecting the car to plough into some unseen obstacle. Arthur recovered the car from the wet grassy verge and straightened it on the road just as a car flashed past travelling in the opposite direction.

Arthur, the voice said, *you didn't think this was all a free ride, did you? I mean, there are consequences to be borne!*

'Consequences?'

Of course! You know that stuff about 'for every action there's an equal and opposite reaction'? It's physics, man. You can't mess with that!

Arthur broke into a sweat. 'Meaning?'

Well, you killed people, so people are going to try and kill you! An eye for an eye and all that, it's only fair! I must admit, I agree with the Bible on that one.

Arthur looked in his rear-view mirror; he could see nothing. 'These rats of yours,' he said, 'what can they do against your old friend?'

Kill him, I hope! Here in this space and time is the only place I can really get him. Thanks to you, Arthur, and that St. Clair bitch for letting me know where they are, I'm about to change the nature of the universe! I probably owe you a drink.

*

The big Triumph howled down the highway like an oncoming tornado, the pan-flat Salisbury Plain now a blur. 'Are you going to try and beat them to the intersection?' Allie asked, looking back and forth from the motorcycles to the road junction. It would be horribly close.

'It's all we can do. If we don't, it could get messy.' Stopping wasn't an option, so they went for it. It got messy.

The Ducati riders beat them by a second to the point where the A303 intersected Countess Road. A huge silver milk tanker, ablaze with lights, also arrived from the north. Neither Michael nor Allie had seen it coming; their attention had been on the riders.

The Ducati rats lay their bikes down at high speed; slithering, scraping and cartwheeling across the intersection in a screaming barrier of bodies and metal. Hitting the big disk brakes of the Rocket III, Michael threw it into a sideways drift. Red machines, some upright, some at crazy angles, flew at them, missing by inches. Allie felt Michael absorb some type of impact and pieces of metal tore at her jacket. Fragments of fibreglass, leather and body parts whirled through the air as time slowed. A fine, blood-red mist sprayed her helmet's visor. More motorbikes hurtled at them. Inexplicably, the tanker also rolled across the intersection and stopped, blocking the road ahead. Motorcycle wheels, exhaust pipes, and broken fittings pinged off the road and the sides of the battered Triumph in a shower of sparks and chrome.

'Hold tight!' Michael yelled.

He leaned the bike down on its right side and slid t under the stationary tanker. Allie's helmet clanged against low-hanging metal and the road tore at her right leg, but she hung on. Sparks from the bike lit up the night as they emerged on the far side of the truck. Somehow, Michael stood the bike up again. Allie knew it was a feat of impossible strength.

The impact as they hit the blue car head-on was unlike anything she'd experienced. Her helmet mashed itself against Michael's back and crumbled to nothing as they were catapulted over the roof of the car. Her breath smashed out of her; the road, then the sky, then the road again, filled her vision. This was it. Images of her crash just two nights ago came rushing back. She thought of her sister and brother and of her little friend, Isabelle, killed all those years ago in the waterskiing accident. She said, 'Sorry, Jacinta,' aloud and closed her eyes.

The impact with the hard black bitumen never came. Opening her eyes, she found herself gently hovering, perhaps a hundred feet above Stonehenge. She was dead and the druids would be coming for her in a moment.

'Don't get too carried away, although I guess you just have been.'

Michael. He held her aloft. Her helmet was gone and a gentle breeze ruffled her hair. She looked down again at the ancient stone obelisks. Of course! They were on Salisbury Plain. The intersection was just down the road from the famous ancient site. They descended gently into a green grassy field; the lights from broken motorcycles and the milk tanker stabbing the darkness at crazy angles.

'The people in the car?' she asked Michael.

'They're okay. Unconscious and with laps full of broken glass and the headlight from my bike, but otherwise, they're fine.'

'Am I in some kind of shock? Because I feel *good*,' she said, checking out her limbs for the second time that week. She looked up at him and saw that he wasn't, though. 'Oh my God, you're bleeding!'

'I suppose I am,' he said, feeling his cheekbone. 'Half of an exhaust pipe from one of those Ducatis tore through my helmet.'

Her hand flew to her mouth as she saw blood soaking through his shirt.

'Michael, is that yours?' She reached a hand out to comfort him, but he stepped back.

'Yes, it's mine. Something very sharp is in my chest. We'd better get this job done fast, Allie.'

She gasped and turned away, emotion welling up in her own chest. 'Michael, I don't know what to say! Can you *die* from this?' Looking down at his increasingly red sodden shirt, he shook his head.

'It'll take a hell of a lot more than this. C'mon, let's go.' He strode off toward the carnage at the T-junction.

Reaching the road, they each picked their way through the wreckage. Some of the rats were stirring, while others lay very broken and dead in crooked piles. Michael heaved a rat off a bike.

'This one's all right. You ride this.' He kicked down its stand and searched for another bike. He found one with a faring hanging off, but otherwise rideable. It started easily. Allie fumbled with the gears on hers, never having ridden a Ducati before. It started and ran well enough. None of the bikes had pillion seats, so there was no option but to ride separately and that meant she was vulnerable. She checked her watch, which miraculously, hadn't been torn from her. It was 11:25 p.m.

Cars arrived from various directions. She booted the sports bike, all safety considerations relegated to the back of her mind. There was no time to worry about helmets and speed limits. They pushed the lightweight bikes as fast as they could go, Allie keeping up with Michael through all but the tightest turns.

The route to the festival site was convoluted. Despite its name, the festival itself wasn't at Glastonbury. It was held on a farm at a little place called Pilton. They shot past the hamlets of Corsley Health and Tytherington and a dozen others with quaint names, riding the red racers to their limit on the narrow, twisting roads. Mercifully, the rain eased, then stopped. A bevy of police cars and a solitary ambulance with lights and sirens activated passed them, travelling at speed in the opposite direction. Allie knew where they were headed. Rounding a sweeping curve, they saw Shepton Mallet in the distance. Allie knew this place; it wasn't far now to the festival site.

Jacinta Wilkinson supposed it was oxygen deprivation that had caused her to sleep. That or shock. She woke as music invaded her little prison. She tried to stretch her legs, but of course the confines of the box precluded that. Her back ached abominably and her neck was frozen in the chin-down position. The car motor was still running and she heard muffled conversation. She heard, 'Okay,' and, 'Through there.' The car moved off over rough ground. The music was louder now.

The hubbub of a large crowd sounded some distance away. She banged her head as the car lurched through a dip in the road. Someone talking over a loudspeaker in the distance clearly said, 'Coldplay.' Three hours travel, music, Coldplay. She could be nowhere else. They had taken her somewhere very close to the Glastonbury Music Festival.

The car moved slowly on before rocking over even rougher terrain, the bottom scraping the ground. Tree branches buffeted and screeched against the side of the car, then the sound of bubbling water. The pitch of the motor dulled then fell silent. The steep angle of the car caused the box that held her to slide and smash against another object in the trunk. Sharp pain shot through her back. The stench in the car intensified. The vehicle rocked again and two doors slammed. She heard splashing, then an acrid, unmistakable, eye-stinging smell forced its way into her prison. Petrol.

She held her breath to block out the odour. She listened, not daring to make a sound. But nobody came for her. Despair took hold. Nobody was going to save her. Tears flooded down her cheeks and her breathing came hard. The band played on.

11:50 p.m.

Allie and Michael rode too slowly through hordes of

festival-goers, dodging new-age hippies; kids in wheelbarrows; and painted, wandering minstrels. They moved towards the main entrance, but they were chewing up time. The crowd thickened even more, so they threw down their bikes in the oozing mud and sprinted the rest of the way, pushing people roughly aside. A festival policeman saw the ruckus as they approached and called his colleague to assist him. The two policemen moved to the centre of the track to intercept Michael and Allie. She thrust her warrant card at them before they spoke.

'DCI St. Clair and DC . . . Michaels, from London!'

The senior of the two policemen, a sergeant, acknowledged her. 'Right you are – we were told you were coming, but we thought you'd take a little longer. You did well to get through that nasty pileup near Amesbury so quickly.'

'Yes, well indeed.' She looked at Michael, who gazed around nonchalantly.

'There's been no sign of the blue Mercedes, Wendell or DC Wilkinson, presumably?' she asked, looking from one officer to the other.

'No, not yet,' said the thinner, junior officer holding up the photos on his clipboard. 'Although, we had to send some cars and officers up to the accident, as you would imagine.'

'How many officers do you have left here on site looking for them?'

'I'd say about eight in total.' Eight men – it was nothing.

She ran her hand through her hair, realizing it must look wild and woolly after the helmetless ride. Still, she supposed she'd fit in here at the festival, motorcycle leathers and all. Looking at Michael, she realized he wasn't out of place either. 'That's not a lot of resources,' she said, staring out over the grounds. 'This festival is much bigger than I'd imagined.'

'Gets bigger every year,' the younger officer advised cheerfully.

'Presumably your officers back at the crash site are alert to the possibility that the Mercedes might yet go through there?'

'They are, ma'am.'

Allie flashed a tight smile. 'Sorry, of course they are.' The younger officer grinned back very enthusiastically.

'One last question and I'll try not to insult you. We believe our suspect is here or *will* be here to see Jase Britt's midnight show, as you're aware. Do you have men stationed near his stage?'

The two policemen looked at each other again, clearly embarrassed. The sergeant spoke up. 'No, we don't. Nobody's mentioned that Jase Britt's show was important, ma'am.'

Allie and Michael got directions to the huge stage where Britt would perform. The two policemen had simply pointed to the one hundred-foot-high white cross dominating the centre of the quagmire that was the Worthy farm. She instructed the sergeant to radio his remaining men and deploy them to the stage area immediately. She and Michael ran hard through the mud and slush, the white cross further away than it had first appeared.

Chapter Twenty

Diamond Ray Riley was in his element. He was living his dream – show business. His new management contract with Jase Britt gave him that opportunity in spades. The methods by which he'd coerced Britt into signing with him were not common knowledge, but more than a few music industry heavies were dismayed at the news that Ray Riley had entered the business; it was corrupt and nasty enough already. Britt's Christian branding added something as well, besides irony. Backstage at Glastonbury, he felt the tension that precedes a big show. He stayed close to Britt while roadies and guitar technicians fussed about, swearing and doing last-minute checks. He peeked through the curtains at the crowd for the sixth time.

Thousands of expectant kids; sparkly-eyed, wholesome-looking mums and dads; and bombed-out teenagers stood or sat in the cold rain and the squelchy black mud. Christianity was nothing if not a broad church. Many in the crowd were already holding aloft the little battery-operated plastic white crosses which they'd illuminate at Britt's command during the show. Riley looked to the rear of the crowd enclosure at the one-hundred-foot-high crane which swayed like a giant articulated beanstalk. The camera mounted in its bucket would provide a brilliant overview of the concert.

Images from that and the three onstage cameras would be fed to the mobile recording studio parked immediately behind the three-storey stage. His company,

Firestone Music, would release the live DVD of the show within the month. Riley had millions of dollars outlaid on the kid and it was about to pay off big time.

He felt a hand on his shoulder. Arthur Wendell, carrying a can of coke and a broad smile, greeted him as he turned.

'Arthur! Very pleased you came. Didn't think you would after last night's altercation between you and our boy. Mind you, son, I wouldn't creep up behind me like that again if I was you!'

'Sorry, Mr Riley,' Arthur said, looking about the stage. 'I wouldn't have missed this though. By the look of the crowd, Britt is going to make a fortune for you!'

Riley grinned broadly. 'You better believe it, sunshine. Who'd have thought, eh? Diamond Ray Riley and the new messiah, joined at the hip!'

Arthur flinched as Mr Black said, *Joined at the hip pocket anyway.*

'It's a brilliant move, that's all I can say,' Arthur said, feeding Riley's ego.

Riley's chest puffed out. 'It's a new deal, Arthur. How does Sir Raymond Riley sound?'

Fucking unlikely. Wendell held Riley's gaze despite Black's inner voice.

'Brilliant! The Earl of Chelsea?' Arthur quipped. 'Or maybe The Duke of Earl?'

Riley laughed uproariously. 'Perfect – see to it would you, Arthur?'

Britt swept out of his dressing room outfitted in a simple white cloak, a garland of daisies encircling his head, no shoes on his feet. Frowning, he strode towards them.

'Jesus Christ!' Ray shouted with a laugh.

Britt got straight down to business, ignoring Wendell. 'Have you got it?'

Riley put his arm around Britt and led him to a darker corner. 'Of course,' he said, digging a plastic packet from his jacket. 'Here, go for it.'

Britt snatched it, mumbled his thanks and hustled back to his dressing room.

Riley was all smiles as he came back to Arthur. 'That's what I call total quality management – only the best stuff for the little messiah.'

Arthur heard a snort of laughter somewhere in his brain.

'Would you mind if I took a wander through the stage area, if there's time?' Arthur asked Riley. 'I used to play a bit of guitar. I wouldn't mind a look at the gear.'

Riley looked at his watch and hesitated, but then said, 'Okay, be quick though, we're already running late.'

Arthur said, 'Great,' and disappeared towards the back of the stage as the tech crew left the area, their final checks complete.

Arthur crouched and stole to the front of the darkened stage to the microphone stand that he reckoned had to be the main one for Britt. The heavy curtain hid him from the crowd. He poured most of the can of coke around its base. He lifted the big retro-style microphone off the stand and crept back to the point where the power lead joined the mixing board. He peeked over the top of the board and saw the red power indicator. The light was off. Hidden from view, he unscrewed the base plate from the microphone.

He was pleased to see it was British gear. Electricity, he still loved it. He knew the earth wire would, therefore, be the green and yellow one. He pulled out a tiny pair of electrician's pliers from his trouser pocket and snipped through it.

Nice, Arthur.

He stripped the brown wire – the live one – and made sure it touched the metal of the microphone housing. He bobbed up to look around. The crew were probably shooting up somewhere backstage. He was alone. He straightened up and walked once more to the microphone stand. He placed the mic back in its holder. This would work well with what his partner was doing with the big cable under the stage. He hoped it would rain some more.

'Hey! You! What the fuck are you doing?'

Arthur jumped and looked to his left. A huge man, wearing a denim jacket, ponytail and a name tag, lumbered towards him. Arthur quickly approached him; the last thing he wanted was the security guy spotting the wet floor. 'All okay,' he said, a placatory hand extended towards the very bothered security guy. 'But thanks for being so vigilant.' He struck a conspiratorial pose. 'Just between you and me, Mr Riley asked me to do a last-minute gear check. He's kinda nervous, as this is Jase's first gig under his management. You can understand that, can't you?'

The security guard looked momentarily unconvinced, then smiled.

'You're Riley's man? Okay, yeah.' He laughed. 'He has been jumping about, issuing orders and getting in our way. He's as nervous as a butcher's thumb.'

Arthur laughed and led the guy towards the backstage exit. 'He'll be fine as soon as the show starts. It'll be quite something.'

The hottest act around.

Arthur shook the man's hand firmly. 'Thanks again for your understanding. I'll tell *Ray* he has one security guy who really knows his stuff.'

Ponytail guy beamed and showed Arthur how to exit the stage from the rear stairs. Arthur hurried away through the brown slush. He wouldn't stay for the show; he had another place to be.

'Good God!' Alvira Goodman said to her new boyfriend. 'Is that a *car*?'

Seventeen-year-old Teddy Portman looked to where she pointed. It *was* a car, at least part of one, about fifty feet from where they lay. Lights from the festival perimeter bounced off the water and illuminated the rear-tail reflectors. The car was sinking in the lake with just the rear-end poking above the water. He sighed. So much for getting laid; the mood had been broken.

He looked at perky Alvira. She'd already unbuttoned her floral blouse. He was halfway there, but now she was all excited for the wrong reasons. Coming down here by the lake, which was screened from the main festival area, had seemed a good idea. Although in truth, the grass wasn't as dry as he'd hoped. Alvira buttoned herself up and stood.

'Let's check it out, Ted!'

She really is a child, he thought.

Skirting the slippery bank in the half-light they came to within twenty feet of the light-coloured car. It bobbed gently, popping air bubbles, which escaped from underneath it.

'It's a Mercedes,' Ted observed. 'An old one, but the paint looks good, at least in this light.'

Ted's father was a panel beater at a major London garage and he was still fond of announcing to anyone who cared to listen that, 'When it comes to cars, our Teddy knows the difference between shit and clay.' Mixed metaphors aside, it was true. Ted knew this was no heap of junk abandoned through lack of interest. Ted had one fat roll-your-own 'cigarette' left in his jacket and now seemed as good a time as any to light it.

'Do you have to?' Alvira said, frowning.

'I might as well; there's no reason to save it!'

'You smoke that stuff too much,' she persisted. 'You'll damage your brain.'

He laughed. 'Too late – I'm here with you aren't I?'

She huffed and returned her attention to the car. 'My eyes are stinging a bit,' she said, squeezing them shut. Teddy lit his joint and threw the still-lit match at the water.

She sniffed noisily again. 'What's that horrible smell?' It's not . . . *petrol* is it?'

The farm dam erupted in a fireball. Alvira's lank, dark hair was engulfed in orange flame and Teddy's eyebrows vanished. The heat induced an elemental roar and the nice light-blue paint on the Mercedes blistered.

Allie's head whirled around at the sound of the explosion. 'Jacinta!' she cried. None of the crowd surrounding them took any notice; their attention was on the main stage. Jase Britt's huge backing band had stormed into its massive intro with more sound than Pink Floyd ever managed. But Allie heard the roar and 'saw' the flames. She pointed back behind the striped refreshment tents. '*There, Michael, there!*'

She was at once lifted into the air, straight up, no messing about. She saw the crowd below her look up and applaud, all thinking it was part of Jase Britt's midnight *Touched by the Angels* show. They rose higher and saw the farm dam; it was maybe five hundred yards away. She felt forward movement, then a *rush* towards the fireball at breathtaking speed. Michael's arms were around her waist and chest. She was secure. Within seconds, they swooped low over the farm road fringing the dam.

'Land, land!' she screamed at Michael. He dived to within a few feet of the ground, pulling up like an eagle alighting to a nest. He released his grip and she catapulted out of his arms into the water. The fire tore at her face. She fell forward, her face submerged for a moment. She felt fire scorch across her back. Rising to her feet, she felt a tornado-like wind from behind her. She stumbled forward with the force of it. She looked behind her. The sight left her stunned. Michael, bathed in orange reflected light, stood on the muddy bank bracing himself with his legs apart, rotating simply massive pure-white wings which were perhaps thirty feet across. The gale he produced created waves on the water and pushed the flames up and away from the bubbling, now black, boot of the car. She couldn't tear her eyes from him. It was a vision from both Heaven and Hell.

'Do it!' he yelled.

Snapping out of it, she waded into the water. Steam rose from the car as water was hurled on to it. Bracing herself for the pain, she hooked her fingers under the boot lid, which was now just a foot above the water. The pain was brain-snapping – it felt as though the skin on her fingers was sizzling away down to the bone. An unearthly scream pierced the air and she pulled upwards. The boot lid tore away from its lock, smashing against the rear window housing.

A large silver metal box lay half submerged in the boot compartment. She wrenched it out and, holding it above her head, spun and waded through the waist-deep water back towards the shore, the weight of the box no issue. She saw the two teenagers face down on the bank, just above the waterline. She flopped to her knees and lowered the box into the mud. She tore at the lid. Inside, Jacinta Wilkinson lay scrunched up in a ball; her hair sodden, her nostrils half submerged in brackish water.

'Jacinta!' Allie yelled at her as she lifted her face free of the filthy water in the box. There was no response. Allie looked at Michael with tear-filled eyes. 'She's . . .'

Jacinta coughed. Water spewed from her. Michael reached in, lifted her out of the box and laid her on the mud bank. She gurgled and vomited more water. She opened her eyes and tried to scream.

Allie looked around at Michael; his wings were still out.

'Put them away!' she yelled, pulling Jacinta to a sitting position and shielding Michael from her. She shook her gently. 'Jacinta! You're okay! It's me, Allie!'

Jacinta opened her eyes wide. 'Thank God! Allie . . . I knew you'd find me! I thought I'd died and gone to Heaven. I saw a magnificent angel! I tell you, it was—' She threw up again. Allie hugged her tightly, despite her own seared hands. She looked around as a police car pulled up behind the trees.

'You'd better go, Michael. I'll find you back at the Britt show.'

He looked over his shoulder at the police car, then the stage in the distance. 'Okay, but hurry, Allie; our boy's about to appear.'

She nodded, still cradling Jacinta in her arms. 'Michael,' she said, causing him to turn back to her, 'thank you for this.' He ran through the long grass and disappeared behind the trees.

The sergeant and the PC Allie and Michael had met at the entrance gate scrambled down the grassy bank. The smouldering ruin that was the 1965 Mercedes saloon finally submerged, releasing clouds of steam to roll across the water and join the acrid smell of burned rubber. A long black bag floated to the surface. The PC waded out and returned to the shore with it. He opened it and recoiled. The stench was breathtaking. Allie reached over and peered inside. It was as she thought – it was the bag she'd seen on the Earl's Court CCTV footage. In it, she knew, was poor Georgie Konstanzo's decomposing tongue. The sergeant came to her; the PC raced to the two teenagers now stirring into life some distance away. Allie was relieved to see they were alive.

'An ambulance is making its way here from the other side of the grounds,' the sergeant said. 'It should be no more than three minutes.'

Jacinta looked up at him. 'I'm fine, really.'

'No, you're not,' Allie said firmly. 'Take the ride in the ambulance. You've been through enough.'

Wilkinson smiled and agreed easily enough. Allie helped her to her feet. 'Before I go, tell me what you can about this guy who abducted you. He's Arthur Wendell by the way.' She pointed at the car in the farm dam 'That's his pride and joy under there.'

Jacinta looked back at the spot where the car had sunk.

'There are two of them, Allie.'

'Yes,' Allie said, 'I figured that. Did you get a look at the second guy – assuming it is a guy?'

'Oh yes, it's a guy, all right, but no, I've not laid eyes on him. His voice is familiar though and he sounds . . . organized. He doesn't waste a word.'

'What type of voice?

'Deepish, at least deeper than Wendell's.'

Allie fished out the photo of Wendell from her jacket and showed it to Jacinta, just to be sure.

'That's him, I guess, but that could be his father. He's younger than that. He has more hair and it's darker.'

'A hairpiece possibly?'

'Definitely not. He just looks younger than that photo. That's all I can say, really.'

It confirmed what Sarah Blascombe from the Black Crow had said. It was Arthur and he was *changed.* The ambulance arrived. Despite her protestations, Jacinta was loaded into it. Allie waved to her and turned to the police officers.

'Quick, can you get me back to the main stage area now, please?'

A minute later, Allie jumped out of the still-moving police car, vaulted the fence surrounding the main stage area and pushed her way to where she and Michael had stood fifteen minutes earlier. She found him further towards the front. The crowd went wild as brilliant blue lighting burst from the stage. The music changed to an apocalyptic orchestral arrangement. A bunch of teenage girls nearby squealed when they saw the white-cloaked Britt descending on to the stage from high above. His arms extended to his flock, Britt gazed beatifically about; every inch the new-age messiah.

'Hope he's had his needleful of Christianity,' Allie shouted to Michael.

'You don't have to yell, remember?'

'Sorry,' she whispered. She looked up at Britt and it struck her that here was a hugely popular biblical figure and Wendell was here. Surely, he wasn't going to go after Britt, his employer's protégé? *Not now? Of course he was.*

'Oh Jesus,' she said. 'I've missed the obvious! I was focused on Jacinta!'

Michael turned to her, having read her distress. 'And so you should have. But you might be right. If it makes you feel better, I didn't think of it, either. I'm not picking up anything from a distance . . . must be the music.'

'It *interferes* with you?'

'Yes. I should have remembered.'

'Quick, move to the front of the stage, he'll be there,' Allie yelled again. Michael heaved disgruntled onlookers out of the way as they raced forward. Britt stepped off his chariot from the Heavens and acknowledged the crowd. Another huge cheer went up all around. Without waiting for their cue, the crowd switched the little white plastic crosses to 'on'. It was quite a sight. Britt beamed from the stage and mouthed *thank you* as twenty thousand people swayed to the music; their illuminated crosses moving side to side as one.

Allie and Michael reached the security line in front of the stage. There was no sign of Wendell. A burly security guard came straight for them. Clearly, they'd upset a lot of people fighting their way to the front. Allie flashed her warrant card, which elicited a wave from the advancing guard. He lost any professional interest.

Britt smiled at the crowd and half-turned as an iridescent blue Fender Stratocaster guitar was brought out for him. He threw the strap over his shoulder, causing the crowd to erupt again. The music segued into his new hit song, *Faith Evermore*. The screams and applause were deafening.

'Do you think Jesus ever got a reception like this?' Allie asked, regretting the question the moment it left her lips.

'Yes. They were smaller crowds, though.'

Two more guitars chimed in to mask any deficiencies in Britt's playing. Allie scanned the crowd again; she could see nothing unusual and definitely no Wendell. Her hands were killing her. She didn't dare look at them.

The big black BMW stopped by the dirt track as arranged. The driver's side electric window hummed as it came down. 'Get in,' the well-spoken man said, the sleeve of his gabardine coat just visible to the onlookers. 'I'll take you up there. You can put that contraption in the back.' The boot lid jumped up with a loud click.

'Perfect, thank you,' one of the men said. 'All hell will break loose shortly.'

The driver smiled. 'I'm banking on it.'

The song was an upbeat rocker; for Allie, it was more reminiscent of something by Wolfmother than anything she would normally have acquainted with her understanding of Christian music.

'Wolfmother?' Michael asked. 'Never heard of 'em.'

'An Australian band.'

'That explains it.'

The song ended with a blistering solo from a guitarist at the back of the stage, although the guy in white nearer the audience took credit for it.

'Very Christian of him,' Michael observed.

Britt was relieved of his guitar by a stagehand and pulled his long blond hair back off his face. Teenage girls went into orbit. Fresh rain splattered into the sodden earth. Walking to the microphone stand, he took hold of the mobile mic mounted on top of it. Fans went wild as he launched into a gyrating pseudo-ecstatic dance, not at all in time to the music. Allie grabbed Michael's coat sleeve.

'This isn't right!' she yelled, climbing the security fence.

The crowd hushed as smoke fumed from Britt's slack mouth. Allie jumped for the edge of the stage. Grabbing the metal strip at the perimeter, she levered herself up and rolled on to the stage floor. Britt burst into flames. Sparks flew from his fingertips, but the crowd wasn't fooled. They knew this was real and it was *wrong*.

Allie sprinted across the stage towards the convulsing Britt, his left cheek sagging and melting as she approached. The ragged end of his bitten-off tongue plopped on to the stage. The skin on his hands simmered and smoke burst from his feet. His band members stopped playing, one by one, as realization hit; apart from the bass player, who was in his own world. The dull rolling thump of his bass and the horrified screaming of the crowd produced a macabre soundtrack to a new-age horror show.

She cannoned into Britt in a full-tilt rugby tackle, managing to break his grip on the microphone, but not before collecting a brief jolt through her own system. She and Britt tumbled in a smoking, stinking heap to the stage floor as the control panel at the back of the stage blew up in a shower of sparks. She flailed at the persistent flames engulfing his cloak. The audience screamed and continued screaming as 20,000 volts surged through a bare open-ended cable which led from the control panel to the waterlogged ground in front of the stage. Rivers of blue high-voltage electricity snaked across the ground, running up wet legs and wriggling in to rain-soaked crevices. A spider web of crackling blue pulsed, jumped and hissed through bodies on its way to God knew where.

Allie was spent, but had to heave the smouldering-hot Britt off her. She didn't know if he was alive. In a way, it would be better for him if he were not. She rolled on to her side. Her eyes were drawn to Michael's gigantic frame. He moved to one side of the stage, bent down, then stood in full view; the live cable now bucked in his left hand. The crowd compound went dark and people dropped heavily into the mud. She saw Michael look at her for what seemed a long moment, then close his right hand over the bare end of the wire. He lurched as he took the full onslaught of the massive flow of electricity. A quizzical look come over his face before a blinding flash of white-blue light hurt her eyes. She looked away, the light imprinted on her retina. She heard an explosion behind the stage. All went quiet. She looked anxiously for Michael, but the residual white light swam in her eyes. She tried to look round it, if that were possible. She tried squeezing her eyes shut and opening them again. It worked. Darkness enveloped the stage and the crowd compound. Michael was gone. She hit the stage floor.

Allie woke in an ambulance, her hands heavily bandaged, only her thumbs protruding. Despair gripped her. *Michael!* What had become of him? The consequences of his death would affect all mankind. And she had caused it. He'd sacrificed himself for the people here and not brought his demon to heel. Three deaths and the problem was still out there.

'You're with us, I see!' The cheery paramedic peered hard at her. 'How are you feeling?'

Allie looked away, hiding her tears. 'Nothing. I feel nothing.'

Her phone blipped and her spirits rose like a rocket.

You know where to find us. We have a special treat for you. Don't dally now.

Her shoulders slumped. It wasn't Michael. She should have been elated; it was contact from the murderers. But she didn't care any more about cosmic games and evil spirits or whatever the hell they were. She texted back, her right thumb working overtime.

Go screw yourselves.

From her perch in the ambulance, she watched dull-eyed as police and volunteers attended to fallen members of the crowd. It looked to her as though the majority were okay, but there would be exceptions, of course, especially those who'd been standing closer to the stage. Britt, she assumed, had died. A familiar face poked its head around the corner of the ambulance. Ray Riley.

She turned her head away. A hand gripped her arm. 'What you did there, Allison St. Clair, was the bravest thing I ever saw.'

'Did Britt survive?' she asked, her gaze still averted.

'Fuck *him*,' Riley said with surprising vehemence. 'Self-centred little bastard.'

She was confused. 'Is he dead?' she asked again.

'No. Incredibly, they say he'll survive. Be a veggie of course. His brain is fried, but he was heading that way anyway.'

She was tired and had no appetite for any more talk.

'But *you*,' Riley continued, 'would have been a *real* loss.' He patted her leg and walked away.

'Better get those hands sorted,' he said over his shoulder, his right hand up in the air, waving a flippant goodbye. 'Oh, and sorry about that big minder of yours – ouch, such a terrible way to go.'

She dropped her gaze to the blanket covering her then, after a minute, looked again towards the stage. A fire crew sprayed fried bits of equipment and the roadies stood about muttering.

Her phone chirped. *Go screw ourselves? That's not very sisterly of you.*

She sat up straight. *What did that mean? Sisterly? What the?*

'Oh no, surely not . . .' she said aloud to no one. She thumbed her parents' phone number in. Her father answered. She yelled into the phone, 'Is Robert there?'

'Allie, is that you?'

'Yes, Dad! Is Robert there? It's urgent!'

'No, he's not. He was going to be here for dinner with us all, but he rang this afternoon and begged off. And then you cancelled as well. Your mother's very—'

'*Where is he?*'

'He's gone with that music group of his to our old stomping ground. I never thought he'd ever want to go back after the accident.'

'Glastonbury,' Allie said in a barely audible voice, an unbearable tiredness weighing on her.

'Yes, of course – Glastonbury.'

Three men sat quietly in the back of the black BMW saloon. Another, much bigger and unconscious, was scrunched into the boot alongside the chrome and rubber contraption. Two of the men in the back of the car didn't feel like talking and the third was gagged. The driver said nothing as they approached the exit gate. The police who'd previously manned it were attending to the injured and dying at the main stage area. The car slid unobserved out of the car park and on to the road to Glastonbury township, just a few miles away; the back of the car hanging low, unable to cope with the massive rearward weight.

Holy fuck, Arthur. Did you see that guy's eyeballs poach back there? And the crowd! Talk about electric blue! Woo-hoo!

Arthur Wendell didn't acknowledge the voice in his head. He stared straight ahead past the driver to where the headlights illuminated the wet, narrow road.

Arthur? C'mon, man, don't tell me you didn't get a 'tingle' out of that? Too 'shocking' for you, was it? Hahahaha.

'Fuck you.'

Arthur's partner turned to him. 'Don't let him goad you.'

'The psychopath who lives in my head, you mean?'

'Yes. Mr Black. We're old friends. Sorry, I lied to you earlier about that.'

Arthur laughed. It was a harsh, cynical sound.

'And here's me thinking I'm the only one who's nutso. We can travel to Hell together when this is done.'

'That'll be three of us, then,' the driver said quietly. The gagged passenger in the backseat tried to scream, but the shiny silver tape stifled all sound.

Chapter Twenty One

The young PC drove Allie St. Clair toward Glastonbury. His name was Trevor Gordon and he'd been a policeman for exactly one year. He looked twelve years old and in need of orthodontic work.

'Where would you like to go exactly, Chief Inspector?' he finally mustered the courage to ask as they approached the main road.

'To the Tor.'

He frowned. 'Mind if I ask why? In this weather, you'll see nothing.'

'It's not a sight-seeing trip, PC Gordon. Drive as fast as you can.'

'Right.' Despite the curtain of rain, he pushed the Vauxhall well beyond the speed limit. She glanced at him. He still had adolescent pimples and she guessed he'd be lucky to weigh ten stone. She wouldn't expose him to any danger, but she had to get to the hill fast. She'd arranged armed backup which she hoped was already gathering at Glastonbury.

Water ran in shallow rivers across the road, the rain again falling hard, filling the crude agricultural drainage culverts to overflowing. One mile from the town that sat at the foot of the strange hill, lightning rent the sky. The

Tor was clearly visible in the blue flash, rising five-hundred vertical feet above the township in a gothic tableau worthy of Mary Shelley. St. Michael's Tower stood at its peak, every inch an ancient sentinel.

'Gives you the shivers, doesn't it?' PC Gordon asked.

'It does. It always has.'

Constable Gordon was keen to engage in further conversation. Picking up signals was not his strongpoint. 'Did you know it's supposed to have been where King Arthur lived?'

'The way my week's going,' Allie replied without enthusiasm, 'he probably still does.'

She saw him look at her, unsure whether or not she was kidding.

'I used to come here as a child,' she explained. 'It's where it all begins and ends.'

Trevor Gordon felt in his pocket for his St. Christopher medal.

'Stop when you see Wellhouse Lane, please – I'll get out there.'

'We're almost there, actually,' he said, peering through the pelting rain on Coursing Batch. 'In fact, the corner is . . .'

The bent figure in the white trench coat stood in the middle of the road, the headlights of the car throwing a jaundiced glow on his angular face. The police car, with lights flashing, was right on him. PC Gordon wrenched the wheel violently to the left, putting the car into a spin, the slick road offering no traction. The car somehow missed the man, but spun completely round, ploughing into a low dry stone wall, hitting hard on Gordon's side.

Allie was shaken, but unhurt. But Gordon was unconscious, his head hanging limply towards her. Blood ran down the driver's window. The man from the middle of the road opened her door, startling her.

'Are you all right?' he asked, concern clearly evident on his long face. 'I'm terribly sorry, my damn dog has run off.'

Allie unbuckled her seat belt and felt the young police officer's neck. His pulse was weak, but regular.

'Do you have a mobile phone?' she asked the stranger.

'Yes, yes!' He fumbled madly in his sodden coat for it.

'Ring an ambulance, please. I have to go.' She looked up towards the Tor. 'When the police arrive, tell them I'm up there.'

The man looked aghast. 'In this weather? Good heavens, what's going on?'

'Just tell them, *please!*'

She levered herself out of the car, putting a hand on the man's shoulder. 'Thank you.'

'Right you are,' he said. 'Don't worry. I'll tell them.'

Allie sprinted across the road toward the copse of ancient oak trees which she knew masked the start of the paved track to the summit of the steep-sided Tor. The man in the trench coat watched her until she disappeared from view. He bent down and checked that the driver was still unconscious. He smiled, straightened and threw his phone into a drainage ditch that barely contained the near-flood waters. He turned and walked the short distance back to his big black BMW.

Away from any lights, the night was black as tar. She should have grabbed a torch. She'd been too worried about poor Trevor Gordon back at the wrecked car, but at least he'd be spared whatever it was that waited for her up at St. Michael's Tower. She looked up at the Tor as lightning crackled, suffusing the air with electricity. Thunder followed immediately overhead, echoing across the low land of the Somerset plain all the way to Stonehenge. Her stomach tightened as she contemplated the Tor. She stepped on to the track and started the long run to the summit.

She dropped into a rhythm quickly. It allowed her to think about the myth and legend which had surrounded the Tor for thousands of years. Her father had made the Tor his special area of study and had regaled her and her sister, Jo, with tales of King Arthur and Avalon, the Isle of Glass, paganism and the supposed ley lines, among other mysteries ascribed to 'that funny hill in Somerset'. Now she knew why. He'd been educating her for this moment. But it had been one character he'd talked about who had disturbed her the most and she knew her brother, Robert, also found him frightening – the 'Scary Faerie' as she and Robert had named him, Gwyn ap Nudd, the Lord of the Underworld.

Thoughts of him had given her cold sweats in her sleep for years after her father had stopped telling them the Celtic Welsh tales. She'd never told her father about it. It was no surprise to her that Gwyn ap Nudd loomed large for her now. She remembered the dream she'd had last night about the black creature in the cave, the giant snake, the river, and Robert drowning. She was halfway up the hill when her thoughts locked on to the picture of her tenth birthday with Michael in the background, and the strange lights on the Tor about which her father had been interviewed by BBC4 earlier this week. Tears came as she saw again her little friend Isabelle disappear under the speedboat at Middlemoor Water Park, which she knew was only a short drive east from where she now jogged. She quickened her pace.

St. Patrick, her forebear, about whom *The Promise of Maewyn Succat* had been written, was real for her now too. She thought of his pact with the Archangel Michael, *her Michael,* after whom the ancient cathedral on top of the Tor had been named, of which only the tower now remained. St. Patrick's pact had become her obligation. Vinculum infinitas – she understood it now. *Bonded forever.* It all came down to the Tor. This was where it would end for her and Robert. This had always been their destiny.

She felt no fear as her run took to the top of the Tor, St. Michael's Tower now only thirty feet further up the track. It should have been raining at the summit, but it wasn't. Breathing hard, she looked back to see if police reinforcements had arrived at the foot of the hill. A heavy mist surrounded the lower reaches of the Tor, obscuring her view of the town and road below. She stood on an island surrounded by white – the legendary Isle of Glass.

She knew deep within her that reinforcements weren't coming. She looked at her watch. It had stopped at 00:01 a.m. Her phone, too, wasn't picking up any signal, its time also frozen at 00:01; the date, May 1st.

She laughed out loud and yelled breathlessly, 'Playing magic tricks now, are we?'

The night swallowed all sound. There was no echo. A clammy silence reigned. She walked quickly to the tower, her footsteps mute. She stood in the narrow archway, her spread arms spanning it, her hands flat against the cold black stone walls. She was alone. Looking through the arch, she pictured the old church to which the tower had originally belonged. Beyond that, she saw a circle of white stones; a recently discovered remnant of an earlier time.

The white mist rose, encircling her, the sky above now clear, the moon bright through the mist. There were no stars. She stood still and listened hard. Nothing. Dropping to all fours she put her ear flat against the worn flagstones of the tower. Sound bubbled up from below. Running water; and there was an echo to it. Beneath the tower there had to be a hollow space. She stood again, examining the floor of the tower. She'd stood here many times as a child; played here in fact. She moved to the eastern wall and crouched down; there were her and Robert's initials: AS and RS, carved in the third stone from the bottom. The third stone. *The number three*. She put her hand to her face. Is this what the murderer had been alluding to?

She cast her mind back to her tenth birthday. It had been after carving their initials all those years ago that Robert had become secretive. She remembered now; they'd been called back from the tower to go to the local pub for her birthday party. Robert had been funny all through it until he'd sneaked away after the birthday cake had been cut. Her dream hadn't been a dream, at least the part about following Robert. She peered at the stone then, in an inspired moment, reached for her phone. She couldn't call, but the phone should still emit enough light to see by.

It was difficult to hold the phone, her bandaging cumbersome. She stood and unwound the long ribbon, shoving the long strips of bandaging into her pockets. She crouched again, moving the small amount of light from the phone across the surface of the third stone. Five long minutes later, she'd found nothing. Her initials stood out like they were carved yesterday, but the black surface of the stone yielded nothing else. Her legs were aching. She half-stood and then saw it.

As the light hit the stone from an oblique angle, a thin spider web of lines was visible. She crouched again and held the phone at a forty-five-degree angle to the stone. She remembered now, it had been an early lunch on her tenth birthday. They'd planned to go swimming later. The sun, therefore, wouldn't have been directly overhead. She looked out through the archway, imagining where the 11:00 a.m. sun might have been on her birthday and tried to relate it to the new angle of her phone. It would have been near enough to a match, she decided.

The lines were a map. No doubt about it. The Tor and the cathedral upon it were clearly distinguishable. It was drawn as an aerial view, which in ancient times was unusual. She thought randomly that her father would love this little discovery. Or perhaps it wasn't so little. The map showed a pathway leading from the Tor down the northern side to what looked like a clump of trees. In an almost modern 'exploded' view, it was clear – she fell on her backside, her eyes wide. She crouched once more. The map showed a king on a throne. She knew who it was. Gwyn ap Nudd, of course. It showed a river snaking its way to something she couldn't make out. But it was enough for her to realize that her dream from last night had been more. It was *memory*. She had been in that cave. It existed . . . and it was where she had to go now. She quickly stood, her head colliding with the heavy leather boots of a man hanging above her.

Allie fell back against the wall of the Tower. The hanged man was dressed as a monk or perhaps an abbot. His long cloak was resplendent with intricate piping around the sleeves and hem. And he wasn't yet dead. His legs twitched, his boots swung wildly. She moved around and away from him, backing out of the archway. The moment she did, he disappeared. Again, silence pervaded. She stepped back into the tower. He reappeared, gurgling and flailing. She nodded cynically; she knew who this man was or was *supposed* to be.

'I'm not falling for this!' she yelled to the silent mist. 'If you're selling this as Richard Whiting, the last abbot of Glastonbury, I'm not buying!' She expected someone or something to step out of the white, but nothing did. She walked back into the tower. The abbot was gone. It was all part of the game, and the game dictated that she find the entrance to the cave just like Robert had twenty years ago, of that she was certain.

She ran blindly into the mist, a vivid picture of the wall map from the tower in her head. Her iPhone had a compass – she would use it. The phone was dead. She smiled ruefully; what had she expected? But even the cotton-wool mist couldn't disguise the slope of the Tor. Down was down whether you had a compass or not and she knew she was on the correct side of the hill. She felt the undulations in the surface as she ran down the hill, barely keeping her balance in the ancient furrows encircling the hill which had been worn by centuries of pilgrims ritually winding their way to the summit, St. Patrick himself among them.

She ran into a wire farm fence. Her right foot kicked the heavy post before she saw it, her body cannoning into the wire. She backed off and turned right in accordance with the map. She would walk the rest of the way. By her reckoning, she had about forty yards to go before she entered a clump of . . .

She walked into a tree and cursed. It was an oak – tall, chunky and old. At least she was in the right area. Staying as close to the fence line as she could, she counted out another twenty steps before turning right, back up the hill. She stopped at the point she had determined. There was nothing but grass. She walked another five yards – still nothing; more grass, but longer. She retreated down the hill to the fence line and paced another ten yards along it, once again with no result. Her heart rate rose; she was wasting time. She took another step, but stopped. With supreme effort, she calmed herself. Then she *heard* something. It was to her right. She moved carefully towards the sound, realizing her feet were tracing a flat path under the spongy, wet grass. Moments later, she confronted a scrubby patch of bushes. Wheel marks disappeared below them. Robert. She recognized the bushes immediately from her dream. She took another deep, calming breath and pulled at the bushes. They came away too easily in a mat of earth and dangling roots. They'd recently been disturbed. A hole large enough for her to crawl through beckoned. Her old friend, claustrophobia, revisited her just as it had twenty years earlier.

She scrambled through the damp hole, ultimately sliding down on to a set of stone steps, skinning her knees before landing on smooth, cool stones.

'Welcome, Miss St. Clair, it's been a while.'

A deep, mellifluous voice, not at all unpleasant, resonated through the cavern. She looked up, planning to eyeball the man who had kidnapped her brother. But he wasn't a man. Not strictly speaking. He was tall, about the same height as Michael had been, almost black, but with albino-white hair. Piercing yellow-brown eyes examined her from under a creased, leathery forehead. He was from her world of dreams.

'Cat got your tongue?' It was said with an amused lilt. Not threatening.

'No, but a demon has my brother.'

He clapped his bony hands together. 'Bravo! Spunk, I love that! I knew you wouldn't disappoint!'

Allie stood, dusting herself off, going easy around her bloodied knees. 'Where is he?' she asked, as if asking directions to a public lavatory.

'Your brother? Over there,' he said just as casually, pointing a disproportionately long appendage towards the back of the cavern, its source of soft light a mystery.

'Do you know,' he continued conversationally, 'that the humans in this enclosure now, and one other from long, long ago are the only humans to ever set foot in here? Can you believe that?'

'Well, gosh.'

He tilted his head curiously at her. 'Do I not impress you?'

'Not favourably, but hey, let's give it time. Say another minute before Robert and I leave you to your . . . hole?'

'Extraordinary,' he said, clasping his hands together like a pleased parent at an Eisteddfod. 'You really are something!'

'I told you she was.' The voice came from the back of the cave. Her brother was being pushed towards her; his wheelchair was scratched and decorated with clumps of earth and grass. It had been roughly shoved through the hole in the bushes and smashed against the stone steps. Robert though, appeared to be unharmed. She breathed a sigh of relief. It was short-lived. They came closer, into the light. The man in the dark-grey suit was immediately familiar to her. He laboured at the effort needed to move the wheelchair over the rough-hewn surface. His long, craggy face was contorted as he puffed hard at the exertion.

Commander Bradley Whitcombe attempted a breathless smile. It was more a sneer. 'St. Clair,' he wheezed. Allie fought to stay calm. She was expecting Arthur Wendell and even at some level, Mathew Connors, but *Whitcombe!* She hadn't seen *that* coming, but she would brazen this out.

'I would apologize for not introducing you two,' the creature said, 'but of course you do know each other. You should now know that Bradley is a vital part of my network and has been assisting me with my enquiries for many, many years. Get it, Chief Inspector – *assisting me with my enquiries?*'

She kept her eyes fixed on Whitcombe. 'Have you been a practising psychopath for long or is this a new thing?' she asked.

Whitcombe shoved Robert forward, smashing his right leg against a jagged rock. Allie knew Robert's paralysis would shield him from the pain.

'You're a long, long way from cloistered Belgravia now, Chief Inspector,' Whitcombe gloated. 'How ridiculous, *Chief Inspector* at your age. I can't believe I agreed to it – the Devil must have made me do it. Anyway, I wouldn't be too relaxed about this if I were you.'

Allie stared at him. 'Relaxed? No, I'm not that. The thought of you and Arthur Wendell sawing Paula Armstrong in half during a theatre matinee keeps me focused. That and the fact you have my brother leaves me at a slight disadvantage, of course.'

Whitcombe laughed; it was a phenomenon rarely witnessed. He was at home in his true skin. 'I should advise you, too, that there'll be no reinforcements coming. As far as the local constabulary is concerned, you're having a mental breakdown of sorts.'

'I figured that. But they'll not be persuaded by the carnage at the festival?'

'Well, who knows, but it won't matter anyway.' He made a show of looking round the cavern. 'They won't find you, be assured of that.'

'I won't be relying on that, *Bradley,* be assured yourself. I also suppose that it was you who told Strauss and Connors that Jacinta Wilkinson had been found safe and sound?'

He inclined his head. 'Very perceptive of you.'

She turned away from Whitcombe, not wanting to tell him Jacinta was alive; that was something he seemed not to know. It was a win. 'So, here we are . . .' she said to the creature.

The tall black figure bowed, 'I'm sorry . . . please allow me to introduce myself, I'm a man of . . .'

'Wealth and taste,' she finished the line from the Rolling Stones song for him.

'So young, yet you know the line! Really, Allison, may I call you Allison by the way? You really are impressive.'

'And you're freaky and just a little too hairy, to be honest. Were you not given a choice about that?'

'Hey, no need to descend to personal vitriol! Where I come from, I'm considered quite a catch. *The* catch, let's be honest.'

'People are hunting for you?'

His laughter reverberated through the labyrinth. 'Please, are you playing here all week? Brad, what do you think? She could join us could she not? Hmmm?'

'She could not.'

'Darn,' he said, snapping his fingers. 'There goes that idea.'

Allie sneaked a look at Robert, who hadn't made a sound. A wet stain against his white trousers told her all she needed to know.

'And that,' the creature said, pointing at the stain, 'is precisely why he wasn't *the one*, Allison.' He leaned in closer to her, sniffing loudly, his breath abominable. 'Hmmm, no little stains on your knickers now are there?'

'What have you eaten?' she asked, recoiling. 'A rat's nest?'

'Yes.'

She studied him. There was something almost familiar about him, not from her dream, but in some other way.

'Something wrong, Ms St. Clair?'

She opened her mouth to answer, but felt a prickling in the back of her brain. A voice, faint, but definitely there, was trying to reach her. She looked around the cavern, then back at the creature.

'So where is our principal murderer Arthur?' she asked. 'Didn't have him for supper, did you?'

'No, no, he's here. He's joining us for breakfast, it is edging towards morning, you know.' The voice in her head grew louder. Her heart thumped so hard she looked at the creature in case he heard it. *Michael.* He was here.

'Of course he's here, Allison,' said the creature, reading her thoughts. 'Why else do you think I'm here? Or you, for that matter?'

She feigned a confused look. 'A séance?'

This time he didn't laugh. 'You know, you're not far off the mark there. Well done.' He was more English than she was. But it was an act; she supposed he could be Armenian if he chose.

'Dutch is toughest,' he said. 'All that guttural stuff, sounds like you're coughing up fur balls.'

'So where is he?' she asked, returning to the core subject.

'Arthur or the Lord Protector of Heaven and Earth and all Points in Between?'

'Either. Let's start with Michael, then.'

'Oooh, *Michael* is it?' He affected a strange pose that didn't quite work, but she got the idea.

'Yes, Michael, or are you bluffing on that one too?'

He spun and ushered her to the back of the cavern. She didn't move. 'C'mon, Roly won't eat you!' he said with a chuckle.

'Roly?' A slimy suspicion tugged at her as they walked toward the narrow, fast-running river that had carved its path through the granite of the cave.

'Ah yes,' he said, 'we never forget our old friends. He's been waiting for you. *Just you*, I might add, all these years. It really is a hell of a compliment.'

She was led beside the river towards the back of the cavern, the creature leading the way, Whitcombe following her, pushing Robert along. The river bent left, revealing a new arm of the cavern. The hollow under the ancient Tor was much, much larger than she'd imagined. They skirted a huge boulder, which left little room between it and the river. She put her hand on it to steady herself and knew immediately she'd repeated her mistake from twenty years ago. Roly's bloated body twitched in response. A ripple ran through his sticky skin and on to the seared nerve endings of her fingers.

'Ugh!' It was an involuntary response. She jumped back.

'Say good morning to Roly, please, Allison,' the man-creature said, not breaking stride. She looked past him to an illuminated area that stood higher than the rest of the cavern. It was a crude altar. Something lay on it. She was distracted by a movement to her right, in the cleft of rocks. A man sitting disconsolately on a ledge looked up and sprang to his feet. 'Thank God!'

'Arthur,' the creature said, 'may I introduce Allison St. Clair?'

'Detective Chief Inspector, actually,' she said.

Arthur stood wringing his hands. 'I am so sorry. I never wanted to hurt them, I swear to you.'

Allie waved a dismissive hand. 'But you did and you'll be taken into custody. You had a choice, Mr Wendell, you know you did.'

The creature turned, an amused expression on his pinched face.

'You'll "take him into custody", will you? You *are* an optimist, St. Clair, but then, so many of you St. Clairs have been. God, I remember old Peter, now he was a cracker, never gave up until his heart did. It was on a stake over there by the throne by that time, but nevertheless, he had persistence. You have to admire that.'

Peter – she'd seen mention of him in the Maewyn Succat book. So he'd been the other human visitor from long ago. He'd lived in the eighth century, if she remembered correctly.

'Close,' the creature said. 'Ninth century, 816 to be exact. He was a nice man, by all accounts.'

She stepped closer to the altar. Her breath caught. Michael lay on his back on a thick oaken board, his body spanning the entire length of the plinth. Long wooden stakes protruded from each shoulder. He was pinned left and right. She looked at his feet. Each was staked the same way. She couldn't see any blood. She studied his chest for signs of movement. There were none, but she knew he wasn't dead. Her head swam; she felt faint.

The creature, oblivious to her condition, addressed her. 'We picked him up. That is, Arthur and Bradley here picked him up from behind the stage area after the fireworks. What a show! The smell of it is still in my nose and, let's face it, I have quite a nose!' He looked closely at Allie and winked. 'And you know what they say about people with big noses . . .'

'You're not a person.'

He winked. 'Bits of me are near enough, Allison.'

Touch me. The voice was clear in her head.

The creature seemed not to have tuned in to the communication. He continued his rant, waving a hand toward Michael.

'Yes, he was lying crumpled and broken near a coffee stand, wasn't he, Arthur?'

Wendell nodded. He was crumpled and broken himself.

'You were there,' Arthur said in a sulky tone.

'Well, yes, I was still riding with you at that time, but you've been so quiet since we parted company, so to speak, that I thought you might like to add something.'

Wendell stared blankly at the rising river. The creature ignored him and continued boasting about his prize catch.

'A gazillion volts will do that to you, no matter who or what you are. Fabulous stuff, electricity, some other places could do with it.'

She pointed at Michael. 'What are your plans . . . Mr Black?'

'Mr Black,' he said. 'So you *have* heard of me.' He said it again as if trying it on for size. And he rolled it around again for good measure, like a Shakespearean actor running through his tongue exercises. 'Mr Black. Miiissteeerr Bbbblack! You know, I still think it sounds nicer when *you* say it,' he said, eyeing Allie like a prime rib. 'I told Arthur my preferred stage name, but he rarely used it. Yes, Mr Black it is. Oops, sorry, what are my plans for Mr White over there, you were asking?'

Allie sighed theatrically. 'Yes, that was the question.'

Mr Black put a hand to his ear. 'Can you hear that?'

She listened, at first hearing nothing. Then slowly, a sound seeped in, a giggling sound. Dread engulfed her. 'Oh no!' she moaned despite her resolve to stay calm. 'Not those lemur things!'

'Oh yes. They have to eat you know, just like any other household pet. But they have a particular fondness for meat. They look like tree dwellers, don't they? But in a funny quirk of nature, they're not. They tunnel and live underground all their lives, hence those freaky black eyes. Farmers around here often find a strange soil subsidence on their properties. They're actually tunnels and they're big enough for a decent-sized cow or person to be dragged down. Amazing really, when you think about it. I don't usually have to feed them at all when I visit, except on very special occasions. And there's Roly to think about too, don't forget. He travelled through the tunnels all the way from Peru twenty years ago and you disappointed him greatly then.'

She spun around to check where the loathsome snake-thing was. It was nowhere in sight. Robert started whimpering. She couldn't resist running to him any longer.

She cradled his head in her hands. 'I'm so sorry, Robert. All this is my fault.'

He shook his head and spoke, the oxygen deprivation from his near drowning all those years ago slowing and slurring his speech, but his mind was sharp.

'Not . . . your . . . fault. Mine. I shouldn't have assumed I was *the one*.' He swallowed hard and with a huge effort, spoke again, very quietly. 'Save him. You must save *him*.' Allie nodded, her tears now a river. 'Stop crying! *Save him!*' The harshness of his words stunned her. Robert glared at her. She got the message. She put her hand in his, something she hadn't done for too long. She squeezed it and stood, brushing away her tears. Time was up. Vinculum infinitas and all that.

'God, how do you understand him? Or do you pretend just to make him feel better?' Mr Black goaded.

'I pretend. Okay, let's have your lemur things out here. What do you call them?'

'Lemur things,' he answered. 'You're keen to get the final show on the road, are you? Good girl! I'll say this for the St. Clairs . . . No I won't, I changed my mind. Bradley, open the gate over there in the corner, would you? Good man.'

'Oh my God!' Allie gasped theatrically. She pointed to the tall wooden chair behind the altar. 'Is that the throne of Gwyn ap Nudd, the mythical Faerie King?'

Mr Black turned towards it. 'Yes. Well, I, of course, am Gwyn ap Nudd, among other things, but you guessed that, I'm sure. Nothing mythical about me, though!'

'Can I see it?' She stepped forward, out of Whitcombe's reach, and lurched towards the altar as if to sit in the prehistoric chair.

'It's incredible!' she shrieked. Mr Black looked again at it. She grabbed Michael's hand just for an instant as she stumbled past.

'Sit in it if you want,' Mr Black said, motioning towards it. But she could hardly move, her life force was instantly depleted, her battery drained. She staggered to the chair and flopped in it. Mr Black cocked his head at an angle. He walked in a low crouch to her, peering into her eyes. 'What have you done?'

A high-pitched screech filled the cavern. The stripy lemurs bounded into the cave and then did what Allie had hoped – they wheeled around and fell upon Bradley Whitcombe first. He screamed and tried to bat them away, but there were too many. Their giggling and chattering intermingled with the sound of cracking bones and spurting liquid. Taking advantage of Mr Black's fascination with Whitcombe's struggle, she stole a look at Michael. His chest rose and fell almost imperceptibly, but she saw it. The stripy lemurs were already losing interest in Whitcombe. The entrée had been served and enjoyed. She looked again at Michael; she needed him to get moving now! The lemurs moved as one towards them; slashes of red coated some of them from paws to tail, while others carried pieces of flesh in tiny razor teeth.

'Cute, aren't they?' Mr Black said, dragging his eyes from the macabre spectacle. 'The piranhas of the underworld, are they not?'

'Whatever you say,' she said, knowing what she had to do next and hating herself for it. It was all about buying time. She caught Arthur Wendell's eye. She nodded in the direction of the advancing animals.

'It's the least you can do, Arthur.' She gave him a sad smile. 'Salvation is hard won.'

He stared at the creatures, then back at Allie. He smiled and mouthed the words, *Thank you.* He understood she'd given him a shot at eternal redemption. No guarantees – just a shot. He stood and walked calmly towards the salivating pack.

'Extraordinary!' Mr Black exclaimed, looking at Allie. 'You really should be one of us. It's not too late you know . . .'

Arthur Wendell went down without a fight. It was his penance for succumbing to Mr Black. He looked at Allie St. Clair as the first of the creatures reached him. It tore the flesh from his cheek and raked a claw down his neck. He didn't flinch. The pack descended and Allie saw her brother staring in horror as Arthur Wendell's clothes were ripped to pieces, his body stripped of skin and connective tissue, his hair torn out by the roots. Still Wendell looked, pleading, at Allie. He sank slowly to the floor, his gaze never wavering. Allie felt rage at his inhuman attacks on Georgie and Paula and yet now he stoically bore the brunt of this nightmarish attack. Somewhere deep within her she wished she had the power to forgive him; it was clearly what he sought. She turned away.

Robert yelled; a moaning drone of a noise. He flapped his arms and rocked his chair from side to side. Mr Black was captivated, but Allie knew what Robert was doing. He was distracting Mr Black. She quickly glanced at Michael. His left arm was raised, his hand on the wooden stake in his shoulder. He pulled it out; his face contorted in agony.

She ran to Robert, prolonging the show. 'Robert! What's wrong?' she yelled.

'I'd say that, despite his mental deficiency, he's worked out that he's next, my dear. Doesn't take a genius, does it? I mean,' he said, turning to the altar, 'there's only your brother, you, me and . . .'

Michael was gone. 'Oh, you clever little bitch,' Mr Black said, his yellow eyes burning into her, his chest and shoulders growing. He clapped his hands. 'Roly!' he called in a thunderous voice. 'Now!' He smiled at Allie. 'It's been fun. No really, it has, but I gotta go.' He hissed and spun around, his huge head swivelling in search of Michael.

Roly came at her fast. Water splashed behind her and she jerked her head around. The huge serpent towered above her, its wide head standing ten feet out of the muddy water of the river, its slit eyes fixed on her. It lunged. Allie fell backwards, the skin of the snake rasping against her clothes as it overshot. She rolled behind a jagged stand of stones. Movement caught her eye on the other side of the cave. The stripys had finished with Arthur Wendell. Now they hunched, heads low to the ground, eyes fixed on Robert. She ran to him, her eyes scanning for the motley serpent as she skirted the river.

Roly catapulted out of the water again, knocking her to the ground with the force of its attack. It rose, back arched, ready for the killer blow. Allie grabbed her brother's arm, both of them helpless to stop the inevitable. She saw the reptile's muscles twitch, the strike imminent.

Michael landed on the huge neck, his fingers searching for the eyes. The serpent recoiled, swaying from side to side in an attempt to rid itself of the annoyance. Michael tore an eye from its socket and stretched for the other, his wings folded behind him. He gripped the neck with his feet and reached both hands into the remaining eye of the snake. A bloody, beach-ball-sized eye was wrenched from its dark hole, hanging by a thread of muscle and sinew. It swung like a pendulum as the beast frantically fought to throw him off. It dove into the brown river, Michael still clinging to its neck. Allie stared at the water, willing him to come up. The lemurs reached them.

With no more time to think, she grabbed Robert and threw him and herself into the water. It occurred to her she hadn't seen the lemur-things in the water. As she and Robert bobbed to the surface, the stripys lined the bank, chattering and jumping up and down, but not jumping in. It was their chance; the demented lemurs *hated* water. Robert clung to her and looked desperately about. Roly was down under them somewhere. Mr Black stood by the bend in the river, watching intently. Michael and the serpent burst from the water, a gaping hole in the throat of the beast. Allie supposed he was trying to drown it.

'Get out!' he yelled to them, water cascading in torrents off his body and wings. 'Get into the light!' He was taken under the water once more.

'Robert!' she yelled, gulping for air. 'Let the water take us towards the cave opening. Hold your breath!' She pulled him under the water. They would be taken over the top of Michael and the huge serpent, but it was a risk they had to take. The current whisked them away quickly. They rolled and tumbled as if they were in a giant washing machine. The skin of the serpent tore a strip off her leg. She squealed under water, a stream of bubbles escaping her mouth. Kicking to the surface, she saw Robert was desperate for air and convulsing. He didn't have her lung capacity. They'd have to stay on the surface. Blood erupted from somewhere beneath them. It spurted high above the surface of the water. She prayed it was from the serpent. She prayed hard. Her shoulder smashed against a rock. She winced and looked ahead; they were nearly at the cave opening, the dangling rooftop tree roots marking the spot.

'Allie!' Robert screamed, his eyes fixed on the water ahead. She saw what concerned him and she heard it.

The river simply disappeared before them, its roar as it descended into the underworld growing louder as they were swept towards the vortex. She kicked higher in the water to try to get a better look. She froze. The water plummeted underground through a narrow fissure, nothing more than a slit. They would be trapped by it, crushed and drowned.

'Robert!' she yelled over the roar of the water. 'Let go of my arms! Hang on to my waist!' He tried, but he was tired.

'I can't, my arms are numb!'

An errant tree root loomed into view. It was close to the water. It would be their only chance. Allie broke an arm free from Robert and lunged for it. The tips of her fingers brushed it. She stretched and her hand closed over a thin strand. Pain burst through her as her burnt and blistered skin protested at the effort, but her grip held. The force of the water was irresistible. It slammed into her chest and gushed up her nostrils. Shaking her head to clear the water, she yelled to Robert over the all-pervading roar of the underground waterfall. 'You'll have to climb up over me to the bank!' Her one-handed grip was failing, and she was still far from fully recovered from 'recharging' Michael. 'Do it now!' she screamed. He didn't move. She looked questioningly at him.

'Allie,' he said, I can't . . .'

'Don't say that! You must! Try, *come on!*'

But Robert didn't try. He rested his head on her shoulder. They stayed like that for perhaps half a minute, both understanding what this meant. The last of his strength left him. He looked at her and tried to smile. He let go.

Allie wailed as the brown water surged through the narrow opening. Robert was gone. She hung on until she felt the root start to give way. She spun around and grabbed the larger roots, hauling herself out on to the earthen bank. The lemurs were sitting on the bank facing away from her, all of them watching the water where Michael and Roly battled. Mr Black paced up and down near them, his attention on the water as well. They'd given her up for dead. The sound of the rushing water changed and it rose where it entered the underground waterfall, banking up towards her. It was Roly, but not as he was. His head lay pinned against the rock face, a split running between his empty eye sockets. A still-attached eye bobbed to the surface. A dead, cloudy eye if ever she saw one. Adrenaline coursed through her. She had to assume Michael was all right. Checking again to see that she remained undetected, she ran for the steps which would take her to the opening and the world above.

A bellow echoed through the cavern. She'd been seen. The chattering escalated. The stripy lemurs came for her. She hit the steps at full pace and sprawled headlong on to them, gashing her forehead on the stone. She scrambled again for traction. Something grabbed her ankle. Hungry black eyes stared into hers. She kicked at it, but it hung on. She wondered why it didn't bite her; it had the equipment. Then she got it. It wasn't the leader, it was just the first to arrive. She rolled and pushed on for the opening, dragging the creature with her. Another ran up her back. She twisted her upper body, throwing it off. The mat of earth and roots was barely ten feet in front of her. The pack arrived. The creature on her leg seemed unsure of what to do next. She punched it on the back of the head. It bared its razor teeth and hissed, but still didn't bite. She pushed at the earth covering. It lifted, the bushes above swinging upwards with it. Cold air rushed in. The lemur let go; the boundary of its world couldn't be breached it seemed.

She scrambled up through the hole and stood. She turned to close the earthen door. A lemur sprang out of the hole at her. She ducked and its momentum carried it above her. It landed on all fours, facing her. She looked down into the hole; the rest of the pack sat there staring up at her, not daring to breach the underworld. This one, she guessed, was the leader – Mr Black's little general. Well, Mr Black's little general was going to die. At least this she could do for Robert. The first pale stirrings of light nibbled at the darkness in the east as they circled each other among the trees.

'Come on, then,' she said, flapping her fingers back and forth. 'Make your move, stinky.' It cocked its head as a dog would and as Mr Black had. *Interesting*, she thought.

It bobbed its head up and down, then jumped up and down on the spot, working itself into a frenzy.

'In your own time,' she announced in a tired tone

It jumped at her, teeth bared, claws out. She twisted her upper body and rammed her elbow into it as it passed over her shoulder. It hit the ground with a thump, rolling twice before regaining its balance. It circled her again. Allie decided to let it think it had made it behind her by stealth. She let it crab around until she couldn't see it. She closed her eyes. She *felt* it. In her mind's eye, she watched it crouch, preparing to spring at her back. She watched it finally jump at her. She waited a millisecond, then spun away, grabbing the creature as it sailed past at head height. She followed it to the ground and forced her hands around its neck, her elbows pinning its clawed hands to the ground. It squirmed and bucked under her weight. Its bared teeth inches from her face, it hissed and spat at her as she increased the pressure around its furry neck. She felt sinews and muscle crunch under her thumbs. Her burnt hands screamed in pain, but it was nothing to her. She felt a pop as its windpipe collapsed. She squeezed harder; the thing stopped thrashing about, its claws stilled. The black light in its eyes went out. She tightened her grip and hung on until she could grip no more. She wept, her tears splashing the unseeing eyes of the creature. She had lost Robert and killing this foul thing had done nothing to bring him back. She rolled off and stood. In a rage, she grabbed the lemur, strode to the hole in the ground, lifted the bush canopy and hurled the dead thing at the rest of the pack. They scattered in a chattering, dishevelled rabble. She slammed the bushes back into place and faced the paling sky.

Michael. What had he yelled? Get into the light? She looked up at the hill, the tower not visible from this angle, although a mist of sorts still clung to the top. That was where she would go, St. Michael's tower. Scrambling through the still wet and slippery long grass, she reached the mist-enshrouded summit, the tower a ghostly edifice at the limits of her vision. Pausing but a moment to catch her breath, she walked the remaining few yards and stepped inside. No dead abbots hung from unseen wooden beams. She stood still, deep in contemplation. There seemed nothing else for it but to wait, for *something*. The mist thinned. *It will be a nicer day tomorrow*, she thought idly. Then she wondered how she was going to tell her parents that she'd lost Robert. Despair and grief gripped her. She was safe, but . . .

A rumbling caught her ear. Again, she got down on all fours and listened. All hell was breaking loose beneath her, literally. She jumped back off the floor and backed out of the tower. Nothing happened.

Then Michael and the black creature burst through the floor of the tower, flagstones ricocheting off walls, mortar and razor sharp chips of stone scattering in an instant across the grass. Mr Black disentangled himself from the rubble first and flew to one side of the tower archway, alighting on the wet grass. Michael stood on the other side of the tower nearest her. The protagonist and antagonist slowly circled the tower, staring unblinkingly at each other. It was Allie and the lemur-thing revisited.

She saw now that Mr Black, or Belhor or Gwyn ap Nudd, whatever and whoever he chose to be, had black wings, but not like Michael's. They were leathery and crinkled like fabric which had been left folded too long in a dark closet. They were shorter, more angular, and bat-like. She backed away closer to the mist. Michael raised his arm; Mr Black did likewise. Mr Black changed direction; Michael mirrored it. It was a ritual she suspected had been played out many times before. It was probably all part of the game without end. They were as much prisoners of it as she. This was a fight to the death – about that she had no doubt. Their movements continued in unison, but she noticed Michael edging closer to his quarry, for that was what Mr Black was, the hunted. Whether or not he understood that, she didn't know. Michael's eyes never left those of his prey. No words passed between them, at least that she could hear or comprehend. As if she'd commanded it, she was suddenly plugged in to the audio between them. Michael nodded at her. He'd let her in on the action. Mr Black glanced at her. Again, they'd both taken their eyes off each other as though there'd been an unspoken agreement to do so. The Rules. Michael had alluded to them on the first night of this horror show.

'It's time, old friend. You know it as well as I,' Michael said to Mr Black.

'I like it here! The locals are so friendly and the food is a delightful surprise.'

'Pack it in. The sun is nearly up, there will be witnesses.'

Mr Black jerked his thumb towards Allie. 'There already is, thanks to you.'

'It can't be helped. If it wasn't for her, I wouldn't be here.'

Allie shook her head as if to clear it. *What's going on here?*

Michael rushed through the archway at Black, who jumped straight up, his stubby wings holding him airborne with frenzied beating, the whooshing of air from them disturbing the grass thirty feet below. He moved to the side of the tower Michael had occupied. Michael slowly and silently rose to the same height, but still on the opposite side of the tower from Black. His was an effortless ascension, smooth and practised; his pure white wings barely moving, the albatross to Black's hummingbird. Mr Black breathed hard.

'You can't keep this up,' Michael said. 'This isn't your domain. You belong with the rats and the blind worms. Even this crisp morning air will probably do you in.'

Black wasn't amused. Allie sensed his desperation. *Careful, Michael.*

'*Careful, Michael,*' Black mimicked in a pansy voice. 'Christ, next you'll be ironing his handkerchiefs.'

'At least they'll fit his nose,' Allie said. Black looked around at her, the childish insult stinging. Michael used the distraction and struck. Hurtling around the top of the tower, he snared one of Black's wings, but only just.

Black shrieked and tried to fly up. He was a giant, wounded bat. Michael clung to Black's wing tip as they flew around the top of the tower in faltering, dipping circles like two wounded prehistoric birds. Black suddenly heaved against Michael, sending him smashing into the stone abutments of the tower. It was a show of strength Michael seemed not to have anticipated. Allie saw the anguish on his face. Black threw himself on Michael, pinning his wings to his sides. They plummeted to the ground, Black riding Michael all the way down. Breath exploded from Michael as he hit the earth with a deep thud. Allie's heart raced. This wasn't what she'd expected. Black had Michael flat against the ground, neither Michael's arms nor legs could be freed. Allie rushed to help him.

'*Stay back!*' Michael yelled to her. She stopped. Michael looked into Black's eyes and simply said, 'It's time.' Michael turned his head sideways, then struck upwards with his teeth, sinking them deep into Black's throat. Black howled, the shrill sound an echo of the lemurs. They stayed like that for a half minute; frozen figures in the mist. Allie saw no blood. No sound now came from either of them. All strength abandoned Black; his body fell limp, and he toppled to one side as Michael withdrew his teeth from his throat, revealing a ragged hole. Michael wrapped his huge arms around Black's waist and lifted him up. He slowly rose to his feet, supporting Black until he could stand firmly. They were locked together. This was how it always had to end. Michael's wings beat rhythmically and, slowly, the two beings rose into the air, the slab sides of the tower barely three feet from them. They reached the top, Michael's wings beating harder now, Black's hanging limp and wasted by his side, his head still to one side under the unrelenting grip of Michael's jaws.

A cold mass formed in Allie's chest as she watched Michael move across to the tower and stand on its edge, Black firmly locked in his grip. He disengaged his jaws from Black and looked down at her, his extended wings brilliant and luminescent in the half-light.

He nodded to her. She stared back at him, knowing this was farewell. She wanted more. This wasn't how their farewell should be. Not after all they'd been through. She could do nothing. He looked over his shoulder towards the road. She heard it now too: people, still hidden from her by the mist, were coming up the track. He looked back at her. She thought she saw a glistening in his eyes, but it might have been a trick of the light. He looked up to the Heavens, the stars now pale in a brightening sky. His massive wings beat faster now. Mr Black stirred and locked his arms around Michael's waist as he was lifted to the sky. Michael turned his gaze toward her once again. She waited for the words, but there were none. Michael and Black started to spin, slowly at first; black, white, black, white, then blurred to grey before a single, brilliant white light prevailed. For a moment the light suspended above the ancient tower brought her father's words back to her. He'd told her of lights being seen above the Tor since ancient times and, of course, just four days ago. It was part of the ancient ritual with the Tor as the portal from this world to another. As the light faded, Allie St. Clair knew The Game was over.

The driver of the black BMW cursed when he saw the white light. He punched the ignition key into its socket and fired the eight-cylinder motor into action. He engaged 'drive' and let the torque of the motor move the car almost silently down Coursing Batch, then left into Ashwell Lane, where its ancient oaks and bucolic charm still hid in darkness, the sun blocked from this area by the mass of the Tor. He nursed the car along to number 13 and turned left into the long earthen driveway. The little farmhouse at the end, with its tiny garden tucked up against the lower reaches of the Tor, looked exactly the same as he'd last seen it thirty years before, when at sixteen years old, he'd finally discovered his birthplace.

He checked his watch, 5:46 a.m. He knew the single occupant of the house would be boiling the kettle in the tiny kitchen at the rear of the house. Who knew, the occupant might even have witnessed the epic struggle above St. Michael's Tower and the ascending white light. It didn't matter now. He exited his car, leaving the door open. He pushed open the moss-covered wooden gate at the side of the cottage and walked to the rear corner, his expensive black shoes crunching against the fine gravel. He kicked in the ancient wooden back door, not worrying now about being seen or heard; the shrubbery obscured any external view of the back garden. The door shattered and flew from its hinges, the termite-ridden doorframe collapsing with it. He confronted the startled old man who stood at the wooden bench, steaming cup in his hand. 'Hello, Dad. Long time, no see.'

Albert Mortlock stared at the face of the man who had burst into his kitchen. He recognized him immediately: the firm jaw, jet-black hair and sharp nose. Even the way he stood with that peculiarly Germanic bearing. The man was his wife Marion reincarnate. So the boy hadn't died. Well, well. They stared at each other; neither showing fear, anger nor any emotion. The intruder nodded. It was time. They both understood the rules, but that didn't mean Albert had to give up his position timidly. That was not his way. His father would be proud of him . . . maybe his son now, too. He sat his cup down on the bench and faced his child.

The old man fought hard and had been surprisingly strong, but in the end, his backbone had snapped loudly like a twig and the light had left his eyes without another word exchanged between them. They'd reconvene in Hell one day. The son buried his father next to where he knew his mother lay; under the willow tree in the corner of the garden. He turned and faced the Tor which stretched above him to the night sky. He bowed. After a minute, he strode to the weathered garden shed and placed the shovel behind the rickety wooden door.

He backed the black car out of the lane and pointed it towards London. The setback at the Tor this morning meant there had to be a new strategy. Ending his father's life meant he would now be the only conduit for *him*. The future would be different; he'd see to that. He smiled. His father's name now had a literal meaning; the bastard, Albert Mortlock, who'd adopted him out and from whom his own name, Lock, was derived, now really was a deadlock. He floored the accelerator. The BMW lifted its nose and charged down the blacktop. Jason Lock would be back in London sitting at the board table at Cranston Lock in two hours.

Epilogue

Seven days later

Allie St. Clair slumped against the cool green metal of the riverside bench, her bandaged hands limp in her lap. Putney Bridge spanned the Thames to her right, the university rowing clubs already alive at 6:30 a.m. and stretching away to her left. She'd not slept for four nights. Two funerals in seven days had taken its toll: first George Houghton, then her brother, Robert. If it hadn't been for her friends, Greg and Phoebe, holding her up, she'd have collapsed to the floor at the foot of Robert's empty casket. Allie, her father, and reluctant mother had collaborated to present Robert's sudden death as a consequence of his long-standing and well-known disability. It was a necessary lie that sat heavily with her and compromised her ability to properly grieve for him. And worst of all, it dishonoured him.

She'd been sent on leave after barely one week in her new job and now depression had taken hold. Carr had insisted she'd benefit from trauma counselling. It had been a week from Hell and Ellen Carr had recognized that.

Allie had completed all of her reports detailing events at the festival and the Tor. Despite the difficulty in identifying the remains of Whitcombe and Wendell in the Tor cave due to the savagery of the striped lemur frenzy, Whitcombe's DNA, along with Arthur Wendell's, was arrogantly smothered all over the remains of Paula Armstrong. Reports from Connors and Strauss had explained how Whitcombe had impeded the investigations at Tottenham Court Road area, endangered Wilkinson's life through his own actions and had sabotaged St. Clair's instructions to the local police at Glastonbury.

The severely concussed but determined young PC Gordon, had woken from the car accident at the foot of the Tor with enough awareness left to realize that no police backup had arrived for Allie and had rung for help. When the backup he'd instigated eventually arrived at the mist-shrouded summit of the Tor, they found a stunned DCI St. Clair staring into space, and the floor of St. Michael's Tower completely destroyed.

Archaeologists were even now pawing over the tower and the underground chamber. Sensational documentaries would soon be aired and Allie supposed her father would be involved. It wouldn't be long before tourists invaded the underground chamber and not one of them would care that her brother had lost his life there. Buying a brochure, a plastic Tor memento, and a donut would be greater priorities.

She and her father had spoken briefly at Robert's funeral, but hadn't spoken further about Michael. She'd had three subsequent calls from her father, but hadn't felt ready to respond. Her mother hadn't spoken to her at the funeral, nor since. Her accusatory glare had left Allie in no doubt as to whom she blamed for Robert's death.

Robert. They'd not been close, until the end. Robert, it seemed, had always enjoyed some sort of exalted status at home. Her mother had consulted him about what Celtic legend-based children's story elements excited him most and he was often invited to book launches where he was laughingly trotted out to the media as the 'detailed research' behind each new book. It had hurt her at the time, but she'd said nothing. For all that, he'd been loyal to her, even after the childhood incident at the Tor which she'd somehow blocked from her memory for decades; or it had been blocked from her. She now admitted the possibility that other forces may have been at work. She realized he had, in his own insular way, been deferential to her, but had never sought her company. A distance had grown between them, to the extent that she'd been unaware of his interest in music and blogging and, consequently, she'd not seen the danger to him from ancient forces which she now knew travelled with and fought against her family. No matter how you dressed it up, she'd let him down in the ultimate way. His life had been forfeited in a game understood in a different time and realm, but which had, since time immemorial, touched the St. Clair family and seemed destined to do so in a future in which she did not care to be involved.

Her thoughts drifted to the problem of Mathew Connors. He'd finally, and reluctantly in her view, explained his absences and aberrant behaviour during the investigations as they chatted briefly at Sergeant George Houghton's funeral. He claimed he'd been suffering inexplicable blackouts for the past week and had been secretly seeking medical treatment. The confession might just have saved his career. But there was a greater issue. She'd felt something radiating from him; something angry and unfulfilled. It had required an act of will for her to remain close to him during their two-minute chat. She'd felt something tugging at her, pulling her away from him. Just a week ago she'd accepted his good wishes on her promotion. Now her skin crawled at the thought of working with him. She shivered and hugged herself. Maybe she was just spooked and suffering some kind of post-traumatic stress, and perhaps it was just a matter of him receiving the proper medical treatment to resolve his issues.

Contrails were already etched in the eastern sky above the city and the first of the full-bellied jumbos bound for nearby Heathrow had already passed low over suburban Putney. A motorbike roared across the bridge from Fulham. She stared at it, aware that her heart had jumped in hope just a little bit. She was reminded of the Ducati rats that had attacked her and Michael near Stonehenge. The media would never hear about all the empty cycle suits which lay draped over more tha twenty broken red motorcycles – the occupants never found.

She thought back to the standing ovation she'd received on entering the office on Monday morning: Ellen Carr weeping openly, embracing her and apologizing quietly later for not being there for Allie when it counted. Apparently, a tiff with her partner from some big law firm had sent her into a spin. Allie had been gracious and humbled by her colleague's acclamation. Even Rachel Strauss had sought her out afterwards to express her admiration. Maybe her friendship with Strauss might yet survive, provided Allie stayed in the force, but after seven days of contemplation, she had serious doubts about that.

The world, she'd learnt, was not as it seemed. There were forces at play about which 99.9 per cent of humans knew absolutely nothing. She watched as two young rowers walked past her carrying their long watercraft overhead; a boy and a girl, perhaps sixteen years old, going about their daily lives in the naïve belief that being 'good, decent, loving and honest' would protect them, and that their future would be bright; full of children and good times. *That is*, Allie thought, *if it's okay with those who 'played The Game'. And if the one that can destroy the fabric of life for everyone on the planet never gains the upper hand.* She knew her father and ancestors had played this Game and of course, she would talk to her father about it all sometime, but not yet.

Blackness settled heavily over her. Sighing, she stood and shuffled along the embankment past the rowing clubs, threading her way through the cars, slim rowers and enormous pointed shells and the inevitable dog walkers. It was bin day and big black bags overflowing with household waste lined the short walk to her door.

A blanket of heavy grey clouds appeared from the west and covered the sun, a chill breeze accompanying them. *That would be right*, she thought, *it'll rain soon.*

She passed the mangled wreck of her motorbike which still degraded a parking space in front of her apartment. A red council sticker adorned one of the few pieces of undamaged metal. She'd remove the wreck within the week. No more bike riding for her.

She slipped on the score of brochures, mail and newspapers that littered her entryway, not bothering to stoop to pick them up. She trudged up her narrow stairs, thought about making a coffee, but flopped into her lounge chair instead. The room was dark, the shutters closed; as they had been for the past week.

She dozed fitfully for an hour. She awoke to the sound of her email pinging on her laptop. She didn't recall turning the thing on. Begrudgingly, she levered herself up out of the chair and walked to the tiny desk. She stopped short. A brilliant, long white feather lay on her keyboard. She picked it up, sure it hadn't been there the night before. Goose pimples rose on her skin and she opened the email. There was no name, just a message:

What does a guy have to do to get your attention? Fancy a coffee at Victor's?

She straightened and looked at herself in the mirror for the first time in days, brushing a stray hair from her face. Dark circles underscored her eyes and her skin was pasty white. She looked like hell.

So the relationship with Michael would continue after all. The St. Clair history chronicled in *The Travels of Maewyn Succat* was the blueprint for her future. There was no escaping it. She truly believed that now.

She threw open the shutters and took a deep breath. The sun streamed in through the lime green foliage of the young elm tree outside her window. London waited out there; every crazy, chaotic, architecturally fraudulent, pompously self-interested, over-regulated piece of it. But it was a city she loved in a country peopled by decent, upright folk who relied, unknowingly, on the few who made their lives safe for them and their children. She'd been called to serve in a way few humans had ever been and she would die in service either on the streets as part of the Metropolitan Police Service or in some nightmarish place battling some unimaginable . . . *thing*. She turned back to the mirror and, inexplicably, a laugh burst from her.

What the hell, she thought. *What was I going to do, anyway? Marry a banker, have two point three kids and buy a beige-coloured dog?* She strode to her desk and sat at the keyboard. Latin was never her strong point, but she knew what vinculum infinitas *truly* meant for her now. She looked again at the message: *Coffee at Victor's?*

She did what a warrior committed for life to The Game Without End would do.

She typed in: *Sure, why not?*

Cave diabolus redit

Fade to Black

More Books by Steven Bannister

Back to Black
The Black Net

The Red Shoes

Find out more at:

www.stevenbannister.com

17641325R00226

Printed in Great Britain
by Amazon